Kennedy's Revenge

The Election of 2016

Stephen L Rodenbeck

This is a work of fiction.

ISBN-13: 978-1522913979 (CreateSpace-Assigned)

ISBN-10: 1522913971

A Message from your Author

The goal of this offering is to change the world…for the better.

Some may accuse this novel of being un-American. Nothing could be further from the truth. This is an attempt to reorient the American perspective of its own history. If that can be accomplished, the problems facing this great nation (debt, healthcare, immigration, security, etc.) can be solved – not bandaged over with useless rhetoric and stale ideas. Some American sacred cows get demolished in the process – think of it as roadkill on the highway to truth.

This book was written in the summer and autumn of 2015. The story revolves around fictitious events in 2016 and 2017.

Enjoy!

Chapter 1 (October 2016)

Why am I doing this? I don't even like humanity. Fitzgerald Cavendish was having his first panic attack, his first failure to focus in over a year. *Why am I doing this?* Was it to avenge the death of his father, whom he never personally knew, or was it to simply right a perceived wrong? Whatever the reason, Fitz needed to concentrate or he was going to fall flat on his face in front of 70 million people. His plan had worked perfectly to this point: his engineered overnight fame and the use of it to catapult him in front of a televised audience surpassed only by the Super Bowl. His opponents were grizzled veterans, who were not only used to the spotlight, but also embraced it. The good news was that the expectations for Fitz, at least as far as the media (and most viewers) were concerned, were low. He wasn't even a candidate. But based on his performance over the next ninety minutes, he could change all of that. He could change everything.

Even though his plan had worked to perfection so far, it was not without sacrifice. He had given up his peaceful anonymity for celebrity -- planned, but never desired. More importantly, he had given up his love – hopefully, only temporarily -- for this moment that he was now beginning to question.

"Your twitter followers are now over 24 million." Polly Preston, his publicist and fast confidant, snapped him out of his funk with news he never thought he would hope to hear: Fitz was now more popular than Miley Cyrus. Cavendish knew that the only reason he was in the position to espouse his views to a large American audience -- in a presidential debate, no less – was due to his popularity and unique background (along with the desire of the networks to get their ratings up.) Popularity was a necessary evil. Polly tightened his yellow Hermes tie, perched on his Brooks Brothers French-cuffed blue shirt, underneath his dark suit. Polly told Fitz that the blue shirt and yellow tie combination made him appear more honest, according to some study conducted by the FBI. Polly had a calming influence on Fitz which is exactly what he needed at this moment, backstage at Wright State University's Nutter Center. Preston's ability to placate Cavendish was amusing to him because it was sourced in the fact that she couldn't stay still for two seconds. She only seemed right when her hair was on fire.

By contrast, the scene backstage at the Nutter Center was fairly subdued given that representatives of the two most powerful political families (Bush and Clinton) were about to square off in the first of a series of presidential debates. In fact, Cavendish had yet to see either candidate, not that he really wanted to, given the ambush he planned to unleash on them over the subsequent hour and a half. His closing speech tonight would be as important as the one that set him on his journey.

History Lesson #1

Chapter 2 (1763)

History is a big lie; a lie of omission -- at least the version taught in classrooms around the country, blasted over the airwaves, and printed by the press. History is a lie that is edited and censored by the winners. In a country where freedom of the press is trumpeted as one of the rights protected by the first amendment to its Constitution, investigative journalism is all but dead in the United States. This is because the media are controlled by the winners. So is public education. The United States won its freedom in the Revolutionary War and its citizens have slowly given it back over the course of the past two centuries, initially with a fight, but now by ignorant consent. So what does this have to do with the price of your caramel macchiato at Starbucks, you ask? Answer: Quite a bit. For the avoidance of doubt, this lacuna has nothing to do with a perversion of the past, a glorification of your imperfect forefathers that give your children an ideal to aspire to. And it is not the loser's side of the story. Yes, your ancestors committed genocide by obliterating at least twelve million Native Americans, which is brushed under the rug and excused in fifteen minutes of classroom discussion about Manifest Destiny. That history is well established. What the 99.9% of you don't know about is not taught by your schools or discussed in the media. This is by design. Your trust in the system has been abused. You have been indoctrinated to believe that the news anchor, the doctor, and the scientist purport the truth. It isn't the truth, or at least not all of it. It is a message from the winners. History, after all, is written by the winners. What follows is what the winners don't want you to know. Why should you care? Answer: because if you're not educated, you will never understand the root causes to such problems such as the debt, the healthcare crisis, and terrorism and it might be too late for you to change a damn thing when you come to realize that you have been had – or worse yet, if Henry Kissinger has his way, you will be so brainwashed that you will consent to your own enslavement.

The American Revolution was not about taxes or freedom from tyranny. It was about money and banking. Riding high on the success of the American colonial economy, Ben Franklin decided, in retrospect, rather naïvely, to share with the British Board of Trade and the Bank of England in 1763, the secret of the colonies' success. That secret was *debt-free* money, otherwise known as Colonial Script. The shareholders in the Bank of England were none too happy to hear about this. The Bank of England was a debt-based, privately held, central bank. A central bank is an entity responsible for overseeing the monetary system for a nation. The shareholders had already waged a successful campaign against their rival currency, *debt-free* money known as tally sticks.

Tally sticks were simply polished pieces of notched wood that served as currency. It was an acceptable form of money – and for a long time, the only acceptable money -- for payment of taxes from the time of King Henry the First (1100) until the end of the 17th Century. The tally sticks worked because the populace had confidence to accept these wooden sticks as money, because the kings accepted them for tax payments. However, when Henry VIII eased usury laws – that allowed for the loaning of money with interest – in the 17th century, the bankers, with their gold and silver coins, launched a quiet war against the *debt-free* tally sticks. The culmination of their efforts occurred in 1694, when the Bank of England was formed to loan money to the British government, left in financial ruin from 50 years of war, brought about by those same bankers. Ironically, shareholders purchased interests in the bank with *debt-free* tally sticks. Yes, you heard that correctly (for a third time): the Bank of England has shareholders. It is privately held! Private individuals loan money to the British government. The original shareholders were a "society of about 1,300 persons" that included the King and Queen of England – their shares were likely free of charge – others who understood the scam (the bankers), and people with titles such as Duke, Lord, or Earl. What the Bank of England issued was debt-based money, and profited from the interest charged on that loaned money. Who is ultimately responsible for the loans? Answer: the population of England.

Taking a quick detour, what you were not taught in school is that there are two types of money: 1. Debt-based, which is the kind of money that is in existence today. Money that comes from a printing press (or a stroke of the computer) that is then loaned into existence by a bank. If your government needs to wage war, it may have to spend more money than it collected in tax receipts, so it borrows the difference from a central bank. The central bank then cranks up its printing press and gives your government money to wage its war, and charges your government interest on that money. 2. *Debt-free*, like the Colonial Script of Ben Franklin's

6

day. Similar to debt-based money, this currency came from a printing press (or in King Henry the First's case, a piece of wood.) However, unlike debt-based money, this money was issued by the government itself, not by a central bank. When the government needed to pay for something, it cranked up *its* printing press and produced paper money (or tally sticks). This system operated just like the debt-based money except that there was no bank involved. And since there wasn't any bank involved, the money wasn't loaned into existence and no interest was charged. *Debt-free* money was merely part of the economy – an aid in the exchange of goods -- not a claim on it. Both forms of currency can be "backed" by a precious metal, such as silver or gold, but this is unnecessary and unwise. 'Fiat' currency is actually superior for reasons you will understand later. The entire history of the United States (and to a great extent, the world since the 1700s) is about debt-based money versus *debt-free money*. News flash: the debt-based money people won and you are indoctrinated with their version of history. In fact, until you read this, you probably didn't even know there was debt-based and *debt-free* money. The difference is the difference between your thralldom and your freedom.

Getting back to 1763, when Ben Franklin was queried by the British about the prosperity in the colonies, he offered,

> "That is simple. In the colonies we issue our own money. It is called Colonial Script. We issue it in proper proportion to the demands of trade and industry to make the products pass easily from the producers to the consumers [i.e. as a medium of exchange, as an alternative to bartering]. In this manner, creating for ourselves our own paper money, we control its purchasing power, and we have no interest to pay to no one."

Once the Bank of England knew that the reason for the colonies' prosperity was a direct threat to its existence, it pressured the British crown to pass the Currency Act of 1764. This act essentially made it illegal for the colonies to print their own money. Money, in the form of silver and gold coin, now had to be *borrowed* from the Bank of England. What ensued is best described by Franklin:

"In one year, the conditions were so reversed that the era of prosperity ended, and a depression set in, to such an extent that the streets of the Colonies were filled with the unemployed."

This contrasts greatly with his statement in 1763 when asked by English officials how it was the Colonies managed to collect enough taxes to build poor houses, and how they were able to handle the great burden of caring for the poor:

"We have no poor houses in the Colonies, and if we had, we would have no one to put in them, as in the Colonies there is not a single unemployed man, no poor and no vagabonds."

In one year, a currency act forcing debt-based money on its subjects had driven the prosperous British colonies into a depression. Ben Franklin sited this as the chief cause of the Revolutionary War:

"The colonies would gladly have borne the little tax on tea and other matters had it not been that England took away from the colonies their money, which created unemployment and dissatisfaction. The inability of the colonists to get power to issue their own [debt-free] money permanently out of the hands of George III and the international bankers was the prime reason for the Revolutionary War."

As you will see, the institutions that issue this debt-based money are responsible for your education, your news, and the price of your caramel macchiato.

Chapter 3 (August 2015)

Fitzgerald Cavendish was born a poor black child. Or so his politically incorrect prep school classmates labeled him for not having a father and knowing nothing about him. When he petitioned his mother, Mary Jane Scott, about his father, she would only reply with, "He was a great man," and infuriatingly to Fitz, nothing more -- *ever*. His mother, although strikingly attractive, never married, rarely dated, and spent her life working as an administrative assistant in a middle school that Fitz never attended. But she doted over her Fitz and his education, and although she had a relatively low paying job, money was never a problem in the Scott household. His prep school (Andover) was paid for, and although he had received some academic assistance through scholarships – Fitz's test scores were extraordinarily high – his college education (Brown – his mother's alma mater) was also taken care of. In fact, when his mother died suddenly in a gruesome car accident in 1990, Fitz inherited over $5 million. It was a huge shock to him – not only that his mother had died so suddenly, but also that she had subsisted so modestly, held a position that was a gross mismatch with her education, and did it all with a quiet grace that belied a much deeper bankroll and that must have belied an even deeper misery. But if it did, Fitz never once saw it bubble to the surface. And what was she doing with all this money? Answer: obviously nothing; or, investing it very well.

To be sure, Cavendish was white, 6 feet, 1 inch, 185 pounds, and owned some of the striking features – long eyelashes, vibrant skin, and high cheekbones -- that defined his mother. His eyes were chameleon. They would change from green to dull blue to brown to hazel depending on the color of the clothes he was wearing. With a headful of fine, brown hair, Fitz had little problem passing for thirty-six at fifty-two (born August 9, 1963). The responsibility for this good fortune fell equally on his healthy lifestyle and youthful complexion. He normally found himself in the company of women a generation (or more) his younger. However, Fitz had never found the 'right' one and had accepted the possibility that he would never wed. When playfully queried by his friends about his marital status, he would respond, "I will settle when it doesn't feel like a compromise." For him, it wasn't an issue of intimacy; it was just a numbers game. If five hundred women were in a room, he might find one who possessed both winsomeness and a magnetic disposition. Put five hundred "attractive" women in a room and one might find Fitz an appealing match. Put fifty of those women in the same room and maybe only one wouldn't want to have children, like Fitz. That math put the chances of a match at 1 in 12.5 million.

Despite those long odds, Cavendish courted many women. But the truth of the matter is that he always found it difficult, if not impossible, to account for his family background. He could talk about his fifteen years on Wall Street, most of which were spent as a partner with Volpe, Brown, a small, west coast investment banking boutique that was purchased in 2000 by Prudential Securities. When Prudential failed to lock up some of the partners and all of the employees with multi-year employment contracts, Fitz took it as an opportunity to "pursue other opportunities", which for him meant traveling the world and playing golf. Between the inheritance from his mother and the buyout of his firm, Cavendish was quite well off. Again, this part of his life he *could* talk about. But not knowing his father's name – was it Cavendish? Was it Scott? -- proved to be a field of broken glass in his attempt to run barefoot through the past. Because of this obstacle, he would detour the conversation in other directions for fear of showing vulnerability. His uncomfortableness displaying weakness was interpreted by some of his lovers as a fear of intimacy. Fitz believed this not to be the case – it was just a game of numbers. But in the end, he wasn't always the final arbiter and found himself on the outs in many a relationship. Whether he would admit it or not, his unwillingness to father children was rooted in the fact that he was never 'fathered'. His only chance at being 'fathered' was blotted out when his maternal grandfather, an accountant at PepsiCo in New York City died suddenly when Fitz was five. He was told that he had died of a stroke. And Fitz obviously never had contact with his father's side of the family. He would claim that he enjoyed his freedom and that children were simply a ball and chain -- which was how he really felt. The question was whether he had reached this conclusion on instinct or as a result of circumstance.

Fitz knew that he was part English and part German, as those were the nationalities of his maternal grandfather and grandmother, respectively. His grandmother, Gertrude, had just passed, but she seemed to have moved on the day her only child was killed. If the sudden passing of her husband in 1968 was a blow to her solar plexus, the tragic death of her daughter in

10

1990 was a brickbat to her resolve from which she never recovered. At the reading of his mother's will, Fitz found Grandma Gert not disconsolate, but rather, disconnected. He tried to keep in touch with her immediately after Mary Jane's death – they were the only family each other had – but she wouldn't pick up his calls, or anyone else's for that matter. She was quickly slipping into a state of oblivion. When he stopped by to check in on her a few days after the funeral, she wouldn't come to the door. He had to use his mother's key to gain entry into Gertrude's Oceanport, NJ house, but once inside, found that he no longer had access to Gertrude's inner sanctum. Fitz watched her stare at the ceiling from her bed, unable to respond to any stimulus. She would not eat and she had laughed her last laugh. Knowing that she was broken, Fitz had her admitted to a hospital, and eventually to an asylum where, with the help of an IV, blood coursed through an unresponsive shell for another twenty-five years.

The reading of Gertrude's took thirty seconds. Fitz only partially attended to Gertrude's affairs (property taxes, lawn maintenance, etc.) when she was institutionalized, in vain hope that she would return from the void. There was once optimism in May 1994 when after nearly four years of nothingness, she seemed to snap to one day, responding to something she had seen on television, but no one could understand what she was mumbling, as if she had learned an entirely new language in her four years as a zombie. After that brief interlude with consciousness, she quickly relapsed and was never heard from again. She had left most everything to Fitz's mother, except for $50,000.00 that went to a local animal shelter (that was still functioning in 2015) at which she volunteered until Mary Jane's death. Gertrude's possessions were now the property of Fitz. Fitz wanted to sell her house and give away the remaining possessions to her friends. The problem was since she had died twice, and the second time at ninety-four, she had no friends left.

Before Fitz put Gert's house on the market, he paid it a visit to gather up any remaining clothing for the Salvation Army and to give it the once over for anything of value. He had had the interior of the house painted by a childhood friend about five years prior, and that was the last time he remembered being inside Gertrude's house for more than five minutes. There wasn't much to clean out except some old tax returns and some property tax receipts he found when he lifted the desktop of her Davenport. The 19th century desk, as well as some other furniture, and an antique Victor Safe & Lock Company combination safe probably had value, but he didn't want to be bothered with an estate sale. He would just sell it as part of the house. As he emptied the contents of the desk into a trash bag, he noticed a 3.5" x 6.5" manila envelope. Fitz grabbed the unmarked envelope and felt a key inside. Figuring it to be to the desk, he was about to put it back, but decided to check its contents. Out came a key, and with it, a small piece of folded paper. Fitz read its contents: "For FC upon JO's death -- Box 103 Ocean Federal Savings and Loan 701 Arnold Ave. Point Pleasant Beach, NJ." He knew that "FC" was himself. He had no idea who "JO" was, or whether he or she was dead, but the key was now his, as were the contents of that box. With this mystery key on his person, Cavendish headed to Point Pleasant Beach.

On his way down, Fitz rummaged through his mind as to why Gertrude would have a safe deposit box in Point Pleasant Beach. She had lived in Oceanport since Fitz could remember and Point Pleasant Beach was a good twenty miles south. When he arrived at 701 Arnold Avenue, he discovered that Ocean Federal Savings and Loan was now Ocean First Bank. He also found out that even though he had the key to the box, he was denied access. The box was actually his mother's and Gertrude was listed as a joint-renter -- this made sense as he remembered spending childhood summers with his mother on the Jersey Shore. When he explained to the bank personnel that he was the only surviving family member, they looked at him with suspicion given that his name, "Cavendish", was not a match with Gertrude or Mary Jane "Scott". It was going to take a lot more lawyering for Fitz to obtain the contents of the box. The good news was that Fitz had time, money, and intense curiosity. *What is in that box?*

Since Mary Jane and Gertrude had separate attorneys draw up their respective wills, the case of the mystery key wasn't all that mysterious, but a bit confusing. Fitz's mother had opened a safe deposit box back in 1968. The fee for the box was paid for out of a trust account that she had established concurrent to its opening. On the chance that her death occurred before "JO", the lawyer would release the key to Fitz when "JO" passed. On the chance that Mary Jane's death occurred not only before "JO's", but also before Gertrude's, the key would be passed to Gertrude, who would then make Fitz the joint-renter, and pass the key to him upon "JO's" death. If Gertrude then died before "JO", the key would pass to

12

Fitz. The break in the chain occurred when Gertrude essentially 'died' at the same time as Mary Jane. As a result, Gertrude never established Fitz as the joint-renter of the box or the beneficiary of its contents upon her death. The trust account continued to pay for the box and the key never moved from the Davenport after Gertrude returned home from the reading of Mary Jane's will. Gertrude simply deposited the envelope in her desk and soon slipped into the shell-shocked state that was her final twenty-five years. Fitz didn't remember the envelope at the reading of his mother's will, but his mind was understandably elsewhere at that time.

Fitz was able to arrange a meeting with Mary Jane's lawyer – fortunately, he was still practicing – and after a relatively short probate process, was granted custody of the safe deposit box. Curiously, the lawyer was ignorant when Fitz inquired as to whether "JO" was still alive – Fitz guessed that the lawyer didn't give it much thought when he passed the key to Gertrude over two and half decades ago. He immediately drove back to Point Pleasant Beach. At the bank, he found that the key was for a 5" x 10" x 24" box. Inside it, were two large manila envelopes; one marked "For Fitz". Fitz opened the "For Fitz" envelope and found two hand written pages and a signed photograph, the contents of which would alter the course of history.

Chapter 4 (1769 - 1796)

Mayer Amschel (M.A.) Rothschild did not invent the concepts of debt-based money and central banking, but he saw their potential to make him wealthy and powerful beyond his or anyone's imagination. He, more so than anyone else, is responsible for the price of your caramel macchiato. Originally a rare coin dealer, Rothschild leveraged his relationship with a rare coin collector, William I (then Count of Hanau-Munzenberg, later Landgrave of Hesse-Kassel and Elector of Hesse) into a job managing William's estate and tax-gathering for William's father (Fredrick II). Fredrick was one of the wealthiest men in Europe and made part of his fortune by loaning out 16,800 young Hessian soldiers to King George III (of England) in his battle against the American colonists – a transaction arranged by Rothschild. M.A. used William's bankroll to start a banking business which proved very profitable to William, but even more profitable to Rothschild. M.A. soon learned that lending to businesses involved risk, whereas lending to monarchs involved little risk. Businesses could fail, putting the repayment of a loan in jeopardy, but if a government went bankrupt, the "nobility" could simply increase taxes on its "subjects", essentially guaranteeing the loan's repayment.

At the same time Rothschild was becoming a force in international banking, a disenfranchised professor of canon law at the University of Ingolstadt named Adam Weishaupt, formed a then secret society, now famously known as the Order of Illuminati. The time was May 1, 1776. The stated goal of the Illuminati was to teach people to be happy by making them good. This would be accomplished by enlightening the mind and freeing it from the dominion of superstition and prejudice – certainly anomalous to the teachings of the Catholic Church. However, the 'real' intentions were brought to light on September 9, 1785, and could be summarized as the call for the destruction of monarchies; traditional families; religion; inheritance; patriotism; and the concept of private property. In short, its objective was the yet to be coined 'communism'. Weishaupt became a freemason in 1777 and used this organization as a means for recruiting Illuminati members. For the avoidance of doubt, Rothschild never joined the Illuminati – a few of his sons did -- but his benefactor William I, was a very influential and connected member – so much so that the Illuminati Congress in 1782 was held at his home

(Wilhelmsbad) in Hanau, Germany. When William's father died in 1785, he inherited one of the largest fortunes in Europe. This massive bequest allowed the talented Rothschild to become one of the most influential international bankers in Europe. It isn't a stretch to see how William's Illuminati beliefs rubbed off on Rothschild.

While Rothschild was growing his fortune and perfecting modern-day debt-based banking, he was also growing his family. He had five sons (Nathan; Amschel; Salomon; Carl; and James) whom he sent to the five major European financial centers (London; Frankfort; Vienna; Naples; and Paris respectively) to pursue the family's goal of financial supremacy. He knew the ability to create money was power and passed that principle on to his five sons. By the time of M.A.'s death in 1812, the Rothschild's family goal wasn't simply financial domination, it was total domination. This was achieved through loaning money to kings and queens so they could wage wars.

Getting back to the Illuminati, the society was first 'outed' when in October 1783, Joseph Utzschneider, a lawyer who had dropped out of the Order in August, presented to Duchess Maria Anna a document which detailed the activities of the Illuminati. He was embittered because he felt he was worthy of a more lofty position in the underground organization, whose endgame was the takeover of the world by toppling all existing governments. The Duchess gave the information to the Duke, who took this organization so seriously that on June 22, 1784, the Elector of Bavaria issued an Edict for its suppression. Many of its members were fined or imprisoned, and some, including Weishaupt, were compelled to flee the country. Three more disillusioned members came forward in 1785 with more detailed information, including membership lists and the aforementioned communist goals, which were formally disclosed at the Court of Inquiry on September 9, 1785. The Edicts of the Elector of Bavaria were repeated in March and August, 1785, and the Order began to decline, so that by the end of the eighteenth century it had ceased to exist...or so you are told in the history books.

The Illuminati actually went 'underground' as part of Freemasonry. It was this element of Freemasonry -- and more specifically rumored Illuminist Louis Philippe II -- which was responsible for the ignition of the French Revolution. Philippe II created an artificial food shortage in France by buying up all the grain and shipping it out of the country. Famine ensued and the monarchy of France was wrongly blamed. Populations will endure many hardships in the name of patriotism, but once they are deprived of food, revolution is usually the result.

The French Revolution was an example of the Hegelian Dialectic (even though Hegel was seventeen and years away from introducing the concept): 1. Create a crisis (food shortage); 2. The crisis creates a reaction (revolution); 3. Offer a solution (replacing a monarchy with a form of socialism) and have the populace accept the solution, usually one that it would not have endorsed before the crisis, resulting in the relinquishment of some of its freedom or control. 300,000 perished in the French Revolution. The Hegelian doctrine and Communism have been the instruments of the winners many times since.

Replacing the Monarchy of Louis XVI and Marie Antoinette was a ruling Directorate of five, including Illuminati Paul François Jean Nicolas, vicomte de Barras. The Former Commander-in-Chief saw an abundance of military talent in a young Freemason named Napoleon Bonaparte. The future emperor would come to learn the evils of debt-based money and his eventual defeat would make your caramel macchiato that much more expensive.

Chapter 5 (August 2015)

Fitz started to read, but the contents were so unexpected that the reality of the moment didn't sink in until he saw the picture. The letter read:

"My Dearest Fitz, I know that I have kept the identity of your father from you all these years. It has broken my heart to do so, but I hope you understand why I did it. Your father was John F. Kennedy, 35th President of the United States. I was working as an aide to Congressman Dominick V. Daniels out of school, when one day in August 1962, Congressman Daniels asked me if I'd like to meet the president. Of course, I jumped at the opportunity. During our brief meeting, Jack invited me to a luncheon and pool party the following day. I was star struck. My boss (Daniels) gave me the whole next day off. At the luncheon, Jack took me for a tour of the White House. The tour ended in his bedroom. Our affair lasted several months and at some time in November 1962, I became pregnant with you. By the time I was sure (in mid-December) I was back at your grandparents' house in Oceanport. I was mortified. I felt like a harlot and felt terrible for his wife and I just didn't know what to do. I was truly in love with Jack and I think he had very deep feelings for me. But this type of scandal would bring down his presidency.

"Over the holiday recess, I reached out to Congressman Daniels and explained my predicament. My boss was quite perceptive and was aware of our affair. He advised me not to return to work and to 'lay low', and that he would reach out to me. To his credit, within a week of returning to the Hill, Congressman Daniels contacted me. He said that Jack had called the office several times looking for me. He had given me Christmas gifts – a strand of pearls, a lock of his hair (my wish), and a card. (They are all in the other envelope.) I'm sure he wanted to know what I thought of his gifts. When Congressman Daniels requested a private meeting to discuss my 'situation', Jack immediately made room on his schedule. To the Congressman's surprise, he reacted rather calmly to the news. Jack said that he would 'make things right' in return for *complete* silence. A trust fund was set up for

17

me to take care of you. If I didn't make it to term with you, the money was still mine. Congressman Daniels took care of it all. I was devastated, but what was Jack or I to do? I was also very scared, especially after what had happened to Marilyn Monroe – Jack confessed that affair to me. As much as Jack cared for me, he was very powerful, and I just knew that my silence was probably the only way you and I would survive. I never spoke to your father from that moment on. He and the congressman became friends after this incident, and an occasional note was passed from Jack to me through Mr. Daniels. One was a letter of apology; one was a tacit acknowledgement of your birth; and the other one, which I received shortly after his death, was a bit more mysterious and prophetic. I saved them all. They are in the other envelope.

"As you probably know, he was killed a few months after you were born. What you probably don't know is that at about the same time you came into the world, Jack and his wife Jackie had a boy, Patrick, who was born prematurely on August 7th. He died two days later – on the day you were born. Your birth and his death occurred almost simultaneously. I took that as a message from God. Even if I wanted to go public with my story after Jack was killed, I could never do that to Jackie, who lost her child at the same time I was giving birth to you. It was all too much. I dearly loved Jack and was sickened and deeply depressed by his death. I promised to keep my word until the day Jackie passed. That is why I waited until now to tell you. It is now your decision as to how you wish to handle this very unique situation.

"Not that Jack was one for 'pillow talk', but he did share with me a lot of very personal feelings, especially the realization (not fear) that he would be killed. The Cuban Missile Crisis was an 'awakening' for Jack. He saw the heart of darkness in many who were serving his administration and the country. He said that he was barely in control of many situations and that was concerning to him because he was the 'leader' of the free world. Your father was a deeply flawed man, but he loved his country and its people and he knew who and what he was up against. I know he would have loved you. And as I told you every time you asked, he was a great man!

I love you,

Mom"

Fitz then looked at the black and white picture of his mother and JFK with their arms around each other. They were both smiling. His mother was quite stunning. He could see why Kennedy was attracted to her. On the back of the photo was written, "My Mary Jane, With Love, Jack". Fitz filled with a confluence of relief, pride, confusion, awe, and most of all, curiosity. Without opening the other envelope, Fitz left the bank in Point Pleasant Beach and drove back to his co-op in New York City.

On the drive up, Fitz tried to place the last pieces into the jigsaw puzzle. He now understood the identity of "JO": Jackie Onassis, but he was also confused. He knew Jackie Kennedy Onassis ("JO") died a long, long time ago. *Why didn't I find out about the identity of my father back then?* He then punched Jackie Onassis into his smart phone and discovered that she had passed after his mother, on May 19, 1994. The timing of her death coincided with Gertrude's last dance with consciousness. She was likely telling the staff at her long-term care facility that she needed to give the key to Fitz.

Fitz tried to comprehend the ramifications of this revelation. He debated whether or not to tell any of his friends. He wondered if there was any way to prove that JFK was his father. Ironically, before this moment, he never gave JFK much thought. If asked to summarize him, Fitz would have said "an overrated, very popular president, who kept the United States from the brink of annihilation in the Cuban Missile Crisis; killed by Lee Harvey Oswald or some conspiracy; with a reputation for sleeping around." Now Fitz could add "father" to that narrative, as well as "mistress" to the characterization of his mother. He never bore a grudge against his mother for her silence regarding his father – he surmised there must be a good reason – and now he was quite grateful that he had not. He also had one comedic spasm: he now owned the best pick-up line in the world.

These thoughts and questions drifted in and out of his head. What stayed was the natural curiosity that would grip someone who had just learned the identity of his father. The great news for Fitz was that his desire for knowledge could be quenched a thousand times over. His father was one of the most popular figures of the 20th century. He could feel this interest boiling into a passion during the hour and thirty minutes it took to make the trip back to his residence in SoHo.

Once home, he immediately opened the other envelope. Inside was a very long strand of pearls mentioned in his mother's note, along with a glass tube that was designed to hold collar stays. Inside was the lock of hair that looked to be in an advanced stage of disintegration. Also contained in the envelope were the Christmas card and three notes written on presidential stationary, all addressed to "Dear Mary." The first note, dated February 14, 1963 said quite simply: "Dear Mary, I wish this could all be different. Bye Mary, Jack." The second note, dated August 10, 1963, said: "Dear Mary, My heart is pregnant with pain. In one day, I have lost two. Bye Mary, Jack." Fitz recognized this note as the "tacit acknowledgement of your birth" with "two" being a reference to the death of his son Patrick and to the birth of Fitz, the son he would never know. He now knew why his name was "Fitzgerald" – the "Cavendish" name was still a mystery.

The third note was odd, very odd. Dated November 19, 1963, it said:

2^2

3^3

10,91,529,___

Nov 19

Dear Mary:

I spoke of my killers
and they are near.

..Bye Mary 30

"Dear Mary, I spoke of my killers and they are near. . _ _ _ Bye Nary 30," with, "2^2 3^3 10, 91, 529, ____," at the upper right of the page. It wasn't even signed. Fitz reasoned that JFK knew his fate was sealed and was cryptically telling his mother the identity of the 'sealers'. Mary Jane loved a good puzzle. But under those circumstances -- with a new-born baby, a dead father who had talked at length to her about his 'enemies', and a vow of silence -- this one was better left unsolved. Fitz also loved a good puzzle, but it was 'Greek' to him on initial inspection. As intriguing as this letter was, Fitz had thousands of other sources to reference. He went to his computer and ordered up a dozen books on JFK in an attempt to better "know" his father.

Chapter 6 (1799 – 1815)

Having achieved military successes throughout Europe and Egypt on behalf of France, Napoleon Bonaparte turned his attention on the Directorate that had bankrupted his country by borrowing money at interest (i.e. debt-based money) to finance his military campaigns. Napoleon successfully engineered a coup on November 9, 1799, eventually resulting in the founding of the Bank of France in 1800. The Banque de France issued *interest-free* loans to its citizens, which were a direct threat to the Rothschild debt-based model. Although Napoleon did borrow at interest from banks, he was strongly opposed to central banking, so much so that in order to finance his imperialist ambitions throughout Europe he sold the Louisiana Purchase to the United States for $3 million in gold in order to avoid the banker's unwanted influence. Napoleon was quoted as saying:

> "When a government is dependent upon bankers for money, they and not the leaders of the government control the situation, since the hand that gives is above the hand that takes. Money has no motherland; financiers are without patriotism and without decency; their sole object is gain."

This may sound like sour grapes, but his campaigns throughout Europe from 1803 – 1815, more commonly known as the "Napoleonic Wars", were a threat to the debt-based central banking practices of the Rothschilds and the Bank of England. On March 17, 1808, Napoleon drew another line in the sand against the bankers (specifically, the Jewish bankers) when he issued the Infamous Decree. It annulled all debts owed to Jews by married women, minors, and soldiers and voided any loan that had interest rates exceeding ten percent. At every step along the way, Napoleon battled a country that was being financed by the Rothschilds.

Ironically, when his campaigns across Europe proved to be too aggressive for his bankroll, he borrowed money from Rothschild banks. It was from this point forward that central bankers funded both sides of every major conflict in Europe, with the stipulation in many instances, that the victor guarantee the debts of the vanquished. As M.A. Rothschild adjudged a few decades prior, war was a great business for central banking. Countries borrowed at any amount to insure victory, and as the losing side became desperate, it used up any remaining resource in an attempt to alter its fate, and with the victor guaranteeing its debts, central bankers couldn't lose. As the countries became more indebted fighting off Napoleon, the central bankers became wealthier. Napoleon's defeat at Waterloo not only ended the last serious threat to modern debt-based central banking in Europe, but also placed the Rothschild family in commanding control of central banking.

Before the age of the telegraph, news traveled slowly. The primary way to obtain information was through courier services. The Rothschilds employed their own couriers, who enjoyed special privileges, such as safe passage through naval blockades, to aide in the conduct of business. One courier in particular would be instrumental in amassing the greatest financial fortune of all time. Before the Battle of Waterloo began, its outcome was anything but assured. Napoleon's forces totaled 74,000, while the armies of the Seventh Coalition numbered 68,000 under the command of the Duke of Wellington and 50,000 Prussians under the guidance of Prince Blucher. With hostilities set to commence on June 18, 1815, Nathan Rothschild placed a courier named Rothworth at the battle scene. Once Napoleon's defeat was all but assured, Rothworth raced to a boat in Ostend, Belgium, through naval blockades, and back to Folkstone Harbour in Kent, England to deliver the news to Nathan Rothschild on the morning of June 20, 1815, a full day ahead of Wellington's courier.

Armed with this information, Nathan went to the stock exchange. Already, a hugely influential figure in finance, observers watched his every move. So, when he started to sell British consols (bonds), other brokers and speculators assumed that Rothschild had received word that Britain had lost the Battle of Waterloo. A defeat at Waterloo would be disastrous to British financial markets. Panic selling ensued and the consols' values plummeted. In the crowd, Rothschild placed agents who started quietly buying up nearly all the consols at a fraction of the previous day's closing price. When word arrived from Wellington's courier, a full day later, trumpeting Napoleon's demise, consol prices skyrocketed at least twenty-fold – some estimates are much greater -- making Nathan a vast fortune. Nathan parlayed this engineered financial stampede into a controlling position in the Bank of England. From this point forward, the Rothschilds dominated Europe. Some portraits of the family say that they achieved their wealth through the sheer scale and sophistication of their operations. All true, especially after 1815. Some biographies say that they didn't want wars and were against lending to belligerent states. Nothing could be more disingenuous. They made money financing wars; they made money financing the post-war reconstruction; and they made money trading on 'inside information' regarding the outcomes of wars. Yes, they financed trade, and that trade could be interrupted as a result of conflict, but they made money off the conflict as well. An article in April 1887 Quarterly Journal of Economics summed up the situation that has menaced Europe from the early 1800s onward:

> "A detailed revue of the public debts of Europe shows interest and sinking fund payments of $5,343 million annually [$5.343 billion]. M. Neymarck's conclusion is much like Mr. Atkinson's. The finances of Europe are so involved that the governments may ask whether war, with all its terrible chances, is not preferable to the maintenance of such a precarious and costly peace. If the military preparations of Europe do not end in war, they may well end in the bankruptcy of the States. Or, if such follies lead neither to war nor to ruin, then they assuredly point to industrial and economic revolution."

Under a debt-based money system, bankruptcy of countries (and its citizens) is the inevitable consequence -- if you don't believe this statement, just look at the current public debt of every country. This dynamic is accelerated through the war process: 1. Bankers advise European governments to build up their armies and navies. (Why wouldn't they, given the inter-state distrust cultivated from prior conflicts?) 2. Military buildup throughout Europe breeds an atmosphere of paranoia. 3. The cost of this escalation becomes a burden on the population of each nation-state. 4. Governments and their leaders become less favored. 5. Seeing their grip on the population slipping, the governments of nation-states create an enemy image in the form of other nation-states, whipping up patriotism. 6. War is declared. The bankers enrich themselves on interest from money they initially created out of thin air. Rinse and repeat until Europe is so war weary and bankrupt that they will look for an alternative: a European Union, the first step in a one-world government. Your caramel macchiato keeps getting more expensive.

Chapter 7 (September 2015 – February 2016)

Fitz decided to tell no one about his 'discovery'. He spent weeks inside his dwelling researching his father. He discovered that the name Cavendish was the last name of a JFK brother-in-law. *She left me a clue.* JFK had a remarkable life. Born into excessive wealth, he was a Harvard grad, a best-selling author (*Why England Slept*), a Pulitzer Prize winner (for *Profiles in Courage,* although it was probably ghost-written), a war hero, U.S. Congressman, U.S. Senator, and 35th President of the United States. At every step along the way was the influence of an obsessed father. *Maybe that ardent influence is what it takes. If I had that kind of wealth, I would be summering on the French Riviera.* Fitz then realized he *had* spent summers on the French Riviera, thanks in part to the wealth he 'inherited' from *his* father. Despite weeks of searching, Fitz never saw a mention of his mother in any publication or online forum.

However, Fitz discovered that his father possessed a deep and unending appetite for women and the wherewithal to satisfy his hunger. He had a veritable trove of lovers: assistants "Fiddle" and "Faddle", his wife's press secretary, a suspected East German spy, the wife of a CIA officer, a mob moll, Marilyn Monroe, Marlene Dietrich, just to name a few -- and, of course, Fitz's mother. In fact, he impregnated another woman -- Judith Exner – who elected to have the pregnancy terminated. To be sure, Jack wasn't the only one sleeping around. Jackie's affairs were more discreet, but included William Holden, Fiat heir Gianni Agnelli, and quite possibly Jack's brothers post mortem – *so, that's how it is in my family.* To be fair, Jackie's affairs were probably a heartbroken response to Jack's extracurricular activities. JFK's proclivity for the ladies made Mary Jane's belief that JFK "had deep feelings" for her a little less believable. There was no way to avoid it. Mary Jane was just one of dozens of affairs that the 35th President enjoyed. However, that answer didn't explain the third and final note – an abstruse correspondence written before and received after his death. *Maybe he respected my mother's discretion – they already shared a profound secret (me). If he didn't die in office, she would never reveal this moment of resignation (or fear). Or maybe he respected my mother's ability to solve puzzles. If he did die, she would solve the note's hidden message and reveal the killer's identity.*

In addition to his predilection for women and drugs – JFK was always on 'uppers' and 'downers' for chronic back issues – he had a knack (bordering on talent) for making enemies everywhere he turned. Although loved by the citizens of the United States, everyone in a position of power seemed to loath Jack. Until now, Fitz had no idea as to the number of books written on his father's assassination, with the vast majority claiming a conspiracy – even the U.S. House Select Committee on Assassinations in 1979 concluded "that Kennedy was probably assassinated as a result of a conspiracy." The list of potential killers was long. During his research, Fitz found no fewer than six individuals or groups that could have wanted JFK dead. That list did not include Fidel Castro or Nikita Khrushchev, both with whom Jack retained 'back channel' communications; or Lee Harvey Oswald. The suspects included:

1. Lyndon Baines Johnson, 36th President of the United States. He was being dropped by Jack Kennedy as the Vice-President on the 1964 ticket. Jack's brother Bobby, then Attorney General, was leaking information to *LIFE* magazine regarding LBJ's suspicious business dealings with Bobby Baker -- who had just resigned as Secretary of the Senate during an ongoing investigation concerning claims of bribery and arrangement of sexual favors in return for votes. The Senate investigation into Baker's and Johnson's questionable financial activities was going to be the lead story of the December 6, 1963 issue and there was a good chance that LBJ would end up in jail once these revelations were made public and thoroughly investigated. After the assassination, any investigation of LBJ as part of the Bobby Baker scandal was dropped. *LIFE* magazine's December 6, 1963 issue covered the funeral of JFK with no mention of LBJ or Bobby Baker.

2. J. Edgar Hoover, Director of the FBI. He was going to be 'forced' into retirement when he reached the then mandatory retirement age of 70 on January 1, 1965. Although, this may seem a minor point, he disliked Jack, detested Bobby, and was good friends with LBJ. He also had the "dirt" on every political figure in Washington D.C. – including the Kennedys -- and he was a little over a year away from being stripped of his power. After the assassination, LBJ made Hoover Director of the FBI for life.

3. The Mafia. JFK won the 1960 election by the slimmest of margins over Richard M. Nixon. He won the election because he carried the state of Illinois. He won Illinois by 9,000 votes (out of 4.75 million cast) because he won Chicago in a landslide. He carried Chicago because of some help from the Mob. That help was negotiated by Jack's father, former Ambassador Joseph P. Kennedy. According to Sam Giancana's daughter, former Ambassador Kennedy agreed to kill the Eisenhower Justice Department's efforts to extradite Santo Trafficante and Carlos Marcello, two prominent mob chieftains, in return for the mob's help in Chicago. Giancana delivered Illinois, but Joe wasn't willing to help the Mob until he received 50% of the action at the Cal-Neva Casino in Lake Tahoe, Nevada to keep up Giancana's side of an earlier deal. Meanwhile, Attorney General Robert Kennedy (Jack's brother) was carrying on a very public crusade against organized crime. Giancana made good on the Cal-Neva deal, but soon after, Joe had a stroke, leaving him unable to communicate with his sons. As a result, the 'heat' on the mafia continued, including a short-lived extradition of Marcello, rumored to be the top don in the United States.

Also, when Castro took over Cuba, the mafia lost their hotel and casino properties. Its best chance of recovering those assets came and went with the Bay of Pigs fiasco, which the mob blamed on Kennedy for failing to provide air support – something he never promised. After the assassination, the 'heat' on the mob decreased significantly.

4. The CIA. After the disastrous Bay of Pigs incident, JFK threatened to "splinter the CIA into a thousand pieces and scatter it into the winds." Whether he actually intended to do that to the agency is a subject of debate. What is not subject to debate is that he asked for (and received) the resignations of CIA chief Allen Dulles, Deputy Director Charles Cabell, and Deputy Director for Plans Richard M. Bissell Jr. The CIA was not pleased with the direction that JFK was taking the country. After the assassination, the CIA continued to flourish and operates a 'shadow government' to this day.

5. Texas Oil. JFK decided that the oil tycoons were not paying their fair share of income tax. They exploited many loopholes in the tax code and Kennedy vowed to close them. He succeeded in October 1962 with the passage of the Revenue Act of 1962 that eliminated the distinction

between repatriated profits and profits reinvested abroad. This provision specifically hurt the oil industry, which had drilling operations throughout the world. If the Revenue Act of 1962 angered the oilmen, JFK's proposal in January of 1963 to do away with (or at least cut) the oil depletion allowance made them seething mad. During the 1960s campaign, JFK supported the depletion allowance claiming that he appreciated "the value and importance of the oil-depletion allowance. I realize its purpose and value... The oil-depletion allowance has served us well." To be fair, he also said (in a 1960 presidential debate with Vice-President Nixon) that "if there is [sic] any inequities in oil or any other commodity, then I would vote to close that loophole." His proposal in 1963 was taken as a betrayal by the Texas Oil men. After the assassination, any talk of removing or reducing the oil-depletion allowance ceased.

6. The Military-Industrial Complex. This nexus of senior military brass and top executives in the defense industry had a vested interest in keeping America at war. Kennedy's NSAM (National Security Action Memorandum) 263 called for the removal of 1,000 military personnel from South Vietnam by the end of 1963. This was the first step in a larger plan to completely withdraw from the Southeast Asian state. Starting with the Cuban Missile Crisis, JFK maintained a secret dialogue with Soviet Leader Nikita Khrushchev. A trust grew between the two publically adversarial world leaders. Kennedy's famous "Peace Speech" at American University on June 10, 1963 was directed at Khrushchev -- "if we cannot now end our differences, at least we can make the world safe for diversity" – and resulted in the Partial Nuclear Test Ban Treaty which, went into effect on October 10, 1963. The military-industrial complex was not in accord with Kennedy's actions – be it for philosophical or financial reasons. After the assassination, NSAM 263 was essentially reversed by LBJ's NSAM 273 and the Vietnam War followed. The military-industrial complex made a fortune from the war that took 58,000 American lives. Many say that NSAM 273 was drafted by Kennedy before he left for Dallas, but that just isn't true. McGeorge Bundy drafted that memorandum while Kennedy was in Texas and Kennedy would have never approved. When JFK's national security advisers met in Honolulu on Nov. 20, 1963, their briefing books reiterated the plans for withdrawal from South Vietnam without victory. In fact, Kennedy said to his Assistant Press Secretary Malcolm Kilduff the day before his assassination,

"We're losing too damned many people over there [Vietnam]. It's time for us to get out. The Vietnamese aren't fighting for themselves. We're the ones who are doing the fighting. After I come back from Texas, that's going to change. There's no reason for us to lose another man over there. Vietnam is not worth another American life."

Fitz was moved by an article written by Robert F. Kennedy Jr. – *my half-cousin* – for *Rolling Stone* on December 5, 2013. One section in particular convinced him that Kennedy was pulling out of Vietnam,

"By the summer of 1963, JFK was quietly telling trusted friends and advisers he intended to get out following the 1964 election. These included Rep. Tip O'Neill, [Secretary of Defense Robert] McNamara, National Security adviser McGeorge Bundy, Sen. Wayne Morse, Washington columnist Charles Bartlett, Canadian Prime Minister Lester Pearson, confidant Larry Newman, Gen. Taylor and Marine Commandant Gen. David M. Shoup, who, besides Taylor, was the only other member of the Joint Chiefs that JFK trusted. Both McNamara and Bundy acknowledged in their respective memoirs that JFK meant to get out – which were jarring admissions against self-interest, since these two would remain in the Johnson administration and orchestrate the war's escalation.

"That spring, JFK had told Montana Sen. Mike Mansfield, who would become the Vietnam War's most outspoken Senate critic, 'I can't do it until 1965, after I'm re-elected.' Later that day, he explained to Kenneth O'Donnell, 'If I tried to pull out completely from Vietnam, we would have another Joe McCarthy Red scare on our hands, but I can do it after I'm re-elected.'"

To be sure, JFK made other enemies. The anti-Castro Cubans, who also blamed him for the Bay of Pigs, would have liked him 'removed' from office. However, as far as Fitz was concerned, none of these groups individually had the ability to commit the crime and cover it up. The CIA could've 'outed' the FBI and vice-versa. If the mob acted alone, some agency or Bobby Kennedy would have gotten to the bottom of the crime of the century and the mafia would have been rooted out once and for all. If this was LBJ's brainchild alone, he would have been figured out by the investigatory agencies (military and/or civilian) and then either charged with JFK's murder or (as it turned out) compromised during his tenure as president. Fitz was confident that Lee Harvey Oswald's role in the assassination was that of the 'patsy'. *There has to be more to the death of my father.*

Chapter 8 (1791 -1835)

While Napoleon was waging war in Europe, battles continued in the United States between the debt-based money cabal and the *debt-free* money coalition. Having fought and won the Revolutionary War over the ability to produce their own *debt-free* money, citizens soon became fearful of government issued *debt-free* fiat (meaning not backed by a precious metal) currency when the 'Continental' failed. The Continental was the *debt-free* fiat currency issued by the colonies to finance their war of independence against the British. The currency failed due to a massive counterfeiting campaign instigated by the British during the Revolutionary War. That is why you heard the slogan, "not worth a Continental" in high school history class. The currency was essentially worthless because the British produced 'fake' Continentals in many multiples of the 'real' Continentals, destroying its value. It did not fail because it wasn't backed by gold, silver, or another commodity (i.e. because it was fiat) and it didn't fail because it wasn't debt-based -- funny how you were taught about the Continental, but not about the actual source of all the unnecessary economic downturns throughout history.

Because the Continental's collapse was fresh on citizens' minds, Alexander Hamilton was able to push through the deceptively named First Bank of the United States. This bank loaned money to the government and was owned by private individuals. Even though the main point of the Revolutionary War was to get rid of debt-based money creation, Hamilton sold other lawmakers on the idea that only the debt-money issued by private banks would be accepted in dealings abroad; thus a national bank was necessary to stabilize and improve the credit of the callow, fledging United States government in the eyes of the rest of the world. What he failed to mention is that a country doesn't need to have its credit 'improved' if it is operating under a *debt-free* money system. If the government needs more capital, it can just produce more, as opposed to having a bank 'just produce more' and charge interest for it. This bank was approved over the objection of Thomas Jefferson, framer of the Constitution. Jefferson argued,

> "The incorporation of a bank and the powers assumed [through legislation] have not, in my opinion, been delegated to the United

States by the Constitution. They are not among the powers specially enumerated."

He realized that by giving the responsibility of money creation over to a private bank, a government was handing over its sovereignty to the bankers. Despite his arguments, the act was passed and the bank created.

Within five years, prices in the United States increased by 72% as the government borrowed $8.2 million from the bank. This prompted Jefferson to declare,

> "I wish it were possible to obtain a single amendment to our Constitution. I would be willing to depend on that alone for the reduction of the administration of our government; I mean an additional article taking from the Federal Government the power of borrowing."

By the time the bank's charter was due for renewal in 1811, there was a movement afoot to kill the bank, as people saw the inflationary consequences of a government borrowing from a private bank. Summing up this movement, Jefferson later stated,

> "[The] Bank of the United States... is one of the most deadly hostility existing, against the principles and form of our Constitution... An institution like this, penetrating by its branches every part of the Union, acting by command and in phalanx, may, in a critical moment, upset the government. I deem no government safe which is under the vassalage of any self-constituted authorities, or any other authority than that of the nation, or its regular functionaries. What an obstruction could not this bank of the United States, with all its branch banks, be in time of war! It might dictate to us the peace we should accept, or withdraw its aids. Ought we then to give further growth to an institution so powerful, so hostile?"

The charter was not renewed by the slimmest of margins.

Allegedly, in 1811, a quote was attributed to Nathan Rothschild, "Either the application for the renewal of the charter is granted, or the United States will find itself involved in a most disastrous war." The source of this quote has never been determined. Regardless of its authenticity, it seems odd that the British would want to entice the United States into a war when it was busy with Napoleon in Europe. In fact, British Prime Minister Spencer Perceval was against the idea of war with the United States. To remove resistance to the War of 1812, Perceval was slain by an assassin named John Bellingham. To say that the influence of the bankers was not at play here would be akin to sticking ones head in the sand. With Perceval out of the way, hostilities commenced five weeks later. The war ended in a stalemate for the United States and Great Britain. The winners were (as always) the bankers, as the United States and Great Britain both spent $100 million US (approx.) on the war and watched their debts expand by $80 million and 25 million pounds respectively. Even though the United States had successfully ended the First Bank of the United States, it didn't have the resolve, the insight, or the votes to print *debt-free* money to finance the conflict. As a result, the US government borrowed heavily from Barings Bank, *based in London, England,* to fight Great Britain.

After the War of 1812, the United States was heavily indebted to banks abroad, with unregulated currency running rampant at home. President Madison, who fought against the bank his entire political life, was at crossroads. He had vetoed the charter for the Second Bank in 1814, but desperately needed to get the country's fiscal house in order. Seeing no pragmatic alternative, Congress passed and Madison -- citing necessity, not principle -- signed into law a charter for the Second Bank of the United States in 1816, marking another victory for the debt-based money cabal. Four thousand private investors held 80% of the bank's capital, including one thousand Europeans. The bulk of the stocks were held by a few hundred wealthy Americans. Despite this quasi-democratic ownership, it was widely known that the principal investor in the Second Bank of the United States was Baron James de Rothschild of Paris (one of M.A.'s sons) through his 'agents' in the United States and Europe.

Andrew Jackson, War of 1812 hero, realizing the unconstitutionality of the Second Bank commented, "If Congress has a right under the Constitution to issue paper money, it was given them to use by themselves, not to be delegated to individuals or corporations." What followed was a speculative boom and bust known as the Panic of 1819 – which was brought about when specie payments (i.e. gold and silver) were due on bonds that financed the Louisiana Purchase in 1803. A severe, three-year recession followed. Even though Rothschild protégé Nicholas Biddle righted the bank and the economy in the mid-to-late-1820s, Andrew Jackson, who understood the fundamental flaw of debt-based banking, was sowing the seeds for its demise.

Chapter 9 (February 2016)

Fitz's research continued unabated for months to the exclusion of everything else. Besides a ritualistic visit to the gym or an occasional trip to the grocery store, the normally chipper Cavendish had not been seen by one friend in New York City for five months -- since he had made that transformative trip to the safe deposit box. The El Nino winter was mild, making less convenient, less credible excuses for his social absenteeism. He had learned so much about his father and his sudden demise, but he had yet to solve the rebus left by JFK in his final correspondence to Fitz's mother. His failure to solve it was starting to wear on him.

Fitz's smart phone flashed. He had kept it on silent mode for months and the voice mails had piled up. He returned the voice mails with text messages, but hadn't had any conversations with most of his cadre for months. The call was from Chuck Schilling, a partner at a small advertising/public relations firm, and friend from Brown who had recently divorced, and was probably looking to get out. Fitz answered liked sports radio personality Jim Rome, "Hey Chuck. What is UP?"

"Not much. What is up with you? Are you alive? Rumor has it that you are shacked-up with some 22-year old smoke show. When are you going to bring her out in public?"

"I wish it were true. Just been doing a little research and trying to stay warm."

"No lady? What is UP?"

The result of the conversation was an agreement to attend a fund-raiser in the Gramercy Park area. Fitz needed a break and these philanthropic events always brought out a bevy of young, very attractive husband shoppers. A decision was made to meet at the Edition Hotel lobby bar on 24th and Madison before heading to the gala.

Chuck was waiting at the bar when Fitz arrived. A big hug was exchanged and 'catching up' ensued. Schilling discussed his latest dates – it seemed he wanted a serious relationship. Fitz was enjoying the small talk. He did not share his 'revelation' with Chuck, but throughout the conversation, he realized that a weight had been lifted from him. He now knew the identity of his father and that filled him with a quiet pride. Although social, Cavendish was never an extrovert. He rarely imposed himself on any one, but tonight he felt a certain confidence, bordering on temerity. After a Krome Vodka and club soda, his self-belief elevated some more.

Before he had a chance to feel any better about himself, Fitz's scan of the room suddenly turned into laser focus. There *she* was. He didn't know her yet, but there *she* was. Chuck's voice drifted into the background. *She*: 5'8", size zero, black hair, dark brown eyes, and legs like a gazelle, full b-cups, and a countenance like New York Eyewitness News anchor Liz Cho, with a hints of Halle Berry and Eva Longoria. Those were the specs, but to Fitz it looked as if God had summoned Da Vinci, Van Gogh, and Rembrandt, daring transcendence until they had arrived at her. This was not a thing of the flesh. This was a motor response, yet it was a suspension of innervations – no response. Many who have had near-death experiences describe 'meeting Jesus'. They describe a feeling of blissful nothingness, so overpowering that they tell Jesus they don't want to go back to the physical world. Fitz was 'meeting Jesus', but was still thirty feet from talking to her. And *she* had a potential suitor chatting her up. Even though *she* was two inches shorter – the guy was 6'1" and her heels made her 5'11" – *she* seemed to be looking down on him, like a queen listening to a request from a member of her court. It wasn't condescending. It was playful, as if *she* might burst out in laughter at his first absurdity.

Fitz's cabin was depressurizing. He was trying to pay attention to Chuck, waiting for the right moment to respond to whatever he was talking about, but his blankness moved Chuck to look over his left shoulder and eyeball the source of Fitz's distraction. After a quick inspection, Chuck turned back to Fitz and simply said, "Whooow."

"Yeah," was all Fitz could muster. This wasn't a one in five hundred. This was one in five hundred thousand, perhaps more. Fitz surmised he could ride a beam of light to the other end of the universe and never find something so stunning. Suddenly, it appeared that *she* and her girlfriends – whom he hadn't even noticed -- might leave. *No!* Fitz hastily moved toward her in an attempt to stop her before *she* left. But before he could get close to her, he realized that her group wasn't headed for the exit, but rather to the bathroom located just off the lobby. Fitz dragged a slightly surprised Chuck to a place away from the bar so he could eye her re-emergence from the loo, on the chance that it was just a quick detour before *she* left the hotel. The guy *she* was talking to was now nowhere to be seen. Although a lot of thoughts were running through his head, his mind was not racing. Fitz was in a trance. *She* then emerged with her friends and, to the relief of Fitz, was on her way back to the bar. About five feet from the bar, Fitz stopped her with a tap of his right index finger on her shoulder. "Excuse me. Who are you? What were you before? What did you do? And what did you think? And may I buy you and your friends a drink?" Like a prize fighter struck with a punch, *she* had an "unconscious moment". It wasn't the line -- stolen, though pretty good – but the seriousness with which it was delivered. For Fitz, it wasn't a line, and it was as serious as serious could be. *She* recovered weakly with, "Okay. Sure."

"What would you and your friends like?"

"Two Grenaches and a Pinot Noir."

"Chuck. You need?"   Chuck had engaged her friends in conversation.

"Yes. I'll take an IPA."

After several trips to and from the bar, Fitz emerged with her Grenache and his first question. "Hi I'm Fitz. Fitzgerald Cavendish. What is your name?"

Fighting an urge to laugh at such a pretentious name, *she* got out, "Ann. My friends call me Annie."

"May I ask you your last name Annie?"

"Van."

Annie Van. I will never forget this moment. "So, Annie Van, who are you? Tell me about yourself. What gives you fulfillment?"

All she could get out was, "I love my dog. Would you like to see a picture?" She wanted to scream at herself for the overtly nervous, idiotic response. The silly reply had the effect of pulling Fitz out of his trance, and bringing a smile to his face. Fitz, an animal enthusiast, was eager to see her dog.

"Absolutely! What kind of dog?"

"He's a Jack Russel Terrier. His name is Oliver."

Fitz melted when he saw the dog pictures on her smart phone. However, he was so taken with Annie, her dog could have looked like an armadillo, and he would have thought it cute. Any creature with Annie was going to have an adorable quality to it, Fitz decided. Annie and Fitz were inseparable the rest of the evening. Like Fitz, Annie's father was a mystery to her. He had passed away when she was one and her mother rarely spoke of him. When Fitz told Annie that he also never knew his father – which after five months of research, was beginning to feel like a lie – there was an empathetic look in each other's eyes that brought them even closer. It turned out that Annie's opening response to Fitz belied her intelligence. Annie graduated from NYU *summa cum laude*, and was working as a teacher at the United Nations School – she hated it – and she spent her free time volunteering at various animal shelters, which she loved. Her pulchritude belied her age. Fitz figured her for twenty-seven. She was thirty-eight. Her eyes were almond shaped and the dark brown irises seemed to occupy an inordinate amount of their space. She had never been married. Why? This alembic of elegance must have been the target of a hundred courting requests every year. Could it be? *Indeed!* Her tenure at the UN School had the effect of birth control. She was not interested in producing offspring. *Jackpot!* Neither Fitz nor Chuck ever made it to the fundraiser. Chuck was entertaining Annie's friends in the hopes of securing a date, or at least a phone number. Cavendish was making plans for a show and dinner – and the rest of his life.

Chapter 10 (1829 – 1837)

Andrew Jackson, seventh President of the United States, said the debt-based Second Bank of the United States was a "hydra of corruption" that made "the rich richer and the potent more powerful." As president, he worked tirelessly to undermine it. In his first annual address to Congress on December 8, 1829, Jackson asked it to review the bank's charter on the grounds of its constitutionality. Although Congress found nothing wrong with the bank's constitutionality, Jackson would not be deterred. In his second annual address to Congress on December 7, 1830, he proposed a replacement to the central bank: a *debt-free* bank that would have no private shareholders. It would not make loans or purchase property, but issue bills of exchange (*debt-free* money) to support its operation.

Rothschild agent Nicholas Biddle, president of the Second Bank of the United States, saw that the re-chartering of the bank was now not only uncertain, but also a very public matter. Pro-bank Senators and Whig party members Henry Clay and Daniel Webster saw a chance to paint Jackson into a corner by pushing for the re-authorization of the bank four years early, during an election year, and convinced Biddle to support their strategy. The bill to re-charter the bank was introduced on January 9, 1832, and after much debate and animosity, passed both houses of Congress on July 3rd. The following day, Jackson said famously to the future eighth President of the United States, "The Bank, Mr. Van Buren, is trying to kill me, but I shall kill it." Jackson vetoed the bill on July 10th saying,

> "The many millions which this act proposes to bestow on the stockholders of the existing bank must come directly or indirectly out of the earnings of the American people....It appears that more than a fourth part of the stock is held by foreigners.... Is there no danger to our liberty and independence in a bank that in its nature has so little to bind it to our country?"

A subsequent override vote fell short. Jackson had prevailed.

Jackson was re-elected as the Whig Party plan backfired. He killed the bank by depositing federal money into 'pet' state banks. In defeat, Biddle massively contracted the money supply in an attempt to cause a financial retraction and blame it on Jackson. The president's reaction to the bankers was not measured,

> "You tell me that if I take the deposits from the bank and annul its charter I shall ruin ten thousand families. That may be true, gentlemen, but that is your sin! Should I let you go on, you will ruin fifty thousand families, and that would be my sin! You are a den of vipers and thieves. I have determined to rout you out, and by the Eternal, (bringing his fist down on the table) I will rout you out!"

The defeated Whig Party rallied for and succeeded in obtaining a censure of President Jackson for "violating the Constitution" – how unfairly ironic. It was rescinded in 1837.

But that wasn't all: on January 30, 1835, in the same month that Jackson made the final payment on the United States debt, Richard Lawrence, an unemployed house painter from England, attempted to assassinate Jackson, but his pistol misfired. Lawrence pulled out a second pistol, which also misfired. [Talk about your lucky day!] At his trial, Lawrence blamed Jackson and his decision to end the Second Bank of the United States for the loss of his job. He was deemed insane and was institutionalized. Jackson knew that the European debt-based banking cabal was behind it. Richard Lawrence even bragged that he was put up to this presidential assassination attempt – the first ever in the United States – by powerful European banking interests.

Jackson became the only president in the history of the United States to pay off its debt, because he understood the dynamics and shortcomings of debt-based money. After "killing the bank", the United States government enjoyed a $50 million surplus and the economy initially boomed. Unfortunately, because he issued an executive order known as the Species Circular, many outstanding loans had to be paid back in silver and gold. Since there was not enough silver and gold circulating through the economy, many investors were unable to pay off loans backed by gold and silver. This action, in and of itself, would have contracted the economy. However, when the Rothschild-controlled Bank of England suddenly refused to accept any US securities as collateral or redeem them for cash, the United States securities market seized up, causing a massive contraction of credit, leading to the Panic of 1837, and another six years of economic hardship, which was wrongly blamed on Martin Van Buren.

To review: *no central bank means no debt*!! Were you taught this in history class? For a couple of years, you caramel macchiato didn't get more expensive.

Chapter 11 (February - May 2016)

About two and half months had passed since their first date that included roses and a note, "When God created the rose, he was thinking of you", "The Book of Mormon", dinner at One if by Land, Two if by Sea, and a meet and greet with Oliver, whose shiny, short white coat, light brown patch encircling his right eye, light brown spotted right ear, and light brown left ear qualified him as the cutest dog in New York City, and a perfect complement to Annie. Since that time a routine developed: Annie would teach on the weekdays, while Fitz did his research. Fitz would spend the weekday nights at Annie's, while Annie and Oliver would spend the weekends at Fitz's. They would both spend Saturday morning and early afternoon volunteering at an animal shelter; Saturday late afternoon grocery shopping; and Saturday night at Fitz's, consuming whatever bounty Annie crafted. Oliver, Annie, and Fitz would cuddle on the couch until someone fell asleep, which prompted all three to go to bed. Sunday was lazy and unscripted. It included brunch with friends – Chuck had a budding romance of his own with one of Annie's friends, Wendy – and walks around the city with Oliver. Annie and Fitz were undeniably in love, and Fitz was conflicted as to whether or not to tell Annie his 'secret'. Fitz considered never telling anyone and taking his discovery to the grave. What good would it do him to let the world know? Publicity was not an aim of Fitz's, especially now. He was content to spend every day with Annie and Oliver and retreat into blissful oblivion forever. Annie certainly didn't care. How could she? However, her brilliance would accidentally change their plans forever.

It was a rainy Sunday morning, May 1st. Annie, usually the last to stir, went to the news stand to get the *New York Times*. They both wanted the *Sunday Times* for the magazine section. Fitz was amazed at how fast she could finish the Sunday crossword and Annie was equally impressed when he solved both KenKen puzzles in less than ten minutes. But it was the puzzle that was sitting on the coffee table under a magazine that spurred Annie's curiosity. It was in Fitz's hand writing:

(J, AM, EO, WT, ATT, EMT, ETM, ETTT) Bye (M)Nary 30

$$2^2$$

$$3^3$$

$$10, 91, 529,$$

Annie quickly deduced that 2^2 and 3^3 were 4 and 27. The other two clues were going to take thought. Oliver emerged from the bedroom with Fitz in tow. Annie asked, "What's this?" Fitz, still clearing his eyes, focused on the paper, quickly cursed himself, calmly recovered, and lied to Annie for the first time ever,

"It's a puzzle a friend of mine gave to me."

"Who gave it to you? Were you able to solve it?"

"Evan (Spring)...and I haven't given it much thought yet." (Lies two and three.)

"Really? Every time I see you with a puzzle you can't put it down until you solve it."

"Okay. I haven't solved it yet. Have you?"

"Well, I think I have it mostly complete."

Fitz couldn't believe what he was hearing, "How so?"

"Well, ignoring the top line for a moment, the first two parts are obvious: 4 and 27. The third clue seems to be a numerical sequence. 10 is a product of two prime numbers: 2 and 5. 91 is the product of two prime numbers as well: 7 and 13. The same can be said for 529, which is 23 squared." Fitz was impressed that she had figured this out so quickly, but he wasn't hearing anything new. He still couldn't believe that he was so sloppy, leaving out a good bit of the most puzzling (and potentially most important) part of his research. He felt like an ass for lying to her. He quickly snapped to when she continued her reasoning,

"If you line up the prime factors, you get:

2	5	for 10
7	13	for 91
23	23	for 529
?	?	for ?

2 is the first prime number; 5 is the third; 7 is the fourth; 13 is the sixth; and 23 is the ninth."

Fitz saw the flaw in her logic. "That's not right. One is first prime number."

"No Silly. For a number to be considered prime, it must have two different factors."

"Really?"

"Didn't they teach you that at Brown?"

"Apparently not -- or at Andover. Wow that changes everything."

"Wait. Let me finish my train of thought before you chime in." Fitz shut up and Annie continued to talk and write, "So that lineup translates into:

1	3
4	6
9	9
?	?.

So, it would logically follow that the next two numbers would be 16 and 12, which means the 16th and 12th prime numbers should be multiplied together." After a brief pause to tabulate the corresponding prime numbers on the same piece of paper that contained the original puzzle, Annie continued, "37 times 53 is the missing sequence."

"One thousand nine hundred sixty-one," Fitz was able to blurt out before Annie could calculate it with a pen and paper. It was his feeble attempt to regain the cerebral high ground, a foregone lost cause.

While Fitz was patting himself on the back for his quick multiplication, Annie was already one step ahead of him. "Four; twenty-seven; nineteen sixty-one -- the first three clues are a date in history. Did anything significant happen on that date?"

Damn, she is quick. Downright unfair that God put a superior brain on the vessel of a goddess. Fitz prided himself on being great (not good, but great) with numbers, yet he didn't know that one wasn't a prime number, causing him wasted months of consternation with JFK's riddle. *Idiot!*

She picked up her smart phone and googled, "April 27, 1961". "Apparently, Kennedy gave a speech that day on secret societies," Annie quipped casually.

Fitz's head almost exploded. *Holy shit!!! Remain calm.* It was a good thing that Fitz was standing behind Annie, who was sitting on the couch with Oliver. 'Ol' was now requesting his special time with 'Mama'. Annie seemed content to take a break from her remarkably quick deciphering of the cryptogram and cuddle with Oliver. The morning ritual consisted of Oliver facing Annie, sitting up on his hind legs on her lap, with his front paws out to the side – penguin-like – with his head tucked under her chin while she whispered sweet nothings in his ears, such as "Jack Russell's live forever". For Fitz, the moment was pure magic. It usually lasted five minutes. Today, it gave him time to compose himself.

As much as Fitz wanted to read and dissect Kennedy's speech at that very instance, he thought it better to start on the other part of the puzzle to not potentially blow his mind (or cover to Annie) with JFK's speech. It did dawn on him that his father didn't waste his Harvard education. This puzzle required some skill. The 'Bye Mary' or 'Bye Nary' had him confused. He thought that 'Nary' was a misprint or misspelling of his mother's name. 'Nary' meant not any. 'Mary' meant his mother. Either way, he made as much progress as Oliver did with his nose buried in Annie's jugular notch for five minutes.

"Any headway, dough brain?"

"None, oh sage one." Oliver stepped off the couch and headed back to the bedroom. Annie returned to the puzzle.

"What do "M" parentheses "N" stand for?"

Fitz was afraid to give her too much information, but answered, "The clue said 'Nary' but I thought it was a misprint. I thought it was 'Bye, Mary'"

"Why would you think that?"

"It was just the way I read it. It looked as if the person was saying goodbye to someone named Mary," *as in my mother!*

"Well, if it's 'Nary', then I interpret it as 'binary' as in binary logic."

Fitz was dumbfounded again. If he wasn't so convinced that this was a misprint, he would've seen it right away. *Double Idiot!*

Annie continued, "Binary 30. What is 30 in binary numbers?"

Fitz, feeling intellectually emasculated, scrambled to type in binary 30 into his smart phone. "One, one, one, one, zero."

Annie responded, "What do these other letters represent?"

"They represent several different combinations of the same Morse code."

"Type each one in with one, one, one, one, zero and see what you get."

Fitz typed in the first two options ('J' and 'AM') into Google search with no meaningful results. When he typed 'EO', Google produced another stunner. He couldn't lie to her about what the search produced since she could google it herself. "It appears to be an executive order issued by JFK," Fitz replied as nonchalantly as he could.

"Wow -- a Kennedy speech and a Kennedy executive order. Are they related?"

"I'm not in the mood to read speeches or executive orders," Fitz lied for the fourth time. "How bout I take that superior noggin of yours to brunch?"

"How bout we get rations at Whole Foods in Tribeca and I make you brunch, that way you can take my body too?"

"How exactly do I deserve you?"

Chapter 12 (1861 – 1867)

Czar Alexander II did much more for the United States than Christopher Columbus ever did, but the land of the free and the home of the brave has a holiday celebrating a man who came upon the Caribbean Islands on a continent that had been discovered centuries before by the Vikings. Native Americans must have shuttered when Franklin Delano Roosevelt signed into law Columbus Day as a national holiday in 1937. A creation of the Knights of Columbus, the holiday gave the country a Catholic holiday. Even if it was just a feast for Italian Americans, couldn't they find someone more deserving? A review of Columbus: he never set foot on the land that is now the United States of America. He discovered Hispaniola. Upon initial landfall, he was greeted by the peaceful Native Taino/Arawak. Columbus found them so tranquil he surmised that, "They are very gentle and without knowledge of what is evil; nor do they murder or steal." He would go on to say, "They would make fine servants.... With fifty men we could subjugate them all and make them do whatever we want."

Under his stewardship of the island, pillage, rape, and murder were permitted. When he returned on his second voyage, Columbus found that the peaceful Natives had rebelled against these barbaric practices, murdering the thirty-nine sailors he had left behind from the first expedition. Upon discovering the fate of his former crewmen, Columbus turned the atrocity level up a notch. In addition to plunder and rape, Columbus allowed contests where his soldiers – 1,200 in total – would test the sharpness of their swords by cutting Natives in half. Soldiers also roasted them on spits, hung them en masse, or beheaded them for sport. Natives were also dropped in boiling vats of soap. Babies were mutilated and fed to dogs in front of their horrified mothers. Reports of soldiers shoving swords up young boys' rectums are also in the written record.

The Natives were either shipped off to Spain as slaves – many died on the voyage – or used similarly in the Antilles gold mines. If an imposed gold quota wasn't met over a three month period, the slaves had their hands chopped off, causing them to bleed to death. An estimated 10,000 Natives met this fate. Others were forced into sex slavery, as young as nine. To be sure, not everyone who came over with Columbus approved of such heinousness. A royal commissioner had Columbus arrested in 1500 and taken back to Spain, where he was promptly pardoned and given financing for a fourth voyage. Estimates vary widely for the total population (from 500,000 to 8,000,000), but in a thirty-year period after Columbus' arrival, the population of Taino/Arawak declined by 80 to 90%. They died from disease, famine, suicide, and murder. A census fifty years after Columbus' arrival revealed that *only 200* remained. Specifically, the Taino became extinct as a distinct population by the end of the 16th century. History is a fable constructed by the winners. Nice going FDR.

While Columbus Day parades are now the norm in the New York City, a much more deserving parade was once thrown down Broadway – during the Civil War -- in honor of a munificent gesture by your Russian ally, Alexander II. Alexander's uncle, Alexander I, was instrumental in blocking the European Union 184 years before its actual formation. After the Napoleonic conflicts, most European governments were war weary and in great financial debt to Rothschild banks and the Bank of England (soon to be under the control of the Rothschilds). Under the guise of making peace and reestablishing old boundaries, the Congress of Vienna convened in September 1814. The Rothschilds' ulterior motive was to form a federation of equally powerful European states under their financial and political influence, with the neutral state of Switzerland acting as its banking repository. This federation would create an uneasy equilibrium in Europe to be exploited by the Rothschilds for further wars and rebuilds. It was for these reasons that Gutle Schnapper, wife of Mayer Amschel Rothschild, was reputed to have said, "If my sons did not want war, there would be none." Alexander I saw through this scheme and countered with the signing of the Treaty of Holy Alliance in 1815, entering Russia into a partnership with Prussia and Austria, effectively killing any chance of a Rothschild-dominated, European Union.

Despite its failed attempt at confederation, the Rothschilds banking dynasty flourished in Europe for the next half century. The family was the undisputed owner of Europe. However, plans to get a permanent central bank into the United States proved challenging when 10th U.S. President John Tyler vetoed two additional national bank bills in the early 1840s. Remember, this was in a period --until 1853 -- when bribing members of Congress was legal, and lobbyists did so freely. Even after bribes were outlawed, congressmen could still receive "consulting fees," which they did until well into the twentieth century. In this environment, the Era of

Free Banking continued until the Civil War. Although overt attempts at regaining a foothold in the United States failed, the European Central bankers were working behind the scenes to split the country in two, so much so that in 1876 Chancellor of Germany, Otto Von Bismarck reflected,

> "The division of the United States into federations of equal force was decided long before the Civil War by the high financial powers of Europe. These bankers were afraid that the US, if they remained as one block, and as one nation, would attain economic and financial independence, which would upset their financial domination over the world."

On the same subject he furthered,

> "The voice of the Rothschilds predominated. They foresaw the tremendous booty if they could substitute two feeble democracies, indebted to the financiers, to the vigorous Republic, confident and self-providing. Therefore they started their emissaries in order to exploit the question of slavery and thus dig an abyss between the two parts of the Republic."

The plan was for France and Britain to enter the war supporting the South. Once the war was won, France would control the South and England the North. Central banking would then be established once and for all in the "former" United States.

Before endeavoring to accomplish these ends, France and Britain thought it prudent to include Russia in their plans. Having just fought Russia in the Crimean War, Emperor Napoleon III and English Foreign Secretary Lord John Russel were leery of leaving themselves vulnerable in the European theater while their military resources were focused across the Atlantic. However, Alexander II would not be a party to their schemes, and as early as 1861, alerted the Lincoln government of their plans to promote a joint UK-France-Russia intervention in favor of the Confederacy. In fact, he would eventually tell the plotting countries that any intervention on either side of the American conflict would be taken as an act of war against Russia. To back up his words, Alexander II sent part of his Baltic Fleet to New York -- where they arrived on September 24,

1863, prompting the aforementioned parade – and part of his Far East Fleet to San Francisco, which reached the West Coast on October 12, 1863. Some historians have said that this was purely self-serving on the part of Alexander II: he wanted to make sure his fleets didn't get pinned down by a superior British naval force if war broke out in Europe over Poland. If that was solely the case, then why did he give Lincoln control of his fleets if hostilities commenced with France and/or England? This bold stroke by Alexander II -- along with Lincoln's Emancipation Proclamation that made it political suicide for the English bankers to support the South – kept England and France out of the American Civil War, inspiring U.S. Secretary of the Navy Gideon Wells to write, "Thank God for the Russians!"

If newly elected President Lincoln did not believe the warning issued by fellow emancipator Alexander II – he liberated 23 million serfs in 1861 – he would change his mind once he tried to obtain financing for the war. The New York-based, Rothschild-backed banks were willing to lend Lincoln money for the war effort, but only at usurious rates (24% - 36%). Lincoln declined. With advice from Col. Edmund D. Taylor, Lincoln instead petitioned Congress to pass a law authorizing the printing of full legal tender zero-interest Treasury notes ('Greenbacks') to pay for the War effort, stating,

> "The government should create, issue, and circulate all the currency and credits needed to satisfy the spending power of the government and the buying power of consumers. By adoption of these principles, the taxpayers will be saved immense sums of interest. Money will cease to be master and become the servant of humanity."

In other words, he was asking Congress to allow the U.S. Treasury to print *debt-free* money. Lincoln recognized this stroke of genius after its passage on February 25, 1862, writing, "... (We) gave the people of this Republic the greatest blessing they have ever had – their own paper money to pay their own debts..." The green ink on the back of the bills birthed the term 'Greenbacks'. The bills were *debt-free*, fiat, and accepted as legal tender. $449,338,902 of Greenbacks were eventually printed to pay for the war. The other difference between the Greenbacks (*debt-free*) and regular banknotes (debt-based) was that the regular banknotes were "backed" by

51

gold. This is actually a misnomer as the banks loaning out the banknotes only owned a fraction of the gold that backed the loans represented by their banknotes; thus the term/scam, "fractional reserve banking". [See Appendix A if you'd like to learn more about this ignoble concept.]

Recognizing Lincoln's brilliant move, an editorial appeared in the Hazard Circular, a newsletter written by Charles Hazzard to every bank in New York and New England during the autumn of 1862. He stated,

> "The great debt that capitalists will see to it is made out of the war must be used as a measure to control the volume of money; to accomplish this...bonds [i.e. debt-based money] must be used as a banking basis. We are now waiting to get the Secretary of the Treasury to make this recommendation to Congress. It will not do to allow the 'greenback,' as it is called [i.e. *debt-free* money], to circulate as money any length of time, for we cannot control them, but we can control the bonds [debt-based money], and through them the bank issue."

Hazzard knew that Lincoln's Greenbacks were a direct threat to the debt-based banking practices. He obviously didn't care about the fate of the country, just about his share of the profits from the war. The Secretary of the Treasury referenced was alleged Rothschild agent, Salmon P. Chase – more on him shortly.

The Hazard Circular printed another commentary on the Greenback that has been alleged to have been reprinted in the London Times sometime in 1865:

> "If that mischievous financial policy [Lincoln's Greenbacks], which had its origin in the North American Republic, should become indurated down to a fixture, then that Government will furnish its own money without cost. It will pay off debts and be without a debt. It will have all the money necessary to carry on its commerce. It will become prosperous beyond precedent in the history of the civilized governments of the world. The brains and the wealth of all countries will go to North America. That government must be destroyed, or it will destroy every monarchy on the globe."

In essence, the op-ed was correctly purporting that *debt-free* money was a blessing for mankind, and immorally concluding that it needed to be destroyed. Also, monarchies were not at risk; bankers were. The moral compass of that quote was, without question, pointing south.

Getting back to Salmon P. Chase, his job was to force a bill (the National Banking Act) through Congress, creating a federally chartered central bank that had the power to issue U.S. Bank Notes (debt-based money). With the bankers' assistance, he partially succeeded in 1863. For the avoidance of doubt, due in large part to the uncertainty regarding the outcome of the war and a campaign waged by the bankers to devalue the Greenback -- speciously invoking suspicion of another Continental debacle -- the Greenback plummeted in value versus coin during the conflict. This eroded Lincoln's ability to persuade Congress into issuing more Greenbacks. Instead, ignorantly fearing a recurrence of the Continental, Congress passed the National Banking Act, creating privately owned national banks (not a central bank) that issued interest bearing (debt-based) national bank notes. This act also provided that the Greenbacks should be retired from circulation as soon as they came back to the Treasury in payment of taxes. Lincoln, unable to obtain the authority to produce additional Greenbacks, needing additional capital to win the war, facing an election year, and seeing that his veto would be overridden, begrudgingly signed the act into law.

If all this talk of debt-based versus *debt-free* money systems seems confusing, that's because it is supposed to be. If Congress fully understood the ramifications of the different money systems, only corruption could allow for the passage of such an act. Banker John Sherman, a Rothschild protégé in London, summed it up in a June 25, 1863 letter to fellow U.S. bankers,

> "The few who understand the [debt-based money] system will either be so interested in its profits or so dependent on its favours that there will be no opposition from that class, while on the other hand, the great body of the people mentally incapable of comprehending the tremendous advantage that capital derives from the system will bear its burdens without complaint and perhaps without even suspecting that the system is inimical to their interests."

Sherman was implying that the "mentally incapable" citizens of the United States would ultimately be responsible for the loans. He was partially wrong. It was their ignorance, not their dullness of mind, which would bind them. The people who control you to this very day, can only do so through your ignorance, and that is why your version of history is always missing this critical discussion of debt-based versus *debt-free* money, because as Henry Ford said, "It is well enough that people of the nation do not understand our banking and monetary system, for if they did, I believe there would be a revolution before tomorrow morning."

To his credit (or possibly to just save face), Salmon later admitted, "My agency in promoting the passage of the National Banking Act was the greatest financial mistake in my life. It has built up a monopoly which affects every interest in the country."

In a letter found a couple of years after the Civil War, addressed to Col. William F. Elkins, and dated Nov 21, 1864, Lincoln saw foreboding in the dismantling of his 'blessing':

> "The money power preys upon the nation in time of peace and conspires against it in times of adversity. It is more despotic than monarchy, more insolent than autocracy, more selfish than bureaucracy. I see in the near future a crisis approaching that unnerves me, and causes me to tremble for the safety of our country. Corporations have been enthroned, an era of corruption will follow, and the money power of the country will endeavor to prolong its reign by working upon the prejudices of the people, until the wealth is aggregated in a few hands, and the republic is destroyed."

The attribution of this quote to Lincoln is in much dispute. Regardless of authorship, you will come to see that never more prophetic words have been spoken.

Lincoln was not going down without a fight. Having freed the slaves, he wanted to free America from the slavery of debt-based money and planned to introduce legislation calling for the repeal of the National Banking Act and a return to *debt-free* money once the war with the Confederacy ended. Lincoln stated, "I have two great enemies, the

Southern Army in front of me and the bankers in the rear. Of the two, the one at my rear is my greatest foe." He won the war, but was killed by the bankers. John Wilkes Booth struck the fatal blow for the debt-based financiers at Ford's Theatre.

Booth was portrayed as a man who was deeply committed to the Southern cause, and killed out of emotion. To be sure, Booth claimed to be pro-South, but never took up arms for the Confederacy or owned a slave. He was a mercenary, plain and simple, and part of a larger conspiracy. At the trial of his co-conspirators – four of whom were sentenced to death – the true nature of the conspiracy came to light. At the trial, Booth's friend Samuel Knapp Chester told the court that Booth had pressed money upon him and had assured him,

> "that if I would do it [participate in the Lincoln's assassination] I would never want again as long as I lived; that I would never want for money. He said there was plenty of money in the enterprise."

John Greenawalt, a witness at the trial, also portrayed the fiendish endeavor as being monetarily motivated.

However, because the testimonies of Richard Montgomery and James B. Merritt were not published as part of the original public record of the trial, the portrait of John Wilkes Booth, mercenary, was incomplete. According to Montgomery's testimony, Jacob Thompson, one time Secretary of the Interior in the American government and now agent for the South, had informed him during the winter of 1865 that he and his associates in Canada had been approached to organize and carry out the plan which resulted in Lincoln's assassination. Montgomery swore that Thompson had informed him in January, 1865, that: "He knew the men who had made the proposition were bold and daring men, able to execute anything they would undertake without regard to the cost." Montgomery also swore that he was told that Booth had been employed to organize and carry out the actual assassination.

Merritt, a physician practicing in Canada, corroborated Montgomery's testimony. He testified that a Southern agent in Canada, George N. Saunders, had told him about the plot and of Booth's connection with it. Saunders also informed Merritt "that there was any amount of money to accomplish the purpose".

According to Richard Mitchell Smoot, Booth had $6,500 on his person at the time of the assassination – a considerable sum for those days. Smoot seemed to have intimate knowledge of the entire affair, being that he unwittingly sold his boat to Booth co-conspirators John H. Surrat and George "Andrew" Atzerodt. Due to the terms of the transaction – Smoot would get final payment after the boat was put into use – Richard kept in touch with the co-conspirators up to the day of the assassination. Because of Booth's broken leg Smoot's boat was never employed – it was chopped to pieces and the wood burnt. Smoot, however, was briefly arrested, and later testified at Surrat's trial. Since Booth was in possession of so much money, yet never on the payroll of the Confederacy, to call this assassination an act of the Confederacy is likely disingenuous.

Booth, according to his granddaughter, made one trip to Europe and was seen in the company of a few Europeans stateside prior to the assassination. From his trunk, a coded message was found that linked him directly to Judah P. Benjamin, Confederate Secretary of State and Secret Service director, and acquaintance of Solomon Rothschild, who deemed Benjamin, "the greatest mind in North America". Benjamin, the true puppet master of the South, burned all of his papers relating to the Confederate's Secret Service. Fortunately, he was not one hundred percent successful covering his tracks. The key to decode the message found in Booth's trunk was discovered in Benjamin's office.

Whether Booth (or more likely someone else) died in the tobacco barn is not germane to the central issue: when Lincoln died at the hands of the bankers, so did any attempt to resurrect the Greenback. Even though the Greenback regained most of its value versus coin by the end of the war, there would be no momentum for the issuance of anymore. The death knell for the Greenback came when the Contraction Act was passed on April 12, 1866, allowing the Treasury to retire some of Lincoln's *debt-free* currency. What followed was a severe contraction of the money supply and an ugly, three-decade economic nightmare. For most, the Reconstruction period was not a joyous time. Prices dropped because the money supply was contracted. When part of the money supply being contracted is *debt-free*, the debt associated with the balance of cash in circulation grows more than proportionally; strangling the economy like a noose, after the trapdoor of the gallows has been released. Your caramel macchiato didn't get more expensive in absolute terms – in fact the consumer price index plunged from 15.79 in 1865 to 8.04 by 1899, a 49% fall -- but with less currency in circulation per capita due to a restrictive monetary policy, a growing population, and rising output, your ability to purchase it (as you will soon see) took a massive hit.

After the war and assassination, Alexander II bestowed the United States with one more gift. In debt to the Rothschilds – these leaders never understand – he sold Alaska to the United States for $7.2 million, or two cents an acre. When Congress was debating whether to approve the purchase, orchestrated by Secretary of State William H. Seward, some members were convinced that this "purchase" from the Russians was just a golden payback for the naval blockade. Seward's Folly was approved and a transfer ceremony took place in the town of Sitka on October 18, 1867. In the span of four years, Alexander II's actions not only preserved the sovereignty of the United States, but also increased its size by 21%. And Christopher Columbus was responsible for the extinction of an entire race of people.

Chapter 13 (May 2, 2016)

Monday morning couldn't come soon enough. Fitz was never excited to see her leave, but Annie's departure for school meant that Fitz could study the Kennedy speech on secret societies and his executive order. After walking Oliver, Fitz sat down to his desktop and pulled up the contents of Kennedy's speech. On April 27, 1961 the President of the United States gave a speech to the American Newspaper Publishers Association at the Waldorf-Astoria Hotel in New York City. Fitz read intently. After a couple of light opening remarks about Karl Marx, Kennedy's administration, and the press, JFK got to the heart of the matter,

"The very word "secrecy" is repugnant in a free and open society; and we are as a people inherently and historically opposed to secret societies, to secret oaths and to secret proceedings. We decided long ago that the dangers of excessive and unwarranted concealment of pertinent facts far outweighed the dangers which are cited to justify it. Even today, there is little value in opposing the threat of a closed society by imitating its arbitrary restrictions. Even today, there is little value in insuring the survival of our nation if our traditions do not survive with it. And there is very grave danger that an announced need for increased security will be seized upon by those anxious to expand its meaning to the very limits of official censorship and concealment. That I do not intend to permit to the extent that it is in my control. And no official of my Administration, whether his rank is high or low, civilian or military, should interpret my words here tonight as an excuse to censor the news, to stifle dissent, to cover up our mistakes or to withhold from the press and the public the facts they deserve to know.

"But I do ask every publisher, every editor, and every newsman in the nation to reexamine his own standards, and to recognize the nature of our country's peril. In time of war, the government and the press have customarily joined in an effort based largely on self-discipline, to prevent unauthorized disclosures to the enemy. In time of "clear and present danger," the courts have held that even the privileged rights of the First Amendment must yield to the public's need for national security.

58

"Today no war has been declared--and however fierce the struggle may be, it may never be declared in the traditional fashion. Our way of life is under attack. Those who make themselves our enemy are advancing around the globe. The survival of our friends is in danger. And yet no war has been declared, no borders have been crossed by marching troops, no missiles have been fired.

"If the press is awaiting a declaration of war before it imposes the self-discipline of combat conditions, then I can only say that no war ever posed a greater threat to our security. If you are awaiting a finding of "clear and present danger," then I can only say that the danger has never been more clear and its presence has never been more imminent.

"It requires a change in outlook, a change in tactics, a change in missions--by the government, by the people, by every businessman or labor leader, and by every newspaper. For we are opposed around the world by a monolithic and ruthless conspiracy that relies primarily on covert means for expanding its sphere of influence--on infiltration instead of invasion, on subversion instead of elections, on intimidation instead of free choice, on guerrillas by night instead of armies by day. It is a system which has conscripted vast human and material resources into the building of a tightly knit, highly efficient machine that combines military, diplomatic, intelligence, economic, scientific and political operations.

"Its preparations are concealed, not published. Its mistakes are buried, not headlined. Its dissenters are silenced, not praised. No expenditure is questioned, no rumor is printed, no secret is revealed."

Fitz continued to read. The speech went on to talk about the responsibility of the press during the Cold War. His initial interpretation was that Kennedy was expressing concern for the threat represented by the Soviet Union. But, if those were JFK's "killers" alluded to in his note to Fitz's mother, something didn't add up. JFK had just signed a Partial Nuclear Test Ban Treaty with Khrushchev and was planning a withdrawal from

Vietnam. To be sure, Kennedy and Khrushchev had philosophical differences, but Kennedy was likely closer to Khrushchev than he was to members of his own Joint Chiefs of Staff. However, this speech (unlike his note to Fitz's mother) was given shortly after Kennedy was in office. He had yet to meet Khrushchev and the Bay of Pigs fiasco was still front and center in the countries' collective consciousness. The note to his mother was written just before Kennedy was assassinated. *The "killers" couldn't be the Soviets.*

Why would a sitting president, the leader of the free world, speak of "a monolithic and ruthless conspiracy"? Fitz would find other presidents who spoke of such conspiracies. Woodrow Wilson, in his campaign speech book, *The New Freedom: A Call for the Emancipation of the Generous Energies of a People* said,

> "Since I entered politics, I have chiefly had men's views confided to me privately. Some of the biggest men in the United States, in the field of commerce and manufacture, are afraid of something. They know that there is a power somewhere so organized, so subtle, so watchful, so interlocked, so complete, so pervasive, that they better not speak above their breath when they speak in condemnation of it. They know that America is not a place of which it can be said, as it used to be, that a man may choose his own calling and pursue it just as far as his abilities enable him to pursue it; because today, if he enters certain fields, there are organizations which will use means against him that will prevent his building up a business which they do not want to have built up; organizations that will see to it that the ground is cut from under him and the markets shut against him. For if he begins to sell to certain retail dealers, to any retail dealers, the monopoly will refuse to sell to those dealers, and those dealers, afraid, will not buy the new man's wares."

Fitz discovered the copyright on the book was 1913 – Wilson's first year in office. He also found quotes from other sitting presidents, including Teddy Roosevelt -- "Behind the ostensible government sits enthroned an Invisible Government owing no allegiance and acknowledging no responsibility to the people." -- and FDR, stating that the government was owned by a conspiracy.

Fitz then examined Kennedy's Executive Order 11110. Its implementation resulted in the production of $5 *debt-free* silver certificates by the U.S. Treasury, not debt-based money by the Federal Reserve. *Oh, my God!* The pieces of the puzzle to his father's death began to fall into place. Fitz, for the first time in his life, welled with a sense of being and mission. He picked up the phone and called Chuck.

"What is UP?"

"Chuck, who is the best PR person you know?" Fitz inquired tersely.

Momentarily taken aback by the odd question, especially without Fitz's normal niceties, Chuck recovered, "Of course, *we* are." Chuck was talking about his small firm, Skinner & Weiss, at which Chuck was a partner.

Realizing that he probably just made a huge miscalculation calling Chuck, Fitz back-peddled and rephrased his question, "Which firm is second best?"

Still puzzled, but understanding the seriousness in Fitz's voice, Chuck answered, "If I were to recommend one I would say Preston and Associates."

"Thanks Chuck! I can't get into detail now, but will clue you in when I can. Talk soon."

"Ah, okay. Ciao." Fitz hung up, thus terminating the shortest conversation he ever had in his life with Chuck.

After a quick search on the net, Fitz found the number for Preston and Associates and made an appointment for Wednesday, May 18th at noon. He had sixteen days to make up his mind. Chances were that if he walked into Preston's office on that Wednesday, Fitz would be shutting doors behind him that he would never be able to reopen.

Fitz had one other problem. He made another search on the web and placed a call to DNA Diagnostic Centers. It was time to prove that he was JFK's son. This turned out to be a bigger obstacle than he ever imagined. The lock of his father's hair was useless – it couldn't be used as

61

a source of DNA, and even it could, there was no proving that the lock belonged to JFK. He needed a blood or saliva sample. There was only one place he could go: to the sitting U.S. Ambassador to Japan. Because he matriculated at Brown, overlapping with John F. Kennedy Jr. for two years, he had friends who were friends with the Kennedy family. *Was this why my mother wanted me to go to Brown? So I could attend school with my half-brother?*

His next call was to Evan Spring. A partner at a New York private equity firm, Evan was the only non-valedictorian in his family, which could be excused to the fact that he graduated high school in three years. Evan, happily married to a brilliant professor (Tracy), had two brilliant children, who were attending Johns Hopkins and Cornell. As the Guinness commercial would proclaim, "Brilliant!" Fitz knew that Evan could keep a secret, but telling him the nature of his call and request felt akin to standing atop a building with a megaphone and announcing it to the world. Even though he was unveiling part of his plan to Evan, he decided not to tell Evan *everything*, and Evan's role in *everything*.

Cavendish caught Evan at a good time -- while he was on a layover at Miami International Airport. Evan listened intently to Fitz's seemingly incredulous tale about his mother, the safe deposit box, and the letter outlining the affair. Evan also sensed a tap of desperation in his voice when he brought up the idea of getting a DNA sample from Caroline. Evan responded that he had not spoken to Caroline in months and had not seen her in two years, but that he would make the call. Evan, perceptive as always, asked, "If Caroline agrees to the test and your mother's story checks out – which I have every reason to believe – what are you going to do with this information?"

Cavendish fibbed, "Besides enjoying my peace of mind? I'm not totally sure."

Chapter 14 (1868 – 1900)

Question: What do Pink Floyd's Dark Side of the Moon and the Coinage Act of 1873 have in common? Answer: The Wonderful Wizard of Oz. [Read on.] The notion of a European Monetary Union is, to most of you, a very recent phenomenon with a vintage of 1999. It isn't. As previously discussed, the Rothschilds were engaged in an attempt at globalization since 1814. Their next major attempt at a European Union – at least currency union -- occurred during the second half of the nineteenth century, with the formation of the Latin Monetary Union on December 23, 1865. This currency union, sold under the guise of facilitating European inter-nation commerce, was a pretext for one of the great swindles of all-time. The United States' role in the crime being the Coinage Act of 1873, and you, the American citizen, unwittingly financed the misconduct, thanks to the laziness, lawlessness, and ignorance of your congressmen and President, the treachery or criminal stupidity [choose the former] of U. S. Senator John Sherman [not the same Rothschild banking protégé John Sherman of Chapter 12] and the bribes of Rothschild agent Ernest Seyd. More importantly, it is a lesson in why pegging a currency to a precious metal is foolhardy. It seems the only item of worth bestowed on the average American citizen from this deplorable episode in history was a good movie.

Backing up a bit, when Alexander Hamilton was arguing for debt-based money, he was also arguing for it to be in the form of gold and silver coins. The Coinage Act of 1792 essentially allowed for both gold and silver to be used as currency with gold being fifteen times more valuable than silver. This concept is known as bimetallism. Back then, you could literally bring your gold or silver ("specie") to the mint and have it converted into currency, and at the time for no charge (or "seigniorage"). Initially, in return, you would receive coins; later on you could receive coins or paper currency. The fixed ratio (15-to-1) had the effect of making the American dollar backed by the cheaper metal. Since both gold and silver had other uses in industry, as jewelry, and as foreign currency, they were subject to the laws of supply and demand; the actual market ratio would fluctuate. For example, if a massive discovery of silver in the United States increased its supply, the market price of silver would decline relative to gold (say to 15.5-to-1). If you owned gold in this price environment, you would be much better off playing the arbitrage by converting your gold into silver in the marketplace and then taking your silver to the mint (where the fixed 15-to-1 ratio still applied) versus taking your gold directly to the mint. Since initially silver was slightly cheaper than gold (relative to this imposed ratio), the mints were flooded with silver and the United States was essentially on a silver standard until 1834.

That changed when Andrew Jackson was trying to kill the banks. With the help of Congress, he altered the fixed ratio to 16-to-1 at the mints. With the market ratio being less than 16-to-1, gold became cheaper than silver, and by default, the standard. Jackson did this to reduce demand for bank notes which were circulating based on the old ratio. The scheme worked, and with the gold discoveries of the 1840s and 1850s in Australia and California increasing its supply – thus decreasing its value -- gold remained the standard until Lincoln circulated the Greenbacks to finance the war effort. Even though no more were issued after the war – because of Lincoln's assassination -- the *debt-free* and fiat Greenbacks became the standard. The debt-based money cabal would not sit still for this. The first assault on the Greenback came when the aforementioned Contraction Act was passed on April 12, 1866, allowing the Treasury to retire some of Lincoln's *debt-free* currency. While putting the Greenback out to pasture, the debt-based cabal was devising another plan to steal the nations' populations of their wealth.

Getting back to Europe and Latin Monetary Union, the idea of a common currency in Europe was practical: a Belgian trader could accept Italian lire for his goods with confidence that it could be converted back to a comparable amount of francs. This pragmatic construct was also synchronistic with, and a step towards the Rothschild's plan for world government. The Latin Monetary Union was the collaboration of four countries: France, Italy, Belgium, and Switzerland. Their currency was unified with respect to their gold and silver coins.

A duplicitous attempt to exploit this union was made at the International Monetary Conference of 1867 in Paris. Claiming that any attempt at monetary unification was futile under dual standards of value, the bankers in attendance, who owned the majority of the gold, wanted to demonetize silver, which was employed more amongst the poorest of the population. Think of it this way: at that time, on a per ounce basis, gold was worth sixteen times more than silver. If you are wealthy, would you rather carry around a huge roll of $1 bills or a much smaller wad of $100 bills? Please keep in mind there were no credit cards during this era. If you were wealthy, like the bankers, you conducted your financial affairs in gold. Silver was for the poorer class. You can look at it another way: the speculators of this world are the creditors and the working classes are the debtors. The debtors benefit from an abundance of money: for when there is more of it in circulation, they have a greater chance of paying off their loans. The creditors don't benefit from abundance (or cheapening) of money (i.e. inflation); the buying power of the money they lent out has been reduced by the time it is paid back. If silver, through its gradual devaluation versus gold, was removed as money, the money supply would be contracted, with the benefit inuring to the creditors (i.e. the bankers).

The debt-based money cabal doesn't like to lose so they devised a scheme at the conference in 1867 to severely constrict the money supply by eliminating one of the mediums of exchange, which would enrich them two ways. First, they would now possess an even greater share of the money, since they owned most of the gold. Second, because gold would become the only metal available as a medium of exchange, demand for the metal would surge slowly, but with the intensity of a tidal wave, making their gold reserves even more valuable. Remember, wealth is not created, nor destroyed. It is simply transferred. The history books will say the conference was an attempt to abandon bimetallism for the gold standard, because it was less complicated. At its essence was a scheme to transfer wealth, making the rich richer and the poor poorer. Rubbing elbows with the debt-based money cabal at this conference was U.S. Senator John Sherman, of Ohio. He was Chairman of the Committee on Finance in the Senate.

The history books will also tell you that the conference failed because the logistics involved in achieving a unified currency were too cumbersome to overcome. The real purpose of the conference – mapping out a strategy to enrich the debt-based money cabal by demonetizing silver – was eventually achieved. Sherman returned to the United States and on January 6, 1868, he introduced, in the Senate, "a bill in relation to the coinage of gold and silver" which would establish a gold standard in the United States. In addition to pitching this legislation on the pretense of "abandoning the impossible effort of making two standards of value", it was also pitched under the absurd notions that it was an American idea [not true, but so what?] and that gold had intrinsic value, thus making it a fixed standard for the world [and silver does not?]. This "impossible effort" had been taking place without much controversy for multiple decades in the United States and Europe. Sherman's full-frontal assault on silver failed to engender any support in his own Senate Committee on Finance, and was never brought up for a vote.

Undeterred and wiser from his initial failure, Sherman decided that the best way to demonetize silver was through subterfuge. With this in mind, he introduced another bill, calling it the "Mint Bill" on April 28, 1870. Unlike his first, straight-forward bill that consisted of ten paragraphs, this piece of legislation contained sixty-eight paragraphs and masqueraded as an attempt at uniformity and quality of coinage at the different U.S. mints. It also went into such minutia as mining reforms, salaries for officers of the mint and assay-offices, and whether there should be an eagle on the larger denomination coins. However, the act conveniently omitted the silver dollar from coins permitted to be struck for currency, putting the United States, by default, on the gold standard. Since this galumphing and tiresome bill was relatively unimportant – at least as it was presented -- it had difficulty getting any attention, and collected cobwebs for two years. Enter Ernest Seyd:

> "I went to America in the winter of 1872-73, authorized to secure, if I could, the passage of a bill demonetizing silver. It was to the interest of those I represented — the governors of the Bank of England — to have it done. I took with me £100,000 sterling [$500,000 US], with instructions if that was not sufficient to accomplish the object to draw for another £100,000 or as much more as was necessary. I saw the committees of the House and Senate and paid the money and stayed in America until I knew the measure was safe. Your people will not now comprehend the far-reaching extent of that measure — but they will in after years. Whatever you may think of corruption in the English Parliament, I assure you I would not have dared to make such an attempt here, as I did in your country."

This quote was from a conversation he had at his London residence with an American friend named Frederick A. Luckenbach in February 1874.

Seyd's treacherous endeavor succeeded. The plan was brought to the floor of both houses where the omission of the silver dollar as money was not discussed. Most of the discussion centered on reforms at the Bureau of Mines and the mints. Those not the recipient of Mr. Seyd's generosity, voted in favor of the bill, not because they had read it, but because they trusted the recommendations of the congressmen that allegedly had. Indulge yourself with the following quotes:

> "Perhaps I ought to be ashamed to say so, but it is the truth to say that, I at that time being chairman of the Committee on Appropriations, and having my hands over-full during all that time with work, I never read the bill. I took it upon the faith of a prominent Democrat and a prominent Republican, and I do not know that I voted at all. There was no call of the yeas and nays, and nobody opposed that bill that I know of. It was put through as dozens of bills are, as my friend and I know, in Congress, on the faith of the report of the chairman of the committee; therefore I tell you, because it is the truth, that I have no knowledge about it." — Congressman and future U.S. President James A. Garfield, as reported in the Congressional Record

> "This legislation was had in the Forty-second Congress, February 12, 1873, by a bill to regulate the mints of the United States, and practically abolished silver as money by failing to provide for the coinage of the silver dollar. It was not discussed, as shown by the Record, and neither members of Congress nor the people understood the scope of the legislation." — Illinois Congressman and future Speaker of the House Joseph G. Gannon, in the House, July 13th, 1876.

> "I know that the bondholders and the monopolists of this country are seeking to destroy all the industries of this people, in their greed to enhance the value of their gold. I know that the act of 1873 did more than all else to accomplish that result, and the demonetization act of the Revised Statutes was an illegal and unconstitutional consummation of the fraud." --- Kentucky Congressman and later Senator James Beck, January 10th, 1878.

"I have before me the record of the proceedings of this House on the passage of that measure, a record which no man can read without being convinced that the measure and the method of its passage through this House was a 'colossal swindle.' I assert that the measure never had the sanction of this House, and it does not possess the moral force of law." — Indiana Congressman William Holman, in the House, July 13th, 1876.

These quotes could go on for hours, but the most telling was from the president who signed it into law:

"I did not know that the act of 1873 demonetized silver. I was deceived in the matter." — 18th President of the United States Ulysses S. Grant.

The bill passed in the House by a vote of 110-13 without it being read. [Where were the other 120 representatives? Were they being entertained by Seyd?] It then passed the Senate without the line concerning the demonetization of silver being read.

Many European countries adopted the gold standard around the same time as the United States – shocking coincidence! Since most of our elected officials were oblivious – some were well compensated for their "ignorance" -- to the theft that was transpiring, it is easy to see how the masses were unaware for a couple of years as to what was occurring. Silver still maintained a "market value" that initially remained close to the 16-to-1 ratio. But since there was no longer demand from the mints, silver steadily dropped in value versus gold. [It became so obvious in time that Sherman would introduce bills forcing the government to buy silver, so the ratio didn't fall completely off a cliff.] Because the mints no longer redeemed at the previously mandated 16-to-1 ratio, the speculators could no longer play the arbitrage and silver's value versus gold dropped to 30-to-1 over the next two decades (and nearly 40-to-1 in the early 1900s). Also as important, the increased demand for gold created by this congressional sleight of hand outstripped its production, resulting in rising gold prices. Since the dollar was pegged to the price of gold, the value of the dollar dropped. Couple this with a rising output of goods and services on behalf of the Industrial Revolution, and you have a recipe for massive deflation. Simply put, when part of the money supply is removed from circulation, deflation will result. Prices decreased at a rate of 1.7% a year in the United States from 1875 to 1896 – some estimates were as high as 3% per annum in the agricultural sector. As a consumer, this sounds terrific. But since most of the producers of this world are debtors, the decrease of the money supply meant there was less money to pay off debts. Since there is never enough money to pay off debts in a debt-based money system to begin with, for the debtors, demonetizing silver was akin to playing musical chairs at double speed, with massive business failures being the result.

The Coinage Act of 1873 was not only responsible for the Panic of 1873 and subsequent six-year depression, but also partly responsible for the Panic of 1893 and subsequent depression, both of which featured widespread business bankruptcies and a run on U.S. gold reserves. The bottom line was deflation was rampant and unemployment was extremely high during this wonderful time to be alive. Unemployment did dip in the 1880s when Gilded Age titans Rockefeller, Carnegie, and Vanderbilt were hiring labor to toil long hours for little wages at their refineries, steel mills, and railroad and shipping operations. However, unemployment returned with a vengeance in the 1890s and by one estimate was 18.4% in 1894. Although GDP rose during this period – because of the Robber Barons -- the number was merely a smokescreen, hiding the fact that 10% to 20% of the population's net worth had been transferred to a few wealthy bankers and industrialists during the two decades following the Coinage Act of 1873 while prevailing conditions resembled that of the Great Depression. In 1873, the average price of silver was approximately $1.47 an ounce; in 1899 it had fallen to $.60, while the price of gold, in dollar terms, remained constant. Remember, just because you owned silver, converting it into gold wasn't obvious or automatic. People weren't watching CNBC noting its slow deterioration. This subtle decline amounted to the wealthy dipping into the pockets of the poor, periodically eroding their wealth like rushing water on soft rock. Grover Cleveland said it best when he stood before a special session of Congress on August 8th, 1893,

> "At times like the present, when the evils of unsound finance threaten us, the speculator may anticipate a harvest gathered from the misfortune of others, the capitalist may protect himself by hoarding or may even find profit in the fluctuations of values; but the wage earner – the first to be injured by a depreciated currency

– is practically defenseless. He relies for work upon the ventures of confident and contented capital. This failing him, his condition is without alleviation, for he can neither prey on the misfortunes of others nor hoard his labor."

After the train left the station, people like William Jennings Bryant ran on a bimetallism campaign platform that entreated for a return to bimetallism and the 16-to-1 ratio. It was a noble gesture, but the crime had already been perpetrated and the deal was sealed when the United States officially went on the gold standard with the passage of the Gold Standard Act on March 14, 1900. If after reading this delightful story, you are still convinced that money should be backed by a precious metal, get your head examined.

The period following the Panic of 1893 inspired author L. Frank Baum to produce an allegory. It was entitled *The Wonderful Wizard of Oz*. For the uninitiated, read Hugh Rockoff's, "The *'Wizard of Oz'* as a Monetary Allegory". In his essay you will be taught about Dorothy as America, on the yellow brick road (the gold standard) with her dog Toto, the teetotaler who was pro silver (as it was a part of the teetotaler platform) on their way to the Emerald City (Washington D.C.) to visit Oz (short for ounce of gold). On their journey they meet President Grover Cleveland Alexander portrayed as the Wicked Witch of the East, who is killed when Dorothy's house lands on her as a result of the cyclone, with her silver shoes becoming Dorothy's, courtesy of the Good Witch of the North – the shoes weren't originally ruby as in the popular Judy Garland movie version; the western farmer as the Scarecrow; the working man as the Tin Woodman; the Populist Democrat William Jennings Bryant as the Cowardly Lion; and President William McKinley as the Wicked Witch of the West. So when you put on your *Dark Side of the Moon* CD and pop in the *Wizard of Oz* -- observers playing the film and the album simultaneously have reported apparent synchronicities, such as Dorothy beginning to jog at the lyric "no one told you when to run" during "Time" -- know that you are watching the story of the Populist movement of the 1890s and its futile quest for the resumption of bimetallism. More importantly, learn that men behind the curtain (i.e. the debt-based money cabal and its secret societies) have been plotting your demise for a long time.

70

Chapter 15 (May 7, 2015)

Fortune favors the bold. The 29th United States Ambassador to Japan was going to be home in New York City during early May. Evan Spring, true to his word, reached out to Caroline Kennedy, and arranged a dinner meeting for all three at Locanda Verde at the Greenwich Hotel on May 7th. The dinner would take place in the drawing room of the Greenwich Hotel, away from the bustling atmosphere of the restaurant proper. This marked a break in routine for Fitz and Annie, who usually spent Saturday at his place. Annie wanted to get over to Jersey City to see her mother and she wanted Fitz to come. Fitz agreed but said that he wanted to meet up with Evan in the city that evening. A plan was agreed to where Fitz and Annie would volunteer at the animal shelter in the morning, and then head over to Jersey City with Oliver for lunch with Annie's mother, Diane. Annie and Oliver would spend the evening in Jersey City and Fitz would head back into the city to meet Evan. Fitz conveniently omitted the other guest who would be accompanying Spring or the actual motive for the dinner. Fitz wanted to tell Annie everything, but he didn't know down which path this was all going to career.

By the time the sheep' milk ricotta had arrived and a bottle of 2009 Marion Amarone delle Valpolicella had been half consumed, it was obvious to Fitz that Evan had not told Caroline the entire story regarding his presence. After the opening introductions, Fitz faded to the background as Evan and Caroline got reacquainted with their respective lives and occupations. Evan was now with a private equity firm in New York, even though he was commuting from Duluth, Minnesota where his wife was a professor. Caroline's kids were slightly older and graduates of Harvard and Yale. Commuting from Tokyo to New York to Washington D.C. didn't sound all too appealing, but she seemed to enjoy the position and the Japanese people. Fitz tried to interject where he thought appropriate, but as long as the two were catching up, Fitz was content to sip on the Amarone.

Finally, when the main courses arrived, Evan segued from one family discussion into another, "Caroline, I know that this is going to come as a shock to you, but there is a good chance that you and Fitz here are related."

Caroline's fork, full of steamed black bass and initially headed for her mouth, reversed course, and landed without incident on her plate. "Come again."

"Fitz, I think it best that you take it from here."

"Caroline. I apologize for what I'm about to tell you. I have a story and a request. I sure hope, for my sake, that what I'm about to tell you is true. I don't mean this as an ambush in any way, I just…"

"It's okay. Evan had given me some advanced notice. I just wasn't notified as to the specifics of your story."

Both Caroline and Fitz looked over at Evan. Then Fitz continued, "My mother, who has been dead since 1990, apparently had an affair with your father when he was in the White House and I was the result. I was never told about it while my mother was alive. My mother only referred to your father as "a great man" and that is all that I was ever told about my father, ever. I was supposed to be informed upon the passing of your mother, but because of some strange happenstance around my mother's passing, I was never informed until nine months ago when I stumbled upon a key to a safe deposit box. Inside it was this note and picture." Fitz removed the contents from the envelope and handed them to Caroline. She looked at the picture briefly and then read the note. She seemed to wince ever so slightly while reading the note. Fitz speculated that she was going places that she would rather not explore or re-explore.

When she finished reading the note, she looked back at the picture of her father and Fitz's mother, and then looked up at Fitz. After a long pause, she said, "You do look like John John."

With that, both Evan and Fitz breathed a sigh of relief. Fitz recovered, "As you can imagine, I have spent almost every waking hour since this revelation researching JFK. The one thing that has shone through from this research is that although flawed, your -- our father was a 'great man'."

Her service as an ambassador had conditioned her to requests. And though she was still in a state of bewilderment over Fitz's claim, she was able to assume his request: "Let me guess. You want me to provide a sample for a DNA test?"

Shocked by her social graces – by simply not throwing her glass of Amarone in his face – Fitz was even more floored that she knew the essence of his solicitation and phrased the question in a manner that prevented his request from turning into a plea. "Yes. That is my wish."

"Are you going to go public with the news if I agree to the test and we're a match?"

"I can't lie. Yes. And it is for reasons that won't be abundantly clear. I don't want fame, but I believe I owe something to your, I mean, our father."

"…to smear his name?"

"No…quite the opposite. Although I understand what would go through most peoples' minds' initially, or at least I think I do. I do not want this to reflect negatively on you; however, I understand why you believe it might."

"Listen. You're a friend of Evan's, you look like you could be my brother, and you don't look like a scam artist." With that, she looked back at Evan. "Admittedly, if you came up to me out of the blue and presented me this information and petitioned me for a DNA test, I would have notified the Secret Service." Everyone smiled. "But why do you want to go public if you're not interested in fame?"

"Have you done much research into your father's assassination?"

"I've always been curious. My uncles were both convinced that it wasn't Oswald, but why do you want to dredge that up?"

"Because you father's death was the fulcrum upon which this country teetered into the abyss."

"You believe this country is headed in the wrong direction?"

"Nearly $20 trillion in debt? Absolutely. I know that you are part of the government and I am getting way out of line, but if – at the risk of being presumptuous -- our father had served out two terms and our uncle two terms thereafter, this country, and dare I say this world, would be completely different -- for the better."

"So our father would have retired the debt?"

"Possibly...he knew the reasons why we had a debt in the first place and he knew who was behind it."

"Who is behind it?"

"The answer to your question is complicated, but it all starts with the central bankers."

"So the Bank of International Settlements was behind my father's death?"

"Indirectly, yes."

Fitz detailed the cryptographic note that JFK had sent his mother and the answer that he and Annie had derived. Fitz explained the dots he had connected between the puzzle's answer and his research. Evan was temporarily spellbound and Caroline was in a suspended state between "this guy is a lunatic" and "this guy is a genius". When Fitz had finished his explanation, Caroline queried, "So what is the end game?"

Without hesitation, Fitz replied, "To get the truth out."

"You realize that what you are purporting isn't contingent on you being my half-brother?"

"Actually, I agree and I disagree. Whether or not I'm JFK's son is irrelevant -- agreed. However, if I'm not JFK's son, no one is going to care what I have to say and consequently the message will not have a large enough platform to effect change. I'm just another guy shouting into the wind. I feel as if I owe our father this version of history. Would you be willing to participate in the test? I promise that I will not drag his name through the mud, although I can't control how the media will react."

"What do you think Evan?"

"If you don't fear the truth, I say do it." *Thanks Evan!*

"Okay. I'm in."

Chapter 16 (1911 – 1913)

Even though the Rothschilds owned Europe, they were more infamous than famous. Given that their wealth was derived from bankrupting countries, the lower classes of society hated them. The aristocracy viewed them with respect, but also sneered behind their backs for their lack of sophistication and social graces. They also inbred (as a matter of family policy) in the early to mid-1800s to keep the fortune in the family. The Rothschilds were aware that bad publicity might be a consequence of their enormous wealth. To that end, the Rothschilds took a significant financial interest in the three major wire services in the second half of the 19th century. By purchasing control (through investment bankers) of Reuters International News Agency, based in London, Havas of France, and Wolf in Germany, the Rothschild essentially controlled the dissemination of all news in Europe. From that time forward, the Rothschilds' affairs and any anti-Rothschild sentiment faded from the headlines. They now controlled the message. This wasn't the only way the family stayed out of the spotlight.

George Peabody, who operated the Georgetown slave trade market and a dry goods business for two decades, moved to London in 1835 to open a satellite office. Through a connection with Brown Brothers, he was introduced to Nathan Rothschild, who offered him a deal. Since the London aristocracy disliked the Rothschilds, they wouldn't attend Nathan's parties, which was bad for business. Part of this hatred may have stemmed from a graceless quote Nathan was alleged to have proclaimed at one of his parties,

> "I care not what puppet is placed upon the throne of England to rule the Empire on which the sun never sets. The man that controls Britain's money supply controls the British Empire, and I control the British money supply."

To stem the loss of business, Nathan would bankroll Peabody, who would throw lavish parties that would be the hit of London's privileged class. Through these events, Peabody obtained much business on behalf of the Rothschild dynasty, unbeknownst to the attendees. This mutually beneficial relationship continued unabated for decades. Peabody, who never wed, chose an agent in New York, Junius Spencer Morgan, to assume his role as Rothschilds' front man in London. When Peabody retired in 1864, the name of the firm changed to Junius S. Morgan Company. Junius' son John Pierpont Morgan eventually assumed the role as Rothschild agent – this relationship became more 'public' after an 1899 meeting at the International Bankers Convention in London. He became a banking luminary in the United States – if you consider perpetuating the lie of debt-based banking 'luminous' -- but the source of his wealth and power was in London. In fact, the later named J.P. Morgan banking enterprise in the United States was *bankrolled and majority-owned* by the Rothschilds.

One of J.P. Morgan's other business ventures involved his bankrolling of White Star Line. The White Star Line owned a ship named the *Olympic*, captained by Edward Smith. The *Olympic* was involved in an incident on its fifth voyage when it collided with the British warship *HMS Hawke* in the Solent, a strait separating the Isle of Wright from the British mainland, on September 20, 1911. Lloyd's of London Insurance would cover the repairs necessary only if the *Olympic* was not found at fault in the subsequent inquiry. Not surprisingly, it was posited by the Royal Navy and ultimately decided that the suction from the *Olympic's* large displacement pulled the *HMS Hawke* into her starboard side causing severe damage to both vessels. The *Olympic* was deemed to be at fault and was responsible not only for the repairs to its own ship, but also for the repairs to the *HMS Hawke*. The repairs needed to make the passenger ship seaworthy were enormous. They included patching up two massive holes in the hull, one below and one above the waterline, which resulted in the flooding of two watertight compartments, a twisted propeller shaft, and a bent keel which produced a pronounced list to port. In fact, it took two weeks to perform emergency repairs to the *Olympic* in Southampton just so it could sail back up to Belfast for more permanent repairs. What did the *Olympic's* woes have to do with debt-based money you ask? Answer: more than you think.

Because of this incident, it was rumored that White Star was facing financial ruin: 1. it had to pay for the repairs to the *Olympic* and the *HMS Hawke*. 2. It suffered the loss of anticipated revenue from the recently built *Olympic*. 3. It had to pay for the soon to be launched *Titanic* (you've heard of the *Titanic*.) *Titanic* was actually the second of three Olympic-class passenger ships built by Harland & Wolff in Belfast for White Star lines. These three ships were commissioned by White Star to compete with the ships of its main rival, Cunard -- one of which was the ill-fated *Lusitania*. White Star raced to get the *Olympic* back out to sea. In doing so, they used a propeller shaft from the *Titanic* which delayed its maiden voyage. On November 20, 1911 *Olympic* was back in service. However, there remained serious questions as to whether it would ever pass another inspection. In addition to the propeller shaft, steel struts were welded onto the *Olympic* to brace the keel -- which didn't completely solve the listing to port issue. And to patch up the holes, Harland & Wolff replaced plates along one-third the ship's length. If *Olympic* was designated not "seaworthy" in its next inspection, it was likely that the repairs to get it back to seaworthiness would be so prohibitively expensive that the ship would likely be scrapped. It is likely that the keel would had to have been replaced. The keel laying is the first part of a ship's construction (and the time of the initial payment to Harland & Wolff from White Star). Replacing the keel would have been a huge undertaking, and probably not economically practical. Given its $7.5 million price tag to construct, the hit to White Star Lines and J.P. Morgan would have been massive, and quite possibly fatal. To add more insult to an already tenuous situation, *Olympic* was involved in another incident returning from New York in February 1912. In this incident the ship lost a propeller blade and suffered vibration damage. The necessary repairs took place in Belfast during late February and early March. Those repairs took place in a slip adjacent to the nearly completed *Titanic*.

The ships were nearly identical and many of the distinguishing items (e.g. crockery, linens, tableware, etc.) were White Star issue and not specific to each ship. If the two ships could be "switched" during that first week of March, and the *Olympic* (disguised as the *Titanic*), was to sink, the insurance money could be collected and the *Olympic's* seaworthiness would no longer be an issue since it was actually the *Titanic*. *Olympic* could then generate revenues for decades to come. The alleged "switch" is in dispute, but below are some interesting items for consideration:

Prior to its maiden voyage, *Olympic* was open to the public for inspection in Belfast and Liverpool. *Titanic* was not.

Olympic's sea trials lasted two days. *Titanic's* was conducted over one morning with no strenuous maneuvers required.

In the middle of a coal strike, passengers were queueing up to get work on the other side of the Atlantic, yet the *Titanic's* maiden voyage was only two-thirds-subscribed as White Star seemed to discourage passengers from taking the journey. This contrasts with the *Olympic's* fully subscribed maiden voyage.

Only two firemen (a.k.a. "boliermen" or "stokers") remained on in Southampton (from Belfast) for the trip across the Atlantic in the middle of a coal strike, when work was extremely scarce. What did they observe? Answer: Most likely a fire in coal bunker #10, which, instead of being extinguished, was topped off with 400 additional tons of coal. Somehow, the inspector missed this fire, which is understandable since the sea trials for the *Titanic* lasted only one morning. The *Titanic*, after all, was new, and essentially identical to the *Olympic*. What was there to inspect? The inspectors didn't even go down to the engine room. What the firemen probably also noticed was that the boilers were not new.

The *Californian*, a British steamship, also owned by J.P. Morgan (via his International Merchant Marine Company) set sail from the port of London on April 5th, *with no passengers* (again, in the middle of a coal strike), and a cargo of 3,000 woolen sweaters and blankets. Once it entered the North Atlantic ice fields on April 14th, it stopped. It then relayed its position to the *Titanic* three times. *Californian's* Captain Stanley Lord decided to spend that fateful evening sleeping fully clothed on a five and a half foot couch in the chart room. He was six feet tall. Was he expecting to be called into duty?

Fifty first class passengers, mostly friends of J.P. Morgan, including Florence Ismay, wife of White Star chairman, J. Bruce Ismay, cancelled at the last moment.

J.P. Morgan also cancelled his room on the ship, citing illness, even though he was spotted two days after the sinking at a French resort with one of his mistresses, in fine health. He also had bronze statues removed from the Titanic one hour before departure.

Titanic's Captain Stanley also rested fully clothed in the ship's chart room on the evening of the iceberg collision. Was he expecting to be called into duty?

79

The ship had "a noticeable list to port" according to a message sent by a passenger aboard the *Titanic*, just like *Olympic* would have with a bent keel.

Most of the ships owned by International Merchant Marine Company were "self-insured" (i.e. IMMC created its own insurance pool). However, enormous projects like White Star's Olympic class liners were partially insured by major insurance companies. *Titanic's* $10 million value was insured by Lloyds of London for $7.5 million. However, an additional $5 million policy was purchased for the *Titanic* just before its maiden voyage. How fortuitous.

When the wreck was discovered 1985, a coat of grey primer paint was seen beneath the top black hull coating. This grey primer coat was a feature of the *Olympic*, and not the *Titanic* (black undercoat). Also, the ship at the bottom of the North Atlantic featured longitudinal bulk heading in the stern. This did not appear in the original plans for either ship – both had lateral bulk heading. The location of this 'additional' bulk heading suggests a repair to the ship (perhaps the steel struts) to strengthen the keel, possibly one damaged in a collision with the *HMS Hawke*.

After the tragedy, Lloyds of London paid out the $12.5 million insurance claim (others purport a lesser amount was collected and White Star took a big hit). The *Olympic* passed its seaworthiness inspections and sailed on for many decades, eventually being retired for scrap. To be sure, many valid competing counter claims and evidence exist purporting the *Titanic's* existence on the bottom of the North Atlantic, and not the *Olympic's*.

However, what cannot be denied is the unbelievable coincidence that a ship owned by Rothschild agent and debt-money master J.P. Morgan sank, took the lives of John Jacob Astor IV, Isidor Strauss, and Benjamin Guggenheim, the three wealthiest and most influential opponents of central banking in the United States. Even if the *Californian* was supposed to be the rescue ship and the miscalculations (as to the position of the *Titanic* in relation to the *Californian*) by fourth officer Joseph Boxhall led to the unnecessary loss of life, the *Californian* was not big enough to rescue everyone, even if time allowed for two trips with the available lifeboats. In an era of chivalry, "woman and children first" would have still meant the demise of Astor, Strauss, and Guggenheim – in fact, J. Bruce Ismay was castigated the rest of his life for not going down with the ship. Whether or not it was part of an insurance scam (or a Jesuit plot as charged by others) is not completely known. What is known is that the last well financed opposition to the Federal Reserve Act was removed on April 15, 1912.

Chapter 17 (May 9 - 18, 2016)

It was decided that Caroline and Fitz would meet Tuesday morning at the DNA Diagnostic Center in Lower Manhattan. Fitz made sure that he was plenty early. He did not want Caroline to have any excuse to back out, but sure enough, she arrived right on time. Fitz reached out to greet her – *is a handshake appropriate?* She met his hand with hers and said, "Hey Brother." Fitz decided to play it safe with a toothy grin and a simple, "We'll see."

After some long stares from some of the staff at the clinic, an assistant in a white lab coat named Carl greeted them. He explained the procedure (known as a buccal swabbing) involved rubbing a cotton-like swab against the inside of the patient's cheek and nothing more. The procedure would be quick and pain free. The samples would be taken to the lab where a half siblingship test would be performed. Results would be back in five days. When they were finished, Fitz asked Caroline how she wished to be contacted when the results came back. To Fitz's surprise, she gave him her cell number. The puzzled look on Fitz's visage was detected by Caroline who explained, "If you're my half-brother, then you are part of my family. It's okay to have my phone number – as long as you don't give it out to the press when you go public with the news."

"How are you so sure that I'm your half-brother?"

"For some reason, you remind me of Dad."

"I'm embarrassed."

"Don't be."

****

Five days later the news came back: positive. Fitz was indeed Caroline Kennedy's half-brother. They shared the same father. It was official. Fitz felt empty. The visit to Preston and Associates would mean the end of his relationship with Annie and her little Oliver of which he had grown so fond. He didn't even know how to say goodbye. He was devastated. And she was likely to be very hurt to hear that he was taking a leave of absence from the relationship. They had never been in an argument. He would miss the way she would smile with her lips pursed. It reminded him of a sunflower catching the first ray of morning sunlight. He would miss the scent of her flesh – the redolence of a dew drenched honeysuckle with a hint of Baby Doll perfume. He would miss the enchanted transformation from elegant and sexy when she returned from a night on the town to infantine and adorable when she slipped on her pajamas and talked to her dog like Dorothy to Toto. She was a thaumaturgic celebration of the senses. Never mind the fact that she was brilliant.

Before he decided how he was going to approach Annie, Fitz picked up his smart phone and dialed Caroline.

"Hello Brother."

"How did you know?"

"I would have received an apologetic text otherwise."

"You're right."

"You don't seem too enthused. Is there anything wrong?"

"No…not at all. Caroline, there is so much that I want to ask, but…"

"You want your share of the inheritance?" she said jocundly.

"Oh God, no. My/our father took care of me and my mother. No. This has absolutely zero to do with that. First of all, I have never thanked you for doing this, which was incredibly rude, so Thank You Very Much."

"You're very welcome."

"I do have two questions to ask. Would you prefer to be in Japan when this goes public?"

"Actually, yes."

"When do you head back?

"In five days."

"Perfect. I will wait until then. Caroline, when you see or hear me on the news, please know that there is a reason for what I am doing, which should become clear in a few months. Please don't judge me until then. During those first few months, I am going to make no attempt to contact you, which you will probably be pretty happy about."

"You said that you weren't going to drag our father's name through the mud."

"I won't. The reasons for my behavior will crystallize by late September."

"You sound like a man with a plan."

"I just hope I can execute."

"Good luck and don't feel awkward about contacting me."

"Thanks for everything Caroline."

"Good-bye Fitz."

That phone call was easy. The upcoming discussion with Annie would be excruciating.

****

The offices of Preston and Associates were busy with very attractive twenty and thirty somethings – exclusively women as far as Fitz could tell – walking purposely through the office. Fitz's view of the firm was all-encompassing from the glassed-in conference room situated in the middle of the office. He had been escorted to the "fishbowl" by the receptionist and was now awaiting the arrival of Ms. Preston. Before he had time to absorb the strange environment, Polly Preston burst into the conference room with a giant white smile and a half out of breath, raspy salutation, "Hi! I'm Polly Preston. And you are Fitzgerald Cavendish?!"

Standing about 5'4" with banged blond hair, beautiful big aqua blue eyes, and mouthful of teeth that appeared artificial because they were so perfect, Fitz half expected Polly to break into a high school pep rally cheer. He could certainly feel the energy in her voice. Polly was extremely attractive – certainly a one in five hundred, Fitz quickly concluded; and extremely energetic. "Yes. Hi Polly. It is a pleasure to make your acquaintance."

"What can I help you with?"

"Polly, this may appear odd, but before we can discuss my situation any further, I need you to sign this." Fitz pulled a Non-Disclosure Agreement from his attaché case. "It is an NDA. I hope you don't mind. I know that your job is publicity, but if after I explain my circumstances to you and for whatever reason we decide that we are not a match, I need to keep this a…"

Polly interrupted, "Not a problem. Now you have me very intrigued." Polly gave the boiler plate two page NDA the once over. She appeared to be reading the document, but Fitz quickly got the sense that her attention span wouldn't allow for its total comprehension. Fitz was wrong, as she quickly spotted the "one million dollars in damages" clause regarding unauthorized dissemination of confidential information without a signed contract in place.

"Wow! That's a lot of money. Do you have the nuclear codes?"

"Funny you should say that."

"Why?"

"Sign and I'll tell you why."

Without further protest or ado, Polly snatched the pen out of Fitz's hand and signed the document. "Why?"

"My father is John F. Kennedy."

"Whoa! And you have proof to back up this claim?"

"Sure do. My half-sister, the U.S. Ambassador to Japan, and I had our buccal swabs last week and the results were positive."

"How did you get Caroline Kennedy to agree to this?"

Fitz pulled out a copy of the results and laid them on the table for Polly to see. "We have a mutual friend. I went to Brown and overlapped a couple of years with her brother."

"John John! You knew John John!?" Polly sounded more like an excited admirer than publicist.

"Not really. I was introduced to him a couple of times by our mutual friend."

"Why have you kept this secret for so long? This is truly incredible!"

"A long story, but I didn't find out until a few months ago."

"So how can I be of help?"

"I want the world to know who I am, and I need to become very popular. It is all a means to an end which I will explain shortly. You came highly recommended. Once I lay out my end game, I will give you time to put together a proposal. I am not going to go to another PR firm in the meantime. The only people who know my real identity are Caroline and me, and now you. I haven't even told Evan, our mutual friend, although Caroline may have."

"What is the endgame of this sought recognition?"

"I need to get a message out to the United States of America. The best platform for this message is the first presidential debate. I don't wish to be a candidate, but as a "Kennedy", if you can make me popular enough, I think we can create a groundswell for a Kennedy voice at the debate. Contingent upon my performance at the debate and its reception with the viewers, I would consider running as a third-party candidate."

Preston just had an "unconscious moment" of the business variety. She was being handed a dream job. She recovered to blurt out, "Making you popular is going to be very, very easy. Making you the next president will be a bit more of a challenge."

"You have two days to put together a proposal of how you get me into that debate, and if my message resonates with America, the proposal

86

must include next steps for the White House. You are supposed to be the best, so...."

"Who told you I was the best?"

"A friend of mine at Brown who is a partner at Skinner, Weiss."

"Are you talking about Chuck Schilling?"

"I am. Do you know him?"

"Yes. May I ask why you are not using Chuck?"

"Good question. And it brings me to the last part of my presentation. My message is going to create enemies in extremely high places. I will come under attack. Your firm may come under attack. The more popular I become, the more danger you could potentially face."

Polly did not completely follow. She was still in awe of what she was seeing and hearing. "I'm not concerned."

"You should be. That is why I came to you first. Chuck is a good friend. He is going to hate me for giving this bid to you – if I like your presentation that is -- but I do believe that this will be perilous work."

"What is your message?"

"That is the question I wanted to hear." Fitz detailed to Polly his discoveries about his father's death, and the message that he endeavored to broadcast to the American people before it is too late. Polly listened to it all and promised to be ready in two days with a proposal when Fitz returned.

Chapter 18 (1891 – 1913)

With no "new world order" in place and no central bank in the United States, many secret and less secret societies formed during the late 1800s in pursuit of changing the status quo. They were secret back then, but are known today through quotes/confessions of their "chattier" members. The most important of the group was the Society of the Elect.

Formed in 1891 by diamond magnate Cecil Rhodes, the society's goal was to "absorb the wealth of the world" and to "take the government of the whole world". Not surprisingly, debt-based bankers were involved. Amongst the group were powerful Rothschild banking agent, Chief Rhodes trustee, and later Governor-General and High Commissioner of South Africa Lord Alfred Milner, Lord Lionel Rothschild, and Lord Arthur Balfour, who will figure prominently later. The goal was a one-world government, wrapped in socialism, and run by the Elect.

Your Wikipedia version of history will tell you that Rhodes abandoned that "noble" cause to pursue the foundation of the Rhodes Trust, which was formed upon his passing in 1902 to provide the capital for the extremely prestigious Rhodes Scholars. The recipients of the scholarships were foreigners (initially just men) selected to study at Oxford College. It doesn't appear that Cecil completely abandoned his plans for world domination (even in death) as the Rothschilds became the trustee for the fortune that handed out scholarships which were used to recruit young minds of similar ilk.

Like all of these organizations and foundations, the young members were enticed with the misleading headline of "humanitarian ideals". However, the most suitable initiates were let in on the real goal of these groups: world government. These insiders were then given influential positions in the government, banking, and education. In the example of the Rhodes Trust, Lord Milner used his influence to get these scholars jobs in prominent positions in government and finance, where they became a dominant force in England's domestic and foreign policy. They became known as Milner's Kindergarten.

Getting back to the Society of the Elect, it formed a larger and less secret group named the "Association of Helpers" which went on (through the guidance of Lord Milner) to form the Round Table Groups – more on them shortly. Association of Helpers member Arnold Toynbee, a world famous British historian, revealed in a June 1931 speech to the Institute for the Study of International Affairs at Copenhagen:

> "We are at present working discreetly with all our might to wrest this mysterious force called sovereignty out of the clutches of the local nation states of the world. All the time we are denying with our lips what we are doing with our hands, because to impugn the sovereignty of the local nation states of the world is still a heresy for which a statesman or publicist can perhaps not quite be burned at the stake but certainly ostracized or discredited."

These Round Table Groups -- created when Association of Helpers merged with members of the Fabian (Socialist) Society (which included the since deceased Cecil Rhodes and Andrew Carnegie) and "the Inquiry" (a group formed by President Woodrow Wilson's chief advisor, Col. Edward M. House) -- include the Council on Foreign Relations (in the United States) and the Royal Institute for International Affairs (in Great Britain). The goal of these Round Table Groups, as stated by Toynbee, is simply a socialistic one-world government. Through these groups and various foundations, the government of the United States would be usurped and turned into a full-fledged criminal organization. Before they could achieve their sinister ends, the debt-based money cabal and its like-minded minions had to install a central bank in the United States.

The challenge facing the debt-based money clique was substantial. People in the United States had an almost nascent distrust for the banking system. Vehement anti-banking voice William Jennings Bryan was the Democratic Presidential nominee three times in a twelve year period from 1896 to 1908. Despite being outspent on the campaign by the debt-based money supported Republican Party by as much as 10 to 1, Bryan still managed between 43% and 47% of the popular vote. The only way a central bank was going to be achieved was through subterfuge.

The first undermining of the American resolve against central banking came with the Panic of 1907. Many reasons are given for the panic and to be sure, the San Francisco earthquake of 1906, the Hepburn Act (which capped railroad rates and crushed railroad stocks – the backbone of the stock market), a failed New York City bond offering, and a failed attempt to corner the shares of United Copper Company all greatly contributed to an unstable environment prior to the panic. The panic itself was triggered on October 21st, when J.P. Morgan-controlled National Bank of Commerce announced it would not serve as clearing house for (its competitor) the Knickerbocker Trust Company. Because it had former ties with Otto Heinze, F. Augustus Heinze and Charles Morse, who had failed to corner the shares of the aforementioned United Copper, it was rumored (incorrectly) that Knickerbocker Trust provided the financing for this failed scheme and consequently was in financial trouble. By 'announcing' that it was forsaking its clearing house duties for Knickerbocker, National Bank of Commerce gave credence to these rumors, thus causing a run on Knickerbocker, the third largest trust in New York City. This bank run triggered other bank runs and the stock market, already in a protracted decline, collapsed.

J.P. Morgan traveled to New York City to lend assistance, and in short order arranged for financing that kept the stock markets open and solvent, most trusts solvent -- not Knickerbocker -- New York City solvent, and a buyout of Tennessee Coal, Iron and Railroad Company by U.S. Steel. Again, he was hailed as a savior, which gave him a platform, along with many other financial titans of the day --Schiff, Warburg, Rothschild, and Rockefeller -- to call for the formation of a central bank to prevent crises like the Panic of 1907 from ever happening again.

The wool was being pulled over the populace's eyes. In May 1908, Congress passed the Aldrich–Vreeland Act that established the National Monetary Commission to investigate the panic and to propose legislation to regulate banking. Senator Nelson Aldrich (R–RI), a shill for the debt-based banking interests, was named the chairman of the National Monetary Commission. He then traveled Europe for nearly two years to study its countries' banking systems. This was all a ruse as Senator Aldrich would convene a secret meeting at the Jekyll Island Club (owned by J.P. Morgan) off the coast of Georgia, to discuss monetary policy and the banking system in November 1910. Paul Warburg (representing Kuhn, Loeb & Co.), with the help of Aldrich, Assistant Secretary of the Treasury A.P. Andrew, soon to be President of the Rockefeller-controlled National City Bank of New York Frank A. Vanderlip, Senior Partner of J.P. Morgan Company Henry P. Davison, President of the Morgan-dominated First

National Bank of New York Charles D. Norton, and Benjamin Strong (representing J.P. Morgan), wrote the bill that would become the Federal Reserve Act of 1913. Keep in mind that Senator Aldrich's daughter, Abagail, was married to John D. Rockefeller Jr. Aldrich published his "findings" in a report of the National Monetary Commission on January 11, 1911. Not surprisingly, the report called for the formation of a central bank in the United States. This became known as the Aldrich Plan; however, the 'plan' faced strong opposition.

27th President of the United States, Republican William Howard Taft, was a popular leader and presided over generally prosperous times from 1909 through 1912. The prevailing wisdom was that he would be re-elected in 1912. This was one of two problems facing the debt-based money gangsters: 1. Taft may have been popular, but probably wasn't strong enough to force the Republican-sponsored Aldrich Plan for a central bank through Congress. 2. The Aldrich Plan was very unpopular with the American populace as it was perceived as a Wall Street scheme. To solve this problem, the bankers secretly sponsored a bank bill by the democrats called the Federal Reserve Act. Elisha Garrison, an agent of Brown Brothers, wrote in his 1931 book *Roosevelt, Wilson and the Federal Reserve Law* that,

> "Paul Warburg is the man who got the Federal Reserve Act together after the Aldrich Plan aroused such nationwide resentment and opposition. The mastermind of both plans was Baron Alfred Rothschild of London."

Remember, Warburg was also the author of the Aldrich Plan. The Democratic Party candidate, Woodrow Wilson, said he would support the Federal Reserve Act, which was essentially identical to the Aldrich Plan, except in name – how easily the public was duped. If the debt-based money cabal could get Wilson elected, chances for passage of a central bank bill would increase significantly. To get Wilson elected, the bankers exploited a schism that had developed in the Republican Party between the progressives and the conservatives, represented by Taft.

Taft won a contentious Republican nomination over progressive Teddy Roosevelt. Playing on Roosevelt's ego, the bankers backed his third party presidential bid through the Bull Moose Party, with publisher

Frank Munsey and its executive secretary George Walbridge Perkins, an employee of banker J.P. Morgan, providing the financing. This team made the newly formed party candidate not only exceptionally well capitalized, but also very well covered by the press – more so than Wilson and Taft combined. With conservative Teddy Roosevelt seen as a viable candidate, the bankers were able to split the Republican vote. To be sure, the other candidates were substantially supported by the banks as well. In fact, in the firm of Kuhn Loeb Company, Felix Warburg was supporting Taft, Paul Warburg and Jacob Schiff were supporting Wilson, and Otto Kahn was supporting Roosevelt. Their plot played out to perfection with Wilson winning the 1912 election in a landslide, even though he received fewer votes than Democrat William Jennings Bryan when he lost his three elections. Wilson received 41.8% of the popular vote, while Roosevelt and Taft combined to garner 50.6% of the vote. Because of the split Republican vote, Wilson received 435 out of 531 electoral votes, despite the fact that he won a majority of the popular vote in only 11 of the 40 states that elected him.

To be sure, this wasn't the only stratagem that Senator Aldrich and his debt-based money cabal had up their sleeves. What good was a central bank without the authority to tax its citizens? Until 1913, customs duties (tariffs) and excise taxes were the primary sources of federal revenue. Income taxes were imposed, but they were technically unconstitutional. Aldrich introduced Joint Resolution No. 40, which called for the 16th Amendment to the Constitution, giving Congress the power to tax incomes. On July 12, 1909, Congress passed the resolution which was sent on to the state legislatures for a vote. On February 3, 1913, Secretary of State Philander C. Knox declared the amendment ratified and on October 3, 1913, the Revenue Act was passed imposing a graduated income tax with rates ranging from 1% to 7%. In very short time, income tax would surpass tariffs as the primary source of government funding. Now the only obstacle remaining was the opposition to the Federal Reserve Act.

Remonstration to the bill was vocal. Minnesota Congressman (and father of the famous aviator) Charles Lindbergh Sr. argued correctly that,

> "This is the Aldrich Bill in disguise…This Act establishes the most gigantic trust on Earth. When the President signs this bill, the invisible government by the Monetary Power will be legalized.

The people may not know it immediately but the day of reckoning is only a few years removed. .. The worst legislative crime of the ages is perpetrated by this bill."

Senator Aldrich and Paul Warburg waited for the most appropriate time to pounce. The date was December 23, 1913, when nearly 30% of the U.S. Senate was home for the holidays, and after dozens of revisions and compromises were pushed through in the wee hours of the morning, the bill was passed 43 to 25 with an astounding 27 not voting. Hardly any senator read the revisions. The "worst legislative crime of the ages" was enacted into law when Woodrow Wilson signed the Federal Reserve Act later that day.

From that point forward, the population of the United States has been officially enslaved by a debt-based money system. Think about it: for every dollar in circulation, there is an interest rate attached to it. M3, which is the broadest measure of money in the United States, is currently around $18 trillion dollars. It should come as no surprise that that figure closely resembles the national debt. The interest on the national debt was over a $430 billion in 2014, which is $1,343 for every man, woman, and child in the United States. Ignore that staggering interest statistic for a second and just consider that if you paid off the national debt out of M3, there would be no money in circulation (i.e. no money to pay off corporate and private debt). You're screwed and you don't even know why. How does that caramel macchiato taste now? Central banking is the sham of the ages.

The saddest part is the way the banksters made the legislation sound like it was a government entity: The Federal Reserve. Nothing could be closer to the truth. The Fed consists of 12 regional banks, but the majority of the authority rests with the Federal Reserve Bank of New York, which sets interest rates and directs open market operations, thus controlling the daily supply and price of money throughout the United States. It is the stockholders of that bank who are the real directors of the entire system. If you are still deluded with the notion that this is a public entity, below is a partial list of the *private shareholders* of the Federal Reserve Bank of New York when it was formed:

National City Bank	30,000
National Bank of Commerce of New York City	21,000
First National Bank	15,000
Chase National Bank	6,000
Marine National Bank of Buffalo	6,000

Total shares issued in the Federal Reserve Bank of New York: 205,053. In total, the New York banking interests owned over 50% of the shares on the initial offering. The owners of these 'owners' included the Rothschilds, Lazard Freres (Eugene Meyer), Jacob Schiff, Paul Warburg, Lehman Brothers, Goldman Sachs, the Rockefeller family, and J.P. Morgan Jr. As you will see, these 'owners' are the rulers of you. These people fund and establish all of the 'Round Tables' that dictate American policy, mandate your 'choices' for political office, and tell you what to think -- all for their good, and not yours.

With all of the different banking and money systems and all of the bankers' schemes to bilk the U.S. population out of its wealth that transpired in the 1800s, prices in 1913, as measured by the Consumer Price Index, were essentially the same as they were in 1793. Setting aside supply and demand dynamics specific to coffee, your $1 caramel macchiato in 1793 cost $1 in 1913. In 2014, thanks to the implementation of a central bank, your caramel macchiato cost $24.66.

Chapter 19 (May 20 - 24, 2016)

Preston's presentation prevailed. Fitz would be entering an arena he never desired: notoriety. Before going public, Fitz had to break-up with Annie. He decided that he would do it at her residence, a one-bedroom apartment in Tribeca. Once he arrived at Annie's, Fitz found her in the kitchen preparing dinner. He cut right to the chase by saying that the past three months had been the most magical time of his life and he wanted to spend the rest of it with her, but before he could do that, he had to take care of some unfinished business. Annie, initially of the mind that she was about to receive a marriage proposal, was in a state of confusion. Confusion birthed bewilderment when Fitz said that he would have to have zero contact with her for the next five (to possibly eight) months. Fitz's voice was cracking, "You will always know my whereabouts, but it's essential for your safety that you never acknowledge the relationship to anyone. It is also vital that our friends who know of our relationship don't mention it to anyone."

"Why?" a rapidly despondent Annie queried.

"To do what I have to do, I can't do if I'm worried about your safety. I love you more than anything in this world. Please believe in me. I swear I will return for you and Oliver. I know that eight months is going to feel like forever – it will for me."

Annie was hoping that this was just a nightmarish phantasmagoria, maybe even a sick practical joke, but the verisimilitude of Fitz's breaking face and the whimpers from her ever perceptive dog meant otherwise. "I don't understand. You're not making any sense."

"I know I'm not right now. And it may not be abundantly clear until I explain everything when I return. But it just has to be this way. I love you. I…" He grabbed her trembling hand which was partially covered in Old Bay Seasoning – dinner was going to be Shrimp Sauté, until Fitz ruined everyone's appetite – and squeezed it like a nervous golfer over a three foot putt. His voice cracked again, "I'm sorry." Both began crying rivers. He hugged her as if he was going off to war. She tried to respond in kind, but love was disordered with shock and despair. The future was suddenly uncertain. She began to question in her mind this bizarre arrangement with the promise of his return around the end of the year. *Why can't I be part of your life during this time? Do you have a wife in Indiana and a whole separate life? What do you actually do during the day? What are you really researching? What am I going to do this summer? How will I always know your whereabouts?*

She tried to compose herself. "So I guess this is goodbye?"

"I'm sorry. I promise I'll be back for you…and when I return, it will be forever. I love you."

Annie released herself from his smothering embrace and whimpered, "Goodbye."

****

When President Bill Clinton ensnared himself in the Monica Lewinsky affair, his staff marveled at his ability to 'compartmentalize'. It didn't seem to matter that his world was caving in; he could focus on the assignment in front of him, to the exclusion of everything else. Fitz was going to need this talent to put Annie out of his mind for the uncertain journey ahead. Polly Preston would prove to be perfectly suited for the development of this capacity in Fitz. First, she would have him on such a frantic schedule that he would not have time to think about anything else, except for what was in front of him. Second, Polly's corybantic personality only operated on overdrive, which was a pleasant distraction to Fitz during the few gaps in his itinerary.

The journey of a thousand miles started with a Sunday phone call to TMZ. Polly thought it best that the news be broken by a celebrity-news medium that possessed over three million Twitter followers, rather than the more conventional route of CNN whose breaking news account had nearly thirty million Twitter followers. The rationale for such a move was that CNN operated on the 24 hour news cycle and Fitz could be "here today, gone tomorrow", whereas TMZ had the ability to keep Fitz relevant, like it did with Paris Hilton and Lindsey Lohan during their party days. To be sure, TMZ ('Thirty-Mile Zone', which encapsulated the Hollywood, CA studios) has a reputation for accuracy with their celebrity scoops, including the death of Michael Jackson, Britany Spears' divorce from Kevin Federline, pictures of a battered Rhianna, and the elevator video of Ray

Rice hitting his fiancé – all such endearing memories. With half-sister Caroline back in the relative obscurity of Japan, it was time to let the world know that there was another direct descendent of former president Jack Kennedy. After a brief conversation with the TMZ office, Polly's cell phone lit up with an incoming call from Harvey Levin, creator and editor of TMZ. After a brief discussion, Polly emailed a .pdf file of the lab results to Harvey. Harvey wanted to verify this story with Caroline, but that would have to wait until daybreak in Japan. Polly also explained that she was not looking for money in exchange for the exclusive, but as Fitz's publicist she was looking for publicity, the more favorable the better. She also informed Levin that Fitz was very attractive and charismatic, and single. Polly also sent over two pictures of Fitz that she had professionally taken the morning Fitz broke up with Annie.

Fitz's phone rang just shy of midnight. It was Polly. Caroline had confirmed the story. TMZ was to break the news in a few hours -- during breakfast on the east coast. Fitz was to board a plane with her to Los Angeles the next day. She wanted him near the paparazzi and she was quite sure that an appearance on the Ellen DeGeneres Show was in the offing. Preston had already secured the Twitter account @FitzCave and asked Fitz if he had ever sent out a 'tweet' or 'followed' anyone on Twitter. Fitz reassured her that was not the case. Polly reassured Fitz that he would have to get the hang of not only Twitter, but also of Instagram, Flipagram, Facebook, and other forms of social media. Fitz politely informed Polly that that was specifically the reason he was paying her so much money. He also politely informed her that it was passed midnight and that he would see her at the airport in the morning. Fitz shut off his phone and went to sleep.

When Fitz awoke at 7am in his SoHo residence, he made himself breakfast which consisted of an omelet and a smoothie. He showered, dressed, packed, and before he headed for the airport, he logged into his desktop and clicked on the Google Chrome icon. There it was. On his default page Yahoo.com was a headshot of himself, and the headlines, "JFK's Other Son". "TMZ is reporting that JFK had a son out of wedlock who was born shortly before JFK was assassinated by Lee Harvey Oswald – [*they're really still pushing that nonsense.*] According to TMZ, U.S. Ambassador to Japan Caroline Kennedy has confirmed the story. TMZ also claims to possess the genetics test that backs up its assertion. The offspring's name is Fitzgerald Cavendish. He is 52, lives in New York City, and leads the life of an international playboy." – *What?!* The story continued on about how Fitz made the discovery. Fitz was quickly uninterested. He turned off his computer, turned on his phone, and headed for the door with his luggage. As he entered the elevator his phone came to life. Fifty emails – a little above average – Forty-two text messages – ridiculous – and seventeen voice mails – not possible. It was as if Fitz was the last to know about the news he broke. One of the text messages was from Polly who said that she was downstairs in a car outside his building. Sure enough, when Fitz exited the lobby of his co-op, a black Lincoln Town Car pulled up with a grinning blonde, head halfway out the window like a happy dog. "Hey Fitz!!"

"Top of the morning Ms. Preston."

"I figured it would be cheaper to commute together, plus we could get some work done on the way over."

"Good thinking. Aren't we going to have five and a half hours of flight time to get work done?"

Ignoring Fitz as he put his luggage into the back trunk and slipped into the back seat, Polly asked, "Did you see the news?" As Fitz nodded that he had, Polly continued like an excited tween-ager on her way to see Taylor Swift, "This is so exciting!!"

Fitz, buried in his smart phone and noticing a text from Chuck Schilling that simply said, "????", responded to Polly, "It's not that exciting to Chuck Schilling right now." Polly didn't answer. She didn't have to. Fitz quickly followed, "That was unfair. I hired you for your eternally optimistic outlook, your boundless energy, and because Chuck recommended you."

Polly added, "And because I have a kick ass plan to get you to the White House!"

"Indeed you do. By the way, what is this international playboy stuff?"

"I need for women to want you. You may eventually get 2% to 17% of the female vote because they are attracted to you, not because of what you have to say. A little James Bond image is not going to hurt. And besides, you've summered in the Côte d'Azur."

Now listening to his voice mails, Fitz queried, "How should I respond to all of these requests? Good grief. Word travels fast."

"If you're okay with me going through your phone, I'll take care of it."

Realizing that he had nothing to hide, Fitz handed the phone over to Polly. "I'm in your hands now."

****

Still in a depressed state over the bizarre events of the evening prior, Annie was struggling not only to process what had happened, but also to plan her summer. Would she get a place in the Hamptons with friends or would she stay in the city and pick up some tutoring jobs? It was hard to concentrate, but Oliver was always good at keeping her mind active, now barking at passing bicycle riders near the Warren Street dog run. Once Oliver calmed down, she noticed that her phone was vibrating quite actively for 7:15am. She started to see some pretty bizarre messages concerning her and JFK. One of them provided a link, which she clicked on. It connected her to a Huffington Post article, and although the picture was hard to make out, she immediately realized that it was about Fitz. Her heart raced as she read it – *international playboy? JFK's illegitimate son?* Some of the tumblers were starting to fall into place, but others – *why didn't he tell me?* – weren't. She snapped to and remembered that Fitz had told her to censor her friends – she now understood the meaning of that instruction. She immediately went into 'muzzle her friends' mode, texting them back not to tell anyone about her relationship with Fitz – deny it as a practical joke if you've already told anyone about us. It is very important – even though she didn't know why.

Chapter 20 (Recess)

You need a break. That was a lot to digest. Just to review:

1. There are two types of money creation systems: *debt-free* (good) and debt-based (bad). Your world currently employs the bad one. The battle between these two systems is left out of your history books.

2. The Revolutionary War was fought because King George III, at the urging of the Bank of England, took away the colonists *debt-free* money creation system. Because the British massively counterfeited the *debt-free* Continental currency, causing its demise, your government chartered the First Bank of the United States, a debt-based money creation bank that loaned money to your new government.

3. Mayer Amschel Rothschild brokered a deal to send Hessian soldiers over to fight against the Colonists. He perfected the art of loaning debt-based money to countries for military buildups before wars, to conduct wars, and to rebuild their economy after wars. In short, he slowly bankrupted nations by lending to them and collecting the interest.

4. M. A. Rothschild was likely influenced – his sons certainly were – by the teachings of Adam Weishaupt, who founded the Order of the Illuminati. The Illuminati wanted to take over the world and institute a communist-style regime.

5. Napoleon was leery of debt-based bankers and fought against a Rothschild-backed army at every turn. If he had triumphed, the money creation system in place would likely look a lot different than it does today. Debt-based money systems have dominated Europe ever since [except for Hitler -- more on that forthcoming.]

6. Nathan Rothschild, already extremely wealthy, made a vast fortune by obtaining first information of Napoleon's defeat at Waterloo.

7. The War of 1812 was likely the result of the United States not renewing the charter for the First Bank of the United States (debt-based money). Shortly after the war, the Second Bank of the United States was chartered.

8. The Rothschild's first attempt at a one-Europe government was thwarted by Alexander I at the Congress of Vienna in 1815. As a side note, Alexander was later poisoned to death.

9. Andrew Jackson vetoed the renewal of the Second Bank of the United States' charter in 1832 and eventually paid off the debt. He is the only president in the history of the United States to accomplish this feat.

10. Abraham Lincoln was assassinated because he introduced the *debt-free* Greenback to the United States to finance the Civil War. He was assassinated because he was going to introduce legislation for more Greenbacks after the war was won.

11. Lincoln's assassin, Johns Wilkes Booth, was very likely a paid mercenary of the Rothschilds, not a wildly pro-South activist. He never took up arms for the South and he never owned a slave.

12. Christopher Columbus was one of the worst human beings in history. Alexander II was likely the greatest friend the United States ever encountered.

13. Since the European banking interests were unsuccessful implementing a central bank in the United States, they robbed its population by demonetizing silver through the corrupt passage of the Coinage Act of 1873. It is the first lesson on why backing your currency with a precious metal is just a dumb idea.

14. To keep their names out of the press, the Rothschilds bought the press by taking a controlling stake in three major wire houses in Europe during the mid to late 1800s.

15. J.P. Morgan & Company was actually a Rothschild front -- another attempt to keep the Rothschild name out of the news. J.P. Morgan was passed off as a financial luminary.

16. The sinking of the *Titanic* may have actually been the sinking of the *Olympic* in a monumental insurance scam. On that fateful voyage, the wealthiest opposition to a central bank in the United States died.

17. A Rothschild-backed group of bankers met at J.P. Morgan's Jekyll Island Club in 1910 to write (what would become) the Federal

Reserve Act, the debt-based central banking model that is the root cause of all the world's money problems today.

18. Because they couldn't get it passed with Taft in office, the bankers financed Teddy Roosevelt's Bull Moose Party run to split the Republican votes, allowing Woodrow Wilson to become the president. Wilson signed the bill into law in 1913 on the same day it was passed by the Senate. 30% of the Senate didn't vote on the bill as it members were home for Christmas. Most likely, an even greater percentage of those who voted on the bill did not read it. The passage of the Federal Reserve Act marked the final death knell for a *debt-free* money system in the United States.

19. Not by coincidence, the sixteenth Amendment to the Constitution (Income Tax) was also passed in 1913. What good is a debt-based central bank if you can't tax the citizens to make its owners rich?

In your next history lesson, you will see the impact that the debt-based money cabal (and its Federal Reserve) has had on the United States and the world. The bankers could not achieve one-world government on their own, so the titans of business joined in their ignoble cause. Through their organizations, foundations, wars, and criminal acts, the bankers and the corporate socialists run the government like a marionette operates a puppet. Every string they pull is designed to make them wealthier and more powerful (by bringing the world closer to global governance).

Chapter 21 (May 24 – 26, 2016)

By the time Fitz landed in Los Angeles he was *cause célèbre*. It was one thing that John Fitzgerald Kennedy, the 35th President of the United States, fooled around; it was completely another thing that his trysts produced offspring; very handsome, make the ladies swoon offspring. His half-brother John Jr. was incredibly famous, so much so that former love interest Sarah Jessica Parker said that she had no idea what real fame was until she dated him. Fitz was no John Jr. yet, but the intrigue of another Kennedy kid was enough bait for the major news networks to bite hard on a slow news day. His story would be a nice segue into the presidential campaign news. Polly had alerted the major outlets that Fitz would be arriving in Los Angeles and leaked just a little bit of the story of how Fitz discovered the identity of his father. By the time that he and Polly had landed, talk show and interview requests were coming in by the dozens. Fitz had no clue how Polly had pulled that off. *How do they even know how to get a hold of her?* Coached by Preston to not reveal too much, Fitz exited LAX terminal 4 dressed in a pair of blue jeans, an untucked white button-down Ralph Lauren Polo shirt (small logo), and an olive green plaid blazer. He just paddled out into Waimea Bay when it was forty feet and closing out. Boom!

"Fitzgerald. Is this a hoax?"

"When did you find out?"

"Where's Caroline?"

"Do you have any illegitimate kids?"

"Are you really 52?"

"Is this your girlfriend? I heard you were single."

"Where are you going?"

"Are you really a playboy?"

"Is it true that you are dating Courtney Cox?"

"Do you know who killed your father?"

"Do you have a job?"

"Do you watch porn?"

"Where did you get that pretentious name from?"

A dozen reporters, as many news cameras, and twice that of paparazzi, all wanted a piece of Fitzgerald Cavendish. Fitz, stunned by the avalanche, managed to utter out, "Hi everybody. Yes. I am Fitz Cavendish and I promise that I will tell my story in its entirety soon. Right now, Polly and I are going to check into our hotel. We will get back to you."

Unsatisfied, the typhoon of questions upgraded to a category 3. He said no to the Courtney Cox rumor – "have never met her" – denied that he was a playboy – "I do like to travel, but am not a big partier" – confirmed that Caroline knew and that he had met her – "I promised her I would wait until she got back to her post in Tokyo before I revealed the news. She is incredibly sweet and has been very supportive throughout." He then denied that he was gay -- "no I'm not gay, but don't have any issues with anyone who is" – confirmed that his mother was deceased – "she died in a car accident back in 1990" – confirmed that he met John Jr. at Brown – "yes I met him at Brown, but did not know him personally. We had mutual friends." Polly did an end around of the proceedings and managed to work her way to the limo. The driver, a tall, older Italian gentleman with a hint of attitude – although it seemed mostly a put on, like a fake Mafioso – opened the driver's side door for Polly. She jumped in and slid across the backseat and opened the passenger side door. Fitz managed to see Polly's actions through the throng of media and made for the car with his duffle and garment bags. After his third "Excuse me," Fitz saw some daylight, handed his duffle bag to Polly, who quickly moved over as Fitz jumped into the limo. He shut the door quickly, but carefully, not wanting to destroy anyone's equipment. The last two questions he heard were, "what is your favorite restaurant?" and "where are you staying?"

Once inside, Polly gave Fitz and unrequited hug, "You were AWESOME!"

"Thanks Polly. That was not what I expected, but it wasn't that bad."

"Hey, I'm sorry I didn't get the door for you. I had no ideer that I was picking up a celebrity."

"I'm not a celebrity. But you don't need to apologize. What is your name?"

Polly interrupted, "You are too a celebrity. You already have 22,000 twitter followers!"

"I'm Mike. My friends call me Mafia Mike -- a pleasure to make your acquaintance."

"Fitz Cavendish. The pleasure is all mine. I apologize about that craziness. I had no idea. Polly. How do I have 22,000 twitter followers?"

"You have 23,000 now. I had my tech people make sure that when 'Fitzgerald Cavendish' is searched online, your twitter handle is at the top of the first page."

"You did tell me that Polly...my apologies. Mafia Mike, what does your schedule look like the rest of the week? Would you like to be our chauffeur for the balance of the time that we are out here?"

"It would be an honor." Mafia Mike reached into his coat pocket and produced a card with his number. "You can just text me. I will confirm receipt of the text and be on my way."

"What do you charge?" Mafia Mike, sensing that he was on to something good replied, "When I drop you back off at the airport you can make the determination as to what my services are worth."

"Deal." Fitz liked this guy. He had a little bit of that "don't 'f' with me" in him. He seemed well spoken, and he didn't wear a turtleneck that was the fashion blight of the limousine world, but rather a white buttoned down shirt. He was probably close to seventy but could pass for late fifties. He was tall and lean and looked like he could take care of himself.

By the time they had reached the hotel, Polly had Fitz booked on the Ellen DeGeneres show. Polly promised that 'Ellen' would be the first to interview JFK's -- up 'til now -- unknown son. It was noontime

Tuesday in Los Angeles and Fitz would not be making an appearance on Ellen until Wednesday, which would air on Thursday. Polly warned Fitz not to say too much until he got on the Ellen show. In fact, she made sure to tell everyone who had followed them to their hotel (the Four Seasons at Beverly Hills) that Fitz would be appearing on Ellen to tell his story and that he would be not be available for any further comment until then. She simply smiled when asked if she was Fitz's love interest.

Once inside the hotel, she wrote Fitz's first tweet. It concerned his appearance on the show. Once up in their hotel room – one room, two beds – she proudly announced to Fitz that he now had over 30,000 followers. Fitz, ignoring the fact that he probably now had more 'followers' than Jesus Christ did when he was alive, asked Polly about the sleeping arrangements. She quickly pointed out that another room would have been an extra $3,500 for the four nights they were going to be in Los Angeles. Fitz was wealthy, but he did not have money growing out of his ears. He agreed with Preston's logic and promptly put is head on the hotel pillow for a nap.

In addition to her logic, Preston had connections. She arranged a dinner for two at Nobu Malibu on short notice – no small feat, even if you are being escorted by the most popular man *du jour* in America. TMZ and others were awaiting Fitz's arrival. Fitz was polite and friendly, but offered nothing of interest to the inquisitive shutterbugs. Fitz wondered what Annie thought of all of this – every time there was a camera recording events, Polly was next to him.

****

Annie was excited, addled, and not talking to anyone, except Oliver and her mother, whom she strongly admonished not to talk to anyone about the relationship. Her love of the last three months – and of her life -- was now plastered all over the media and she wasn't allowed to contact him. He would come for her. And she was essentially supposed to deny there was any relationship, even to her friends. *Yet he was returning for me in eight months, possibly less, and that would be forever? And who was this attractive blonde chic with the toothy smile?* Annie couldn't tell if she was part of a greater scheme or if she was just being played. At least

Fitz was honest about the part where he said that she would know where he was. She made plans to be in front of the television at 4pm Thursday.

****

Ellen was selected by Polly as Fitz's initial public offering platform because: 1. she was well viewed (3.9 million a day). 2. Her audience was overwhelmingly female and Fitz had Hollywood good looks. 3. Fitz's total air time would be less than seven minutes – enough time to give the viewing audiences a small taste, with the hope that they would want more.

After Fitz explained how he had come about his discovery in the safe deposit box, Ellen asked him why he decided to go public with his discovery. Fitz responded that he really wasn't interested in fame. In fact, he did tell anyone for six months, but wanted to set the record straight for the sake of history – JFK, after all, was one of the most popular figures of the twentieth century. This, of course, would have been impossible if not for the college connection to Caroline Kennedy and her gracious cooperation. After a few more softball questions, Ellen decided that it was a good idea, since no one knew anything about Fitzgerald Cavendish, to play "Never Have I Ever" with him. In this game Ellen starts a statement with "Never have I ever…" and finishes it with a statement that may reveal something heretofore unknown (and potentially embarrassing) about the guest. As a good sport, Ellen plays along as well. Both Ellen and the guest have paddles that have the words "I HAVE" on one side and "I HAVE NOT" on the other side. When the statement is read, Ellen and her guest raise their paddles with the appropriate side showing. When "I HAVE" is the response, Ellen will ask the guest to expound on the situation where the "I HAVE" came about.

Ellen: "Never have I ever told an inappropriate joke." Ellen looked at the question with a disapproving smirk as if to say, "of course I have". Both Ellen and Fitz displayed "I HAVE" to the audience. Fitz continued, "And I have to confess, I thought it was very funny." The audience laughed – it was an easy crowd.

Ellen chimed in, "I wouldn't be here today without telling inappropriate jokes. Jeez that wasn't very revealing. Okay. Never have I ever dressed up in women's clothing." Fitz immediately raised the "I HAVE NOT" side of the paddle. Ellen continued, "Is my creative team suggesting I dress like a man? Wow! Fitz, never?"

"I can't help you there."

"Not even on Halloween?"

"Not my thing."

"Okay. Hopefully these will get better. Never have I ever sent a naked selfie." "I HAVE NOT" sides of both paddles were shown. Ellen quickly interjected upon seeing Fitz's negative response, "Would you please consider it?" Coming from a lesbian, Fitz found it humorous. The audience went crazy.

Fitz smiled and repeated, "Not my thing."

The audience responded with an, "Aww."

Feeling a little more at ease, Fitz interjected, "C'mon Ellen, you and Portia...never?"

Ellen feigned a little nervousness and replied, "Not my thing." The audience laughed. "Okay, last one. Never have I ever pretended to be James Bond." Fitz's paddle displayed "I HAVE". Ellen responded, "Do tell..."

"I spent a summer on the French Riviera a few years back and was seeing a very nice lady. Under the guise of attending a gala in Cannes, we got dressed up – she in a very attractive blue gown. I was dressed in a tuxedo. Instead of going to the gala in Cannes, I had a helicopter waiting in St. Tropez to take us to Monte Carlo. We gambled in the casino while I had a Bond Street Gin martini, shaken not stirred. We then dined at Le Louis XV at the Hotel de Paris and took a limo back to St. Tropez."

"Wow! You are some date! I'm sure she was impressed!"

"She threw up in the limo."

"Oh my! Sounds messy."

"It was, but I managed to get her head out of the window so most of it was 'on the limo' as opposed to 'in the limo'."

"I'm sure there was a lot of fooling around when you got back to St. Tropez."

"Not exactly…to be sure, the food was incredible. I think it was a case of one too many libations at Le Bar Américain."

"Now let me get this straight. You don't have a girlfriend at the moment?"

"No." Fitz did not like the sound of that and he was sure that Annie was not going to like the sound of that, but *that* was how it had to be.

"You're the son of JFK, single, and this good looking? You sir, are the most eligible bachelor in America. Thanks for coming on and telling us your incredible story." The audience roared with approval.

Once backstage, Polly gave Fitz a big hug, this time requited, and said, "You were awesome! You are making my job very easy! When this airs tomorrow, we will have requests from every major magazine in America! Not that we don't already. You will have over a half a million followers!"

"You really think that went well?"

"That James Bond story was perfect. Did that really happen?"

"Indeed."

History Lesson #2

Chapter 22 (World War I)

World War I, like all wars, was a banker's war. With the national debts of most European nations burgeoning due to a banker induced 'arms race' and popularity for those debt-ridden governments waning, any excuse – like the assassination of the Austrian Archduke Franz Ferdinand – was *casus belli*. A sense of patriotism was kindled by each country's press, and off to war they went.

However, the war had very little momentum in Germany, mostly because the country did not have the wherewithal to feed itself under wartime conditions, mostly due to the fact that Great Britain had imposed an economic blockade on Germany and its occupied countries. One of countries that Germany 'occupied' was neutral Belgium. Belgium only had enough home grown food to feed approximately 25% of its population. It relied on imports, and with the Great Britain infarction now binding, the population of 11 million was on the brink of starvation.

Enter Belgium Relief. The Commission for Relief in Belgium (or CRB) was organized by Emile Francqui, director of a large Belgian bank, Societe Generale, and run by future U.S. President Herbert Hoover. It was an international commission, but was largely run and supplied by the United States. On the surface, it was an organization created to feed the citizens of Belgium – a very noble cause. However, the CRB was a front to feed Germany and its soldiers. If the Germans were fed, the war could continue and the bankers could profit immensely. The German newspaper, *Nordeutsche Allgemeine Zeitung*, made several notes of the food arriving from Belgium into Germany. Gustav Friedrich von Schmoller, founder and leader of the Association of German Academic Economists, produced an economic journal called *Schmoller's Yearbook of Legislation, Administration and Political Economy*. In 1916, the publication shows that one billion pounds of meat, one and a half billion pounds of potatoes, one and a half billion pounds of bread, and one hundred twenty-one million pounds of butter had been shipped from Belgium to Germany in that year. Without those rations, war in Europe was not possible.

Edith Cavell, a British woman who operated a hospital in Belgium, became aware of this subterfuge and exposed it on April 15, 1915 in the leading nursing journal in Great Britain, the *Nursing Mirror*. Sir William Wiseman, head of British Intelligence, and partner of Kuhn Loeb Company, feared that the continuance of the war was at stake, and secretly notified the Germans – most likely fellow banker and German Intelligence head Max Warburg -- that Miss Cavell must be executed. Max's brother Paul was a partner in Kuhn, Loeb and the primary author of the Federal Reserve Act of 1913. The Germans, who didn't really care about what Ms. Cavell had to say in a British nursing journal, bowed to Wiseman's pressure, arrested her, and had her executed by firing squad on October 12, 1915 on trumped up charges. The flow of food into Germany through Belgium continued unabated until America's entry into the conflict. This is just one example of how Great Britain and the United States supplied its enemy during World War I. They would supply a 'neutral' country (such as Switzerland, Belgium, Holland, Denmark, Norway and Sweden) with war supplies which would then be funneled to Germany. Rear Admiral M.W.W.P. Consett, who was the British Naval Attaché in Scandinavia, authored a book, "*The Triumph of Unarmed Forces 1914-1918*" (1923) that details this stratagem.

Even though the CRB raises obvious questions (and suspicions), the biggest question of World War I was simply: how is it that an American populace that wanted absolutely nothing to do with the Great War in Europe, end up losing over 100,000 military personnel to it? At the onset of the war, thousands of Americans tried to enlist in the German army – almost half of the United States populace at that time was of German descent. [Do you remember all those Hessian soldiers that Rothschild brokered to fight the colonists? Many of them decided to make America their permanent home.] The Irish American community absolutely hated the British, because they wouldn't allow independence for Ireland. President Woodrow Wilson, not only declared neutrality, but would not permit loans by American banks to "belligerent" countries. This policy didn't sit well with the bankers who bought him the White House in 1912. By 1915, Wilson buckled to pressure from his moneyed backers and allowed American banks to lend to Europe. J.P. Morgan bank, a Rothschild front, loaned heavily to the governments of Britain and France. Secretary of State William Jennings Bryan – the same one who lost the bid for the White House three times – said it best: "The large banking interests were deeply interested in the world war because of the wide opportunities for large profits."

Please keep in mind that "Rothschild front" means that the Rothschilds actually had controlling interest in the bank, not "financial luminary" J.P. Morgan. When J.P. Morgan Sr. died in 1913, his wealth was estimated to be has much as $100 million or more. In 1901, his commissions alone from the U.S. Steel consolidation were north of $50 million. It was later disclosed there were only $19 million of securities in the entire estate, of which $7 million was owed to the art dealer Duveen. J.P. Morgan Jr. had to sell off some of his father's expensive art to pay some of the expenses of the estate. The balance of the reputed wealth was actually property of the Rothschild's. For the avoidance of doubt, $19 million was a princely sum in 1913, but paltry considering the stature of J.P. Morgan. The Rothschilds also controlled the houses of Kuhn, Loeb (through Jacob Schiff – who was born in M.A. Rothschild's home in Frankfort) and the National City Bank of Cleveland, which financed Rockefeller's Standard Oil.

Even though lending to Europe was good business, getting the United States directly into the war would be fantastic for the U.S. bankers. It would have been an impossible task without the passage of the Federal Reserve Act and the 16th Amendment to the Constitution. Even with those measures in place, the bankers still faced a difficult obstacle: the citizens of the United States, for the most part, wanted nothing to do with the war. However, the bankers were deeply resourced and richly experienced in the art of swaying public opinion. Taking a page from the Rothschild playbook in Europe, on November 13, 1914, in a letter to British journalist and historian Sir Valentine Chirol, Sir Cecil Spring-Rice, British ambassador to the United States wrote, "I was told today that The *New York Times* has been practically acquired by [alleged J.P. Morgan rival] Kuhn, Loeb and Schiff..." Not to be outdone, Texas Congressman Oscar Calloway claimed:

> "In March, 1915, the J.P. Morgan interests, the steel, ship building and powder interests and their subsidiary organizations, got together 12 men high up in the newspaper world and employed them to select the most influential newspapers in the United States

112

and sufficient number of them to control generally the policy of the daily press in the United States. These 12 men worked the problems out by selecting 179 newspapers, and then began, by an elimination process, to retain only those necessary for the purpose of controlling the general policy of the daily press throughout the country. They found it was only necessary to purchase the control of 25 of the greatest papers. The 25 papers were agreed upon; emissaries were sent to purchase the policy, national and international, of these papers; an agreement was reached; the policy of the papers was bought, to be paid for by the month; an editor was furnished for each paper to properly supervise and edit information regarding the questions of preparedness, militarism, financial policies and other things of national and international nature considered vital to the interests of the purchasers.

"This contract is in existence at the present time, and it accounts for the news columns of the daily press of the country being filled with all sorts of preparedness arguments and misrepresentations as to the present condition of the United States Army and Navy and the possibility and probability of the United States being attacked by foreign foes."

In other words, through the purchase of media assets, the message to America was being controlled by the Rothschild-controlled bankers and industries that could benefit greatly from America's direct participation in the war. Gradually, sentiment in the newspapers turned decidedly anti-German with chronicles of the Rape of Belgium – a true German-made atrocity -- and cartoons depicting German soldiers pitchforking babies.

In addition to the press, pro-banking elements within the government were working feverishly behind the scenes to involve the United States in the war. Woodrow Wilson's chief advisor on European politics, Colonel Edward House – with intimate ties to the banking interests -- had a conversation with Foreign Secretary of England, Sir Edward Grey regarding getting the United States into the war. Grey inquired, "What will Americans do if Germans sink an ocean liner with American passengers on board?"

House responded: "I believe that a flame of indignation would sweep the United States and that by itself would be sufficient to carry us into war."

Enter the *Lusitania*. The *Lusitania* was owned by the Cunard Steamship Company, Ltd. and competed with White Star Line's *Olympic* and *Britannica* – and for a brief moment, *Titanic* -- for the North American passenger trade. In return for British government financing to build the *Lusitania* (and the *Mauretania*), Cunard agreed to turn control of these ships over to the British government in times of war. Ostensibly, that did not appear to be the case, as the Lusitania continued shipping passengers back and forth between Liverpool, England and New York City in 1914 and early 1915. However, as an auxiliary naval ship, the Lusitania was under orders from the British Admiralty to ram any German ship seeking to inspect her cargo – a rather 'guilty' action for an ostensibly 'neutral' passenger ship – as it was illegally running armaments to Great Britain. *Lusitania's* Captain Daniel Dow decided that he wasn't going to be a party to this deception any longer and resigned on March 8, 1915 claiming that he was "tired and really ill". The real reason: he was no longer willing "to carry the responsibility of mixing passengers with munitions or contraband."

Aware of the illegal cargo going to Great Britain, the German embassy attempted to place advertisements in fifty United States newspapers, dated April 22, 1915 with the following warning:

"NOTICE! Travellers intending to embark on the Atlantic voyage are reminded that a state of war exists between Germany and her allies and Great Britain and her allies; that the zone of war includes the waters adjacent to the British Isles; that, in accordance with formal notice given by the Imperial German Government, vessels flying the flag of Great Britain, or any of her allies, are liable to destruction in those waters and that travellers sailing in the war zone on ships of Great Britain or her allies do so at their own risk. IMPERIAL GERMAN EMBASSY WASHINGTON, D.C., APRIL 22, 1915."

However, the publication of many of these ads was inexplicably blocked. George Viereck, the man who placed the ads on behalf of the embassy, protested to the State Department on April 26th that the ads were not being printed. Viereck met with Secretary of State William Jennings Bryan and produced copies of the Lusitania's supplementary manifests. Bryan, impressed by the evidence that the Lusitania was carrying weapons, said that he would entreaty President Wilson to publish the warnings. Some warnings were published, most weren't. It should be of little doubt that Wilson was informed of the illegal cargo on board the *Lusitania*, but did nothing to stop its departure. So with a new captain (William Thomas Turner) at the helm, the *Lusitania* departed Pier 54 in New York on May 1, 1915 en route to Liverpool with 1,959 people aboard.

Awaiting her demise was First Lord of the British Admiralty, Winston Churchill. Keep in mind that England had broken the German war code five months prior, on December 14, 1914, so Churchill had a decent idea of the location of each U-boat. As the *Lusitania* neared England on May 7th, it slowed anticipating the arrival of an English escort vessel, *Juno*. However, Churchill had called *Juno* back to port, leaving the *Lusitania* a veritable sitting duck off the coast of Ireland, with three U-boats in the area. Not surprisingly, the *Lusitania* was torpedoed. *U-20*'s torpedo officer, Raimund Weisbach, viewed the destruction through the vessel's periscope and felt the explosion was unusually severe. This was due to an immediate subsequent explosion of munitions in the ship, causing it to sink in eighteen minutes resulting in a loss of 1,198 lives. However, the sinking of a 'neutral' passenger ship with 129 American lives lost did not ignite the "flame of indignation" that Col. Edward House had predicted, but it did turn sentiment – once anti-British -- decidedly anti-German.

Wilson was re-elected in 1916, due in part to his platform that he had kept America out of the war. It was understood by the public that it was Wilson's aim to bring about a negotiated end to World War I without victory for either side. On January 22, 1917 in an address to the U.S. Senate, Wilson said, "It must be a peace without victory... Only a peace between equals can last." Furthermore, momentum for the continuance of the war was waning as the European population grew weary of casualty lists, food shortages, and promises of victory that never materialized. Germany offered up an olive branch on December 12, 1916. And this was in an atmosphere where Germany would soon be in a position to commit more resources to the Western Front with Russia's internal strife crippling its ability to capably execute a war on the Eastern Front. Yet within five months of Wilson's re-election (and two and a half months after his speech to the Senate), the U.S. had declared war on Germany.

The only answer to this enigma lies in the fact that the banks didn't want the war to end. The Rothschild-sponsored J.P. Morgan and Kuhn, Loeb Company had already loaned out $1.5 billion to the Allies, not to mention the other banks and American businesses that had sold to the Allies on credit. If peace was made, the Allied countries would likely default on the loans as they were bankrupt from spending on the build-up to the war and its prosecution. If they continued to fight on, they could easily lose the war to the Central Powers with Germany now able to concentrate more on the Western Front.; thus another scenario that would result in default to the banks and businesses of the United States. As a stalling tactic, diplomatic wrangling retarded any progress on the German peace overture. Desperate for assistance, the Allies enlisted Rothschilds European banking interests to petition Woodrow Wilson to enter the war. According to Marine Major General Smedley D. Butler, author of *War is a Racket*,

> "An allied commission...came over shortly before the war declaration and called on the President. The President summoned a group of advisers. The head of the commission spoke...'There is no use kidding ourselves any longer. The cause of the allies is lost. We now owe you (American bankers, American munitions makers, American manufacturers, American speculators, American exporters) five or six billion dollars. If we lose (and without the help of the United States we must lose) we, England, France and Italy, cannot pay back this money . . . and Germany won't...'"

[As an aside, during 1933, a cabal of wealthy industrialists plotted a fascist coup to overthrow FDR. The plotters asked Butler to be the leader of the fascist state. Butler, not only rejected the offer, but also reported the plot to the press and to Congress. If the plan had come to fruition, it was all likely a ruse to give FDR more power, with Butler playing the unwitting dupe.] Also, U.S. Ambassador to Britain, Walter Hines Page, whose salary was supplemented by National City Bank, sent a confidential message to Wilson dated March 5, 1917, stating,

"I think that the pressure of this approaching crisis has gone beyond the ability of the Morgan Financial Agency for the British and French Governments...The greatest help we could give the Allies would be credit. Unless we go to war with Germany, our Government, of course, cannot make such a direct grant of credit."

In other words, it didn't matter what the citizens of the United States thought about the war in Europe, it only mattered what the bankers and war related businesses thought. This was an economic decision brought about by American banks over-leveraging themselves (through fractional reserve banking) and putting the American and world economies at risk.

With no meaningful response to its proposal for peace, Germany re-established a policy of unrestricted submarine warfare on February 1, 1917. Even the ill-conceived Zimmermann telegram failed to unify public opinion in support of war. After two American merchant ships were sunk in February and five more in March, Woodrow Wilson seized upon the opportunity to ask for a declaration of war on Germany which was granted by Congress on April 6, 1917. The Selective Service Act was passed on May 18, 1917 conscripting 2.8 million men into service, supplementing the 2 million that had volunteered. American men were brainwashed into fighting a "war to make the world safe for democracy" and a "war to end all wars." It should have been declared that they were actually "bailing out U.S. debt-based banking system". One week after the declaration of war, $200 million of U.S. taxpayer money was sent to Great Britain and $100 million to France. All of that money was applied against the J.P. Morgan loans. In 1936, Senator Gerald Nye's Committee concluded J.P. Morgan & Co. was a "merchant of death" by forcing America into the war on the principle of profit, not policy, after it and other banks lent the Allies $2.3 billion.

With 10,000 fresh soldiers landing in France daily, the American entry into the war helped turn the tide on the Western Front with meaningful advances occurring in August 1918. Despite having won the war on the Eastern Front against Russia, and despite never having fought on its own soil, Germany sought out peace again, as morale for the war back home had disintegrated.

As a result of the war, with Standard Oil supplying about 80% of the Allies petroleum needs, J.D. Rockefeller made $200 million. Other companies did quite well. DuPont, which manufactured gun powder, saw a 950% increase in average annual profits to $58 million. Bethlehem Steel saw an 800% increase in average annual profits to $49 million. Bernard Baruch took time from his banking and fundraising – for Woodrow Wilson -- activities to become the chairman of the War Industries Board, during which time his net worth was alleged to have skyrocketed from $1 million to $200 million. [What selfless service on behalf of the war effort!] Many defense-related industries thrived during the war, but no group fared better than the banks. Estimates vary, but the United States spent between $22 and $39 billion on World War I. All countries participating in the conflict spent approximately $200 billion. Almost all of that money was borrowed. With American aid, the Allies could pay back the loans to their financiers, making J.P. Morgan and Kuhn Loeb enormous profits. Approximately $16 billion in profits were made off of a war that accomplished little, except the deaths of 20 million young men and innocents. Who paid for the American aid to the Allies? Answer: You, the American tax payer. During the war, the recently instituted income tax saw the top rate skyrocket from 7% to 67%. This is just another example of the debt-based money cabal stealing from the citizens of the world. Without the passage of the 16th Amendment to the Constitution and the Federal Reserve Act, there is little chance that the United States could have entered the war.

Any remaining shortfall to the banks would be made up by the Germans. After offering peace two years prior, Germany was now forced to pay for the war by the tenets of Treaty of Versailles. Very odd how Max Warburg, head of the German espionage system (Secret Service) was at the negotiating table on behalf of Germany; very odd how the N.M. Warburg financed Germany's war effort; very odd how Max's brother Paul was not only the author of the Federal Reserve Act, but also a vice-chairman of the Federal Reserve and author of the plan organizing the War Financing Corporation; odder still how Paul was decorated by the Kaiser in 1912 and only became an naturalized citizen of the United States in 1911; very odd how he was a partner at New York based Kuhn Loeb & Co. that profited immensely off of the war; very odd how Max and Paul's brother Felix was a director of the Prussian Life Insurance Company, a company that would surely benefit from a German surrender. And who else do you find at the negotiating table but Baruch.

Despite these oddities, Max Warburg was steamrolled at the negotiations. He opined that Germany should not submit to the Allies' (really France's) impossible war reparation demands as it would result in bankruptcy. He turned out to be correct. Many of the 440 articles of the treaty dealt with how the Germans would pay for the war. The total war reparations tab: $33 billion – three times the value of all property in Germany. A newly installed government faced a declaration of war if it didn't accept all 440 articles 'as is'. Left with no alternative, Germany signed the treaty on June 28, 1919. Germany managed to pay $5 billion before the country went bankrupt. What followed was a period of hyper-inflation, fueled by short-selling of the German mark, known as the Weimar Republic. A German caramel macchiato costing $1 in 1918 would sell for $1 trillion (yes, with a 'T') by the end of 1923. The collapse of the German economy would sow the seeds for World War II – and another opportunity for profit.

As an aside, in return for getting the United States into the war, Rothschild-backed Zionist interests were paid in kind. In 1917 Walter Rothschild, 2nd Baron Rothschild was the addressee of the Balfour Declaration (delivered by then British Foreign Secretary and former Prime Minister Lord Arthur Balfour of Society of the Elect fame) to the Zionist Federation, which committed the British government to the establishment in Palestine of a national home for the Jewish people. There was one problem with this declaration: the land had already been promised to the Arabs in return for their participation in World War I against the Ottoman Empire. This secret treaty (known as Sykes-Picot or Asia Minor Agreement) was negotiated by Lawrence of Arabia in 1916 and promised the Arabs an independent state in the Palestinian territory. The Arabs held up their end of the bargain, but once the agreement became public three weeks after the Balfour Declaration, the French claimed that they were not a party to this agreement, which seems incredulous since Francois Georges-Picot was a French diplomat. In the end, the French and British reneged on Sykes-Picot, laying the foundation of distrust that has pervaded the relationship ever since. The ISIS and ISIL groups that are portrayed in the western media simply as cold blooded murderers – those same ones that the United States fights alongside in Syria and against in Iraq -- are seeking the territory laid out by Sykes-Picot to establish a caliphate.

Chapter 23 (Late May – July 2016)

The 2016 presidential campaign season got off to an early start with candidates throwing their hats into the ring as early as mid-2015. The TV networks deduced that the more they made the quest for the White House look more like a reality show, the better their ratings. One of the many blunders included Jeb Bush's response to the question of whether or not he would have authorized the invasion of Iraq, knowing what we know now. His answers (in the course of one week):

"I would've. And so would've Hillary Clinton, just to remind everybody. And so would have almost everybody that was confronted with the intelligence that they got." [*Okay, we are not talking about what you knew then, but what you know now.*]

"Yea, I don't know what that decision would have been – that's a hypothetical. But the simple fact is mistakes were made, as they always are in life." [*So after more than a decade, you don't know what the right decision would have been to one of the most divisive issues in the United States?*]

"I answered it honestly. And I answered it the way I…answer it all the time, which is that there were mistakes made, but based on the information that we had, it was the right decision. Going back in time and talking about hypothetical – what would have happened, what could've happened – I think does a disservice for them [the troops]." [*Aren't you running – and isn't the population judging you -- on hypotheticals, since you have never been confronted with these foreign policy decisions as the governor of Florida?*]

"Of course, you know, given the power of looking back and having that – of course anybody would have made different decisions." [*What would your decision have been? This is like pulling teeth. Is the question that hard?*]

"Knowing what we know now, I would have not engaged. I would have not gone into Iraq." [*Congratulations! It is very presidential of you to have taken a week to think this through, not to mention the decade you had to reflect on this minor issue. It is hard to imagine that you would have been confronted with this question on the campaign trail or in a debate. You are obviously well prepared.*]

And of course, there was Hilary Clinton. Pick a scandal, any scandal: Benghazi, email-gate, Pardon-gate, Whitewater, missing Rose Law firm documents, Travel-gate, China-gate, Vince Foster, File-gate, using the IRS as a gestapo, covering up Bill's dirty deeds, or looting the White House. It is amazing that someone who is accused of so much misconduct [the number of scandals as of this writing is twenty-two] is a serious candidate for the office of the President of the United States of America. If she was involved in half of the wrongdoing she is accused of and tried to run for mayor of a small rural town in the 1800s, she would have been stoned to death. Dick Morris said,

> "I finally parted company with Hillary Clinton when I saw how she was using private detectives to investigate the women who were linked to her husband – not to change him, not to reform him, not to make him a better person, but to cow those women into silence, so that he could get elected president."

There was Donald Trump, spewing his anti-Muslim venom, making misogynist comments, calling everyone with less money than him a 'loser', calling John McCain "a war hero because he was captured – I like people that weren't." It was as if the American citizens were being asked to vote for a comic strip character. It was as if Donald didn't really want to win, for if he had shown just a tincture of humility, he probably would have won the Republican nomination – not because he had the answers to anything, but because he was famous and he wasn't one of *them* and he was raising some issues that *they* didn't want addressed – like the funding for ISIS and vaccines and their link to autism. He was a breath of fresh air. However, the American public, after witnessing "The Donald" and his egotistically abrasive brand of douche-ness on the campaign trail for months, understandably tired of watching his daily train wrecks rerun on late night talk shows, and decided that it didn't want a caricature running the country. Mercifully, the pugnacious windbag was 'fired'. Bluster of a third party run proved to be just that. Claiming that he didn't want a repeat of Teddy Roosevelt's Bull Moose Party run of 1912, which opened the door to Democrat Woodrow Wilson's election, Trump disappeared loudly from the political scene.

Against this backdrop, Fitz saw an encouraging sign. People didn't really like either presidential choice; they just hated the other candidate more. People voted for Hilary Clinton, not because she was a nice person who would do the country some good, but she was most likely to beat the candidate that the Republican Party nominated. Nobody cared about Jeb Bush, but he was determined to be the person most likely to defeat the candidate that the Democratic Party nominated. This was the reason Donald Trump was so popular early on: he wasn't part of the "establishment". He was a bona-fide outsider, and a wild-card (and a narcissistic jackass) that the real rulers of this country couldn't control. Unfortunately, Donald didn't know much about what actually ailed the country or how the system was rigged – so that he could unrigged it -- but he was sure that there existed a direct correlation between the size of one's bankroll and his intelligence quotient. With that said, he was the only candidate that mattered; the only one who could affect real change.

Fitz surmised that if someone could get in front of a large enough audience and explain exactly what was going on with this country and offer up actual solutions, the American public would flock to that candidate. Fitz's research led him to believe that the only person who had a clue over the past fifty years was Ron Paul, and now possibly his son Rand. The problem for the two of them was that they were public figures and known quantities that the mainstream media could marginalize. Ron Paul would win the debates (according to post-debate polls) when the Republican candidates competed in 2008 and 2012; however, the pundits would dismiss it as "just a bunch of fanatics voting multiple times". *At least he had some fanatics.* The next day Ron Paul, like a middle child, would get next to no media attention, as the story would shift to which candidate screwed up. The Pauls' other obstacle was superficial, yet out of their control: neither Ron nor his son Rand "looked" presidential, but at least they had a notion and actually cared.

****

The Ellen Show proved to be a bonanza for Fitz. His twitter followers jumped to 1.2 million three days after the airing of the show. *Seven minutes with Ellen, with nothing meaningful said, and people ate it up? They want (or care) to know more?* Two bachelor reality shows contacted Fitz to see if he was interested in the starring role – millions were offered. Fitz politely declined. There were appearances on *The Tonight Show Starring Jimmy Fallon* and *Jimmy Kimmel Live!*, both of which displayed the talents of the dry-witted hosts to keep their audiences interested in a person who was promoting nothing (except himself). Fitz's story was interesting, but beyond talking about how he discovered his father's identity, there wasn't much to say. Are you going to write a book about your life? "No" – although a publishing company had contacted him about writing his biography. With hindsight as your guide, did your mother ever hint at the identity of your father – maybe she dropped subtle innuendos that you didn't pick up? "Only my name." The only rejoinder by Cavendish to a question that insinuated his ultimate intention occurred when he was asked, "Who do you like, Hilary or Jeb?" "Actually I'm disappointed. No one seems to have any passion for the ideas that these candidates are submitting as solutions. They are only nominated because they are more likely to beat the other party's candidate, whom the voter despises."

It wasn't until he appeared on Anderson Cooper 360° – *why would he be interested in talking to me? How does Polly procure these appearances?* – that Fitz was able to display another talent: his aptitude for numbers. The show took place on June 4, 2016. Polly had informed Fitz that Anderson Cooper's birthday was the day before and to wish him a belated happy birthday. Once the airing began, Fitz did just that, but took it one step further. He told Anderson that he was born on a Saturday. Cooper started into his programmed "thank you", but stumbled slightly when he realized Fitz was correct. "That's correct. How did you know that? Did you look it up?"

"No and yes -- I looked up the year you were born. It is just something I can do. It's just a dumb bar trick."

Anderson wasn't letting go. "There is nothing about what you just did that would be considered 'dumb'. How did you do that?"

"I would explain, but I think I would put your audience to sleep."

"I thought that only six people in the United States had that gift, and you are one of them?"

"I highly doubt that there are only six people who can do it."

124

"I don't think you would put my audience to sleep."

"I'll do it, but I feel bad, because people tune in to your show for serious reporting. My mathematical ruse is just that."

"I think they would find it fascinating."

"Okay. All we are trying to do is factor out the "extra" days from the year, month, and day of the month to determine on which day of the week your birthday falls. Let's start with the year. You were born in 1967. Each year has 365 days – we will get to the leap years in a moment. That is 52 weeks plus one extra day, so that makes 67 "extra" days. Now, every fourth year there is an extra day. Four divided by the 67 years is 16 with a remainder of 3. 16 is the number of leap years that transpired last century before you were born, so that is an additional 16 "extra" days – the remainder of 3 is unimportant. Now we have to factor out the extra days of the month in which you were born. January is obviously the first month so there are no extra days to factor out. January has 31 days. That is four weeks plus 3 extra days, so the number for February is 3. February has 28 days – we have already factored out the leap years – which is four weeks and no extra days; thus the number for March is 3 plus 0 or 3. March has 31 days, or three extra days. 3 plus 3 is 6; so the number for April is 6. April has 30, or 2 extra days. 2 plus 6 equals 8. 8 is one week plus one extra day; thus the number for May is 1. May has 31 days, or three extra; so the number for June is 3 plus 1, or 4. The number for June is 4. So we have 67 plus 16 plus 4 plus you were born on June 3rd so that is 3 more days. 67+16+4+3 = 90. 90 divided by 7 is 12 with a remainder of 6. Six extra days applies to a Saturday. Anderson, you were born on a Saturday. Zero is a Sunday. One is a Monday. Two is a Tuesday, and so on."

"That was absolutely fascinating. How did you know that 6 is a Saturday?"

"I cheated. There is one assumption you have to make, or know. I looked up the first day of the 1900s, January 1, 1900, and found that it was a Monday. That is why Monday is a 1."

"And you can calculate that in your head or did you look up my birthday before we came on the air?"

"My assistant told me your that yesterday was your birthday. So I looked up the year you were born and calculated it before I sat down on the set."

"How fast can you do it if I just gave you any date?"

"Give me one and we'll see."

"October 13, 1944"

A three second pause and "Friday."

"Wow!"

"Forty-four plus eleven plus thirteen equals 68. October is a zero. 68 divided by 7 is 9 with a remainder of five. Five is a Friday."

"What about July 4, 1776?"

Almost no hesitation -- "Thursday -- that one is a little trickier as it involves a different century. As you go back each century you add one or two extra days – usually two, to reflect that a leap year is skipped at the turn of about 3 out of every 4 centuries. We skip a leap year three times every 400 years to take into account that the sidereal year is 11 minutes and 14 seconds shorter than our 365 day 6 hour calendar year. So we add one "extra" day three out of four centuries to reflect this dynamic and we add one "extra" day per century to reflect that there are 125 "extra" days each century which is one short of a perfect week (18 weeks times 7 equals 126). So 76 plus 19 plus 6 plus 4 plus 4 for the two centuries (since they both skipped the leap year) equals 109. 109 divided by 7 is 15 with a remainder of 4. 4 is a Thursday."

"That is truly astonishing. Do you have any other "tricks" that you'd like to share with us?"

"I'm sure your audience has been sufficiently bored and your ratings have plummeted." Fitz could not be more wrong. The elucidation of his little "bar trick" was re-broadcasted on YouTube and was one of the lead stories trending on Yahoo! Even before anyone knew of Cavendish's performance, one million viewers tuned into to the 8pm cable show, almost double its normal audience from the same time last year. Amongst other questions, Cooper asked Fitz whether he had inherited the instinct for politics. Fitz led out a little more rope with his response: "I think that most of the problems plaguing the United States and the world are completely fixable, but I don't hear these solutions coming from the current batch of candidates." Fortunately for him, his numerical stunt took such a long time to explain that Anderson ran out of time and could not follow up with another question about politics. Now wasn't the time for Fitz to talk about what was wrong with the country. The algebraic antic did create a positive impression about Fitz in the minds of the viewing public. He wasn't just the illegitimate son of a U.S. President who women found attractive. He was now thought of as someone who was entertainingly intelligent.

Two weeks later Fitz appeared on *Live! With Kelly and Michael.* They gave him a series of brain teasers to solve. Fitz correctly answered each one, including a riddle concerning three light switches in one room and three light bulbs in another. With only one trip to the room that housed the light bulbs, Fitz had to determine which switch operated which lightbulb. The solution involved leaving one switch in the 'on' position for 15 seconds and turning it off. When you walk into the room with the light bulbs, the bulb that is not emitting any light and is warm would correspond to that switch. Of the other two switches, one would be in the 'off' position and correspond to the bulb that was not emitting light and cold; and the other switch would be in the 'on' position and correspond to the bulb lighting up the room. Fitz had actually heard this question when he was at Brown over thirty years ago, but didn't lead on that he already knew the answer. After Cavendish's correct deciphering, the normally verbose Michael Strahan could only muster a stupefied "Daaamn!"

Fitz turned the table ten days later when he was invited to appear on *The Today Show* with Matt Lauer and Savannah Guthrie. He told the show's hosts that he would be able to read their minds through a simple exercise. Fitz handed out two pieces of paper and a pen to each co-host. He instructed them to write down any one or two digit number. He then had the co-hosts multiply that number by two. They were then instructed to add five to that number. They then multiplied that number by fifty. He then asked them both if they had a birthday this year. Both shook their heads no. Fitz, ignoring their responses, continued that if the answer was yes to add 1765 to the number; and if the answer was no to add 1764 to the number. His last directive was to subtract from that number the year in which they were born. He then had everyone write that number on a separate piece of paper. He then asked co-host Savannah Guthrie to reveal her number which was 1744. Fitz then instructed her that the number she had been thinking of was 17 and that she was 44 years old. "That's right!" responded a surprised Guthrie. Matt Lauer's number was 558. Fitz told him that he had been thinking of the number 5. Lauer quickly queried, "How old am I?" Fitz shot back "58". He went on to tell them that the last two digits represented their ages and that the number – be it one or two digits – to the left of their age was the number they had initially written down and if that was not the case then they had made a mathematical error. Lauer quipped, "You are some nerd."

Fitzgerald Cavendish was indeed a nerd, but a very popular one. Polly reserved tables at the hottest restaurants in town – New York or Los Angeles – and escorted him almost every time. He was offered money by several nightclubs to simply 'hang out'. Fitz politely declined. TMZ kept Fitz in the spotlight, especially when he was in Los Angeles, with positive vignettes. One in particular, arranged by Ms. Preston, included a trip to an animal shelter where Fitz volunteered all day and left a $5,000.00 check for the organization. When he departed the facility, the paparazzi were snapping away and a few "reporters" peppered him with questions:

"Did you adopt a pet?"

"Did you work there all day?"

"Are you dating someone in the facility?"

Fitz replied, "I have an unending love for animals, so when I can, I like to volunteer at shelters. Nothing breaks my heart more than to see these wonderful creatures homeless and, in some cases, abused. Please adopt and please spay and neuter your animals."

Polly had surreptitiously informed TMZ about Fitz's donation, which it confirmed with the shelter. This story generated more beneficial press for Fitz; and more Twitter followers. Fitz, in the span of two months, had acquired more than 2.4 million fans.

****

One of those 2.4 million admirers wasn't Annie Van. She very much missed Fitz, but stayed away from anything that could be perceived as contact with him. However, she did follow him in the news and determined that the piece on him at the animal shelter was possibly a message to her. However, she could not reconcile the endgame of this publicity stunt. In the three months that they had dated, she never noticed any inkling of notoriety seeking in Fitz. She also did a little research into Polly Preston and found out that she was indeed a publicist, a very engaging, and apparently unattached one. Some celebrity blogs placed the two as a couple, but Annie refused to take the bait.

Annie had decided to stay in New York City for the summer, spending a good majority of her time volunteering at animal shelters, instead of tutoring. It made the time go by faster and kept her away from the Hamptons scene at which she would invariably be spotted or gossiped about as Fitz's ex-girlfriend – something that she wanted to disown, for now. To be sure, her friends invited her out as her friend Wendy, still Chuck Schilling's girlfriend, was weekending at a place he had rented for the summer. She gracefully declined. Still, she was fighting the urge to obsess about Fitz and his odd behavior. She would finally solve the mystery the night Fitz was solving another puzzle as a guest on a late-July episode of *The Late Show with Stephen Colbert*.

Chapter 24 (Communism, Rockefeller, Hitler, WWII Part 1)

World War I saw the first major victory of the Illuminati objective – communism. The old order was destroyed as four 'empires' – Russia, Germany, Austria-Hungary, and Ottoman – lay in ruins, with Russian now under the influence of communism. For the avoidance of doubt, communism is not a competing economic system or even a competing philosophy. It is simply a method of population control and enslavement wrapped in a sheath of false promises such as the common good through the absence of class, property, and religion. It is a monstrous lie conceived by Adam Weishaupt, publicly espoused by Karl Marx and Friedrich Engels, and successfully executed by Vladimir Lenin (Ulyanov) and Leon Trotsky (born Lev Davidovich Bronshtein). Three quick, obvious lies: 1. there *are* two *classes* in communism: slaves and the slave masters who make the decisions for the servant population without their consent. 2. If the state owns the property, the oppressors running the state *own* the property. 3. There *is* religion with communism. Your submission merely switches from a higher being to the "state". Karl Marx called religion the opiate of the masses. Communism is the subjection of the masses. As you will see, it is the endgame of the debt-based money cabal that currently runs your world.

Not surprisingly, the debt-based money cabal was behind the Bolshevik Revolution. One of the biggest historical misconceptions was that it was simply a popular uprising of the downtrodden masses against an unpopular czar (Nicholas II). For the avoidance of doubt, Nicholas II was extremely unpopular thanks in large part to his mismanaging of the war effort. This led to the February Revolution (that actually took place in March) resulting in his ouster and the formation of a provisional government.

However, the October Revolution (the re-revolution) was a scheme decades in the making devised by the European bankers and financed by M.M. Warburg (of Germany), Jacob Schiff of Kuhn, Loeb, & Company (New York), and by the British through Lord Alfred Milner of Society of the Elect fame. Trotsky, in his book *My Life*, mentions a British financier, who in 1907 gave him a "large loan" to be repaid after the overthrow of the Tsar. Schiff's grandson John claimed that his grandfather also contributed $20 million to the cause. The final chapter of the plot had its origins in

1915 Germany. $50 million was supplied by Kaiser Wilhelm II to Lenin, but keep in mind that Max Moritz Warburg, director of M.M. Warburg & Company in Hamburg, was also the head of the Secret Service in Germany. Knowing this, it is pretty easy to surmise from which entity Kaiser Wilhelm II procured the $50 million. The Kaiser's objective was obvious: by fomenting a revolution in Russia, Germany had a much better chance of winning the war on the Eastern Front. This mission was accomplished with the signing of the Treaty of Brest-Litovsk on March 3, 1918, which ended hostilities between the Russian Soviet Federated Socialist Republic and the Central powers.

The United States' role is much more puzzling. Woodrow Wilson provided Trotsky with an *American* passport for his fateful journey back to Russia after the February Revolution. By means never fully explained, Mackenzie King, an agent of the Rockefeller interests and/or Wilson's advisor, Colonel Edward House (of *Lusitania* fame) and/or somebody else obtained Trotsky's freedom from prison in Halifax when he was arrested en route to Russia. Canadian publisher and businessman Lieutenant Colonel John Bayne MacLean said Trotsky's freedom was actuated "at the request of the British Embassy at Washington . . . [which] acted on the request of the U.S. State Department, who were acting for someone else." In New York, on the night before his departure, Trotsky had given a speech in which he said: "I am going back to Russia to overthrow the provisional government and stop the war with Germany." Trotsky's partner in crime Lenin was provided safe passage from Switzerland to Russia (also after the February Revolution) through Germany by Max Warburg, making him a German agent provocateur.

The question remains: Why would Woodrow Wilson want to help dismantle a future ally in the war against Germany? The only answer is that the financial backers of Lenin and Trotsky wanted to see a return on their investment and pressured Wilson to aid and abet Trotsky. Please remember that bankers had succeeded in financing both sides of every war since the early 1800s. Why would this "revolution" be any different? It seems that during 1917, everyone was plotting against Nicholas II, whose country, like the rest of Europe was tired of the war and all the sacrifices (such as starvation) it entailed. Nicholas had deposited a massive amount of family money in European and American banks ($400 million of gold in Rockefeller-controlled Chase National Bank; $500 million in other U.S.

banks; $115 million in London-based banks; and at least $80 million in Paris; and as much as $132 million in Berlin's Mendelsohn Bank). However, when the October Revolution succeeded, all of the Romanovs were executed without trial on July 17, 1918. With no one surviving to claim the money, guess who ended up with the $1 billion +? By skirting escheat laws, the banks kept the deposits and the Rothschilds ended up getting ultimate revenge against the Romanov's for Alexander I's torpedoing of their first attempt at one-world government during the Congress of Vienna in 1815 and Nicholas II's thwarting of their attempt to take over America during the Civil War. Even if they weren't executed (as some contend) no claims were ever made on the bank accounts.

In August 1917, the American Red Cross Mission to Russia arrived in Petrograd despite the fact there was a surplus of medical help and half-empty hospitals in the city. In the mission, there were only five doctors, two medical researchers, and three orderlies. The rest of the contingent consisted of bankers from the Federal Reserve Bank of New York, Chase and National City Banks as well as lawyers and representatives of American industry, at least one with ties to Standard Oil. Together, they outnumbered the doctors three to one. In fact, the doctors, with nothing to do, went home on September 11th. Looks like Trotsky and Lenin needed some financial and technical assistance with the October Revolution.

If you are beginning to think that Woodrow Wilson is a complete buffoon and nothing but a puppet of the banking interests consider this quote attributed to him from Senate documents,

> "I am a most unhappy man. I have unwittingly ruined my country. A great industrial nation is controlled by its system of credit. Our system of credit is concentrated. The growth of the nation, therefore, and all our activities are in the hands of a few men. We have come to be one of the worst ruled, one of the most completely controlled and dominated Governments in the civilized world no longer a Government by free opinion, no longer a Government by conviction and the vote of the majority, but a Government by the opinion and duress of a small group of dominant men."

From that point forward, the Rockefellers controlled the machinations of the Soviet Union. Author Eustace Mullins summarizes it best:

> "The Rockefellers figured in many pro-Soviet deals during the 1920s. Because of the struggle for power which developed between Stalin and Trotsky, the Rockefellers intervened in October, 1926, and backed Stalin, ousting Trotsky...

> "John D. Rockefeller instructed his press agent, Ivy Lee in 1925 to promote Communism in the U.S. and to sparkplug a public relations drive which culminated in 1933 with the U.S. government recognition of Soviet Russia. In 1927 Standard Oil of New Jersey built a refinery in Russia, after having been promised 50% of the Caucasus oil production. The Rockefeller firm, Vacuum Oil, signed an agreement with the Soviet Naphtha Syndicate to sell Russian oil in Europe, and made a $75 million loan to Russia....

> "In 1935, Stalin expropriated many foreign investments in Russia, but the Standard Oil properties were not touched. The Five Year Plans (1928-32, 1933-37, and 1938-42) were all financed by the international banking houses. During the 1920s, the principal firms doing business with Russia were Vacuum Oil, International Harvester, Guaranty Trust and New York Life, all firms controlled by the Morgan-Rockefeller interests."

Like Russia, Germany's domestic situation had deteriorated, due largely to the food shortages caused by the (now enforced) Allied blockade when the United States entered the conflict. Again, when a population cannot eat, it will revolt. Communist insurrections at home and mutinies within its navy were as much a contributing factor to Germany's surrender as were the Allies' advances. Despite not having any of the conflict conducted on its own soil, Germany threw in the towel and was subjected to ridiculous conditions and war reparations, which did not resemble Woodrow Wilson's Fourteen Points, under which it initially laid down arms.

So if you're Adolf Hitler, a soldier on the front, and not privy to the deteriorating situation in your homeland, and your country surrenders without you firing one shot in defense of that homeland, and your country is now burdened (through the Treaty of Versailles) with a stupefying amount of debt that can only result in the economic destruction of your home country, you can see why you would be indignant. And if you see a Jewish banker (Max Warburg) negotiating the debt-laden Treaty of Versailles on behalf of Germany, with his brother Paul occasionally at the other side of the table as part of the American delegation (led by Woodrow Wilson), you can see why Adolph Hitler hated Jewish bankers and viewed this all as a Jewish plot. The American delegation (Wilson, J.P. Morgan Jr., Albert Strauss of J & W Seligman, Thomas Lamont of J.P. Morgan & Co. amongst others) was hosted by Baron Edmond de Rothschild at his Paris mansion. (Col. Edward House stayed at the Hotel Crillon with a personal staff of 201 servants – your income tax dollars at work.) The truth is Max Warburg hated the treaty and recommended not signing it, but the new Weimar leadership was essentially left with no options. The blighted economic landscape that would pervade Germany for the next decade would give rise to Adolph Hitler and the amazing German economy that soared in the face of the Great Depression. Do you know what fueled this amazing turnaround? Answer: *debt-free* money!!

Before you learn what the history books don't discuss about the rise of the Third Reich, it is important to clear up one error about the hyper-inflation that followed the Treaty of Versailles. Textbooks will present government sponsored money printing as the primary cause of the German hyper-inflation -- absolutely false. The source of the money printing was the speculation by foreign investors, who shorted the German mark, betting on its decreasing value. The speculators would essentially sell something they didn't have (German marks) with the hopes of buying it back cheaper. Before the speculators could sell something they didn't have, they had to 'borrow' it. This enterprise was made possible by the Reichsbank, the German version of the Federal Reserve. This privately held central bank made massive amounts of currency available for borrowing. Marks were then created with accounting entries on the bank's books and lent at a profitable interest. When the demand to short the mark turned into frenzy, marks were printed on such as a scale that they became worthless; thus hyperinflation.

Those same history texts will tell you that large public works programs and a military buildup supported by deficit spending – such as the construction of the Autobahn network – stimulated the economy and reduced unemployment in Germany during the mid to late 1930s. If that was the case, why didn't FDR's New Deal turn around the American economy? It is downright peculiar how your textbooks stay away from the root cause of why essentially the same public works program succeeded in Germany and failed in the United States. The real secret to the rise of Germany during the Great Depression was twofold. The first suppressed reason for the German Miracle was the Mefo Bills, or Treasury Labor Certificates. It is debatable whether Adolph Hitler or German Central Bank president (and Bank of International Settlements founder) Hjalmar Schacht initially understood that they were stealing a page from the Lincoln Greenback playbook with the issuance of these bills. Their real motive was a method to hide their rearmament from the prying eyes of the world – a rearmament that was illegal under the Treaty of Versailles. Keep in mind that the Reichsbank was now under the aegis of the Nazi party. It was as central bank, but a government-run central bank and no longer a for-profit, privately-held central bank. This bank formed a shell company (Metallurgische Forschungsgesellschaft, or "Mefo") that issued bills of exchange, that by decree, were exchangeable into German currency (Reich marks). These were issued to the armament manufactures and were used to pay the laborers. These bills of exchange (or money) were *debt-free* and not backed by gold.

The second secret was Hitler's implementation of a system of bartering with its European neighbors and Mexico. This was done out of necessity since it was denied foreign credit because it didn't possess any gold to operate in the international currency markets. Germany put their population to work using Mefo Bills, then exported equipment, goods, and commodities (such as Volkswagens) in exchange for equipment, goods, and commodities (such as oil from Mexico). By doing so, no money was exchanged, thus circumventing international debt-based banking. To be sure, Hitler was also able to negotiate an abeyance of World War I reparations. However, with the use of *debt-free* Mefo Bills and *debt-free* bartering, German unemployment disappeared and Hitler became immensely popular, establishing a cult of personality not surpassed in the 20th century. Hitler later said,

> "We're not foolish enough to try to make a currency [backed by] gold of which we had none, but for every mark that was issued we required the equivalent of a mark's worth of work done or goods

135

produced...we laugh at the time our national financiers held the view that the value of currency is regulated by the gold and securities lying in the vaults of a state bank."

To be sure, the Nazi version of fascism is another form of population control (submission to the state), and in Germany it was downright thuggish. However, with *debt-free* money, the German economy flourished.

Contrast Germany with the situation in the United States. Don't you find it odd that less than sixteen years after the formation of the Federal Reserve -- a central bank that was hailed as a financial panacea, immunizing the United States' economy from the gyrations of the business cycles -- a stock market crash occurred from which the economy didn't recover? Don't you find it odd that when Franklin Delano Roosevelt was elected, he pushed through the Gold Confiscation Act of 1933, which under penalty of $10,000 and/or up to five to ten years imprisonment required the citizens of the United States to return all of their gold to the Federal Reserve in exchange for $20.67 an ounce? Why did your government need all of that gold? Who had all of the gold? The government didn't have any. That is why FDR was forcing U.S. citizens to turn over their gold to the Fed. Why was the government out of gold? Had the Fed bankrupted the government in less than two decades? Why was the price of gold fixed one year later by the Gold Reserve Act of 1934 at $35 an ounce? Doesn't it seem strange that with stroke of a pen, the purchasing power of the dollar decreased by 41%? By not allowing its citizens to own gold, FDR effectively took the United States off the gold standard.

Actually, the United States had gold, but in order to get European countries back on the gold standard, the Federal Reserve lent considerable sums of gold to England and France in the mid-20s. In order to keep that gold from returning to the United States, the Federal Reserve kept money rates artificially low. This cheap money led to the frenzied speculation that resulted in the stock market crash of 1929 and subsequent Great Depression. The reason that the Fed kept rates high during the 30s and FDR confiscated your gold was that it needed that gold in its vault to produce more money – there was a 40% gold reserve requirement at the

Fed. If rates remained low, a further outflow to Europe would have transpired. Former President Hoover understood the score:

> "In replying to Roosevelt's statement that I was responsible for the orgy of speculation, I considered for some time whether I should expose the responsibility of the Federal Reserve Board by its deliberate inflation policies from 1925-28 under European influence, and my opposition to these policies."

That still leaves the question: what happened to Europe's gold that forced it to borrow America's to get back on the gold standard? Answer: it was sitting in the basements of all of those Rothschild mansions. They are the ones who bankrupted Europe through debt-based banking and now had all the gold.

This is another lesson detailing why you should never have a money system backed by a precious metal: the owners of the precious metal control the value of your currency. In 1932, $35 allowed you to purchase 1.69 ounces of gold. In 1934, not only were you not allowed to purchase gold, but if you could, you would only receive 1.00 ounce in return for that same $35 dollars. That, in a nutshell, is inflation.

Another question that should be asked: why didn't the New Deal work? Unemployment in the United States was still at 19% in 1938; it was less than 2% in Nazi Germany. *Debt-free* money is why the German economy sprung back to life in the 1930s while the United States and the rest of the world were mired in the Great Depression. Germany just commanded its government-run central bank to produce *debt-free* money, when necessary, to finance armament projects. Money, when bartering was not employed, was an aid in the conduct of commerce. In the United States and elsewhere, money had to be borrowed from a privately-owned central bank (at interest), and if there wasn't enough gold in the vaults at the U.S. Treasury or any interest in a United States debt (bond, bill, or note) issuance, then the government couldn't produce more money. That is why FDR confiscated your gold in 1933. And when he devalued the dollar by repricing gold in 1934, he essentially stole from you, the American people. Since every dollar is loaned into existence, those dollars represent a lien on commerce.

To be sure, Hitler was initially financed by the international bankers, but the German economy came to life because of international bartering and the *debt-free* Mefo bills. Hitler was initially bankrolled by the debt-based money cabal to counter-balance Stalin, whose rather unexpected rise to power (over banking puppet Trotsky) put an unstable Rockefeller man in the charge of the Soviet Union. In fact, former Weimar Republic Chancellor Dr. Heinrich Brüning (1930 – 1932) claimed in a letter dated August 28, 1937 to Winston Churchill:

> "I did not and do not even today, for understandable reasons, wish to reveal that from October 1928 the two largest regular contributors to the Nazi Party were the general managers of two of the largest Berlin banks, both of Jewish faith, and one of them the leader of Zionism in Germany."

Much has been written about the Kuhn, Loeb, & Company and other banks financing Hitler's rise to power. In fact, it was a meeting on January 4, 1933 at Schroder Bank in Berlin between bankers, industrialists, future CIA chief Allen Dulles, his brother, future Secretary of State John Foster Dulles, and Adolph Hitler that kept the Nazi apparatus functioning (before he assumed control on January 30, 1933.) In return for the bailout, Hitler promised to break the labor unions, which he did in May 1933.

However, little is written about how Hitler turned the table on the bankers with his *debt-free* currency. C. G. Rakovsky, one of the founders of Soviet Bolshevism and a Trotsky intimate, was being interrogated at a Stalin-era show trial in 1938. His quote at that trial is an accurate assessment of events:

> "Hitler took over the privilege of manufacturing money, and not only physical moneys, but also financial ones. He took over the machinery of falsification and put it to work for the benefit of the people. Can you possibly imagine what would have come if this had infected a number of other states?"

Suddenly, Hitler was more of a menace to the bankers than Stalin.

Hitler seemed to understand the import of what he was accomplishing when he hosted British representative Lord Londonderry in late January 1936 for informal talks. Hitler, President Hermann Goering, and soon to be German Ambassador to the United Kingdom Joachim Von Ribbentrop laid their cards on the table to Londonderry. They had learned through their research that the countries of Europe were all part of an international (although they were incorrectly convinced it was strictly Jewish) banking conspiracy that used ever expanding national debt burdens to bring the world under their control by influencing national and international affairs. Hitler's solution was the destruction of Communism (i.e. an invasion of the Soviet Union) and the removal of the Jewish race from the European continent. Lord Londonderry made a report of this meeting to the British cabinet and subsequently wrote Herr Von Ribbentrop:

> "In relation to the Jews...we do not like persecution, but in addition to this, there is the material feeling that you are taking on a tremendous force which is capable of having repercussions all over the world...it is possible to trace their participation in most of these international disturbances which have created so much havoc in different countries, but on the other hand, one can find many Jews strongly ranged on the other side who have done their best, with the wealth at their disposal, and also by their influence, to counteract those malevolent and mischievous activities of fellow Jews."

In other words, we believe in your Jewish banking conspiracy, but we do not believe that it can be stopped. With regards to the Jews, not all are bad, so we are against their removal. This communication convinced Hitler that there would be no alliance between debt-based cabal-controlled Britain and Germany and that it would be his responsibility alone to rid the world of communism and debt-based banking. From this point on, Hitler moved from fascism to the much more radical Nazism. [By the way, that was not exactly a stinging denouncement of Hitler's final solution.]

Chapter 25 (July 2016)

July 2016 went by like a blur. Polly orchestrated a public relations campaign that kept Fitz in the public eye almost every day. As a respite from the talk show circuit, Fitz was seen at the Major League Baseball All-Star Game in San Diego on July 12th and the ESPY Awards in Los Angeles on July 13th, with Mafia Mike chauffeuring him and Polly along the way. Next was the Open Championship at Royal Troon in Scotland from July 15th thru the 17th. Because of Fitz's passion for the game – he was a scratch golfer – he was invited up to the TV tower with the ESPN crew where he was able to provide some insightful analysis of the major championship, impressing both Paul Azinger and Mike Tirico. He pointed out that, for better or worse, the Open Championship winner would be determined by the more fortunate draw. Because of the ever changing conditions on the British Isles -- both wind and precipitation – when a player tees off can be worth three or four strokes over the course of the tournament. Fitz was able to point out that the winner of each of the last ten Open Championships came from the more fortunate draw – i.e. if he teed off early Thursday and late Friday, versus late Thursday and early Friday, or vice versa. The winner always came from the draw that had the lower stroke average, a result of better playing conditions. In other words, luck was eliminating half of the field in each of the last ten Open Championships.

When Fitz returned stateside, one of the companies in which Evan Spring's firm invested was going public, meaning that, in this instance, it was to be listed for trading on the New York Stock Exchange. As part of the pomp and circumstance associated with this company milestone, executives of the listing company and other associated VIPs are invited to ring the opening or closing bell. Evan was invited to the ceremony and passed along an invite to Fitz, which he accepted. Someone from CNBC was tipped off as to Fitz's presence on the NYSE podium and requested an interview. Surprisingly to Fitz, the people at CNBC were unaware of his Wall Street background, which he was quick to politely point out once the interview commenced. Of course, Closing Bell anchor Kelly Evans asked Fitz his opinion of the market to which he replied, "The past two presidents have inherited markets that were in the middle of a free falls. I think the next president may face the same dynamic." Kelly responded with a quick,

"Why?" Fitz bit his tongue. He wanted to communicate what he really thought, but now was not the time. Instead, Fitz talked about the S&P 500 price/earnings (P/E) ratio and the global situation that featured Greece falling into the financial abyss, yet again, and a struggling China. It was the typical analysis from the bear camp: the market was expensive given the worldwide economic environment. It was a position that would make Fitz look informed, without saying anything too radical. When Fitz worked on Wall Street, he used to chuckle over the explanations offered as to why the market was up or down on any particular day. Short of a major shock to the market, the commentary was simply fodder to pass the time away.

Evan and Fitz spent the evening catching up. Evan ribbed him about his recent celebrity – he had a very favorable performer Q score, which reflected the public's familiarity with, and appeal of Fitz. Fitz said he had heard the same from Polly and that he found it amusing since he was not a "performer", unless one considered being the illegitimate son of a former U.S. president "performing". Fitz also told Evan that he may be asking another huge favor of his friend in the future. Evan pressed for further explanation, but Fitz said that the time wasn't yet right to solicit his indulgence.

Two days later, Fitz was on the set of *The Dr. Oz Show* in Manhattan. Oz was shocked to see how young Cavendish looked in person, joking that he was preserved. When queried about his 'secret' to looking young, Fitz talked about 'eating the rainbow', organic if possible. Each color of the food rainbow represented different phytonutrients that your body needs to properly function. He talked about avoiding bleached sugars and bleached flour, which eat away the collagen in the skin. Fitz also explained the benefit of cleanses and described his favorite, the liver cleanse. This nasty regiment included: 1. fasting all day. 2. An 8oz glass of water with a teaspoon of Epsom salt four hours before bed – it tastes awful. 3. Repeat step 2 two hours before bed. 4. Right before bed, chug a 5oz glass of extra virgin olive oil. 5. Immediately chase the olive oil with 5oz of fresh squeezed lemon juice. 6. Immediately lay on your right side for a half an hour – it is okay to go to sleep in that position. This will have the effect of belching gallstones into a vacant digestive tract. 7. Have another 8oz glass of Epsom salt water upon awakening. 8. Have the morning free to expel gallstones. Fitz went on to explain that the gall bladder is a garbage dump for the body, specifically the liver. When impurities enter the blood stream, the liver filters them out, creating liver stones, which are then deposited into the gall bladder. Over time, the gall bladder gets full and the stones at the bottom tend to calcify, creating pressure on the bladder, sometimes causing it to tear. When that occurs, gall bladder surgery is usually the result. It is the number two surgery in the United States which can be avoided by empting it out periodically. Emptying it out the first time requires many cleanses. Also, when the gall bladder fills, the liver has no place to unload its stones, retarding its ability to properly cleanse the blood. When these impurities are not properly filtered out of the blood, they may end up taking a home in other organs, disrupting their functions, causing poor health. Dr. Oz responded, "I see you take this seriously."

The last week of July featured an appearance on the *Late Show with Stephen Colbert*. The quickest wit in television had made a successful jump from parodying Bill O'Reilly on Comedy Central's *The Colbert Report* (pronounced coal-bear re-pour) to replacing David Letterman in a more standard late night format, although Colbert did not stray too far from his prior character when interviewing Cavendish. Fitz was a huge fan of the former show and asked Polly to make the Colbert camp aware of this reverence before the interview.

At the start of the dialogue, Colbert featured clips of Cavendish being interviewed on Golf Central, CNBC, and *The Dr. Oz Show*. This was followed by a clip of him explaining to Anderson Cooper how he figured out what day of the week he was born.

"You know that you are responsible for the loss of $1 trillion?"

"How so?"

"Ever since you made that comment about the stock market, the S&P 500 has lost approximately one trillion in market value." Colbert holds out his hand. "I'm just looking to recapture my share -- $3,000. Pay up." The studio audience laughs. "So let me get this straight. Just because you're Kennedy's kid you think you can offer advice on every topic under the sun?"

Cavendish just smiled, knowing that he was being set up by Colbert -- all he could do was wait.

"Okay hotshot – time to meet your maker." Colbert reached under his desk and produced a Rubik's Cube. The audience howled.

Fitz took it from Colbert, and started to go to work while casually asking, "Do you miss O'Reilly?" What Colbert and his audience did not know was that Cavendish could solve the cube, usually in about two minutes. Most people, who have never solved the cube, are unaware that there are two basic techniques to accomplishing this goal. The first is for the utterly brilliant, who can look at the entire cube and find the quickest way to put it back in its place. These are the people you see doing it in timed contests, maneuvering their hands around the cubes so quickly that it appears to be suspended, defying the laws of gravity. The other method involves solving the puzzle one layer at a time. With this slower approach, many of the same moves are repeated to get certain cubes into their proper position. Once one has solved the cube multiple times, the repetition of the moves becomes programmed into the hands, requiring the decoder to only look at the cube a small amount of times in order to solve it, approximately once for every eight turns of the cube. To the uninitiated, it looks like magic. In fact, with Cavendish looking at Colbert while they were engaged in conversation, it didn't look as if he was actually trying to solve the cube, but as the conversation continued the cube gradually took form.

"No sir. I ask the questions here. What is the capital of Chad?"

"N'Djamena, I think. What is this -- better know an African country evening?" This was a reference to "Better Know A [Congressional] District" that was an occasional feature on *The Colbert Report.*

"Impressive. What is the circumference of the earth?"

"24,900 miles."

"How does the earth wobble?"

"Actually it doesn't wobble; it is just the illusion created by our sun's dual star relationship with Sirius and is responsible for the procession of the equinoxes."

"Oookaaaay." Colbert was impressed. This answer wasn't in his notes, but sounded convincing all the same. It was time to humor the skit. "What color is Donald Trump's hair?"

"Cheetos Orange." The audience approved with laughter. Even Colbert cracked a smile. "You do realize that you are not asking me to solve anything with these questions, just to regurgitate facts?"

Ignoring Fitz's commentary, Colbert continued, "What is the gestation period for a llama?"

"About 350 days."

"How many episodes of *The Colbert Report* aired?"

"I apologize."

"Stumped! Whoaaaaaah!!!!"

"No. I apologize *for knowing* this trivial matter: One thousand four hundred forty-seven." Cavendish -- although never a liberal -- thought the comedy of fake newsmen Colbert and John Stewart was brilliant and had done his homework on Colbert to emphasize his fandom of Stephen's former show. He didn't foresee it being used in this skit. The audience roared as Colbert stared into the camera with his signature counterfeit confidence as if to say, "The fact that he knows this obscure detail about my former show means that I am the superior being."

"Stephen."

"Yes Fitzgerald."

"Do you like apples?"

"May I remind you that I ask the questions here?"

Before Colbert could launch into another query, Fitz produced the completed Rubik's Cube. For once in his life, the host was speechless.

The dazzled congregation roared with applause. Colbert recovered meekly with, "How did you do that? You weren't even looking at it. Did you switch it out for a completed one?"

"If you replay the tape, I'm sure you'll see that it was legit."

"Wow! That was something. Can you solve this nation's debt burden? Maybe we should run you for president." The studio audience roared with consent.

Fitz blushed and then joked, "Do you have any of that Colbert PAC money leftover?" He was referring to Colbert successfully starting his own actual super PAC, "Americans for a Better Tomorrow, Tomorrow," on his prior show. It was portrayed as "100 percent legal and at least 10 percent ethical."

Colbert continued, "We can have a Bush, a Clinton, and a Kennedy to choose from – talk about new families on the American political landscape." The crowd roared with laughter.

"I think it would be fun and possibly very informative to debate the issues with the people who are interested in running this country." More loud applause ensued.

"Cavendish for President!" exclaimed Colbert, followed by more rambunctious cheering.

"Oh no – I would be happy to debate the issues, but I am not interested in pursuing public office. Besides, I couldn't afford it." Cavendish knew he was lying, but he had to.

"Maybe you could take out a loan from the Donald?"

"I think the interest rate just went up with that Cheetos comment."

The music signaling commercial time (and the end of the show) started to play and the show cut away to a break. During the downtime, Colbert leaned over and said to Cavendish in a hushed tone, "That was truly remarkable. In all seriousness, if you want help running for the presidency, even as a faux campaign, I can push the agenda on my show."

"I would be honored to get your assistance getting into that debate. The issues that I would elucidate are radically different than what the candidates are chirping about. With that said, I am not talking about those specific issues until the debate, if I could ever get invited."

Colbert, sensing an opportunity to be kingmaker replied with a sincere, "I'll do my best."

****

When *Late Night with Stephen Colbert* aired that evening, Annie Van almost threw up when she realized what her ex-boyfriend was up to. *Holy Moses...he's going to run for president!* At that moment she remembered the puzzles that she had helped solve a few months back that both related to his father. She knew one was about a conspiracy speech that JFK had given on $2^2 3^3$. She couldn't remember the year, but it had to be one of three. The other was about an executive order that had something to do with binary code. She embarked on a research odyssey of her own.

Evan Spring's reaction was similar to Annie's. Fitz's yet to be asked obligement was taking on a whole new dimension. Evan sent a text to Caroline Kennedy to find out what she knew. Caroline, who was besieged with media requests right after the Fitzgerald Cavendish news broke, had settled back into relative obscurity in Tokyo. She texted Evan that she knew absolutely nothing and had not spoken to Fitz since the day the results came back positive, although she thought the notion was quite prepossessing.

Polly Preston, who was responsible for many of these public relations wins – the visit to the animal shelter, the Rubik's Cube, and the tip off to CNBC that Fitz would be at the NYSE podium – was nearly overwhelmed with tweets from Fitz's fans. Some were asking Fitz for advice regarding specific ailments with which they were burdened. Some people were asking him who was going to win the PGA Championship. He was averaging about six marriage proposals a day. Polly was being inquired about as well – "is your publicist dating anyone?" Now he was receiving hundreds of messages about a run for the presidency. His twitter followers were up to six million and trending towards ten million by the end of August. Because of her carefully timed operation and Fitz's overall appeal, she had engineered an obscure nobody into the most interesting man in America over the course of ten weeks. Fitz's problem solving skills – stupid human tricks as he called them – generated credibility which ate away the audience's normal skepticism, leaving them more receptive to his ideas – not that he had yet expressed the important ones. Polly had exploited America's obsession with celebrity to the nth degree, like a good accountant would with a new loophole in the tax code. It was now time to turn his celebrity into a crusade to get him into the first presidential debate, scheduled to take place on October 5, 2016.

Chapter 26 (The War Against You)

Even though the debt-based bankers and war-related industries prevailed enormously in the 1910s with the establishment of an income tax in the United States, a privately held central bank in the world's largest economy (United States), control of the American press, and a worldwide conflict to enrich themselves, they still wanted more. What they wanted was absolute control. What they wanted was a one-world government in the same vein as the European Union attempted by the Rothschilds at the Congress of Vienna in 1814 - 1815. What they publically attempted was a relatively feckless organization known as the League of Nations spearheaded by President Woodrow Wilson.

The League of Nations failed because many countries, including the United States, were suspicious of organizations that, at their cores, were anti-nation state. In order for a one-world government concept to succeed, nation-states have to submit their sovereignties over to a greater authority, which is in direct opposition not only to most nation-state constitutions, but also to the desires of its citizens. (No wonder clueless Woodrow Wilson was shocked to be booed in the streets of France.) One-world government was, and is still, sold under the bait of ending wars. The rationale embraced by these deceptive bastards is that if there is only one army and only one government then there can be no worldwide conflict. In theory, this may sound appealing; however it is not going to be run by a United States-styled Constitution with a democratically elected government. It is going to be run by the bankers and corporate heads under a Soviet-style regime – the same bastards that have been responsible for, and have profited from every major conflict on this planet for the last 200 years. Without the efforts of the debt-based money cabal, almost every major conflict of the past 200 years would not have occurred.

You may be wondering what the elite's motivation is for one-world government. The answer can be broken down into three schools of thought, all to a certain degree correct. First, they actually believe what they are doing is for the good of the planet. Second, as conservative author Willard Cleon Skousen theorized, "Power from any source tends to create an appetite for additional power... It was almost inevitable that the super-rich would one day aspire to control not only their own wealth, but the wealth of the whole world." Third, as Nelson Rockefeller said when discussing the source of his presidential ambitions, "When you think of what I had, what else was there to aspire to?"

What became abundantly clear to these 'internationalists' after World War I was that the world, despite being war fatigued, was not yet ready for a one-world government. The internationalists may have had most of the world's money, but they did not yet possess the physical means to transform the planet into their personal fiefdom. They decided that best way to achieve their ends was through covert control of the government and the media. With the U.S. government unconstitutionally handing them the money creation apparatus, the internationalists could destroy the world's strongest economy and nation from within, by bankrupting its citizens and by polarizing them through the media on any exploitable issue. After the implementation of the Federal Reserve, every act by this devious cabal had only two goals. The first goal is obvious: to make the internationalists wealthier, generally through engineered economic hardships, wars, and financial leverage.

Now for some dry economic theory: please remember that under a debt-based central banking model, all of the money is eventually going to end up with the bankers – it is only a question of how long the process takes. When the debt level (principle plus interest) is greater than the level of money (principle) – a condition of debt-based money creation -- it is simply a game of musical chairs. [See Appendix A if you are confused.] If there is only $1 million in circulation chasing $1.1 million in debt, not all of the debt can be paid off. Most of you will be able to pay off your debts, where the bankers make interest. Others will be able to borrow more to service their short term debt requirements, which is a double win for the bankers: they not only receive interest, but also increase the debt level, securing even more interest in the future. Lastly, some of the borrowers in this game of musical chairs will be left without a seat which has been taken away by the bankers. The banks will foreclose on them and confiscate their property. In all scenarios, the bankers win. By controlling interest rate levels, the Federal Reserve can engineer booms (by lowering interest rates, thus increasing the money supply) and busts (by raising interest rates, thus decreasing the money supply). The more frequent these boom and bust cycles, the quicker the central banks can shake down their populaces. They will have you believe that keeping a nation's economy on an even keel is an extremely difficile, yet to be mastered science, given the complexities of the modern world. With debt-based money creation, the only onerous task is keeping the public bamboozled about its inevitable result, until it has been completely impoverished. The wealthiest 1 percent of Americans control 35.6 percent of the total wealth of the country; 10 percent control 75 percent – and your standard of living is, generally speaking, better than the rest of the world.

You may think that these are the inevitable results of capitalism. You are wrong – capitalism is fine. In fact, it is as close to perfection amongst the economic systems. These are the inevitable results of a debt-based money creation system and to a certain extent the corporate socialistic economic system currently masquerading as capitalism. Remember, like energy, wealth cannot be created or destroyed. It can only be transferred. Growing a money supply has no impact on aggregate wealth. It only makes each unit of money less valuable. Because you fly around in a plane now -- as opposed to riding in a horse and buggy in the 1800s – has no impact on your wealth. It only increases your standard of living. Those responsible for increasing the overall standard of living generally experience a significant positive wealth transfer -- capitalism. Debt-based money creation systems create a massive wealth transfer to the creators of the money. But the creators of the money did nothing to increase the standard of living. They simply stole from you by charging interest on every dollar in circulation and indoctrinating you into believing that there were no other alternatives. The other methods employed by the banking cabal to speed up this wealth transfer is through the proliferation of wars – which you have already heard about ad nauseam – and through leverage (a.k.a. fractional reserve banking) -- another form of debt-based money creation. [Again, Appendix A if you wish.]

To demonstrate how few people understand the concept of money creation, one need not look further than the actual Federal Reserve Act of 1913. The act is also known as the Glass-Owen Bill, named after its sponsors. The competing bill was known as the Aldrich Bill (or Plan) for Senator Nelson W. Aldrich who convened the infamous meeting on Jekyll Island in 1910. The two bills were essentially identical, but through subterfuge and public ignorance (not stupidity), the Glass-Owen Bill was paraded as a more acceptable, anti-Wall Street reform bill. As part of his original bill, sponsor Senator Robert L. Owen included a mandate for the Federal Reserve to stabilize the purchasing power of the dollar. If Senator

Owen actually understood the concept of debt-based money creation, he would have known that this provision was an absurdity. Again, when money is loaned into existence, the level of debt (principle plus interest) is always greater than the level of money (principle). In order to pay off a debt that is currently greater than the money in circulation, more money has to be borrowed, which in turn creates a greater level of debt. As more money is borrowed into circulation to pay off the debt currently due, the purchasing power of each outstanding currency unit becomes more diluted. In other words, you may have more money to purchase your caramel macchiato, but the price of the caramel macchiato has gone up commensurately -- to reflect the decline in the value of your dollar – and a little bit more to reflect the interest claim on the money in circulation. The price of your caramel macchiato is not only a function of its supply and demand, but also the supply and demand for money. In other words, under a debt-based money system, stabilizing a currency's purchasing power is impossible: it can only go down. If the co-sponsor of the bill didn't even understand money creation, how is the average American citizen expected to be proficient in this area when it is deliberately concealed? Senator Owen's unrealistic provision was struck from the bill that President Wilson signed, and since the Federal Reserve Act became law, the dollar has lost 97% of its purchasing power and America's total debt has grown by $18 trillion.

To demonstrate the level of greed exhibited by the Federal Reserve, you only have to look at the National Banking Act of 1933. Originally, Section 7 of the Federal Reserve Act of 1913 detailed how the earnings of the Federal Reserve were allocated. Paragraph 1 in the initial act says:

> "After all necessary expenses of a Federal reserve bank have been paid or provided for, the stockholders shall be entitled [to] receive an annual dividend of six per centum on the paid-in capital stock, which dividend shall be cumulative. After the aforesaid dividend claims have been fully met, all the net *shall be paid to the United States as a franchise tax*, except that one-half of such net earnings shall be paid into a surplus fund until it shall amount to forty per centum of the paid-in capital stock of such bank."

In other words, the U.S. government participates in the earnings of the Federal Reserve. This is a generous division of the pie to the government given that all of the Federal Reserve Bank stocks are in private hands. However, this section of the act was never observed and with the passage of the National Banking Act of 1933 it was amended to read:

> "After all necessary expenses of a Federal reserve bank shall have been paid or provided for, the stockholders shall be entitled to receive an annual dividend of 6 per centum on the paid-in capital stock, which dividend shall be cumulative. After the aforesaid dividend claims have been fully met, the net earnings *shall be paid into the surplus fund of the Federal reserve bank.*" [Emphasis added.]

The government was officially sliced out. Today, you read stories in the *Wall Street Journal* and the *New York Times* trumpeting a press release from the Federal Reserve in which it states that it returned $75.4 billion of its 2011 earnings to the U.S. Treasury. The Fed will have you believe that this has been going on since day one. Keep in mind that it wouldn't be until August 10, 1993 that another modification was made to Section 7 of the Federal Reserve Act.

The second goal of these groups is to move the country more towards the idea of one-world government. These groups are comprised of bankers and industrialists. If the bankers had their druthers, they would have gone it alone, but the overwhelming success of the industrialists they financed obviated their need for financing. In fact, industrialists like John D. Rockefeller used his profits from oil to finance his own banking enterprises. As a result, the bankers and industrialists, of like mind that they should be in charge of the world, set out to take it over.

In order to achieve these goals, the cabal created tax-free foundations and think tanks to advance the message. These organizations have much more to do with setting policy in the United States (and elsewhere) than any mandate from its population. Some of these 'Round Table Groups' (as previously mentioned) are derivatives of the Society of Elect, such as the Council on Foreign Relations in New York and the Royal Institute of International Affairs in London. A few, such as the now rolled-up General Education Board, are creations of bankers' and industrialists' tax-free foundations (such as the Rockefeller Foundation, Mont Pelerin Society, Brookings Institution, and the Ford Foundation), while others, such as the World Bank and the International Monetary Fund are the creation of the Council on Foreign Relations. Some are foundation and corporation influenced trade associations like the AMA. Some are government organizations that are strongly influenced by these foundations and corporations, such as the FDA, and for good measure, the U.S. Congress – yes, your Congress is paid for by your multinational corporations. In fact, they write most of the laws that your congressmen never read. All of these organizations are motivated by the two goals of profit and control, and nothing else, irrespective of what bunkum they claim to the contrary. In the United States, the Rockefeller family has been the most prominent needle worker that weaves these two themes through their participation, both physically and financially, in these organizations. A very short list would include the Council on Foreign Relations, the American Medical Association, the United Nations, the Bilderberg Group, and the Trilateral Commission. Before you can completely understand the influence of these organizations on your everyday life, one example of the Rockefeller ethos is laid out below – more will follow.

After profiting immensely from World War I, the Rockefeller-controlled Standard Oil of New Jersey began to work closely with German chemical conglomerate, I.G. Farben -- so close, in fact, that the relationship was formalized with the formation of American I.G. Farben in 1929, which was mostly owned and operated by Standard Oil of New Jersey. This relationship seemed to be somewhat one-sided, benefitting I.G. Farben more than Standard Oil. The results of this collaboration became the basis for the development of Hitler's oil from-coal-program which made World War II possible. From this relationship, I.G. Farben was able to acquire knowledge of the quality requirements that are called for by the different uses of motor fuels, mostly through the addition of tetraethyl-lead and the manufacture of this product. In fact, Standard Oil petitioned the U.S. War Department to allow for the licensing of this process in Germany – right before the war. This request was granted. I.G. Farben was also the beneficiary of Standard Oil's polymerization process, not to mention its knowledge of lubricating oils. Also, through I.G. Farben, the Nazi government was able to secure $20 million worth of mineral oils, essential for the production of aviation fuels and aviation lubricating oils. Most of the oils, and the logistics for moving it to Germany, were provided by Standard Oil. Additionally, Germany had no natural rubber, yet in 1938, Standard Oil provided I.G. Farben with its new butyl rubber process. And as late as 1939, Standard Oil's German subsidiary designed a German plant for aviation gas. Tetraethyl was shipped on an emergency basis for the Wehrmacht, allowing the German Luftwaffe to fly. In other words, World War II could not be conducted without Standard Oil's assistance to Nazi Germany's rearmament – illegal under the provisions of the Treaty of Versailles.

You may say that this was all pre-war, and all's fair pre-war – fair enough. But why did Standard Oil, before World War II agreed with I.G. Farben that buna (another synthetic rubber) was within I.G. Farben's sphere of influence, and not business partner, Standard Oil's. In other words, Standard kept the German buna process a guarded secret within the United States, even after hostilities commenced in Europe. Since buna was an essential element of many war-related products, Standard Oil was not only aiding the future enemy, but also, by honoring this agreement, acting against the best interests of the United States. Standard Oil of New Jersey would say that it was in exchange for I.G. Farben not competing with them in the United States. There was little chance of that happening once hostilities commenced in 1939.

Oh but wait…there's more. Undersecretary of the Navy, James V. Forrestal, as late as 1941, authorized the Rockefellers to ship oil to the Nazis. Once the United States was officially 'drawn' into the war, the shipments of petroleum products to Germany (and Japan) continued through Standard Oil companies in Venezuela. Nelson Rockefeller saw to it that Germany had all it needed to conduct the war through his operations in South America. Standard Oil tankers fueled Nazi U-boats in the Canary Islands. If Great Britain complained, Nelson threatened to cut off food supplies from Latin America – the Rockefellers owned very large farms and plantations throughout. He made our future ally pay for these resources in cash, while credit and barter arrangements were made with Germany. When the United States threatened legal action, Standard president William Farish III cautioned that a bottleneck in domestic petroleum production could occur, making it impossible for the United States to conduct the war. Nelson's and Standard Oil's overtly abhorrent behavior would come back to bite them. As the war was winding down,

Nelson's sphere of influence, through his corporate enterprises and position as Assistant Secretary of State for Latin America – he was actually head of Latin American intelligence -- was enormous. Nelson would be able to control the South American votes (nineteen versus Europe's nine) for Israeli acceptance into the United Nations. Nelson, who was a member of the U.S. delegation at the United Nations Conference on International Organization at San Francisco in 1945, saw this as an opportunity to make big money by selling those votes and splitting the proceeds with the leaders of each South American country.

To be sure, Nelson wasn't terribly popular with the US government, but that didn't seem to matter since his family controlled FDR. In 1942, then Senator Harry S. Truman described the activities of Standard Oil as "treasonous" and as president fired Nelson from his government post in August 1945. The United States finally had enough of Standard Oil's bad behavior and seized some contested patents. Standard Oil filed suit on July 13, 1944. On November 7, 1945 the courts ruled against Standard Oil. Standard filed an appeal and on September 22, 1947, Federal Judge Charles Clark issued the following opinion in the civil case: "Standard Oil can be considered an enemy national in view of its relationship with I.G. Farben after the United States and Germany became active enemies." A further appeal was denied.

Nelson also wasn't popular with the Zionists. The Zionists had the goods on Nelson, such as an April 22, 1943 cable from one of Rockefeller's officers to Zurich confirming the shipment of 16.7 tons of fuel to the Axis; or a secret document on June 9, 1943 stating that one of Rockefeller's officers in Venezuela was authorized to continue trading with four enemy corporations. The Zionists, led by soon to be founder of Israel David Ben-Gurion's intelligence chief, Reuven Shiloah, dropped the hammer on Nelson Rockefeller. They had his Swiss bank records with the Nazis, his signature on correspondences setting up the German cartel in South America, transcripts of his conversations with Nazi agents during the war, and, finally, evidence of his complicity in helping (future CIA director) Allen Dulles smuggle war criminals and money from the Vatican to Argentina. In return for the Zionists' silence, instead of blackmailing the Zionists, Nelson agreed to deliver the South American votes for free and on November 29, 1947, the United Nations General Assembly adopted a resolution recommending a plan to partition Mandatory Palestine into an

Arab state and a Jewish state with a common currency, common market, and joint coordinating political authorities. The Balfour Declaration of 1917 became a reality when the British Mandate for Palestine expired at midnight, April 15, 1948, and Israel declared its independence. Israel was admitted to the United Nations on May 11, 1949 by a vote of thirty-seven to twelve with nine abstentions. Of the twenty Latin American nations voting, eighteen voted yes and two (El Salvador and Brazil) abstained. These votes were instrumental in obtaining the two-thirds majority necessary for admission. Was that taught out of your textbook? Probably not, due to the Rockefeller's control of the public educational system in the United States through its General Education Board and the Rockefeller Foundation.

Standard Oil wasn't the only United States Corporation aiding the Nazis before or during the conflict. Other companies collaborated with the Nazis, such as Alcoa (Andrew Mellon), Hearst Corporation (William Randolph Hearst), DuPont (Irenee du Pont), Ford Motor Company (Henry Ford), International Telephone and Telegraph (Sosthenes Behn), General Motors (William S. Knudsen), and Coca-Cola. And Nelson Rockefeller wasn't the only American official under the watchful eye of the United States government for activities that could compromise national security during World War II. Secretary of the Navy and future Secretary of Defense, James Forrestal, future U.S. Senator Prescott Bush – father of George H.W. Bush and grandfather of George W. Bush – and his lawyer, future CIA head Allen Dulles were also put under surveillance by FDR. In fact, Prescott's bank, Union Banking Corporation – of which he was a founding member and director – was seized in October 1942 under the Trading with the Enemy Act for operating as a clearing house for many assets and enterprises held by German steel magnate Fritz Thyssen. Keep in mind the moral turpitude of these men when you see what positions they (or their family members) ascend to. Do you really think for one second that these people have the best interests of the American citizen in mind when shaping U.S. policy? You should be spitting out your caramel macchiato at this point. If you haven't, just wait.

Chapter 27 (August – September 2016)

The Democratic and Republican National Conventions were both held in July, before the Summer Olympics, as opposed to 2012, when both conventions took place after the games. As a result, with Hillary Clinton and Jeb Bush entrenched as their respective party's nominees, and with three months remaining until the general election in November, a malaise settled over the political landscape during August, affording an opportunity to campaign for Fitz's inclusion in the debate.

To that end, Polly had a meeting with Jeff Krupnick of OptIn Technologies. Ms. Preston knew that text messaging is the best available medium to directly communicate with the masses, as 96% of text messages get opened within an hour of receipt compared to 6% of emails and 5% of tweets. Her plan was to have Fitz's twitter followers (and anyone else) "opt-in" to a short code giving them the opportunity to vote yes ("YESFITZ") or no ("NOFITZ") as to whether or not Fitz should be included in the first presidential debate. Jeff and Polly constructed a plan where anyone who opted-in to the short code by voting was eligible to receive a $10,000 cash prize, irrespective of how he or she voted. When Polly and Fitz returned from the Olympics in Rio de Janeiro, the talk show circuit would resume in earnest with Fitz pushing this opt-in medium as a way of petitioning the Commission on Presidential Debates (CPD) to include Fitz in the first debate. TMZ also advertised this vote as part of its usual twice weekly feature on Fitz. If enough positive interest was generated for Fitz's inclusion in the debate and the TV networks could be convinced of higher Neilson ratings from Fitz's participation, together they could push the CPD to include Fitz in the first debate. If Polly and Fitz could accomplish this feat, they would have in essence circumvented the reality show of the past twelve months where candidates vied for the public's approval, with one or two getting eliminated every month or so. The presidential election campaign season was just an extended version of *American Idol*, *The Bachelor*, or *Survivor*, with the final two contestants squaring off in three verbal jousting matches, with their understudies engaging in one debate. The only difference – it was hoped -- was that Fitzgerald Cavendish, my mere force of his celebrity, was going to be the wrinkle included in the first contest.

If successful, this certainly wasn't going to be the first time that notoriety, not career political accomplishments, would get someone elected. Arnold Schwarzenegger became Governor of California with his only two famous speeches being "I'll be back" (in *The Terminator*) and "Your daughter has a great ass" (to Maria Shriver's mother) before his gubernatorial bid. When times are economically bleak, and as a consequence the citizenry is disenchanted with the status quo, a popular non-political figure, especially one that looks like or has played an action hero, seduces the masses with the belief that through power of personality alone, he can solve the world's ills, just like in the movies – except in the movies, the hero usually employs a gun.

Jesse "The Body" Ventura, former Governor of Minnesota, is another example of this phenomenon. The difference with Jesse is that he is much closer to comprehending the core problems of this country and, by further extension, the world. Since his message hits much closer to the heart of the matter, he is marginalized by the mainstream media, which attempts to paint him as a kook. If he says something controversial (and correct) on a talk show, it is never re-broadcasted; his remarks are only re-aired if it furthers the message that he is missing a marble. His cable show, called *Conspiracy Theory*, attracted over a million viewers consistently. But once he started shining light into dark places, like with his "Police State" episode, the show was cancelled. Critics subtly denigrated the show, calling it, "mindless, good fun and a hoot to watch aging action stars still taking action."

Unlike Ventura, Fitz had avoided marginalization. By contrast, he was a media darling: intelligent, handsome, and the son of the most popular president of the 20th century. Women loved him and he had enough James Bond mixed with a modicum of humility that made most men not hate him. People solicited his opinion. He was vying for the opportunity to get his opinion out, not to one million of the already converted, but to seventy million of the ignorant and (hopefully) willing to listen.

Fitz's time in Brazil was spent rubbing elbows with dignitaries from around the world who were in town to watch the festivities. It seemed, even as the illegitimate son of JFK (with a different last name no less), that people were attracted to him, especially the older foreign politicians, because of his father – not that any were old enough to hold any meaningful governmental position when Jack was the president. However, a genuine curiosity was etched on their faces when they saw Fitz. The resemblance to his old man was subtle, yet unmistakable, but his ubiety was identical.

The economies of the world may have been in rapid decline, but wherever Fitz was in Rio, prosperity reigned. Fitz knew that wealth was neither created nor destroyed; it was simply transferred. And it appeared to Fitz that the transfer recipients had all converged on the Olympics. He was fast becoming part of the human tapestry at any VIP event in any town that he visited. However, the over-the-top corporate sponsored events in Rio contrasted greatly with the austerity programs that were currently dominating the world news headlines, being pushed as cures for the ailing economies of the world. Cavendish was tiring of the Rio party circuit and the self-congratulatory nature of the political and economic big wigs. It was as if they didn't have an issue with bankrupting every government on the planet – as long as they were getting theirs. On the rare occasion that the growing world economic turmoil came up in conversation, the solutions offered up to Fitz by these power brokers were incredibly hollow, with a faux wrapping of well-informed reasoning, like a Christmas gift in a big box with forty bows that housed a small turd.

As for the Olympics itself, the irony of a competition that celebrated every country's unique heritage, an event that was a coming together of those unique heritages, a triumph that epitomized tolerance of those unique heritages (except Munich 1972) -- in essence, proof that the current system of nation states could prosper -- all being sponsored by multi-national corporations whose heads were publicly and secretly members of organizations that were actively undermining the current system of nation states was not lost on Fitz.

He may have been bothered by the dissimilitude of the answers propounded by the moneyed and political elite versus what he perceived as the correct ones, but what was gnawing at Fitz was the yawning chasm in his heart that could only be filled by Annie. He had thought about her every day since they parted ways three months ago, but his busy and novel schedule (and his travel companion Polly) had kept his mind occupied enough that Annie couldn't take up any meaningful residence. The vapid, self-centered participants at the closing ceremony hot ticket event had the effect of evicting Fitz's remaining cerebral tenants. He wondered what she and Oliver were doing and how she had reacted to his celebrity and to his absence. He also regressed into what if scenarios. *If Annie had never entered my life, would I be sleeping around? Yes. Would I be in an affair with this one woman pep rally that is Polly Preston? Does Polly think I'm gay?* They had spent about a month and half of evenings in hotel rooms together without either one ever making an advance on the other. Fitz never told Polly about Annie and was not going to until this odyssey was over. It was strictly business for both of them, although Fitz was well aware of the rumors connecting him to Polly. It was only natural. They were always together. Fitz worried how that affected Annie and her feelings for him.

"Great news!" Polly snapped Fitz out of his minor detour into pining.

"We're on an earlier flight out of here?"

Preston always ignored any of Fitz's sarcasm. It was as if her ear was deaf to that tone of voice. "Jeff had a series of meetings with the networks regarding the debate to hammer out the details of his 'text to vote' platform and he broached the subject of you in the first debate and they were very receptive to the idea."

"Who's Jeff?"

"He is the one running the "YESFITZ", "NOFITZ" campaign to get you into that debate."

"How is that coming?"

"That's the other great news. During the first three days of the campaign, without any advertising, except through your twitter followers, 900,000 votes came in, with a 15 to 1 yes to no. Jeff showed the results to the networks."

"And that is what made them receptive?"

"According to Jeff, they were immediately receptive to the idea. When he shared the early results of our campaign, they seemed sold on the idea. They are going to do their own market research over the next few days to confirm its salability – which should be a slam dunk – then they will petition the Commission on Presidential Debates to include you in the first one."

"Wow. That is impressive. You are impressive."

"Thank you." She flashed him a perfect row of white tiles that Fitz still had a hard time believing were not dentures.

"What's next?"

"Colbert has gotten permission from Comedy Central to do a one night return of *The Colbert Report* on *Late Night with Stephen Colbert*. You are going to be the centerpiece of the show and will be interviewed at the end."

"Wow. That's amazing!"

****

Annie was moderately jealous of Fitz's travels. If she ever spoke to Fitz again, "Why didn't you include me on your adventure?" would be her first question to him. He had been to three continents, appeared on numerous talk shows, attended amazing sporting events, and was the darling of the worldwide media - all this, while she and Oliver never left Manhattan, except to visit her mother in Jersey City. She wondered if Fitz even thought about her any more or if he would still find her interesting or attractive after engaging the "Who's Who" of the worldwide stage. There were rumors of him running for the presidency, but after her initial revelation watching Fitz on Colbert's show, that seemed like a longshot, since he hadn't declared and requirements for registering in each state were quite a labyrinth to negotiate, not to mention deadlines, some of which had passed, at least as far as her research could tell. Her investigation into Fitz's JFK-related riddles was informative, but produced little proof of Fitz's ultimate goal. She was unaware of the texting campaign, which would have confirmed her earlier intuition of him running for the presidency, although she would soon learn that her initial instincts about Fitz's endgame were correct. Class was beginning anew at the United Nations School. She hoped that the children and the workload and Oliver would keep her distracted until the winter recess, although that seemed a long, long ways off.

****

Late Night with Stephen Colbert spoofing *The Colbert Report* with Fitzgerald Cavendish appearing as the guest was set to tape on September 8th, but the good news came on September 7th: Fitz would be part of the first 2016 U.S. Presidential debate. Citizen Cavendish would not have an opportunity to address all of the issues presented, but would be allowed to debate any domestic issue and have closing remarks. Polly, on a conference call with the CPD and some network executives, explained that each had something to gain from Fitz's appearance. For the CPD, it would attract more Americans to the television set; thus increasing the relevancy of the CPD; for the networks, it would attract more Americans to the television set; thus increasing their advertising revenues. Her arguments were unnecessary as everyone was already sold. It was almost too easy. For Fitz it was the favorable circumstance to tell the world the truth. For Polly Preston, it was a public relations grand slam home run. Her firm would be the most sought out promotional entity in the country. She had become a celebrity in her own right. However, her work was far from done. The next part involved covertly establishing Fitz as candidate for the election.

Stephen Colbert was masterful parodying himself parodying Bill O'Reilly. The ratings for the show would be its highest ever. The show revolved around Colbert's efforts to position Cavendish into the first debate. There was a vignette entitled "Better Know a Kennedy" which was taped earlier in the day, before the studio audience had arrived, featuring Colbert asking ridiculous questions such as, "Fiddle or Faddle?" referencing two of his father's many affairs. Given that Fitz was the result of a JFK affair, it was a perfectly awkward *Colbert Report* question. Fitz responded, "I would paddle the Faddle and play the Fiddle." While conducting the interview that took place in front of the studio audience, during which he peppered Cavendish with questions about his stances on multiple issues, Colbert pretended not to know that the news about his inclusion in the debate was already out. In the middle of another, "You'll hear my position at the debate" response, Colbert touched his ear, pretending to receive breaking news, jumped up from his seat and declared,

"It's official. Cavendish is in the debaaaaate! Whooaaah!!!" Red, white and blue balloons were released from the ceiling while Colbert ran around the stage like Tom Watson after he chipped in on the seventy-first hole of the 1982 U.S. Open at Pebble Beach. The audience went berserk as "Hail to the Chief" was performed by the studio orchestra. Cavendish sat in his seat with an enormous grin on his face, which broke out in laughter, shaking his head at Colbert's antics.

Colbert's lampoon received hundreds of thousands of hits on the internet by lunchtime on the East Coast. While Cavendish was becoming water cooler fodder, Polly Preston and her staff were working diligently to get the paperwork in order to actuate Cavendish's entrance into the U.S. Presidential election. It was decided when Polly made the presentation to Cavendish in May that running as a write-in candidate was the only alternative. He wasn't getting into the debate as the candidate from the Libertarian party, or the "Bring down the Lawyers" party for that matter; he wasn't getting into the debate as any candidate. Fitzgerald Cavendish was getting in because he was a celebrity citizen whose father was a celebrity politician. In the eyes of the CPD and the networks, Fitz was not a threat to the candidates or to the status quo. He was simply a ratings booster.

Running as a write-in candidate was a longshot of the highest order. First, write-ins for the office of the President of the United States of America are not allowed in eight states: Arkansas, Hawaii, Louisiana, Mississippi, Nevada, Oklahoma, South Carolina, and South Dakota. Secondly, the deadlines for declaring oneself as a write-in candidate had come to pass in certain states: Colorado, Florida, Indiana, North Carolina, and Texas. In other states, the process was not conducive to running in a stealthy manner. For example, in Georgia, Fitz would have to declare himself a write-in candidate in the Atlanta Journal-Constitution by September 2016. Since the debate wasn't until October 5th, it was decided that those electoral votes weren't worth the risk of disclosure. The state of Illinois makes the process utterly cumbersome, requiring the candidate to submit a Declaration of Intent to be a Write-in Candidate form to every county in the state and with each of the 8 Board of Elections Commissioners. There are 102 Counties in Illinois, so the candidate needs to file 110 forms total. Each one has to be signed and notarized individually. Many states require a list of electorates in advance. This was solved by putting out an advertisement offering $250 to residents of a particular state with a permanent home address. First come, first serve. In exchange for the $250, the electorate had to sign a Non-Disclosure Agreement acknowledging his or her silence until Fitz publically announced his candidacy. This was a big expense for someone whose message might ring hollow on debate night. In total, there were only 371 electoral votes (of 538) available to Fitz. He would have to secure 270, or 73% to capture the White House.

There was also the matter of a Vice-President. Fitz figured Evan Spring to be perfect as he was intelligent, well-spoken, well-connected, and didn't really need the job at which he was currently employed -- in other words, he could afford the pay cut. There was the minor issue of Evan being totally ignorant of Fitz's platform and whether or not he would support it. Fitz pitched the idea to Evan over dinner in mid-September. Evan termed Cavendish's platform "provocative and intelligent" and gave it a zero chance of implementation, which was greater than the odds he assigned to his election hopes. Spring also advised his friend that there was good chance that he would no longer be the darling of the media after the debate. Fitz said he understood that dynamic completely and that if he bombed at the debate he could go back to being a private citizen; which is what he preferred anyway. Fitz also promised Spring limited public appearances in the month after the debate and prior to the election – neither Spring nor Cavendish expected to be invited to any more debates after October 5th. Evan, even though he thought Fitz to be a tap mad regarding his ambitious odyssey, agreed to indulge his friend, on the condition that his wife and his partners at the private equity group said if it was okay. Fitz emphasized discretion. Two days later, Evan agreed to be Fitz's running mate stating, "Tracy gives you a much greater chance than I do. I shared your ideas with her – I did not with the PE guys – and she said that she would vote for you."

It was time to prepare for the debate.

Chapter 28 (CFR and the Media)

Most of you have never heard of Col. Edward Mandell House. He was arguably the most influential politician that never held a formal office in the history of the United States. He was Woodrow Wilson's unofficial super-Secretary of State and confidant. Wilson wouldn't, politically speaking, tie his shoes without running it up the flagpole with House. Wilson admitted as much when he exclaimed, "House is my second personality; he is my independent self. His thoughts and mine are one." House essentially chose Wilson's cabinet, steered him into a secret "Gentlemen's Agreement" to enter the war on the side of the Allies in early 1916 – while Wilson was campaigning on the fact that he had kept the United States out of the war. House was the invisible hand guiding the passage of the Federal Reserve Act. He then chose the members of the original Federal Reserve Board and shepherded Wilson away from declaring war on Great Britain – yes, you heard that correctly – even after he had submitted to the Gentlemen's Agreement. This shouldn't come as a surprise since House's father said he wanted to raise his sons to "know and serve England." He also authored Wilson's Fourteen Points.

House also penned a book entitled, *Philip Dru: Administrator: a Story of Tomorrow, 1920-1935*. In this book, a civil war breaks out in the United States and Philip Dru becomes autocrat when his side wins the conflict and he dismisses Congress. As the sole "benevolent" leader of the country, Dru establishes a central bank, abolishes protective tariffs, and imposes a graduated income tax, amongst other reforms. This work of fiction, published in 1912, with the subservient cooperation of the Woodrow Wilson administration, transmogrified into reality. In 1918, Franklin K. Lane, Woodrow Wilson's Secretary of the Interior, stated in a private letter: "All that book has said should be, comes about...The President comes to Philip Dru, in the end." This book is a blueprint for running a "shadow government", where a small group of elite and rich bankers manipulate and control politicians from behind the scenes. They do this in secrecy and through various private groups they create.

Not surprisingly, this hugely influential backstage figure was a member of Cecil Rhodes' and Lord Milner's Round Table Groups, tying him closely to European central banking interests – the same ones who wanted a central bank in the United States and a one-world government.

One of the most disturbing quotes attributed to House, who would also greatly influence President Franklin Delano Roosevelt, originates from the minutes of a 1913 White House meeting with Wilson, before the passage of the income tax amendment and the Federal Reserve Act:

> "[Very] soon, every American will be required to register their biological property in a national system designed to keep track of the people and that will operate under the ancient system of pledging. By such methodology, we can compel people to submit to our agenda, which will affect our security as a chargeback for our [debt-based] fiat paper currency. Every American will be forced to register or suffer being unable to work and earn a living. They will be our chattel, and we will hold the security interest over them forever, by operation of the law merchant under the scheme of secured transactions.

> "Americans, by unknowingly or unwittingly delivering the bills of lading to us will be rendered bankrupt and insolvent, forever to remain economic slaves through taxation, secured by their pledges. They will be stripped of their rights and given a commercial value designed to make us a profit and they will be none the wiser, for not one man in a million could ever figure our plans and, if by accident one or two should figure it out, we have in our arsenal plausible deniability. After all, this is the only logical way to fund government, by floating liens and debt to the registrants in the form of benefits and privileges. This will inevitably reap to us huge profits beyond our wildest expectations and leave every American a contributor to this fraud which we will call "Social Insurance." Without realizing it, every American will insure us for any loss we may incur and in this manner; every American will unknowingly be our servant, however begrudgingly. The people will become helpless and without any hope for their redemption and, we will employ the high office of the President of our dummy corporation to foment this plot against America."

Keep this quote in mind when you come to realize that House would go on to found the Council on Foreign Relations (CFR) when it became apparent that the United States would not officially enter the League of Nations, another of his co-created attempts at one-world government.

The CFR was conceived in 1919 at the Paris Peace Conference and formed in 1921 (along with its European counterpart, the Royal Institute of International Affairs in London) when it was decided that the world was not ready for the establishment of a one-world government. The aim of this membership by invitation only group was to guide the United States in that direction from behind the scenes. This would be no small undertaking, but now with a central bank in place, it was possible. To be sure, House was not the only driving force in this essentially furtive enterprise. Bankers J. P. Morgan, John D. Rockefeller, Bernard Baruch, Otto Kahn, Jacob Schiff and Paul Warburg were all instrumental in its birth. In fact, it was originally staffed by J.P. Morgan men and financed with Morgan money. J.P. Morgan's personal attorney (and later Republican presidential candidate) John W. Davis, was the founding President of the CFR. Paul Carvath, the first Vice-President of the CFR, also represented the J.P. Morgan interests. The council's first chairman was Morgan partner Russell Leffingwell. The CFR was later financed with donations from the Rockefeller and Carnegie Foundations. Carrol Quigley, professor of history at the School of Foreign Service at Georgetown University from 1941 to 1976, published a 1,300 page history of the twentieth century in 1966 entitled *Tragedy and Hope*, in which he stated,

> "There does exist, and has existed for a generation, an international Anglophile network which operates, to some extent, in the way the Radical right believes the Communists act. In fact, this network, which we may identify as the Round Table Groups, has no aversion to cooperating with the Communists, or any other group, and frequently does so. I know of the operation of this network because I have studied it for twenty years and was permitted for two years, in the early 1960s, to examine its papers and secret records. I have no aversion to it or to most of its aims and have, for much of my life, been close to it and to many of its instruments. I have objected, both in the past and recently, to a few of its policies... but in general my chief difference of opinion is that it wishes to remain unknown, and I believe its role in history is significant enough to be known."

Quigley, for the avoidance of doubt, was referring to the CFR, serving as one of many conduits through which the bankers could "create a world system of financial control in private hands able to dominate the political system of each country and the economy of the world as a whole."

To further illustrate, former sixteen year CFR member Admiral Chester Ward explained,

> "The main purpose of the Council on Foreign Relations is promoting the disarmament of U.S. sovereignty and national independence and submergence into an all-powerful, one-world government."

He later states,

> "Once the ruling members of the CFR have decided that the U.S. Government should adopt a particular policy, the very substantial research facilities of CFR are put to work to develop arguments, intellectual and emotional, to support the new policy, and to confound and discredit, intellectually and politically, any opposition...In the entire CFR lexicon, there is no term of revulsion carrying a meaning so deep as 'America First'."

So explain why its members, who are actively looking to subvert the United States Constitution, hold positions such as President of the United States, Vice-President, U.S. Senator, U.S. Representative, Supreme Court Justice, Secretary of Defense, Chairman of the Joint Chiefs of Staff, Secretary of State, Secretary of the Treasury, Director of the CIA, Director of the FBI, Chairman of the Federal Reserve, U.S. Ambassador to the United Nations, almost every ranking member of the U.S. State department, CEO of every major media company, CEO of every major defense contractor, CEO of every major pharmaceutical company, CEO of every major bank, etc.? Doesn't the U.S. President take an oath to "uphold the Constitution" when he is inaugurated? You must see that the entire world is a stage and they are the performers. The thespians are both Republican and Democrat. You are only offered the illusion of choice. Quigley outlines the connivance: "The two parties should be almost identical, so that the American people can 'throw the rascals out' at any election without leading to any profound or extensive shift in policy."

Your confidence in the system has been exploited. Your government has been taken over from within, but how are you to know unless you do some extensive digging. You don't have time for that. You are getting your kids off to soccer practice, working to make ends meet, and dealing with your own personal issues. In short, you are living your life. As a result, you are compelled to trust what is coming through the television set as reality. It is not. It is a message designed to splinter your country in two. Have another debate about a white cop killing an unarmed black kid or talk about the terrorist group *du jour* (financed and armed by the United States government) while it is NEVER mentioned that each citizen of the United States is on the hook for nearly $60,000 for his or her share of the national debt – or if it is, the root cause is never addressed and no solutions offered. You are either a republican or a democrat and the polarity has never been greater, yet you are being led down the road to communism, and both sides are too blind to see it. Once your country is completely broke and when the Federal Reserve, to whom you should pray keeps printing more debt-based money to keep the game going a little longer, stops the music, you will have no choice but to submit the sovereignty of your country over to the United Nations, at which point you will be ruled by the Elite and your enslavement will be complete. Sounds crazy? Keep whistling past the graveyard.

Anyone naïve enough to believe that the United Nations has served its purpose by keeping nation states out of worldwide conflict is a clueless loon. What has kept us out of global war is the nuclear bomb. Even the elite that rule from behind the curtain know that they can't prosper in a world where a radioactive plume menaces the air. So in order to keep their pockets lined with gold and the population submissive, the concept of terrorism has been thrust upon the world. You are no longer fighting a country, but a concept. This intellection is perpetual: you are always in a state of war against terrorism.

This gives your government the ability to strip you of your Constitutional rights through such laws as the Patriot Act. You can be declared an 'enemy combatant' by someone in authority and you now have no rights; no right to a lawyer; no right to a trial; and no habeas corpus rights. It is amazing to think that we can't properly bring to justice those who killed JFK, yet we can pre-determine who is a terrorist and who isn't. What terrible event transpires if a suspected "enemy combatant" citizen has access to a lawyer?

Also, the never ending war on terrorism creates the convenient excuse that war cannot be waged without sacrificing freedom of speech at home, prompting people such as the former Administrator of the ghoulish sounding Office of Information and Regulatory Affairs in the Obama administration, Cass Sunstein, to propose banning "conspiracy theorizing". Cass doesn't seem to understand a few points: 1. Conspiracy theorizing is a right granted under the First Amendment of the Constitution to its citizens, not its government. 2. Conspiracy theorizing was the tactic used by the U.S. government (weapons of mass destruction, anthrax attacks, etc.) as an excuse to invade Iraq. 3. One man's conspiracy theory is another man's truth. Recent examples include the U.S. government illegally spying on its citizens and the U.S. government torturing suspected terrorists. Once decried as a conspiracy theory, these events turned out to be true. [4. "Fuck you Cass Sunstein!" Just exercising the rights to free speech before you take it away.] And as you will see, like Sunstein with freedom of speech, the CFR and likeminded institutions have worked tirelessly to dismantle the freedom of the press.

The Council on Foreign Relations attempts to maintain the pretense of diversity via its Non-Attribution Rule, which allows members to engage in "a free, frank, and open exchange of ideas" without fear of having any of their statements "attributed" in public. This can only be interpreted as some of the most influential people in the United States meeting in secret and deciding policy for the rest of the country. What happened to open debate on the floor of Congress? To be sure, the CFR has a public face in the form of its bi-monthly *Foreign Affairs* magazine, which offers a glimpse into the future foreign policy of the United States.

Republican and Democrats, at various times, occupy the White House, but CFR members never seem to go away. Every Secretary of State since 1940 (save one) has been a member of the CFR or the Trilateral Commission (essentially the CFRs younger, Asian sister). Every Secretary of Defense (or War) has been a member since 1940. Almost every national security or foreign policy advisor position has been occupied by a CFR member since 1940. Almost every U.S. President has been a member as well as the losing party's nominee. Do you find it odd that Bill Clinton and Dick Cheney, allegedly on opposite sides of the political spectrum, participate in discussions that you are not allowed to hear? What do these public figures really think once the light of public scrutiny is switched off?

170

What is Alan Greenspan doing there, besides adjusting his glasses? What about Timothy Geithner? Why is there a media blackout? Why is it that Tom Brokaw, Barbara Walters, (the late) Walter Cronkite, Charles Krauthammer, Les Moonves, Rupert Murdoch, Charlie Rose, Diane Sawyer, Lesley Stahl, (the late) David Brinkley, (the late) Peter Jennings, (the late) Edward Bradley, Dan Rather, Laurence A. Tisch, Jack Welch, Robert MacNeil, Jim Lehrer, (the late) Katharine Graham, William F. Buckley, Jr., George Will, Richard Gelb, and David Gergen (amongst many others) are not producing, interpreting, or reporting the news, but instead meeting in private to plot a one-world government? Can you really trust what is coming out of their mouths when they report the "news"? Corporate media members include Bloomberg, Thomson Reuters, General Electric, and Time Warner, along with individual representation from CBS, NBC, ABC, PBS, *Washington Post*, *New York Times*, *U.S. News & World Report*, Dow Jones (*Wall Street Journal*), Time Inc., *Washington Times*, et al. If the people in power are working towards a global union, can they really be concerned with your Constitutional rights? Have you ever wondered why the first three news stories on ABC World News Tonight, CBS Evening News, and NBC Nightly News are always the same? Even in this day of cable news, the stories are consubstantial; they are just disseminated from a right or left viewpoint, with the purpose of dividing this country down socioeconomic, racial, generational, and philosophical lines.

In the 2008 presidential campaign, Fred Thompson, John McCain, Jim Gilmore, Newt Gingrich, Hilary Clinton, Joe Biden, Chris Dodd, Bill Richardson, and Barack Obama were all members of the CFR – although Obama said he didn't know if he was an 'official' member. (Curiously, JFK claimed the same.) Mitt Romney was not a member, but contributed an article for *Foreign Affairs* in 2007. The entire world's a stage and they are your performers. You are given the veneer of alternatives, but you only have a choice between two lanes on the same corporate socialistic highway going straight to hell – that is, if you define hell as the subjection of your Constitution to a higher authority, such as the United Nations. If you are watching a presidential debate, the moderator and the candidates are generally members of the CFR. This is another artificially eristic production giving you the illusion of choice. The boundaries of debate are already decided before a word is uttered. You will listen to arguments for and against gun control, terrorism, immigration, and healthcare – all very important issues. Few solutions are given as no root causes are addressed. However, no one will dare ask or talk about the debt-based money creation system that has the United States $18 trillion in the hole, or a way to solve it. No one will ask why the presidential debates are complete shams put on by members of the Council on Foreign Relations, a one-world government organization, and as a result, no one will ask about the obvious conflict between the CFR and the United States Constitution. This is why Donald Trump is so dangerous to the internationalists. He is not beholden to them and has enough pomposity, money, and notoriety to ask these fundamental questions. His fame can bring these issues to a larger audience and that is why FOX and the conservatives are attacking him – hard. They make him look like a jackass – although, admittedly, he sometimes does not need anyone's assistance.

Returning to the mainstream media and the CFR, J.P. Morgan (and other) bankers along with war related interests were "controlling the message" as early as the 1910s. With the formation of the CFR by J.P. Morgan interests it is not a huge stretch to conclude that influence over the press was a CFR directive from its origin. This leverage has continued up through present day thanks to a CIA operation devised and hatched by CFR members. The program for media domination was called Operation Mockingbird. Under the guise of keeping the United States safe from the influence of communism, it was initially organized by Cord Meyer (CFR) and Allen W. Dulles (CFR) in 1951. When Dulles became head of the CIA he passed his day to day responsibilities to Frank Wisner (Deputy Director for Plans), who in turn recruited Philip Graham (CFR), owner of the *Washington Post* to recruit other publications and leading reporters into the mix. Carl Bernstein states in his epic Oct. 20, 1977 *Rolling Stone* article "The CIA and the Media":

> "By operating under the guise of accredited news correspondents, Dulles believed, CIA operatives abroad would be accorded a degree of access and freedom of movement unobtainable under almost any other type of cover."

Keep that in mind when your journalists are jailed in Middle East and accused of being spies. He also stated that the *New York Times* (Arthur Hays Sulzberger, CFR) was the most valuable newspaper relationship;

CBS (William Paley, CFR) the most valuable broadcasting asset; and Time Inc. (Henry Luce, CFR) the most valuable magazine company. By siphoning off money intended for the Marshall Plan, the CIA was able to pay over 3,300 employees in this clandestine venture. From the 1950s onward, your message is what the CFR and the CIA want you to hear. It gives new meaning to the *New York Times* slogan, "All the News That's Fit to Print". When you watch or listen to the news, understand that is crafted not to inform, but rather to shape your mind.

This distortion of the news doesn't simply come from the CIA. Saudi Prince Alwaleed bin Talal, who owns the largest stake in News Corp outside of Rupert Murdoch, was able to get a story that Fox News reported as "Muslim riots" changed to "civil riots". Talal admitted as much in a speech he gave in Dubai – he simply made a call to Rupert Murdoch and the subtle change came to pass.

Along those same lines, former Emmy winning CNN correspondent Amber Lyon has accused CNN of accepting money from oppressive Islamic nations in return for censoring unflattering reporting of its conduct. Such was the case when she produced a documentary on the impact of social media during the Arab Spring uprisings. It was not aired on CNN International, because it portrayed the persecution of pro-democracy protesters in Bahrain. Lyon claims that her former employer buried the report because "Bahrain is a paying customer" of CNN.

As an ironic aside – the irony will be discovered later – FBI Director J. Edgar Hoover was jealous of the rise of the CIA and started investigating its members. He discovered that a lot of CIA employees had communist leanings, including Cord Meyer (whose wife had an affair with JFK) and Allen Dulles. He passed this information on to Senator Joseph "Red Scare" McCarthy, who claimed that the CIA was "a sinkhole of communists" that he would root out. In return, Wisner was directed by Dulles to unleash Operation Mockingbird on McCarthy. Many media members (including Walter Lippmann (CFR) and Ed Murrow (CFR)) participated in a successful smear campaign against McCarthy – not to say that McCarthy wasn't clearly on the other end of the political spectrum. It makes you wonder what current CFR member George Clooney's ulterior motivation was behind *Good Night, and Good Luck*. The investigation of Cord Meyer was blocked and McCarthy discredited. During this time,

President Eisenhower became concerned about the growing influence of the CIA and its covert activities. He formed a National Security Council 5412/2 Group to make sure that their actions were in concert with foreign policy objectives. Since Dulles was in the group, he just circumvented the group by not informing it of the CIA's covert operations. In other words, Dulles was operating his own shadow government. This is part of the "acquisition of unwarranted influence, whether sought or unsought, by the military industrial complex" that Eisenhower warned Americans about in his 1961 farewell speech.

Don't think for one second that the CIA just magically abandoned Operation Mockingbird once the Berlin Wall fell. Even if it did, the job of media manipulation has actually become easier with all of the mergers in the industry over the past 30 years. As former FCC Commissioner Michael Copps (2001 – 2011) explained,

> "Ninety percent of the top cable channels are owned by the same giants that own TV networks and the cable system. More channels are great, but when they are all owned by the same people, cable doesn't advance localism, editorial diversity, and competition. And those who believe the internet alone will save us from this fate should realize that the dominating internet news sources are controlled by the same media giants who control radio, TV, newspapers, and cable."

All the world's a stage...

It seems appropriate that a behind the scenes influencer like Col. Edward House was chiefly responsible for the behind the scenes power and globalist agenda of the Council on Foreign Relations. As you will see, the CFR had one other very important conspiratorial role, starting in 1963.

Chapter 29 (October 5, 2016)

Why am I doing this? I don't even like humanity. Actually, those words – backstage before the debate – were a bit hollow. After discovering the identity of his father and researching the reasons for the decline of the American ideal since his death, Fitz no longer blamed the American people for their laziness or for their decline in productivity. It was all by design. It was the inevitable outcome of a system rigged against the American people. Winning two world wars fought on someone else's soil prolonged their predetermined doomed reckoning. It was time to share this story with the American people. It was truly time for a change. After updating Fitz on his twitter followers and fixing his tie, Polly gave Fitz a peck on the cheek and whispered, "You are truly an amazing person. Do your country proud." It was the first time Polly had ever kissed Fitz.

Hillary Clinton and Jeb Bush both entered the backstage area simultaneously, where Fitz was readying himself. Both greeted Fitz very cordially, knowing that there existed a very small percentage of undecided voters that would determine the election, and knowing how fickle the uncommitted faction could be, and knowing that Fitz was more favorably thought of than either of them, an endorsement by him could swing the outcome of the election. Fitz, of course, had other plans.

The three of them walked onto the stage to their respective podiums with Hillary Clinton on the viewing audience's left; Jeb on the right; and Fitz off to the right side of the stage, almost as if he was the one who would be asking the two candidates questions. Diane Sawyer [CFR], the debate moderator started the proceedings, "Good evening and welcome to the first of three debates among the two major candidates for President of the United States, sponsored by the Commission on Presidential Debates. The candidates are Hillary Clinton [CFR], the Democratic nominee and Jeb Bush, the Republican nominee. Also joining us this evening is Fitzgerald Cavendish, son of former president John F. Kennedy. I am Diane Sawyer of ABC News and I will be the moderator for this ninety minute event which is taking place before an audience at Wright State University's Nutter Center in Fairborn, Ohio. Three members of the media will be asking questions tonight. They are David E. Sanger [CFR] from the *New York Times*; Charles Krauthammer [CFR] from the *Washington Post* and *Time Magazine*; and Alan S. Murray [CFR] of the

Wall Street Journal. We will follow a format agreed to by representatives of the Clinton and Bush campaigns. That agreement contains no restrictions regarding the content or subject matter of the questions." *Yeah right*, thought Cavendish.

"Each candidate will have up to two minutes for a closing statement as well as Mr. Cavendish. The first question goes to Mr. Bush. He will have two minutes to answer to be followed by rebuttals of up to one minute each from Ms. Clinton and Mr. Cavendish. Mr. Bush, what is the single most separating domestic issue of this campaign?"

Bush: "The single most important issue would be the economy. There are six million more people in poverty than there were at the start of the Obama administration. There are six and half million people working part-time who want to be working full-time. There is no income growth. Under President Obama we've had tax increases -- $1 trillion to fund Obamacare and an additional $600 billion over the next ten years because he could. We can stop this poverty by growing the economy at 4% and creating an additional nineteen million jobs over the next eight years. These lofty goals can be met by revamping the tax code and making it much more business friendly. We have to get rid of regulations that are not pro-business. We have to remove job killers such as Obamacare. If we properly address the immigration issue, it can provide a major boost to the U.S. economy. We have to embrace the energy revolution in our country. How can this current administration not be for the XL Energy Pipeline? Give me a break. We have to be for these things as this is how we sustain high income growth. When I was governor of Florida we cut taxes every year, totaling $19 billion, creating a much better business environment. We've seen the debt almost double under the Obama administration, whereas when I was governor of Florida our reserves went up tenfold from $1 billion to $10 billion. We are not protecting our entitlement system for the next generation. When I was governor, our pension system was fully funded, so we weren't stealing from future generations. We also reduced the government workforce by 11% during my eight years. Our state was AAA-rated. Under Obama, this country lost its AAA rating. The recovery is the weakest in modern history. Two percent growth is the new normal. Median household income is down over $2,000 over the past seven years. Workforce participation is at a 30-year low. While I was governor, we created 1.3 million net new jobs with median household income going up by over $1,000 and the economy grew by 4.4 percent a year.

"Mrs. Clinton, your response?"

Clinton: "The defining economic challenge of our time is clear. We must raise incomes for hard working Americans so they can afford a middle class life. We must drive strong and steady income growth that lifts up families, and lifts up our country. I will push for broader business tax reforms to spur investment in America and close the loopholes that reward businesses for moving jobs overseas. Another engine of economic growth should be comprehensive immigration reform. We need to establish an infrastructure bank. There is no excuse to not make investment in cleaner renewable energy right now. It is time to recognize that quality child care is not a luxury, but a growth strategy. It is high time that gender and race pay equality becomes a reality. We need to raise the minimum wage and go after employers who wrongly categorize their employees as contractors. Under the administration that I served, the S&P 500 has risen over 130% over the past seven and a half years. Unemployment has gone from over 9% to as low as 5%. More people have access to healthcare than ever before."

"Mr. Cavendish, your response?"

Cavendish: "The defining issue is our system of money creation. What has been offered up by our two candidates are the same two competing economic philosophies that have been given as answers on how to make the economy better for the past fifty years and now we stand here in 2016, nearly $20 trillion in debt. That is over $60,000 for every citizen – every man, woman, and child – in this country. In an extremely artificially low interest rate environment we are paying close to half a trillion dollars annually in interest payments. That is over $1,500 per citizen per year – just on the interest! Do you really believe that the solutions offered up by these two candidates are going to solve the debt crisis? Do you really think we can keep this charade going on much longer? What is being offered up here is a choice between a kidney stone and a canker sore. What you have to realize is that these answers don't address the root cause of the real problem that plagues this country and nearly every country on this planet. The root cause that I am referring to is central banking. Do you understand how money is created? It is created out of debt. I will expound on this further when I have more time."

"Mr. Bush, your response?"

Jeb spent his additional minute eviscerating Obamacare and explaining if businesses were allowed the proper operating environment – i.e. not being subjected to Obamacare and minimum wage hikes -- we wouldn't have to worry about jobs going overseas.

"Mrs. Clinton?"

Hillary spent her rebuttal time defending Obamacare, proposing incentivizing corporations to profit share with employees, and explaining that Jeb's incentives for business would destroy the middle class.

"Mr. Cavendish?"

Cavendish: "The passage of the Federal Reserve Act of 1913 guaranteed that all money is loaned into existence out of thin air – by a private bank. Let me use a quick example to demonstrate. Let's assume that Mrs. Clinton and I are the only two people on earth. But I'm a central bank. And for whatever reason, she wishes to borrow $10 from me. I start up my printing press and produce a $10 bill and charge her 10 percent interest. (Cavendish pulls a $10 bill out of his suit pocket for effect.) So in a year she will owe me $10 *plus* $1 in interest. But there is a problem: *this* $10 (he shakes the bill) that I loaned her is the only money in existence. So how is she going to pay back the $11? Either she is not, whereby I confiscate her property, or she is going to borrow more money from me. That in a nutshell is our system of money creation. That is why the level of debt ($11) is always greater than the level of money ($10). We talk about extinguishing our debt and not stealing from our kids' futures, but under this money system that outcome is impossible. If we were to retire all of our debt -- federal, corporate, and personal -- there would be no money in circulation."

A little murmur enveloped the audience.

Sawyer: "Alright. We move now to the subject of taxes and spending. The question goes to Mrs. Clinton for a two minute answer. The question will be asked by Alan Murray."

Murray: "Mrs. Clinton, can you lock in a level where middle income families will be guaranteed a tax cut, or at the very least, a level of income where they will be guaranteed no tax increase?"

Clinton: "I will not commit to an exact level for a tax cut, but I can guarantee that there will be no tax increase on the middle class. The tax code needs to be simplified. I support the Buffet rule whereby millionaires don't pay taxes at a lower rate than their secretaries. I support the abolition of the carried interest loophole which allows wealthy financiers to pay an artificially low rate. And let's agree that hugely successful companies that benefit from everything America has to offer should not be able to game the system, and avoid paying their fair share; especially when smaller companies that can't afford high-priced lobbyists and lawyers, end up paying more."

"Mr. Bush?"

Bush: "If you create the right environment in which businesses can operate then you can grow the economy at 4%. If the economy is growing at 4%, the level of income will grow, and there will be no need to increase taxes to pay for the entitlement programs or to reduce our deficits. If the economy is growing at 4%, companies will be enjoying greater profits, and as a result, will be paying more in taxes. With regards to middle income people, there will be no tax increases. With regards to the higher income people, we already have the highest progressivity of any country in the developed world. One percent of the people earn twenty percent of the income, but pay thirty percent of the taxes. I don't see a need to change the income tax rate."

"Mr. Cavendish?"

Cavendish: "Abolish income taxes. We will have an across the board 30% sales tax, which can be tweaked contingent upon the good or service being sold. If the good or service sold is harmful to the human condition, like cigarettes, it will be taxed at a higher rate. For example, organic food is taxed at 5%, whereas the garbage that is sold at fast food restaurants and is passed off as food is taxed at 150%. The tax is regressive, so in order to solve that problem, in addition to no income taxes, every man and woman, 18 years of age and older, will receive a check in the first week of January in the amount of $10,000. For those that are on a fixed income such as Social Security, there will be a bump in your benefits. Through this tax, corporate behavior can be controlled. If no one is buying pop tarts because of the excessive 150% tax, then the maker of pop tarts is going to have to revise its formula so that it is at least "all natural", generating a lower tax rate and resulting in greater consumption. Sorry accountants, the true way to economic growth is through productivity. If you want to increase productivity, you have to get rid of unproductive activities, like finding ways to avoid taxes."

A slightly louder mummer enveloped the audience.

"Mrs. Clinton?"

Hillary Clinton, who seemed amused by Cavendish's remarks on taxation, spent her minute talking about the absurd breaks that large corporations receive and reiterated how wealthy Americans should not be paying a lower tax rate than the middle class because of all of the investment class tax breaks.

"Mr. Bush?"

Jeb Bush, who seemed confused by Cavendish's tax proposal, spent his minute backing out of his previous rhetoric concerning the wealthy already carrying enough of the tax burden in America and reiterated that the right business environment is the key to prosperity.

"Mr. Cavendish?"

Cavendish: "The new tax code can be an instrument for addressing other problems at their root cause, such as health care; but more on that later. The absolute number one issue so that we don't end up like Greece and Spain is central banking. Why don't any of the panelists here ask a question like, 'If all of the governments of the world are $70 trillion in debt -- that is trillion with a "T" -- who has all the money?' The answer is your central bankers. The system is rigged so that they end up with all of the money in the end and all governments end up bankrupt. Just like the example I spoke of before with Mrs. Clinton, I earned interest and she has to borrow more money from me or I will foreclose on her. And what did I do to earn my income? Nothing -- except that by law – unconstitutionally, mind you – I have the printing press. That is it. And that is the most absurd notion in the world. But this is the system that we have worked under for the past 250 years. This has to be changed."

Sawyer: "Our next topic will be healthcare. The question goes to Mr. Cavendish for a two minute answer. The question will be asked by David Sanger."

Sanger: "What is your view on healthcare?"

Cavendish: "Did you ever ask yourself why the healthcare system is essentially bankrupt? Is it because now most people die of degenerative diseases -- cancer, Alzheimer's, diabetes, heart disease -- which means people of this generation have long drawn out deaths. For example, 100 years ago, 1 in 30 people died of cancer – some estimates are 1 in 300; today, 1 in 3 die of cancer. The cost to keep the patient alive during the last six months of his or her life is typically north of a million dollars. I can assure you that those people have not paid north of $1 million in insurance premiums or Medicare payments. When 1 in 2 is dying of degenerative diseases, it is easy to see why the system is broken.

How do we fix it? Get rid of degenerative disease. If we get rid of degenerative diseases, the healthcare system will become solvent again. Sounds impossible, right? Well, did it ever occur to either candidate that drug companies have no interest in curing degenerative diseases? If they were ever cured, Big Pharma wouldn't be able to jam painkillers and chemotherapy into our bodies because we would be healthy and they wouldn't make any money. Did it ever occur to either candidate that the American Medical Association has no interest in curing degenerative diseases? If they were ever cured, the need for this sprawling healthcare industry would be greatly diminished and the system wouldn't make nearly as much money. That is why they act like the gestapo when a cheap un-patentable alternative begins to make news, like laetrile. Follow the money! It is very simple. Tax those things that give us degenerative diseases. For example, during World War II the consumption of sugar was banned in Great Britain and diabetes per capita dropped by 40%. Twenty years ago, the rate of degenerative diseases in Europe was one-tenth of that in the United States and they smoke twice as much as we do. Why is this? Many reasons, but fast food and processed food are the biggest ones. Curiously, Europe is starting to catch up to us now that fast food is much more pervasive over there. They don't allow crap like high fructose corn syrup in their food supply. Remember, there are poisons that kill you in 20 minutes, like snakebites, and then there are those that kill over the course of twenty or thirty years, like the 62% of the American diet that is processed foods. Those have to be eliminated from our bodies. I believe that everyone should have access to healthcare; it should be a basic right. (The bell goes off marking the end of two minutes.) I'm all for free choice, but if you want to consume garbage that is going to burden our bankrupt healthcare system, then you will have to pay a lot more to consume that garbage.

"Mr. Bush?"

Bush: "My view on healthcare is that it should be more personal, the patient/doctor relationship. To that end, I would repeal the Affordable Healthcare Act, Obamacare. It is a monstrosity. As far as replacing it, the model would be consumer directed, where consumers, where patients, have more choices, where they have more of a direct relationship; where the subsidies, if there were to be subsidies, are state administered; and if there are to be exchanges, they aren't coercive exchanges; where there's no employer mandate, employee mandate or requirements of services provided that are extraordinary; where people have more customized types of insurance based on their needs; and it's more consumer-directed so that they're more engaged in the decision-making, and they have more choices than what they have today. The role of the government in all of this ought to be to try to create catastrophic coverage, where there is relief for families in our country, where if you have a hardship that goes way beyond your means of paying for it, the government is there or an entity is there to help you deal with that. The rest of it ought to be shifted back, where individuals are empowered to make more decisions themselves."

"Mrs. Clinton?"

Clinton: "I defend the Affordable Care Act, which my Republican opponent seems obsessed with repealing. No real alternative has been offered, only in the vaguest generalities. When Republicans are confronted with evidence on climate change, they say, 'I'm not a scientist.' Well, neither am I. I am a just a grandmother with two eyes and a brain, and I can see that the world is getting warmer. I'm not a doctor, but I can see the good that the Affordable Care Act has done. As president I will work to improve it, to lower out-of-pocket healthcare costs, but providing access to healthcare for every person in this country is not something that should be repealed, not in the least. I would like to remind Mr. Cavendish that life expectancy is a lot greater than it was one hundred years ago."

"Mr. Cavendish?"

Cavendish: "We live a lot longer than we did one hundred years ago because we wiped out childhood diseases such as polio, scarlet fever, diphtheria, whooping cough, measles, and small pox. Back then two of the top four killers we diarrhea and tuberculosis, from which people today don't die. Additionally, in 1900, the U.S. infant mortality rate was approximately 100 infant deaths per 1,000 live births; while in 2000, the rate was less than 7. These are the primary reasons we live much longer than we did 100 years ago. If you made it to the age of 10 in 1900 your life expectancy isn't much different than it is today. It has absolutely nothing to do with Big Pharma and the allopathic method of treatment forced on students in the medical schools of this country. I will add that the United States is remarkable at trauma, and back in the day when you fell off you horse and broke your leg, you could get gangrene and die. That really doesn't happen anymore, because we are world class at trauma. Don't read into this the wrong way. 99% of the healthcare providers are not corrupt; the system under which they operate is corrupt."

"Mr. Bush?"

Bush stumbled through his record in Florida with, "While I was governor of Florida, we had to deal with Medicaid, just like every other governor. We put reforms in place, a defined contribution plan. It increased patient and physician satisfaction and reduced per patient costs."

Hillary for her part, didn't touch any of Fitz's comments, but gave a weak example as to how she was going to lower the out-of-pocket costs for the consumers of Obamacare.

Sawyer: "Our next topic will be immigration. The question goes to Mr. Bush for a two minute answer. The question will be asked by Charles Krauthammer."

Krauthammer: "Mr. Bush, you have been criticized about being soft of immigration. You have called illegal immigration, "not a felony, but an act of love". Do you stand by your support of earned legal status?"

Bush: "I do. A great majority of people come here illegally because they have no other alternative to support their family. But we need to control our border. It is our responsibility to pick and choose who comes in. I've written a book about this and I have developed a comprehensive strategy which reflects what is in the book. We need to deal with e-verify. We need to deal with people who come here on a legal visa and overstay. We need to be much more strategic when dealing with boarder enforcement and security. We need to eliminate the sanctuary cities in the United States. It is ridiculous and tragic that people are dying because local authorities are not following federal laws. There is much to do. I think that instead of talking about this as a wedge issue which Barack Obama has done for seven years, the next president, which I hope to be, will fix this once and for all, so we can turn this into a driver for high, sustained, economic growth. And there should be a path to earned legal status for those who are here; not amnesty, but earned legal status, which means you pay a fine and do many things over an extended period of time."

"Mr. Cavendish?"

Cavendish: "If you really want to get rid of them, abolish income taxes and enact a 30% sales tax. We know they don't pay any income taxes, so if we increase their cost of living here by at least 30%, and 150% on a lot of goods that they consume, it will act as a strong disincentive to enter the country illegally. Remember, since they don't have a social security number, they aren't going to receive the $10,000 checks that are being sent out on the first week of January. Illegal immigration is part of a *plan* to destroy the economic well-being of this country. Having over 11 million people illegally abuse the system increases our debt levels, and with this ridiculous money creation system in place, puts us deeper into a hole – a hole out of which we can't ascend, unless central banking is abolished."

"Mrs. Clinton?"

Clinton: "I do believe that people who are here, and are raising families, and are working hard, deserve a path to citizenship. The horror of separating children from their families, which has happened when a child is at school and her mother gets picked up at work and deported, is just so against the values of what this country stands for that we have to have a path to full and equal citizenship for these people. I am not talking about legal status, which is a code word for second class citizen. Republicans like to characterize immigrants as law-breaking, when the overwhelming majority of them are productive, law-abiding members of our society that deserve a path to citizenship."

"Mr. Bush?"

Bush defended that his plan was a path for full and equal citizenship, but fines had to be paid and hurdles had to be overcome in order to obtain citizenship.

Mr. Cavendish: "So let me get this straight? We have a Constitution in this country and we have laws, yet we don't enforce immigration, yet we run illegal wars all around the planet in the name of keeping us safe from terrorism, and from terrorists entering this country. We have something called the Patriot Act, which gives the government the right to strip us of our Constitutional rights, which by law, is unconstitutional? Does that make any sense? It seems as if the illegals get more out of this country than the regular citizens of this country. You want to give them a path to citizenship? If I was an illegal under this current system, I'd say screw that. I'll take what handouts I can get from this government, not pay taxes, and since my Constitutional rights are a mirage anyway, why bother with citizenship. Citizens, please see what is going on here: neither of these two candidates is addressing root causes with their "solutions", to anything."

Again, the crowd buzzed.

"Mrs. Clinton?"

185

Clinton: "I don't think that it is that we are not enforcing immigration. President Obama has deported some three million immigrants under his administration. It is just that the reality of the situation is such that we have to control it and separating mothers from their children is just not the right way to go about it. If we give them a path to citizenship then they can become people who pay taxes for the benefits that they receive."

Cavendish: "And how is that a disincentive to illegal immigration?"

Sawyer cut him off, "Alright. We move now to the subject of gun control. The question goes to Mrs. Clinton for a two minute answer. The question will be asked by Alan Murray."

Murray: "It seems that the majority of Americans are in favor of some form of gun control. How do plan on getting legislation passed?"

Clinton: "I think that it is an issue that needs to come to the forefront. I don't know how we keep seeing shooting after shooting, read about the people murdered because they went to Bible study or they went to the movies or they were just doing their job, and not finally say we've got to do something about this. I understand that gun ownership is part of the fabric of many law abiding communities, but when a Johns Hopkins study says 89% are in favor of background checks, I think we have a responsibility to listen. There were over 33,000 deaths due to firearms in the United States in 2013. That is unacceptable. I support sensible action to curb gun violence, including universal background checks, cracking down on illegal gun traffickers, and keeping guns out of the hands of domestic abusers and stalkers. As senator, I co-sponsored and voted for legislation to close the gun show loophole by requiring criminal background checks on all transactions taking place at events that sell firearms. I also co-sponsored and voted for legislation to extend and reinstate the assault weapons ban. With regards to getting legislation passed, I will need help from the voters out there. If 89% of you are in favor of greater gun control, elect congressmen who reflect your sentiment. I will sign the legislation."

"Mr. Bush, your response?"

Bush: "In Florida, where I was governor, we are pro second amendment, but we do have background checks, a seventy-two hour waiting period. Criminals can't get access to guns. We have to find a better way to keep guns out of the hands of people with mental issues. That is the common denominator with these entire headline making tragedies. I believe that it is a states' rights issue and should be managed at that level. Rural Florida and New York City are two totally different places and imposing blanket legislation on both places doesn't seem to make sense. The tenth amendment gives the states the power to do this and I think that this is an instance of its proper application."

"Mr. Cavendish, your response?"

Cavendish: "This country was founded on the concept of rugged individualism. The second amendment was put in place so that its citizens had a check and balance against the government in case it started making the same tyrannical missteps as the British crown. When Obama is administering a litmus test for senior military officials as to whether or not they will disarm or fire upon American citizens, I think that qualifies as a tyrannical misstep. I do see a need to keep guns away from people with mental disabilities, and if 89% of the citizens are for more stringent background checks, then we should listen to the will of the people. But in no way should a government 'by the people and for the people' start disarming American citizens."

The audience seemed stunned.

"Mrs. Clinton?"

Clinton went on to emasculate Bush's position, reminding him that Constitution is a federal document and the Second Amendment to that Constitution deals with the right to bear arms. Making it a states' rights issue is an excuse to "kick the can down the road" and do nothing. She also cited an example of someone being denied a gun in Pennsylvania, but getting one in Florida and committing murder.

"Mr. Bush?"

Bush mentioned that a majority (about 21,000) of the gun deaths were by suicide. He went on to clarify the difference between his stance and that of Clinton. He is for states' rights as it relates to gun control and she is not.

"Mr. Cavendish?"

Cavendish: "This country was also founded on the concepts of freedom, individual rights, and the golden rule. It is a terrible tragedy when a disturbed person commits a heinous act. The carnage that results is usually a function of what killing capacity is at his disposal. When these events occur they make the news and tug at our heartstrings. It is natural to want to feel safe and have the government protect us in trying times. And it is common sense to refrain certain people from having the ability to do harm to others. But never surrender your liberties in exchange for safety. As Ben Franklin said, 'Those who surrender freedom for security will not have, nor do they deserve, either one.' That is why the Patriot Act must be repealed. You live with the illusion of freedom and almost everyone one of your daily activities are unaffected, but what if, in the future, you wanted to protest an unpopular war or the corporate takeover of America? You could be labeled an enemy combatant and stripped of your freedoms by some random government official. That is not right. Repeal the Patriot Act."

It was decided in advance that questions of foreign policy would be only directed to Bush and Clinton, who debated the merits of the Iranian nuclear deal, Hillary's role in Benghazi, the takedown of Osama bin Laden, and how to handle Vladimir Putin and ISIS. When the foreign policy question and answer period was over, Sawyer said, "I am going to ask each candidate the same question and they will each have 90 seconds to respond. There would be no period for rebuttal."

Sawyer: "If you are elected president, what is the first issue or issues you will tackle in the White House? We will start with Mrs. Clinton."

Clinton: "I think that the initial focus must be on the American people and the economy. I am going to propose legislation that will provide tax relief for hard working families while making sure that the wealthiest pay their fair share. I will cut red tape for small businesses. Small businesses spend $1,100 per employee and 150 hours complying with the federal tax code. That must be simplified. I will propose comprehensive immigration reform. I will propose legislation that will incentivize the production of clean energy – making us the world superpower in that industry. Through legislation I will encourage businesses to profit share with their employees. I will propose an increase in the minimum wage. I will propose a New College Compact that will invest $350 billion so that students will not have to borrow for tuition at public colleges in their state. I will also invest in our future generations by slashing the interest rates on student loans. I will propose an infrastructure bank that would leverage public and private funds to invest in projects across the country. I will increase funding for scientific research at agencies like the National Institutes of Health and the National Science Foundation."

"Mr. Bush?"

Bush: "I have no idea how she is going to pay for all of these projects. We are already $20 trillion in debt. To that end, I would work for comprehensive regulatory reform. Regulations are like an invisible tax on the economy, to the tune of $1.9 trillion per year; that's $15,000 per family. First, I would set new, reasonable standards for the government agencies that issue rules that choke economic activity and opportunity. For every dollar of regulatory cost proposed, that agency must also propose a dollar of regulatory relief. I will establish a two-year deadline for the federal permitting process, including environmental reviews. Do you realize that the average time taken for environmental reviews of highway projects is eight years? That is ridiculous. I will get to work repealing or reforming the Obama era regulations such as Dodd-Frank, Waters of the United States, the Carbon Rule, the Coal Ash Rule, and Net Neutrality. In short, I will get to work creating an atmosphere where businesses can succeed, and as a result the economy can grow at 4%, which will grow incomes across the country."

"Mr. Cavendish?"

Cavendish: "Well there you have it again. Give away free goods versus letting the corporations run roughshod over America. Not much of a choice – they both take us to the same place. I would repeal the Federal Reserve Act of 1913; repeal the National Banking Act of 1863 and 1864.

Move the printing press back to the U.S. Treasury. As 'the U.S. government debts come due, instead of letting the owners of the government securities roll them over, the U.S. Treasury will pay them off in full (principal plus interest) with U.S. Government Money as opposed to [pulls out a dollar bill] this Federal Reserve Note. This will flood the banks of the world with a lot of money -- which should be inflationary. But as this money finds its way into the banking system, the US Treasury will ratchet up the fractional reserve requirement for banks from its current 10 percent level towards 100 percent as all of the debt comes due. This will keep the money in circulation relatively stationary and inflation in check. A bank that has $10 million in deposits can currently make $100 million in loans; when all of the debt is extinguished, that bank will have $100 million in deposits with which it can make a $100 million in loans. The debt is now gone and we will no longer have to hear the rhetoric of how we are stealing from our children's future. The financial system will be deleveraged so the amplitude of the business cycles will be diminished greatly. In fact, business cycles should cease to exist as they are currently engineered. I would then work to repeal the 16th Amendment to the Constitution (income tax) and send out a check in the amount of $10,000 to every citizen, eighteen years or older. I would then impose the sales tax at different levels based on the good or services' effect on the human condition to regulate business. In ten years about 88% or $17.5 trillion of the debt will be paid off permanently."

The audience broke into applause.

Sawyer: "And now for closing statements. You will have two minutes. We will start with Mr. Cavendish."

Cavendish: "I think that the citizens watching this debate should be made aware of the fact that they are being kept in the dark. You are watching a production of the Council of Foreign Relations that creates the illusion of choice. For example, do you find it odd -- heck, I find it creepy -- that both Mrs. Clinton, her husband, and Mr. Bush's father, the moderator of this debate, the question asking panelists, and five members on the board of the Commission on Presidential Debates all belong to the same organization: The Council on Foreign Relations? Do you find it strange that every president since 1928 has been a member of this organization or beholden to it? For example, Ronald Reagan wasn't a member, but he had over three hundred members of the CFR in his cabinet -- pretty amazing coincidence. Every Secretary of State, save one? Do you know who else is on the membership roll? There are corporate members that include every major investment bank, every major drug company, and every major oil company. But what I find most disturbing is that News Corp, Bloomberg, ABC News, Time-Warner, Google, and McGraw-Hill are also members. So here we have a group of politicians, central bankers, mixed with the big business, mixed with big media. I interpret this only one way: a meeting place where big business is making sure that the politicians bend to its will while the media doesn't report it. The CFR meetings are a sworn secret. According to the 1917 Congressional Record, a J.P. Morgan consortium – one of the driving forces behind the Federal Reserve -- quietly purchased twenty-five newspapers earlier that decade after it had formed a commission to determine which ones were the most influential. Why did he do this? To control the message! How do you think we ended up in World War I? Who profited the most off of World War I? J.P. Morgan and the other central bankers! And this is what the CFR is doing: controlling the message. For those of you that don't find this co-mingling of 4,600 politicians, businessmen, and media disturbing, ask yourself "what is the goal of the CFR?" The answer is one-world government. I'm sure that most of you think I'm insane at this point so let me leave with a quote from the Chairman Emeritus of the CFR, David Rockefeller, as he speaks at another one of his secret organizations, the Bilderberg Group, in 1991:

> 'We are grateful to the *Washington Post*, the *New York Times*, *Time Magazine* and other great publications whose directors have attended our meetings and respected their promises of discretion for almost forty years. It would have been impossible for us to develop our plan for the world if we had been subjected to the lights of publicity during those years. But, the world is now more sophisticated and prepared to march towards a world government. The supranational sovereignty of an intellectual elite and world bankers is surely preferable to the national auto-determination practiced in past centuries.'

"And you thought that our media was fair and impartial? Citizens, remember what you are seeing in Greece and Spain and remember that we (and most of the world) are headed in the same financial direction. This is not by accident. This is by design. These people want to destroy the sovereignty of the United States by bankrupting it. This can be stopped. Step one is by ending central banking. Thank you for this opportunity."

The applause grew raucous. Bush and Clinton made their closing speeches, but no one was paying attention to them. Bush spoke, then Clinton. When Clinton finished her closing remarks, more polite applause ensued. The three met in the middle and shook hands. This time it wasn't as cordial. They were no longer treating Fitz's vote hope well. After a few minutes of glad-handing, Fitz worked his way backstage and was greeted by Polly.

"That was AMAZING! Jeff has sent me the early results of who won the debate and you are receiving 77% of the vote. He also posed the question to the viewers that if you were on the ballot, which one would they vote for and 70% said that they would vote for you!"

"There is nothing like promising a $10,000 check in return for a vote." Fitz joked. "I assume that the pundits have completely ignored what I said?"

"How did you know? My girls just relayed that they were all talking about Hillary and Jeb. CBS, CNBC, MSNBC, and NBC haven't posted Jeff's post-debate results, although ABC and CNN have.

"They will eventually, portraying me as a loon. That's what I get for dumping on the CFR. The good news is that people actually seem ready for a change. How is the write-in process going?"

"We have filed in about twenty-five states and we should be done in at all thirty-six states by the end of the week."

"You already filed in twenty-five states?"

"I arranged to have the filings take place at the close of business today. As you can see, since you are a write-in, no word leaked out. I have you booked on the Alex Jones show. Your twitter account is exploding. Alex Jones, Jesse Ventura, Judge Napolitano, and Ron Paul have all said really nice things about your performance."

"What if I bombed tonight?"

"I knew you would be awesome."

Even though the mainstream media was ignoring Fitz like you would your crazy aunt when she said something embarrassing at the Thanksgiving dinner table, all of America was talking about his performance. College students liked it because it was a totally different voice than the establishment. To that end, a link was sent to Fitz's account that showed a group of people congregated at a bar in Harvard Square to watch the debate, with some unimpressed young ruffians from Medford, MA – or at least that's what their apparel advertised. "Where does this guy think he is coming from?"

A student, who looked the part of a Harvard political science major responded, "From the right, and you should never end your question with a preposition."

"All right, where does this guy think he is coming from, asshole?!"

Many who had recorded the debate were replaying Fitz's statement about repealing the Federal Reserve Act and retiring the debt. Could he actually do that? Would that work? The populace was downright frustrated with the fact that all of the post-debate commentary surrounded Clinton and Bush. People were channel surfing to see what commentators were saying about Fitz and his plan to retire the debt, but maddeningly could not find any. His twitter account exploded to north of 38,000,000. He was now more popular than Kim Kardashian West. The cold shoulder would end when Polly sent out a tweet that Fitz was running for the President of the United States as a write-in candidate and that you could see Fitz's entire platform at his site Fitz2016.com. In addition to his platform, the site listed his upcoming appearances on different media, and instructed voters on how to "write-in" Fitz in each state. He also apologized to the voters in the fourteen states in which he would not be a write-in nominee.

Chapter 30 (AMA, FDA)

Most of you don't know (or care) how George Washington died. He had a sore throat, so he and a few allopathic doctors decided it was good idea to blood let. Approximately three pints were removed. In an already weakened state, the allopathic practitioners at his bed side decided to administer 650mg of mercury, which proved fatal. He died of heavy metal poisoning.

President Garfield was not killed by the debt-based banking cabal, as some claim. He was killed by incompetent doctors who unsanitarily poked and prodded at the non-fatal gunshot wound in his back until he developed a terrible infection that brought on pneumonia and heart issues. He died two and half months after being shot by a delusional Charles Guiteau.

Morris Fishbein, a man most of you never knew, is probably responsible for as many unnecessary early deaths as Joe Stalin.

Back in the 1800s there were two types of medical care practiced in the United States. The type described above is allopathic, or "rational" [how so?], which employs surgery, drugs, and bloodletting. Bloodletting has been phased out, but radio therapy has since been added to the allopathic protocol. Allopathic medicine attempts to force the disease out of the body. The other type is homeopathy, which was the creation of a doctor named Christian Hahnemann in the late eighteenth century. Homeopaths employed the use of non-toxic, natural herbs to stimulate the body's own immune system to return the body to normal health. Midway through the nineteenth century, homeopaths outnumbered allopathic doctors two to one.

In 1847, an allopathic trade group was formed with the purpose of establishing uniform standards for medical education, training, and practice. It was called the American Medical Association. Outwardly, it was a noble pursuit with the end game of instilling more confidence in the American public regarding allopathic medicine. Its real goal was to drive the homeopaths out of business. As Dr. J.N. McCormack of the AMA accurately stated, "…we have never fought the homeopath on matters of principle. We fought him because he came into our community and got the business." They employed different methods of subterfuge, from falsely claiming that French homeopaths were giving up on the practice in 1867, to suppressing reports – also perpetrated by its sister organization, the British AMA -- like the study done on a 1854 cholera outbreak in Great Britain that showed one out of every two cholera patients died at allopathic hospitals as compared to one in six at homeopathic hospitals. However, as the 19th century drew to a close, the allopathic practitioners were still losing out to the homeopaths.

That all changed when John D. Rockefeller entered the scene in the early 1900s. Wealthy beyond anyone's wildest imagination, Rockefeller hired Fredrick T. Gates in 1892 to start giving his money away. However, this philanthropic activity was a front to increase his wealth and more importantly, the Rockefeller family power. This can be best seen through his domination of the American medical education system. Gates and Rockefeller founded The Rockefeller Institute for Medical Research (now known as Rockefeller University) in June 1901. Its first director was Simon Flexner, who supervised the development of research capacity at the Institute. This institute worked closely with the Carnegie Foundation in the field of medical research. The timing of the formation of these entities was perfect for the editor of the *Journal of the American Medical Association*, Dr. George H. Simmons, who took over in 1899. He thought that there were too many practicing physicians. "The growth of the profession must be stemmed if individual members are to find the practice of [allopathic] medicine a lucrative profession." In 1907, he asked the Carnegie Foundation to produce a study of all of the country's medical schools. This study was conducted by Abraham Flexner, brother of Simon. Completed in 1910, the report was a stinging rebuke of the medical school system. Most schools were not teaching sound medicine, which according to Flexner, was the allopathic method. This isn't surprising considering that his study was requested by the AMA and financed by owners of pharmaceutical concerns. Also not surprisingly, Flexner found his alma mater, Johns Hopkins University, an allopathic school founded in 1893, to be the model to which all other medical schools should aspire. His report was music to both Rockefeller's and Simmons's ears.

For the AMA, Flexner called for a culling of the herd as it related to the medical profession. This was to be accomplished two ways. First, physicians would be required to complete at least two years – and in most instances, four years -- of undergraduate education, followed by four years of medical school – by no means an evil stipulation. The cost of school and the investment of time would act as a deterrent for aspiring practitioners. Second, medical schools were required to have laboratories, medical equipment, and a teaching staff big enough to teach four years' of medicine. Many schools could not afford these preconditions and would have to be closed.

For Mr. Rockefeller and the AMA, Flexner called for the allopathic method – this was referred to as a "scientific" approach versus the homeopaths that practiced an empirical approach of observation and experience -- to be sole doctrine taught at these schools, as it was at Johns Hopkins. The difference between the allopathic approach, supported by Flexner's study, and the homeopathic method was that the treatments used by the allopathic physicians could be patented, whereas the treatments endorsed by the homeopaths were from nature, and could not be patented. In other words, there was no money in the homeopathic approach. Rockefeller Foundation's philanthropic endeavor could exploit the allopathic approach to increase its own wealth and power.

Following the recommendations of the Flexner Report, Rockefeller, through his General Education Board, donated millions to medical schools throughout the country. In return, he placed members of his General Education Board, his Medical Institute, or the Rockefeller Foundation – formed in 1913 – on the boards of these medical schools. In this way he could insure that the allopathic approach would be taken by the schools, and a curriculum of employing drugs to force disease out of the human body would be the required teaching. If your school taught homeopathic principles, it would not be the beneficiary of Rockefeller's money and it would not be recognized by the suddenly powerful AMA. In return, the Rockefeller interests bought up a controlling interest in many of the drug companies allowing them to profit from their force-fed paradigm. This report proved to be the death knell for homeopathy. At the time of the report there were 155 medical schools in the country. By 1935, the number had been reduced to 66. With the industry-changing educational standards and licensing regulations, the last school in the U.S. exclusively teaching homeopathy closed in 1920. By 1940, 1,500 chiropractors were prosecuted as "quacks".

From the origin of the Flexner Report on forward, the AMA has protected its allopathic turf with the ruthlessness of the gestapo. One example of this vindictiveness towards the homeopaths is in the area of cancer. Anytime a promising homeopathic alternative started making inroads with patients, the AMA set out to destroy the treatment's and the healer's credibility. God forbid, any cures hit the marketplace. If it did, there would be one less disease for allopathic practitioners to treat with prescription drugs -- $135 billion annually out its and Big Pharma's pockets in the United States alone.

The paradigm regarding cancer is the same as it was sixty-five years ago. It is called molecular theory. That is, cancer is a group of over one hundred diseases characterized by abnormal, uncontrolled cell growth. The cancer cells are unstructured masses of tissue known as neoplasms, more commonly referred to as tumors. Most deaths are caused when those cancerous cells metastasize – in other words, tumor cells enter the circulatory system and take up a home in another part of the body. Most of the research in the second half of the twentieth century has focused on isolating the triggering mechanism in the cell that causes the abnormal, uncontrollable growth.

With the mapping of the human genome, research has now also focused on isolating those genes that may be responsible for different types of cancer. This may be a promising avenue, but it is sure to be a profitable one for the pharmaceutical companies with each cancer patient – 1,658,370 new ones projected in the United States during 2015 – potentially receiving a customized regiment of drugs in line with its human genome. Still, the only approved oncology treatments are surgery, chemotherapy, and radio therapy; two of which are carcinogenic amongst other side effects. According to a meta-analysis (with over 227,000 patients) conducted in Australia and the United States and published in 2004 in *Clinical Oncology*:

> "The overall contribution of curative and adjuvant cytotoxic chemotherapy to 5-year survival in adults was estimated to be 2.3% in Australia and 2.1% in the USA. ... Conclusion ... To justify the continued funding and availability of drugs used in cytotoxic chemotherapy, a rigorous evaluation of the cost effectiveness and impact on quality of life is urgently required. ..."

Yet, all the scientists studying these phenomena have yet to isolate a triggering mechanism and there is no proof that the genetics is the cause of cancer.

With this dismal record against cancer, the question should be asked, "Why haven't alternatives treatments been approved?" The answer, of course lies in the money. Since drug companies can't patent natural remedies, it isn't going to spend $20 million testing something that it not only can't sell exclusively, but also may destroy the revenues from a whole class of its drugs. The FDA, for its part, won't allow anything to be prescribed that hasn't been approved as safe or effective. This paradox insulates the drug companies from a potential cure from ever being approved.

Getting back to the early twentieth century, once the AMA seized control, an aggressive marketing campaign was initiated to associate homeopaths with quackery. In 1922, Rene Caisse, a nurse in Bracebridge, Ontario was curing people of cancer with a mixture of herbs that was the invention of a medicine man from a local Indian tribe. The four main herbs that comprised the solution were Burdock Root, Slippery Elm Inner Bark, Sheep Sorrel, and Indian Rhubarb Root. After initial success, she opened up her own clinic treating people with this herb mixture called Essiac – her name spelled backwards. News of her cure spread. In 1934, the town donated a building so she could set up a clinic, where she cured people of cancer for eight and a half years. The clinic was always full with patients. Caisse treated 300 to 600 patients a week. There was a catch, however: she had to treat the people free of charge and there had to be a doctor's diagnosis for the patients to receive the treatment.

Word of her success traveled to Dr. Richard A. Leonardo, a cancer surgeon in Buffalo, New York. He went to the Caisse's clinic to investigate. He told Caisse that she did indeed have a cure, but "the medical profession will not allow you to do this to us." Soon thereafter, a group of businessmen arrived at the clinic and offered Caisse one million dollars for the cure. She refused as they would not guarantee that her cure would be provided free of charge to anyone in need. She tried to have her cure "legalized" by the Ontario legislature in 1938. She acquired 55,000 signatures on a petition. Despite overwhelming beneficial evidence, the legislature declined it by three votes. As it turned out the Canadian

Medical Association had convinced enough members of the legislature that if the bill was not passed they would then sponsor the appointment of a "Cancer Commission" to hear Rene's case and to give Essiac a "fair" hearing. On December 31, 1939, the Commission into the Investigation of Cancer Remedies issued its report on Essiac:

> "After careful examination of all the evidence submitted and analyzed herewith and, not forgetting the fact that the patients, or a number of them, who came before the Commission, felt they had been benefitted by the treatment which they had received, the Commission is of the opinion that the evidence adduced does not justify any favourable conclusion as to the merits of ESSIAC as a remedy for cancer and would so report."

The number of patients that were willing to testify before the commission numbered over 380. The commission limited the number of patient testimonies to 49 and then used that as evidence that there weren't many patients willing to testify. The commission, comprised of CMA members, then discredited most of the 49 testimonies with incredible nonsense such as the patient was "cured by surgery" when the only invasive procedure involved the biopsy to determine whether or not the patient had cancer, or proclaiming the patient never had cancer and had been misdiagnosed. The commission, in short, was a sham, proving Dr. Leonardo's prediction correct. Caisse kept the clinic open, but no doctors were allowed to send patients to her clinic, and since she was forbidden to provide Essiac without a doctor's diagnosis, she eventually closed in 1942. She then started to treat people covertly in her basement. When word spread, the authorities started harassing her, arresting her on more than one occasion.

Finally, a clinic in Massachusetts decided to study the effects of Essiac in 1958. The study was conducted by Dr. Charles Brush, who was JFK's personal physician. He said it was non-toxic and efficacious and recommended that it be tested for toxicity so it could be approved by the FDA as a cancer cure. However, when Essiac was brought to Sloan-Kettering for study it was bogged down in bureaucratic delays and doublespeak and was never thoroughly tested. To this day, no extensive clinical studies have been performed to determine conclusive evidence that Rene Caisse's herbal formula will alleviate, cure or prevent any disease or condition. Ms. Caisse continued to treat patients in her basement until her death in 1978. On her ninetieth birthday, busloads of patients whom she had cured came up to Bracebridge to thank Rene one more time. You can find Essiac on line.

Then there is the fascinating story of Harry Hoxsey. On his deathbed, Hoxsey's father passed along to him a cure for cancer that his veterinarian father – Harry's grandfather -- had discovered when he put his prize stallion out to pasture. The horse had been diagnosed with cancer. Harry's grandfather noticed that the horse would eat flowers and other plants not part of its normal diet. He noticed that the horse's health stopped declining in three weeks; and within a year, the horse was cancer free. The horse had essentially cured itself. Harry's grandfather gathered up the herbs that the horse used to cure itself and created a compound that he passed along to his son, who was the first to start administering it to humans. On his deathbed, he told his son Harry to make the remedy available to all, even those who couldn't afford it. Because of Hoxsey's wealth and tenacity, the stage was set for a fight with the AMA and its chief, Morris Fishbein. Harry Hoxsey started treating people at his Hoxsey Clinic in Taylorville, Illinois during 1924 with the herbal remedy. Once he announced his findings of efficacy – calling it a cure – the AMA labeled him, "the worst cancer quack of the century". He was arrested more times than any man in medical history, mostly for practicing without a license. Undeterred, Hoxsey got a license for naturopathy and set up clinics in seventeen states, and by the 1950s, the Hoxsey Clinic in Dallas, Texas was the largest privately owned cancer center in the world. His treatment was endorsed by senators and some doctors. Two federal courts upheld its therapeutic value.

James Wakefield Burke was assigned the task by *Esquire* magazine of doing a story to discredit Hoxsey in 1939. *Esquire* was told by the AMA that a charlatan was in their mist and must be stopped. He went to Dallas to visit the clinic. He planned to stay one day. He ended up staying six weeks. He was stunned by what he saw: sick people were entering, and very healthy people were leaving. He outlined a piece entitled, "The Quack Who Cured Cancer". The piece was never published.

It gets better. Assistant District Attorney Al Templeton had Hoxsey arrested more than one hundred times over a two year period. Then his brother, Mike, came down with cancer. Mike secretly went to

Hoxsey. Mike Templeton got well. Al Templeton gave Hoxsey credit for his brother's turnaround. Hoxsey's prosecutor switched teams and became his defense attorney. Hoxsey begged for any federal authority to come down and assess his treatment:

> "All I want is to have them come here – the American Medical Association, the…Food and Drug, the federal government, anybody! Come here and make an investigation, and if I don't prove to them beyond any question of a doubt that our treatment is superior to radium x-ray and surgery, then I will lock the doors of this institution forever."

Hoxsey said that the AMA doctors, including *Journal of the American Medical Association* editor Morris Fishbein, had previously invited him to demonstrate the treatment. Dr. Malcolm Harris, an eminent Chicago surgeon and later president of the AMA, at the behest of Fishbein, offered to buy out the Hoxsey remedy after watching Hoxsey successfully treat a terminal patient. Hoxsey would get ten percent of the profits, according to the offer, but only after ten years. The AMA would set the fees, keep all the profits for the first nine years, and then reap ninety percent of the profits from the tenth year on. The alleged offer would have given all control to a group of doctors, including AMA boss Dr. Morris Fishbein. Just like Rene Caisse, Hoxsey wanted a guarantee that it would be made available to the public for free to anyone who needed it. The AMA declined.

At that point, Fishbein used his position as editor to label Hoxsey a quack. Well financed, Hoxsey and Fishbein had a very public spat for twenty-five years. Hoxsey went to the National Cancer Institute asking them to investigate his therapy, but they refused saying that his records were incomplete. The records were incomplete because Fishbein influenced doctors not to supply the medical records on his patients. Government officials deemed that it would be a waste of tax payer dollars to investigate. Hoxsey upped the ante by offering to pay for the investigation himself. This essentially painted Fishbein into a corner. In 1949, he countered by writing a derogatory article about Hoxsey for the Hearst papers entitled, "Blood Money". Hoxsey sued both Fishbein and the Hearst papers for libel and slander. Fishbein, who failed anatomy in medical school and never practiced medicine a day in his life, admitted in court that Hoxsey's treatment actually did cure external cancer, such as melanoma. Hoxsey became the first person to win a judgement against Fishbein and the AMA – albeit for $2. As a result, Fishbein was forced to resign from the AMA.

Then in 1953, Congressman Charles Tobey enlisted Benedict Fitzgerald, an investigator for the Interstate Commerce Commission, to investigate allegations of conspiracy and monopolistic practices on the part of orthodox medicine. The Fitzgerald Report concluded that organized medicine had "conspired" to suppress the Hoxsey therapy and at least a dozen other promising cancer treatments. Harry's clinic in Dallas now had 12,000 patients. Hoxsey then produced his own movie about his anti-cancer tonic and asked for the government to investigate. Instead, remarkably, with the AMA feckless in its crusade against Hoxsey, the FDA took over the fight.

First, in 1957 it issued notices in all of the post offices stating, "PUBLIC BEWARE!" Underneath it stated (among other things) that, "the Hoxsey treatment for internal cancers has been found worthless by two federal courts." The FDA claimed that it had reviewed all of Hoxsey's records and determined that there was not one documented case of a cure – an obviously blatant lie. Despite the inability of prosecutors to prove that the Hoxsey treatment was ineffective, the FDA claimed Hoxsey was allowing his "untested, potentially unsafe drug" to cross state lines to his various clinics in the different states without legal permission. That violated Interstate Commerce laws. The FDA padlocked his clinics in September 1960. Hoxsey was wealthy, but he did not have the money to go to court in seventeen states. The government had finally won. The ultimate irony is that Hoxsey came down with prostate cancer in 1967. He didn't respond to his own treatment and eventually elected surgery. He died in 1974. Anyone who is stupid enough to state that Hoxsey's physical demise is proof his treatment didn't work, should check in with the 25,000+ patients he cured. To be sure, not everyone who entered his clinic was miraculously cured. Remember, many patients seek alternatives after the allopathic methods have failed, and their immune system has been ravaged by chemo and radiation. These were the patients that the FDA and AMA claimed Hoxsey was killing with his "dangerous" potion. Effectively neutered in the United States, Hoxsey's head nurse, Mildred Nelson – whose mother was cured of uterine cancer by Hoxsey and lived to ninety-nine after the AMA doctors sent her home to die -- crossed the border to Tijuana, Mexico to set up a clinic – with Hoxsey's money -- outside of FDA authority, which is still in operation today.

When Rene Caisse turned ninety, patients that she had cured came from all over Canada by the busload to pay their respects. When Harry Hoxsey was arrested – a very frequent occurrence – his patients would sometimes surround the prison until he was released. It is hard to imagine this type of patient devotion if their methods of treatment weren't effective.

The next cancer cure up for forbearance by the AMA and Morris Fishbein is the Gerson Method. Max Gerson was a German-born physician who had trouble with migraines. He experimented with a diet of raw foods eventually leading to relief from his migraines. He started prescribing this diet for his patients with migraines when one of his patients informed him that it had cured his skin tuberculosis. He then started prescribing the diet for patients with skin tuberculosis. Word of his treatment spread, which attracted the attention of a curious Dr. Ferdinand Sauerbruch. Sauerbruch and Gerson set up a clinical trial that included 450 patients at the Munich University Hospital in 1924. Of the 450 patients, 446 were cured, resulting in the first ever cure for skin tuberculosis.

These results attracted the attention of Nobel Prize winning Dr. Albert Schweitzer. Schweitzer sent his wife, who had lung tuberculosis, to Gerson. He was able to cure her after all conventional methods had failed. Gerson's dietary therapy progressed into heart disease, kidney failure, and type II diabetes. Gerson was able to cure Dr. Schweitzer of his type II diabetes. His next frontier was cancer. With Nazism on the rise, Gerson immigrated to the United States where he became a certified physician in 1938. For twenty years, he received and treated cancer patients who were sent home to die after conventional methods had failed. The treatment aims to detoxify the body through a series of intestinal cleanses, which returns the body to a state where the immune system is no longer compromised and the body can heal itself. This is accomplished through a diet of organic coffee and raw fruits and vegetables. Meats, under this regiment, are strictly forbidden.

His success treating terminally ill patients was such that he was invited to testify – along with five of his patients -- before the Pepper-

Neely Congressional Subcommittee, during hearings on a bill to fund research into cancer treatment. This took place on July 1 - 3, 1946. So convincing was his testimony, that ABC news correspondent Raymond Graham Swing declared on his radio broadcast on the evening of July 3rd that for the first time in history, there was a cure for cancer. This announcement created an overwhelming response from the population -- and a swift reaction from the AMA. Morris Fishbein was already in a protracted struggle with Dr. Gerson over his claims that smoking was bad for health. Fishbein would have none of it since cigarette manufacturers were the number one advertiser in the *Journal of the American Medical Association.* (In fact, Camel used to advertise that "More Doctors Smoke Camels".) For his radio message, thirty year correspondent Swing was fired from his post two weeks later. The Pepper-Nelly Anti-Cancer Bill died without a vote. The committee report of 227 pages, Document No. 89471 was suppressed by Congress. When Don C. Matchan of the *Herald of Health Magazine* asked for a copy of the document, he was informed by a senator's office and by the Superintendent of Documents that there were no more copies left. [Copies do exist.] Gerson was labeled a quack and investigated by the AMA. Again, the same nonsense was put forth: there are no clinical trials [yes, but the AMA won't allow any]; and some of his patients die [yes, but they usually show up after they have exhausted all of the conventional methods and are sent home to die. In other words, they are on death's doorstep when they seek Dr. Gerson's remedy.] The real reason for deriding Gerson, of course, was that a cure meant fewer visits to the doctor, and nutritional therapies could not be patented by the drug industry.

Gerson went on to write a book about his treatment and documented cases. The original draft was stolen and had to be re-written from scratch. The book, *A Cancer Therapy: Results of Fifty Cases* (1958), which detailed the findings of thirty years of clinical experimentation, could not find a publisher in the United States. He continued to treat patients with his forbidden therapy out of his apartment in Manhattan until his death in 1959. Over one hundred scientific studies regarding the Gerson Therapy exist – almost exclusively out of Europe. Gerson's daughter, Charlotte, opened the Gerson Clinic in Mexico to cure people. A Gerson Health Centre was opened during 2009 in Budapest, Hungary.

Medical records are available to anyone who wishes to examine them, but the AMA, the FDA, and Big Pharma aren't interested.

Their mouthpieces continue to denounce the Gerson diet with statements from AMA hacks such as Dr. Dean Edell, "I don't' think Gerson's therapy has ever cured a terminally ill patient. [Have you ever looked at the findings?] People get very confused by this. [No they don't.] If you think of basically what's in Gerson's therapy, you really wouldn't expect it to cure cancer. [Ah, but it does.] But sometimes cancer cures itself. [Yes, after the immune system is repaired to the point where the body can tackle cancer and heal itself, which is what the Gerson diet promotes.] Some people really didn't have cancer. It was a misdiagnosis." [OR, it was cured by the Gerson diet. Go back into your office and continue to kill people with your cut, burn, and poison approach.]

Dr. Wallace Sampson, Emeritus Professor of Clinical Medicine at Stanford University and editor of the rag *Scientific Review of Alternative Medicine and Aberrant Medical Practices* claims that there is no proof that the Gerson method has ever cured anyone because "they won't even release their records". [False.] He also states that, "[Gerson] has to show some reason why it works. [How does a repaired immune system grab you?] We know...how cancers behave, and we know the kind of things that cause cancer. [Then why haven't you cured it?] So they have to come up with some kind of believable theory of why their diet should work [Already have that one covered.], but second of all they would have to convince us that everything we know about it in the past fifty years is wrong, and they're right. Now how are they going to come up with material like that? That's impossible. They don't have it. [Actually, Dr. Sampson, if you pulled your head out of your ass, you would see that over one hundred scientific papers have been published in Europe, but for some reason they aren't published in the United States.]

Then there is the curious case of Dr. Royal Raymond Rife. Rife invented the Universal Prismatic Microscope, which was more effective than electron microscopy for viewing live organisms. He was the first ever to see and photograph live viruses. Rife was able to isolate the frequencies of different disease cells, including cancer. He then broadcast those frequencies back at the cell at a greater intensity – a dissonant frequency -- causing the diseased cell to explode or shatter, like a champagne flute subjected to a high pitched voice. Since the frequencies of healthy cells were different, they were not harmed by Rife's device. By 1934, he had gotten so adept at killing sarcoma and carcinoma in animals that he started curing humans – sixteen in total – that had been declared terminal by conventional means. The Special Research Committee of the University of Southern California confirmed Rife's breakthrough.

Threatened by a potential cure, the AMA and the Rockefeller Institute sprang into action. Dr. Thomas Rivers of the Rockefeller Institute claimed that the grounds for his frequency device, an evolving virus theory which could only be seen under Rife's microscope – not Rivers' electron microscope -- were baseless. Fishbein tried to partner up with Rife in 1934. The terms of the offer are unknown, but given the deal that was offered to Hoxsey, it is easy to see why Rife rejected the overture. Unable to buy him out, the medical authorities made false claims, and multiple lawsuits were brought against Dr. Rife (all of which Rife ultimately won). His lab was ransacked on several occasions and USC's Special Research Committee was disbanded. Marginalized and broke from fighting decades of lawsuits, Rife died in 1971.

Investigative journalist Barry Lynes studied the story of Rife's machine and life, resulting in the publication of a book in 1987 entitled *The Cancer Cure That Worked! Fifty Years of Suppression*. San Diego manufacturer James Folsom took up the cause in 1995 and began manufacturing machines modeled after Rife's research. He claimed to have only satisfied customers, with some testimonials claiming a remission of cancer.

With the reemergence of the Rife device came the reappearance of the health authorities, this time in the form of the FDA. It raided Folsom's home in 2003 under Operation Cure-All, a program to suppress the alternative "quacks". Over 500 instruments as well as many office records were confiscated. He was then arrested in 2007 under charges of selling a medical instrument without a license, except for the fact that Folsom's devices were not medical instruments, but rather biofeedback machines. Even though these machines were in use for seventy years with no harmful side effects, the FDA claimed that the devices were under its jurisdiction, falling under the category of high-voltage medical devices. Some of Folsom's devices were powered by a nine-volt battery. Knowing that the lawsuit was a sham, Folsom was offered a deal to plea to a misdemeanor, pay a $250 fine, and be subjected to one year of unsupervised probation. Knowing that this bogus misdemeanor would ruin his credibility, Folsom went to trial. At the trial, no discussion as to the effectiveness or safety of the devise was allowed, nor were testimonials from satisfied customers permitted. He was convicted by a U.S. Federal Jury on twenty-six counts of fraud against customers, fraud against the government, and misbranding his products. His sentence: 140 years in prison and $500,000 in fines.

How about laetrile? Laetrile, also known as vitamin B17, is found richly in apricot seeds. Without getting too technical, the compound in laetrile, nitriloside, is effective in combating cancer. Certain subsets of people throughout the world don't fall prey to cancer. One such group is the Native American Indian. The AMA actually conducted a special study in an effort to discover why there was little to no cancer amongst the Hopi and Navajo Indians. In the February 5, 1949 issue of the *Journal of the American Medical Association*, the study was published, finding 36 cases of malignant cancer from a population of 30,000. At that time, in the same population of Caucasians, one would expect the number to be about 1,800. Dr. Ernst Krebs research later found that the typical diet for the Navajo and Hopi Indian consisted of nitriloside-rich foods such as Cassava. He calculated that some of the tribes would ingest the equivalent of 8000mg of Vitamin B17 per day from their diet.

In laymen terms, when laetrile comes into contact with a cancer cell, it releases cyanide into the cancerous cells (because of the presence of an enzyme called beta-glucosidase), and leaves healthy cells alone. This is according to the Head of Cytochemistry Research at the National Cancer Institute, Dr. Dean Burk. From his study in 1970, he stated, "When we add laetrile to a cancer culture under the microscope, we can see the cancer cells dying off like flies." Burk would later say of the American Cancer Society, "They lie like scoundrels."

Sloan-Kettering also endorsed the safety and efficacy of laetrile – at least for a short time. Dr. Kanematsu Sugiura was conducting research on laetrile at Sloan-Kettering when he declared that laetrile was more effective in the control of cancer than any substance that he had ever tested. Sugiura concluded in a 1977 magazine interview that laetrile inhibited the growth of tumors, relieved pain, and improved general health.

Sugiura was no "quack". He was one of the foremost cancer researchers in the world. Facing another cancer cure that could threaten its *raison d'être*, Sloan-Kettering pressured Sugiura to retract his statements. He refused. Sloan-Kettering was forced to release a bogus press statement claiming that, "laetrile was found to possess neither preventative...nor curative anticancer activity." However, Sloan-Kettering PR man, Ralph Moss (and his group of colleagues known as Second Opinion), decided not to sit idly by while his employer lied. In July 1977, Moss exposed the truth about Sloan Kettering's conduct at a highly publicized press conference. The next business day he was fired and swiftly escorted to the door by armed guards. Moss has written a book about this incident called *Doctored Results*.

Dr. John A. Richardson had a clinic in the San Francisco area where he was treating cancer patients. Fed up with poor results, he met with Dr. Ernst Krebs Jr. and discussed his "trophoblast theory", which states that cancers arose and grew from a lack of enough pancreatic enzymes – molecular theory isn't the only cancer theory – and the application of laetrile. Richardson began to use it on his patients with excellent results. Word spread and people started arriving at the clinic from all over the country to be treated by Dr. Richardson. He quickly incurred the wrath of the medical authorities because the FDA had not approved laetrile. He protested that it worked and didn't care whether it was approved. He was told that the FDA didn't care that it was efficacious, only that it wasn't approved and he was in violation of the law. Dr. Richardson published a book entitled, *Laetrile Case Histories: The Richardson Cancer Clinic Experience*, which details his patients' experiences and his fight with orthodox medicine.

To be sure, the National Cancer Institute finally agreed in 1980 to test laetrile on 178 advanced cancer patients. These tests were conducted at four major U.S. medical centers, including the Mayo Clinic and Sloan Kettering. *Public Scrutiny*, a medical freedom of choice publication, maintained that these biased trials were designed to fail when it was discovered that 66% of participants were already ravaged from chemotherapy treatments and the laetrile used was of poor quality, containing little or no nitriloside. The FDA used this bogus trial as another opportunity to smear laetrile, posting 10,000 "Laetrile Warning" placards in post offices. Laetrile is still listed as a toxic substance, illegal to sell in the United States [yet chemo and radiation are known carcinogens.]. Jason Vale, who was cured by eating laetrile rich apricot seeds, was arrested and sentenced to five years in prison for peddling apricot seeds in 2003. In the ultimate irony, he was accused of profiting from desperate cancer victims.

Are you getting the idea? An entire book could be written just about this one avenue of deceit conducted by the American medical establishment – and for that matter, the worldwide medical cabal. Similar stories can be written about the anti-angiogenesis qualities of shark cartilage, which the pharmaceutical companies are trying to replicate in the lab so it can be patented; iscador, an herbal remedy from mistletoe that cured Suzanne Sommers; Dr. Tullio Simoncini and his fungal theory of cancer treated by sodium bicarbonate; antineoplaston therapy by Dr. Stanislaw Burzynski; parasitic theory by Hulda Regehr Clark; or Dr. Ryke Geerd Hamer and his theory that cancer is the result of a deep psychological trauma that could not be resolved completely by the individual. These are just some of many that merit further investigation. In every instance, despite strong evidence to the contrary, the doctor is discredited and labeled a quack, and in many cases stripped of his or her right to practice medicine. No studies are allowed to be conducted or are suppressed and the lack of studies/evidence is cited by the FDA, or some medical authority, as to why a potential cure cannot be allowed into the marketplace.

Do not think for one second that the AMA, ACS, FDA and other agencies have your health in mind when they act like the Nazi SS in stamping out "alternative medicine". They don't care about you. With more people living off degenerative disease, than dying of it, all the top medical and pharmaceutical executives worry about is their industry vanishing before their eyes if cures become more widely known and accessible. If that were to occur, what would come of the healthcare trade and to those cottage industries that have grown up around raising money for cancer cures? Who cares! Just remember when you wear your pink ribbons and donate your time and money for a "cure", your charity is going to organizations that look at disease as a business model! Save your money, it's already been cured. Did you ever ask why your government agencies aren't as vigilant at stopping companies from releasing carcinogens into the environment? If they were, there would not be as many degenerative diseases to treat with pharmaceuticals. For the avoidance of doubt, there are many real diseases (such as type I diabetes), and many of you have been cured of cancer through surgery, radiation, and chemotherapy; most have not. However, when one of the therapies approved by the AMA is 98% ineffective, it is time to investigate alternatives. Remember, that 98% figure originates from the 2004 *Clinical Oncology* study. According to the lead epidemiologist from that study, those numbers still apply today. If you believe that cutting, burning, and poisoning are the only effective treatments out there to combat cancer, and if a real cure existed, you would know about it, because it would have to get out, wake up and follow the money.

One example of this media censorship occurred in 2012. Dr. Gilles-Éric Séralini published research findings in the peer-reviewed *Journal of Food and Chemical Toxicology* that demonstrated the toxic impact of Monsanto's herbicide and genetically modified corn on lab rats. However, after the article was published, the journal made the unprecedented move of retracting the article, even though the established criteria for such a move were not met. As it turns out, the article was retracted by the publication after it hired Richard E. Goodman to fill a newly created position of associate editor of biotechnology. Goodman, who worked for Monsanto from 1997 to 2004, was responsible for the retraction. The mainstream media elected not to cover this story on any level. Do you know why?

The answer might lie in another story involving investigative reporters Jane Akre and Steve Wilson. They were employed by WTVT-TV in Tampa, Florida and were tasked with doing hard-hitting stories for the station. One of their first stories involved Monsanto's bovine growth hormone (rBST), commercially known as Posilac. According to Akre and Wilson, the only toxicity study performed involved thirty rats for ninety days. And that study proved very worrisome. The report concluded that the hormone could be absorbed by the body and did have implications for human health. Somehow that conclusion was deleted from the public version of its findings. Canada did not allow it into its borders, which was no small accomplishment. Health Canada scientist, Dr. Shiv Chopra described being "pressured and coerced to pass drugs of questionable safety, including rBST."

Akre and Wilson were prepared to air the story on Monday, February 24, 1997. The station advertised the story – and that proved to be a mistake. Monsanto contacted the station through its legal representation stating its strong concern over the airing of the story. The Fox affiliate decided to hold off on the story. The following week Monsanto threatened "dire consequences" for Fox News if the story was aired in Florida. Fearing lawsuits and the loss of advertising revenue, Fox News caved and decided not to air the story. Akre and Wilson protested. They were told by their superior, "We just paid $3 billion for these television stations. We'll tell you what the news is." Their superior then offered the two reporters the balance of their salaries for the year if they left the station and signed a confidentiality agreement which would not allow them to discuss the story or the station's suppression of the story. They refused but Fox made the mistake of sending them the confidentiality agreement which Akre and Wilson used as leverage over the station. The station, now caught between a rock and a hard place, said to Akre and Wilson that they would run the story with some re-edits. The story was then re-edited *83 times* over eight months before the story was killed. Akre and Wilson were fired. They sued the Fox affiliate under the Whistleblower Protection Act. Akre received a $425,000 ruling from the jury that determined that Fox "acted intentionally and deliberately to falsify or distort the plaintiffs' news reporting on BGH." In that decision, the jury also found that Jane's threat to blow the whistle on Fox's misconduct to the FCC was the sole reason for the termination. Fox appealed and amazingly won when the appeals court determined, "We agree with WTVT that the FCC's policy against the intentional falsification of the news -- which the FCC has called its 'news distortion policy' -- does not qualify as the required "law, rule, or regulation" under section 448.102." In other words, it's not against the law to falsify the news so Akre couldn't sue under the whistleblower act. Remember decades ago, when comedians would joke about the propaganda for news that Pravda produced? You say in can't happen here? It is. Follow the money.

That money trail ends at the Rockefeller "philanthropic" endeavors and its obliged blood sucking agencies such as the AMA, FDA, ACS, and leading hospitals like Memorial Sloan-Kettering. These foundations, agencies, and hospitals are supposed to protect the patient, but instead, regrettably and criminally, protect the industry. Nixon's "War on Cancer"

211

turned into a war on anyone with a natural cancer cure. Thanks to Morris Fishbein, the Flexner Report, the Rockefeller interests, Big Food, the sugar industry, Big Pharma, and their aggressive media campaigns, you are brainwashed into believing that the person with the white lab jacket knows what he is talking about and that the government is looking out for you. Your physician only knows what the AMA and Big Pharma want him or her to know and your government isn't looking out for you. Do you know how many hours of nutrition – never mind health and wellness, but just nutrition – your American doctor gets in medical school? Answer: very little. Only 25% of accredited medical schools even require a course on the subject. As a result of this 'conspiracy', the U.S. population is rapidly becoming a pathetic hodgepodge of obese, overmedicated zombies to be molded like clay by those plotting your demise. 70% of you are overweight and 30% of you are obese. Your overall health is declining, and you continue to lose the battle against cancer and other degenerative diseases. Keep sipping on that venti caramel macchiato with its 40 grams of sugar. You can sip on it at the doctor's office.

The sad part about all of these cures is that most of them would not be necessary if you learned that an ounce of prevention is worth a pound of cure. All degenerative diseases, at the end of the day, are the result of immune suppression. If your white blood cells are hard at work trying to remove mercury from your pancreas, your immune system becomes compromised. If you prevent your body from being bombarded with insult upon insult and if you cleanse out those immune compromising insults (heavy metals, azo dyes, etc.) that have already taken up a home in your body, degenerative disease and the need for a cure would be greatly diminished.

Chapter 31 (October 2016)

Fitz's announcement forced the mainstream media to change tactics. With articles flooding the internet blogosphere, his Fitz2016.com website receiving millions of hits, his twitter account tweeting, and references to his performance in the debate and subsequent candidacy being mentioned on unrelated media such as Sports Center, the networks and the newspapers could no longer marginalize Cavendish by ignoring him. It was as if they were the only ones not talking about his candidacy. As a result, the denigration machine needed to be kicked into overdrive: if you can't kill the message, destroy the messenger's credibility.

The challenge facing the mainstream media was two-fold: 1. they had spent the past few months hoisting Fitz upon their collective shoulders. Any smear campaign would likely backfire on the mainstream media, calling into question its own integrity. 2. There wasn't any dirt on Fitz. If there was, nobody was coming forward with it. Even the cheap and easy attack on his vice-presidential selection ("How could he have someone with no political experience so close to highest post in the land?") was hollow since Fitz also had no political experience. This left the media to dismantle his platform issue by issue. Actuating engagement consisted of marching "experts" on the economy, banking, foreign affairs, and healthcare in front of the American people explaining the ridiculousness of Cavendish's platform.

Fitz didn't pay any mind to the mainstream media – he left that up to Polly. He had an engagement on Sunday in Austin, Texas with Alex Jones. *The Alex Jones Show* syndicated radio program is broadcast nationally by the Genesis Communications Network weekdays live from 11am – 2-pm CST and Sunday live 4pm – 6pm CST. Jones, a known libertarian and conspiracy theorist, is best known in the non-conspiracy circles for his January 2013 tirade directed at Piers Morgan on *Piers Morgan Live* regarding gun control, amongst other topics. It was one of the show's most memorable episodes. As for Jones' own program, because he appeals to the younger generation and embraces the technology, he has a larger on-line audience than Glenn Beck or Rush Limbaugh. Fitz was scheduled for the entire two hours, with health and wellness dominating the first half, with a caller Q & A session scheduled for the balance.

Jones: "Good afternoon. We are honored to have on the show, leading presidential candidate, Fitzgerald Cavendish. First of all, I want to thank you for getting the message out to the masses with that performance in the debate. Your plan to get yourself on the dais was brilliant, but not as brilliant as your message. The most encouraging outcome is your standing in the polls. Secondly, I want to thank you for appearing on the show."

Cavendish: "The honor is mine. I've been a big fan of your effort to get the message out to the masses and am thankful for the opportunity to talk about my platform in greater detail with your listeners. I'm sure we will have minor differences of opinion on many matters, but the important thing is that we are always in search of the truth."

Jones: "Amen to that. I know that one of the areas you covered briefly in the debate was the healthcare system. To be clear, you are for some form of socialized medicine, but your plan includes choice."

Cavendish: "I do believe that every person should have access to healthcare, whether he can afford it or not. And on this point I differ from say a Ron Paul, who argues that it should be exclusively in private hands. I am a big believer in choice. You can go to a private doctor or you can go to a government sponsored hospital or clinic. Obviously, a bureaucracy has to be put in place for the government sponsored part of the program, which shouldn't make anyone happy, but I consider it a necessary evil. The much bigger issue Alex is the fact that this country is so mislead by the food producers and the medical establishment. All you have to do is watch the TV commercials to see that something is amiss. You have a fast food commercial, which pushes crap that is processed and by definition, not really food. This food, as demonstrated by the movie, *Supersize Me*, will make you sick. So you have to go to the doctor and get a prescription to mask your sickness. That is commercial number two: Big Pharma is pushing some garbage that has ten side effects but will cover-up – not cure – your original problem. Because of some unforeseen horrible side effect, you have commercial number three, which is some law firm telling you that you are eligible for money if something horrible happened to you or a loved one as a result of taking a certain prescription medication. That in a nutshell is our healthcare economy, and it is a joke."

Jones: "And this has its origins with the Rockefellers."

Cavendish: "It does, since they financed all of the medical schools in the first half of the twentieth century on the condition that the institutions teach the allopathic method, which includes prescribing patented drugs. The Rockefeller interests bought stock in companies such as Sterling Drug and Squibb back in the day, thus profiting from their philanthropic pursuits. However, many of the health issues today go back to a report in the 1977, called the McGovern Report, which said that the recent surge in obesity (back then) was due to us consuming too many fats. Whether there was any malicious intent is unknown to me, but the result of that report, which became government policy, had us consuming foods with less fat. Since fat gives many foods their "taste", sugar was substituted and foods were labeled as "low-fat". However, this entire paradigm is completely wrong, and should be reversed. Then in 1992, the U.S. Department of Agriculture published its Food Pyramid imploring that carbs are good and fats are bad. These two government sponsored recommendations have done as much to ruin health as the practice of strictly allopathic methods by American doctors. In short, our dietary and medical approaches are completely backward. Once these are reversed, the healthcare crisis in this country will cease to exist."

Jones: "I think that is very well said. Now could you provide for our audience some examples of what you are talking about?"

Cavendish: "Absolutely. Let's start with heart disease and cholesterol. Actually, I should state beforehand -- because I may go straight to hell if I don't -- that I am not a licensed physician and that you should consult with your doctor before you follow any of my regiments. Now back to cholesterol. Every cell in your body needs it to properly function, and it is food for your brain. That is why your cholesterol level should be 200 plus your age, so in my case, it should be around 250. People on statin drugs are 50% more likely to come down with Alzheimer's disease. That is because they are starving their brains of their food source. But since statin drugs provide an annual multiple-eleven-figure revenue stream for the drug industry, you aren't going to hear this from conventional medicine. It all starts with the McGovern Report and the food pyramid which tell us to eat carbs. Fruits and vegetables are good for you and the sugars found in them are what are known as left-rotating sugars, which are good sugars. The rotation is in reference to how the molecule reacts when subjected to light. There are studies being conducted

215

right now indicating that cancers feed off of right-rotating sugars, which are the bleached sugars, high-fructose corn syrup, etc. before they feed off of proteins. These bleached sugars – and for that matter bleached salts and bleached flours – are acidic. If you eat a bag of potato chips, your mouth usually feels sore afterwards. That, in my opinion, is the acidity of the bleached salt entering the bloodstream through the lining in your mouth. Once your blood is subjected to acids, its defense mechanisms go to work. Your kidneys pump out bicarbonate to get the pH level in your blood – which should be at 7.4 – back into balance. Acid in the tissues blocks vitamin absorption, creates toxic buildup in clogged cells, slows organ function, prevents proper digestion, creates excess gas and bloating, causes unhealthy weight gain, and speeds the aging process. Getting back to your defense mechanisms, your liver, the major blood filter, starts to produce low-density lipoproteins – known as bad cholesterol, but really a cholesterol carrying protein -- in response to the blood's acidity. If the blood is acidic – relatively speaking, it doesn't dip below 7 for any meaningful period of time, because if it did, you would die of acidosis – it will wear down the lining of your arterial walls, causing lesions. Also, heavy metals and other foreign substances can enter your bloodstream and tear at your arterial lining. The LDLs will stick to the lesions in your arteries, essentially patching them up, keeping you from bleeding internally. Over time, these "patches" harden and sometimes other LDLs will stick to these patches causing a blockage or a hardening of the arteries. So the problem isn't the consumption of fatty foods – which contain the high-density lipoproteins, the good cholesterol. The problem is the consumption of bleached sugar and acidic carbohydrates. Don't get me wrong, the meats and poultry that we consume, unless organic, are mostly acidic garbage as well. Organic grass fed beef is loaded with healthy Omega-3s. Organic eggs are great for you and they are loaded with cholesterol – food for the brain."

Jones: "That is great stuff. As you well know, the lobbyists for Big Food and Big Pharma write the laws that keep the corporations wealthy and the American consumer misinformed and unhealthy. In the debate you mentioned the elimination of degenerative diseases. You have already mentioned the root causes of heart disease and have touched on Alzheimer's. Are there others out there that you'd like to address?"

Cavendish: "Indeed. I'd like to address two more. Since we are already on the topic of sugar, let's talk about type II diabetes. The unbelievable spike in this disease over the past decades has its origins with the introduction of high-fructose corn syrup into the food supply, the McGovern Report, and later with the food pyramid. Nearly thirty million Americans have type II. In my opinion, type II diabetes is curable through diet and exercise. Muscles at work suck up glucose like a vacuum -- the bigger the muscle group you are working out, the more glucose consumed. The legs and glutes are your biggest muscle groups. But when you are fat, the fat blocks the uptake of the glucose into the muscles. As a result, the sugar stays in your bloodstream, causing elevated blood sugar levels, which will eventually damage your arterial system, especially at the extremities. So if you eliminate fat through proper diet and exercise and build your muscles, especially your leg muscles, you will see a dramatic improvement in your blood sugar levels. But because between the doctor visits, the testing kits, and the drugs, the diabetes industry is a quarter of a trillion dollar a year money maker worldwide, you will be uninformed and medicated with drugs that harm your liver. If you are listening to this broadcast and wish to get off your medication, consult your doctor and get off the meds slowly. Improving one's body mass index is the key to solving the type II riddle. For the avoidance of doubt, type I is a real disease and is a pancreas issue involving damage to the islets of Langerhans, but type II is not a pancreatic issue, it is a body mass index issue.

Jones: "That is really groundbreaking stuff. Where did you learn all of this?"

Cavendish: "I have done a lot of research in this area, but Charles Wahlheim and his book, *The Truth: Claiming Your Birthright to Health* is a great starting point in the area of health and wellness."

Jones: "I will have to look into it. You said that there is another degenerative disease that you would like to address?"

Cavendish: "Yes. Thank you. Cancer is the number two killer in the United States behind heart disease. It is still treated with the cut, burn, and poison approach, otherwise known as surgery, radiation, and chemotherapy. Even though these are the only approved modalities, they have had limited success. Meanwhile, there are close to a dozen others that merit further meaningful investigation. However, these modalities are – for the most part – not patentable and are suppressed by the medical authorities. I will list them shortly. My belief is that the body works through polarity. Cells are either north or south polarized. Your brain and reproductive systems are south polarized; all of your other cells are north polarized. Signals are sent to the brain through the nervous system. When you receive trauma – let's say you cut your hand -- the cells that have been traumatized change polarity, in this instance from north to south. That change in polarity sends a signal to your brain which then has the body produce fibroblasts, otherwise known as stem cells. These stem cells arrive at the point of the trauma to repair the damage done by the cut. Once the cut is fully healed, the cells return to north polarity, which sends a signal to the brain to stop sending down fibroblasts. The process is over.

Now let's say that you use antiperspirant, which contains 25% aluminum. Aluminum is pervasive in our household care products, our water, our vaccines (as a preservative), our processed cheese, our baked goods, and the air that we breathe through chemtrails. It is also very bad for human consumption. For some reason, it is allowed in your antiperspirant. Your skin is a two-way street, otherwise nicotine patches wouldn't work. The aluminum enters your body and your bloodstream through the pores of your skin. If your immune system, or if your liver is compromised and not properly filtering the blood -- not trapping the aluminum, forming a liver stone, and depositing it into the gall bladder – the aluminum can take up a home elsewhere in the body. Aluminum seems to have an affinity for the woman's breast and the human brain. Let's say it takes up a home in a woman's breast and starts to oxidize. That oxidation invites fungus that causes inflammation in the cells where the aluminum has taken up a home, triggering a shift in polarity. The cells become south polarized and a signal is sent to the brain to send down stem cells. The problem is that the root cause of the problem, which is aluminum oxidizing in the breast, has not gone away. The aluminum is still there. As a result, the brain continues to send down stem cells to repair the breast. These cells form a mass. When oxidation occurs, pathogens – be it oncoviruses, bacteria, parasites – are attracted to the oxidation. Once that mass is infected with one of these pathogens, meaning that the DNA of the stem cells have been damaged and are now cancer stem cells, it becomes a malignant tumor. Modern medicine says that we cut the breast out, radiate the area, and in some cases prescribe a regiment of chemotherapy. The chemo doesn't kill the stem cells; it kills the daughter cells produced by the stem cells. That is why chemo is only two to three percent effective. Modern medicine is akin to napalming for insects. The insects above ground die, but the insect larvae are underground and unaffected, ready to reemerge. Meanwhile, all the other life above ground has been destroyed as collateral damage. Doctors who dare prescribe anything something other than chemo and radiation are stripped of their licenses to practices. Some doctors receive kickbacks on chemo drugs as the cost for patients is between $10,000 and $30,000 a month. Medicare, for example, pays a kickback of 6% to the doctors, known as a "reimbursement". Imagine paying that kind of money for drugs that are handled by people wearing hazmat suits? Would it not make more sense to remove the root cause of the problem, which is the oxidizing aluminum? Aluminum is very difficult to remove from the body tissue, partly because it doesn't bind to sulfates readily. However, malic acid and silica are effective at pulling aluminum out of the tissue and into the bloodstream where white blood cells or a properly functioning liver can remove it, or sulfates such as alpha-lipoic acid can attach onto it long enough to get it flushed out of your body through the kidneys. That would be a cure for your problem, eliminate the root cause and the need for conventional medical modalities. Heavier metals such as mercury, which seem to have an affinity for the pancreas, can be removed with sulfates such as alpha-lipoic acid, ethylene-diamine-tetra-acetic acid (EDTA), or dimethyl-sulfoxide (DMSO)"

Jones: "What causes the polarity shift?"

Cavendish: "It is still uncertain, but possibly when the cells are traumatized, they inflame, causing them to explode, at which point they release iron."

Jones: "Wow – really remarkable. But as you mentioned, modern medicine isn't interested in any cures as there is no money in it for them. And the aluminum industry surely will go to lengths to keep information like this from the public."

Cavendish: "They have done a pretty good job so far, especially when it comes to fluoride, a by-product of copper, iron, and aluminum production. We are told that fluoride strengthens our teeth, and as a result it was eventually added to our drinking water. The truth about fluoride is a lot more sinister. The American Dental Association conducted a study in the late 1930s that was heavily influenced by fluoride producers. It surmised that fluoride strengthened your teeth. Eventually, in 1945, experimentation was started in Grand Rapids, Michigan at the behest of the Surgeon General, Thomas Parran, Jr. It was then introduced to the water supply as a matter of policy in 1951 by the ADA and the Public Health Service, which was headed by former Alcoa chief counsel, Oscar Ewing. However, after World War II, the United States Government sent Charles Elliot Perkins, a research worker in chemistry, biochemistry, physiology and pathology, to oversee the I.G. Farben chemical plants in Germany. Perkins wrote a letter to the Lee Foundation for Nutritional Research in Milwaukee, Wisconsin, dated October 2, 1954 and if I can indulge your listeners, I would like to quote directly from that letter:

'We are told by the fanatical ideologists who are advocating the fluoridation of the water supplies in this country that their purpose is to reduce the incidence of tooth decay in children, and it is the plausibility of this excuse, plus the gullibility of the public and the cupidity of public officials that is responsible for the present spread of artificial water fluoridation in this country. However - and I want to make this very definite and positive - the real reason behind water fluoridation is not to benefit children's teeth. If this were the real reason, there are many ways in which it could be done which are much easier, cheaper and far more effective. The real purpose behind water fluoridation is to reduce the resistance of the masses to domination, control and loss of liberty. I say this in all earnestness and sincerity of a scientist who has spent nearly 20 years research into the chemistry, biochemistry, physiology and pathology of fluorides. Any person who drinks artificially fluoridated water for a period of one year or more will never again be the same person, mentally or physically.'

As a conspiratorial side note, Parran left his post as Surgeon General in 1948, finding work as the dean of the newly founded University of Pittsburgh's Graduate School of Public Health. That school was started

220

with a $13.6 million grant from the A. W. Mellon Educational and Charitable Trust, the same Mellon who founded Alcoa. Parran worked for the Rockefeller and Mellon interests the rest of his life.

Jones: "So you have Alcoa's fingerprints all over fluoride in the water as a matter of public policy."

Cavendish: "Yes, and in 2012, Harvard University published a meta-analysis funded by the National Institutes of Health (NIH), which concluded that children who live in areas with highly fluoridated water have significantly lower IQ scores than those who live in low fluoride areas. I was actually surprised that study was made public, because there seems to have been a concerted effort over the years to suppress studies that were negative on fluoride. Almost all psychotropic drugs, such as Zoloft, are fluoride products. Fluoride is a member of the halogen family on the periodic chart of elements. So is iodine. Your thyroid needs iodine to function properly. I believe that fluoride is absorbed by the thyroid because of its molecular similarity to iodine. The fluoride screws up the functioning of the thyroid and is probably responsible for many thyroid-related health issues, which then gets treated with prescription drugs. In addition to filtering your water and not using fluoride toothpaste, you should take magnesium, curcumin, calcium, iodine, and boron to chelate out the fluoride that is already in your body."

Jones: "Do you believe that all drugs are inherently bad?"

Cavendish: "No. There are certainly drugs that have benefited mankind, such as the nootropics that enhance brain function. I also believe that not every artificial compound is evil. For example, one of the antioxidant food additives, butylated hydroxytoluene, otherwise known as BHT, is a favorite punching bag of the health and wellness groups. In fact, Chipotle fast food restaurants have put out commercials proclaiming that they don't have BHT in their food. BHT has been bashed as a carcinogen, and this is simply a case of people parroting other peoples' bad research. There was one study conducted back in the 1970s in which lab rats that consumed BHT developed lung tumors. From that point forward, BHT has gotten a bad rap. It turns out the reason that all of the rats contracted cancer was that the rodents' feed had been contaminated with aflatoxin, which is a carcinogen. That experiment has been repeated several times with no harm coming to any of the rats as a result of BHT. In fact, BHT has some potential anti-viral qualities that make it a threat to Big Pharma."

Jones: "How so?"

Cavendish: "BHT breaks down fat. Why does that matter? Many viruses, such as herpes, HIV, hepatitis B and C, West Nile, Ebola – to name a few – are lipid encased. In other words, they are surrounded by a fatty envelope – think of a gel cap. The reason that these viruses are so virulent is due to the inability of the white blood cells to get at the virus. They can't because of the lipid encasing around the virus – like fats inhibiting glucose absorption by the muscles in type II diabetes. Because it breaks down fat, BHT chemically disrupts the physical structure of lipid-enveloped viruses, in essence tearing off the fat shield, exposing the virus to attack from the white blood cells. In theory, this could be a possible cure for many of these viruses.

In fact, a study was conducted on Scottish Deerhounds back in the late 60s and early 70s using BHT. The results were remarkable. These dogs normally die of sarcoma at a young age. In the study, thirty-six dogs were split up into two groups: 1. eighteen receiving BHT daily starting between the ages of one and a half and three; and 2. eighteen not receiving BHT. The non-BHT dogs all lived between four and six years with most of them dying of sarcoma. The BHT dogs lived between eight and ten years while exhibiting much healthier characteristics, like a shinier coat. You would think that this inexpensive compound should be further investigated, but as always, in our corporate socialistic set-up, this will not happen. I take BHT every day. Think about it: chemotherapy drugs which are about 3% effective in treating cancer, are known carcinogens, and are handled by people wearing hazmat suits, are part and parcel of the cancer protocol, but BHT, a potential AIDS cure gets a bad rap because of some flawed study conducted over forty years ago. If I am fortunate enough to be elected president, I will see to it that all of these potential cures are studied more thoroughly, as I believe that this is the path to solving our healthcare crisis."

Jones: "That is truly fascinating. We are here with Fitzgerald Cavendish, making his first appearance since the debate, and we are going to open up the phone lines for some Q & A. Even though we have been

222

talking about healthcare, we are going to open it up to questions on any subject. The first caller is Eric from Houston. What's on your mind, Eric?"

Eric: "I wanted to know what Mr. Cavendish thinks of GMOs."

Cavendish: "Good question. I think GMOs are a scourge. I know that scientists will line up to argue against me, but I think that they are missing the point, and I will use an example to illustrate. There is GMO corn that is resistant to Round-Up, which is Monsanto's insecticide. So when the plant is sprayed with Round-Up, only the insects, which could be harmful to the corn, die. That seems ideal, but that Round-Up ends up in the soil where it is absorbed into the root system and into the corn, not to mention the Round-Up that is already on the plant. As a result, the corn that is harvested contains Round-Up. The corn may be resistant to Round-Up, but humans aren't. Now scientists will tell you that Round-Up isn't harmful to humans because it employs the shikimate pathway, which is absent in all animals. The problem with that logic is that it is not absent in bacteria, and bacteria outnumber cells in our body by a factor of 10-to-1. Also, former US Navy staff scientist Dr. Nancy Swanson collected statistics on glyphosate usage and various diseases and conditions, including autism, dating back to 1990 up 'til 2010. The correlation is staggering. Remember, in 1975, 1 in 5,000 had autism. Now, according to the latest CDC [Center for Disease Control] findings, 1 in 40 has autism. I am for the elimination of GMOs. Think about all of the high-fructose corn syrup out there made with GMO corn – it's frightening. With that said, I am also for choice. However, with my tax plan, foods containing GMOs would be taxed at 150%. That should act as a strong disincentive to buy consumable products containing GMOs. Given the downtick in demand as a result of the tax on GMOs, big food will probably work to eliminate GMOs in most of their offerings."

Jones: "You mentioned before that you were going to mention other cancer modalities that deserve investigation. I don't know if we got to them."

Cavendish: "You are absolutely right -- my apologies. Other cancer modalities that deserve serious investigation are vitamin therapy, laetrile, baking soda/hydrogen peroxide, the Gerson diet, Essiac, the

Hoxsey treatment, antineoplaston therapy by Dr. Stanislaw Burzynski, unresolved psychological trauma theory, iscador/mistletoe, phytonutrient therapy, hemp oil, and anything else that has shown at least anecdotal success. All diseases, in the end, are the result of a compromised immune system. That is why cleansing and eating organically is so important. You have to get the toxins that are already in the body out, and try to prevent toxins from entering in the first place. Eating organic is a step in the right direction, and that is why those products will only be taxed at 5% under my system. Even though we have talked about a lot of silver bullets on this program, it is much more important to put your body in a place where it never requires a silver bullet.

"Also, while it is fresh on my mind, other disorders such as depression and alcoholism, maybe much more physical (as opposed to psychological) in nature than ever thought before. For example, depression in many instances is caused by inflammation. Trans-fats and sugars in the diet promote inflammation. It would logically follow that a diet low in these culprits and rich in curcumin and omega-3 fatty acids would go a long way towards solving depression. Obviously, these remedies cost much less than prescribed antidepressants."

Jones: "Good stuff. Casey from Centerville, Iowa -- what's on your mind, sir?"

Casey: "Yeah. I wanted to know what Fitzgerald thought about vaccines."

Cavendish: "Indeed. Good question. I am for choice. I am not for mandating vaccines. Conceptually, I like the idea of vaccines. They have served a vital purpose, but when you preserve the vaccines with aluminum, formaldehyde, and sometimes mercury, you are doing more harm than good. And then when you are giving the young children a battery of these shots all at once, given their body sizes, that is a lot of poison all at once. Vaccines have a purpose, but you have to change the formula."

Jones: "Dominique in Chicago. Thanks for holding. You're on the air."

Dominique: "Are you going to take our guns away?"

Cavendish: "Absolutely not. The reason I am not taking your guns away is that they are a check on the federal government. They are a check on me if I'm elected. It is also a check on those that want us to subvert our Constitution to a higher authority – a one-world government. That will not happen under my watch. With that said, if 89% of the population is for stiffer background checks, I should bend to their will. But regarding types of guns, I am not interested in regulating that."

Jones: "God bless you, brother. The next call is from Maine and it is from Brett. What would you like to talk to Fitzgerald about?"

Brett: "I think immigration is a big problem and I like your idea regarding the taxes, but if you provide medical coverage for everyone, won't that be an incentive for them to stay?"

Cavendish: "Excellent point, Brett. The only answer I have is that if illegals are still a big problem, then we can just tweak the tax system so the sales tax increases from 30% to 50%, but the rebates are also higher, to $15,000. To be sure, this will be a bit of an inexact science in the first year, so adjustments will be made on both sides, in terms of the tax rates and on the rebates. The ultimate goal is to use this system as a tool to promote better health and prosperity amongst the population."

Jones: "I like that idea. Next up is Tom from South Carolina. What's on your mind, Tom?"

Tom: "Jeez, you sure seem to know a lot about medicine. You know more than that Dr. Oz guy. I had no idea about all of these cures. That's really amazing. I know that you mentioned that liver, or gall bladder cleanse on Dr. Oz. Are there other cleanses that you can recommend?"

Cavendish: "First, thanks for the complement; I'm sure Dr. Oz knows more than I do about health and wellness. Second, just because something works, remember that nothing is 100% effective. Regarding cleanses, I would recommend reading Charles Wahlheim's book, *The Truth: Claiming Your Birthright to Health*. With that said, there is a good heavy metal cleanse that involves R-Alpha Lipoic Acid. ALA is an organosulfur compound, which is a fancy way of saying that it pulls metals out of your tissue, eventually removing them from your body through you kidneys. I would recommend taking 1 gram of R-ALA – the R type of ALA is the kind that occurs in nature, so make sure you get the R type of ALA. Anyway, take 1 gram of R-ALA every three hours for thirty-six hours -- that means getting up in the middle of the night. Drink plenty of water, as you will be reshuffling the deck and you want to flush the metals out of your body. You don't want them ending up in another organ. As you are doing this cleanse, you probably won't notice much change over the first nine to twelve hours. That is because most people are deficient in sulfur and your cells will be absorbing the initial quantities. Once your cells are sated, the remaining sulfur that you put into your body will start to pull the metals out of your tissues. You will know that this is happening when you go to the bathroom; you will literally smell the metals coming out in your urine. The removal of heavy metals is so important to good health."

Jones: "Right on. Let's take another call from Trace in Lexington, South Carolina. What do you have for Mr. Cavendish?"

Trace: "Are you going to reopen the investigation into the death of your father?"

Cavendish: "The first thing I'm going to do is see to it that all of the unreleased documents are immediately available for public review. Once those documents have been digested, I think that there should be a forum consisting of JFK researchers from all viewpoints; it could possibly be a congressional committee. Any person that claims to have information should be compelled to come forward with a guarantee of immunity. I realize that most of the players from that day are now departed, but any additional information would certainly be helpful."

Jones: "What about 9/11 – are you going to reopen the investigation into that false flag event?"

Cavendish: "Yes. There are a lot of troubling issues surrounding that event. For example, there was certainly an explosion in the basement of the World Trade Center seconds before the first plane hit. The collapse of WTC 7 -- that needs to be better investigated. I think that the 9/11 Commission Report left a lot to be desired."

Jones: "What do you say to people who say that we are wasting our time expending energy to go over things that have already been investigated, rehashing the past?"

Cavendish: "Alex, I say that if we don't know the truth about our past, then it is hard to set the correct course for the future."

Jones: "Amen to that. Jim in Eureka, California – you're on the air."

Jim: "Yes. My question for Mr. Cavendish is in regards to his plan to eliminate the debt. Could you go over that again? It was so different from anything else that I had ever heard that I had a hard time digesting it."

Cavendish: "Certainly, Jim. It isn't an easy concept to get one's mind around, since most of us were never taught about it in school. My plan is essentially copied from William Still, who directed a documentary entitled, *Money Masters*, I believe back in 1996. What you have to understand is that all of our money in circulation is loaned into existence. It is either borrowed by the federal government from or through a central bank, or it is created through fractional reserve banking. In other words, when the government needs money that it doesn't have, it produces what we know as treasury securities (bond, bills, or notes) that are given to the Federal Reserve in exchange for money. The Federal Reserve then auctions off these securities through its broker dealer facility. Sometimes the Fed purchases these securities outright. When the Fed purchases these securities, it doesn't have the money, so it creates it out of thin air, with a stroke of the keyboard. Let's say I'm the government and you're the Fed, Jim. I need to borrow $1 million. I produce a treasury security, which in essence is an IOU. You crank out the printing press or stroke your computer and create $1 million worth of Federal Reserve Notes, which is our money. I give you the treasury security and you give me the money. It seems like an even up exchange, except for the fact that you are charging me interest for the money you just created out of thin air. So in one year I will owe you $1 million *plus* interest. I then take this money and deposit in a bank. Because of fractional reserve banking, the institution – and I am cutting out a bunch of steps here – the institution that I just deposited the money into can make $10 million in loans, obviously charging interest on those loans. This is the other instance where money is created out of thin air – the bank didn't have the other $9 million to make those loans. It just created it out of thin air -- all of the money has been loaned into existence: the $1 million I borrowed from you and the $9 million worth of loans made by the bank. Let's say that is the only $10 million in existence, and let's say that all of that money is loaned out at 10% interest. That means that there is $10 million in circulation, but $11 million of debt, comprised of the $10 million in principle and $1 million in interest. In other words, in our money system, retiring all of the debt is impossible. This is the scam of the ages. Most Americans probably believe that our government has been irresponsible, spending more money that it collects in tax receipts. If you remove the interest component of the debt, you will find this to be misleading. In 2003, our government's total debt was about $6.7 trillion. If you subtract out the $7 trillion in interest payments the government had made on the debt up 'til 2003, the government actually ran a $300 billion surplus! The overwhelming component of our nearly $20 trillion debt is due to the cumulative effect of interest payments made on that debt. Perpetual debt and economic collapse under this money system are the inevitable outcomes. When the debt burden becomes too ridiculous – and we are getting close to that level now, the interest on the debt will eat a giant hole, not only in our economy, but in the global economy. History has shown that every great empire of the last two thousand years has collapsed under the weight of its own debt, because of debt-based money.

"My solution, or more accurately Bill Still's solution, involves dismantling the apparatus by which money is created out of debt. That is done by removing the Federal Reserve and moving the printing press back into the hands of the U.S. Treasury, where it belongs constitutionally. That printing press will issue a slightly different currency. We will call it United States Money. That money will be accepted for the payment of taxes and shall be legal tender for all debts, public and private. As the debt comes due, the U.S. Treasury will pay it off with the new United States Money. For example, let's say a mutual fund holds $500 million of three year treasury notes. Normally, as they come due, there is a concurrent auction for more three year securities at which point the mutual fund will present its $500 million IOU and receive $500 million plus the interest which it uses to purchase new $500 million three year notes at the current auction. This is known as a rollover. Under my proposal, when the $500 million comes due, instead of replacing it with more debt, we simply give the holder of the treasury notes $500 million (plus interest) in United States Money. Instead of holding debt, the mutual fund now has $500 million plus in cash. That cash will either find its way into other investment instruments such as stocks or certificates of deposit at a bank.

"Since the government is printing all of this new money to retire the debt obligations as they come due, there is going to be a huge spike in the amount of money in our economy which will be very inflationary. However, as that money enters the banking system, the government will gradually raise the fractional reserve requirement for the banks so that the amount of money in the economy stays stable. For example, let's say Jim's bank has $1 million in deposits and with the fractional reserve requirement at 10%, it can make $10 million in loans. As this new money is printed to retire the government debt, let's assume Jim's bank (and all other banks) realize a doubling of deposits. For Jim's bank that would be an additional $1 million in deposits for a total of $2 million. Under the current requirement (10%) Jim's bank could now make $20 million in loans. This would be very inflationary, so the government is not going to let Jim's bank make these loans. What the government is going to do is raise the fractional reserve requirement to 20%, which means that with its $2 million in deposits, Jim's bank can make $10 million in loans, which is what Jim's bank has currently loaned out; thus no new money enters the economy and the retirement of debt is not inflationary. About 88% of the debt is due in the next ten years, so we will be able to retire about $17.5 trillion in that time period.

"As a side bar, the mechanics of banking don't exactly function like I outlined, but for the purposes of illustration, my example should suffice. I hope this helps. If it doesn't, I outlined the logistics with illustrations on my website Fitz2016.com.

"I can't emphasize this enough: we can debate gun control, abortion, healthcare, immigration, taxation, terrorism, and campaign reform, but the absolute first order of business is to replace our current money creation system with the one I just outlined. We will no longer be in debt to the banking cabal that has owned this country since 1913. We will no longer have to talk about how we are leveraging our children's future. Please understand the Federal Reserve is a private bank, not a public entity. However, since it was created by an act of Congress, the one power the government has over it, is the power to abolish it."

Jones: "God bless you, brother. What is your take on putting us back on the gold standard?"

Cavendish: "Great question, Alex. Unlike most constitutionalists, I believe that backing our currency with a precious metal is a terrible idea. First, it imposes an artificial discipline on the government that I think is unnecessary. Remember, up until about thirteen years ago, without the interest component of the debt, there basically wouldn't be any debt. We have spent a ridiculous amount of money conducting several useless wars, useless that is, unless you are a defense contractor or part of the security state. We have also spent money to bail the economy out of an extremely overleveraged situation back in 2008. With my proposed money system, the economy will be deleveraged, since the banking system will not be allowed to create debt-based money out of thin air.

Getting back to gold, the second reason that is a bad idea is that we are subject to the whims of gold discoveries. For example, if Ecuador discovers a massive load of gold, that would mean Ecuador – and I don't mean to pick on Ecuador – with its relatively unproductive economy becomes one of the wealthiest nations on the planet. That doesn't make any sense. The third and most important reason that you do not want to back a currency with a precious metal is because whoever owns the precious metal can manipulate your currency. Since it is my belief that the European central banking interests own most of the world's gold, they would control the value of our currency."

Jones: "What do think about bitcoin?"

Cavendish: "Since it is a *debt-free* money system, I think it is a great idea, and since the level of money in the system can never increase beyond a certain level, I think it is a great way to measure the value of our currency. I do have one concern with bitcoin, and that is with regards to the Big Brother aspect of it, as all transactions have an electronic fingerprint. Even though it has this traceable element to it, the flip-side of the argument is that it the currency on the dark web, which means for terrorists, drug dealers, and peddlers of child pornography."

Jones: "Bret from Miami is on the line. What's on your mind, Bret?"

Bret: "Isn't the money system you are proposing nothing more than counterfeiting?"

Cavendish: "Great question, Bret. Our current system is a counterfeiting system with the Federal Reserve allowed to counterfeit money and charge interest. Our government unconstitutionally bestowed the Federal Reserve with the power to create money out of thin air – counterfeiting, if you will – and charge interest for all of the money it counterfeits. The system of money I am proposing has money working for us. It is simply an aid in the conduct of commerce – an alternative to bartering -- not a lien on the economy as money is currently. The government will print money when it needs to; hopefully not very often as tax receipts should match tax expenditures. When it does grow the money supply, it should be equal to population growth, so that the money in the economy per capita remains constant."

Jones: "How do you think the global markets would react if you were to implement this system of money creation?"

Cavendish: "The markets will probably act horribly at first because of a combination of ignorance and sabotage. Once people begin to realize that the United States is going to have the strongest economy because it has the fairest and most honest money system and will be retiring its debt, markets should rebound."

Jones: "What kind of sabotage?"

Cavendish: "The central banks of Europe and Japan could dump dollars; the foreign central banks could try to play games such as not accepting our new money for payment, but if they threatened the world's biggest economy with that nonsense, we will retaliate in kind. I don't think it will come to that, but we are prepared."

Jones: "Russ from Milwaukee, you're on the air."

Russ: "How do you plan to get Congress to agree to this? They won't vote for this, even if we vote you in."

Cavendish: "Russ, if Congress doesn't cooperate with the mandate that I would have if I were voted into office under these extraordinary circumstances, then I will submit to you that you will just have to trust me on this one. It will get it done."

Jones: "Next up is Amy from New Jersey, you're on the air."

Amy: "How do you plan to control terrorism?"

Cavendish: "I will invite the so called terrorists to the White House for a sit down. I will find out what their issues are with the United States and see if we can come to some sort of an agreement. My guess is that they want our armed forces out of their homeland for starters. My guess is that 99.99% of Muslims over there want peace and want to be left alone."

Amy: "I think that's absurd to talk to people who film beheadings. Our kids don't grow up to be terrorists."

Cavendish: "That is all semantics. Your kids – and I don't mean your kids specifically – grow up to work at the CIA where they operate drones from Langley, Virginia that drop bombs on an alleged terror suspect in Yemen and kill eight innocent people in a wedding procession. Our killing is just more impersonal. I'm sure that they look at us like we are the terrorists for occupying their homeland with military bases and conducting overt and covert wars on their soil."

Amy: "But they started this with 9/11. We are just trying to contain it so it doesn't happen again."

Cavendish: "That is the version of events that the news reports will have you believe, but we've been poking around in their business since we deposed of the democratically elected leader in Iran and reinstalled the Shah back in 1953. That is why we are so hated. Our corporations enter these countries to exploit their natural resources. When the corporate interests don't get their way, they enlist the CIA to activate regime change. That is why the corporate socialist structure in the United States hated my father. He was for aiding third world countries that had a democratically elected government, irrespective of the chosen ideology. He knew that if we helped them in the development of their natural resources, they would become our ally, which would benefit us immensely in the long term.

Instead, the CIA has conducted its own foreign policy on behalf of our corporate interests for the last seventy years, resulting in the repression of the will of the populace in these countries, breeding enmity towards the United States. Please don't get me wrong. I am for capitalism, but our economy is not capitalistic, it is corporate socialistic. I can assure you that most of the supposed great "capitalists" of our time – the Rockefellers, the Carnegies, and the Harriman's – did not want any competition. They wanted monopolies and total control. That is much more in tune with communist philosophy."

Jones: "Great stuff, Fitz. We are going to take one more caller. Donny in Baton Rouge, you're on the air."

Donny: "Hi Fitzgerald. Are you really going to give us each $10,000?"

Cavendish: "If I get rid of income taxes, impose a sales tax, and not give the citizens of this country eighteen years of age and up a rebate, then the tax will be regressive, meaning that it will hurt the lower income earners more than the higher income earners, so the answer to your question is yes."

Jones: "There you have it ladies and gentlemen, Fitzgerald Cavendish, the next President of the United States, telling it like he sees it, unlike these two phonies debating next week."

Cavendish: "I don't think I will be invited back to those final two debates."

Jones: "The CPD ought to. It was the most watched debate ever, and according to the latest poll you should win the election in a landslide -- 59% Cavendish, 22% Clinton, and 19% Bush. The country doesn't care what they have to say. They want to hear from you."

Cavendish: "Thank you Alex. I am very thankful to you and your audience's indulgence. If you want to learn more, you can go to the website Fitz2016.com, or you can follow on Twitter."

When the interview was over and they were off the air, Fitz asked Alex Jones for any help or suggestions, since Jones was much more connected and in the know. Jones could ask some of his contacts for "the goods" on the people who were likely to connect themselves to Fitz if he were to ascend to the Oval Office.

Fitz knew that the mainstream media was going to have a field day with his comments during the Monday news cycle. "Fitz would negotiate with terrorists." "Fitz thinks he can cure cancer." "Fitz explains his voodoo money system." "Helicopter Fitz wants to buy American votes, $10,000 for each one." "Fitz promises to increase debt by $2.3 trillion." *Let the bashing begin*. The next debate was slated for Wednesday. Fitz had not been invited, nor would he attend if called. Since the latest poll numbers reflected a veritable *coup de maître* for Fitz, the next debate would surely focus on his policies, whether or not he was in attendance.

****

"What is UP?"

"Holy shit – have you seen the poll numbers?!" The reality that Evan's indulgence might result in a move to Number One Observatory Circle was beginning to take hold.

"Has the press bombarded you?" Fitz was surprised that he didn't get one question about his running mate in the one hour of Q & A with Alex Jones.

"I started getting deluged today [Monday]. I haven't returned any phone calls. The people at my firm are looking at me a little cockeyed."

"I assume that you are up to speed with my platform?"

"Yes, and even if I didn't want to be, it is all that any one is talking about. I could obtain it through osmosis at the water cooler."

"What is Tracy saying?"

"She's very excited for you. On the other hand, I'm still in a bit of shock."

"Truth be told, so am I. I thought the country was ready for this message with Congressional approval ratings at 16%, but I had no idea as to the magnitude. Listen, at some point, those who are trying to tear me down – the mainstream media – are going to make you the focal point of the campaign if my poll numbers don't plummet after the next debate."

"Are you participating in that debate?"

"Haven't been invited and don't wish to attend. My guess is that the whole debate will surround my willingness to talk to the head of the terrorist group *du jour* and my money creation system, which I'm fairly certain neither of them understand. I will be back in New York on Tuesday. Let's meet up on Tuesday evening or Wednesday. We are going to be hounded by the press. I will use it as an opportunity to introduce you. It will be your coming out party."

"Terrific," Evan said with more than a modicum of sarcasm.

"Just remember, after they shoot me, you're in charge."

Chapter 32 (World War II Part 2)

The United States participation in World War II was predicated upon the unprovoked surprise attack on Pearl Harbor by the Japanese, or so the lie goes in your history books. What you weren't told is that your beloved FDR was responsible for instigating World War II – not America's involvement, but the whole damn affair. According to the history books, FDR led America through the Great Depression and through World War II until his death on April 12, 1945. The truth of the matter is that his policies never succeeded during the Great Depression because of the debt-based money creation system in place (whereas Hitler's German miracle was the result of the *debt-free* fiat money and barter.) He was the cabal's puppet who stole your gold and whose internationalist policies were aligned with the Council on Foreign Relations, not the American people, whose desires he was supposed to represent.

You've been told that Hitler created a false flag event in Poland that was used as an excuse for war on September 1, 1939; it has little validity. Hitler, rightly or wrongly, was trying to reverse the land concessions that were a consequence of the Treaty of Versailles, and bring all Germans underneath one "umbrella". After the Saar Territory and Rhineland, he annexed Austria on March 12, 1938 – which the Austrians almost unanimously voted for. Then through the Munich Agreement that was signed on September 30, 1938 he occupied the Sudetenland, formerly of Czechoslovakia, where three million Germans lived. Czechoslovakia, a patchwork country birthed in 1918 as a result of the dismantling of the Austro-Hungarian Empire, had over eight million Czechs who treated its German minority as second class citizens. Keep in mind, as part of the Munich Agreement, Poland was allowed to annex Zaolzie, an area with a Polish plurality, and Hungary was allowed to annex the Hungarian section of Czechoslovakia. Hitler's next coveted parcel of land was The Free City of Danzig. This was a semi-autonomous city-state created by the League of Nations so Poland could have access to a developed seaport after the Great War. The population of Danzig was 97% German, which of course meant that the bully on the block would want to annex it. The governments of both France and Britain were very intent on avoiding war. In fact, Chamberlain contended that Sudeten German grievances were justified. However, FDR, from his purchased perch on the other side of the pond, was unhappy with the course of events.

Before the Munich Agreement was even signed – nearly a year before the start of World War II -- British Ambassador to Washington, Sir Ronald Lindsay was summoned to a secret meeting with FDR on September 19, 1938. According to Lindsay, the President told him that if news of the illicit meeting was ever made public, it could mean his impeachment. The conversation concerned a plan to start World War II, with France and Great Britain maneuvering Germany into a declaration of war through a naval blockade of the Atlantic. Roosevelt emphasized that Germany must be goaded into the first shot. Lindsay commented,

> "This method of conducting war by blockade would in his [Roosevelt's] opinion meet with approval of the United States if its humanitarian purpose[s] were strongly emphasized."

FDR would be able to talk the American public into arming the French and the Brits with an eventual endgame of entering the war. What was FDR's obsession with starting the war? This meeting with Ambassador Lindsay was the first in a series of deeply troubling moves by a U.S. President representing an isolationist population.

FDR started giving a series of speeches condemning totalitarianism in Europe. The author of the quote, "the only thing we have to fear is fear itself," began spreading a lot of it. He argued for an expensive military buildup in order to maintain a defensive peace. The Polish Ambassador in Washington, Count Jerzy Potocki saw his speeches in a different light,

> "As a result of the effective speeches of President Roosevelt, which are supported by the press, the American public is today being conscientiously manipulated to hate everything that smacks of totalitarianism and fascism. But it is interesting that the USSR is not included in all this."

It was a valid point. Why was FDR so whipped up into frenzy over Hitler's land grabs, when Stalin was killing tens of millions of his own citizens? More importantly, why was FDR trying to incite armed conflict in Europe when his constituency was unquestionably more interested in domestic economic issues, like 19% unemployment? FDR, truly believing that the American form of democracy was the truth path to prosperity, singled out Hitler, because up until that point, Hitler's record as a leader – they both came to power in 1933 – and homeland popularity were far superior to his. Both leaders attacked their respective economic problems similarly. In fact, Reichsbank President Hjalmar Schacht smugly told the official Nazi newspaper *Völkischer Beobachter* that FDR had adopted the economic philosophy of Hitler. The difference was *debt-free* money. FDR, an economic neophyte who initially thought it best that livestock be slaughtered in the name of keeping prices buoyant when many in his country were starving, was jealous of what Hitler was able to orchestrate, both in terms of economic prosperity and cult of personality.

Continuing this disturbing pattern of diplomatic posturing, American Ambassador to France and very close FDR confidant, William C. Bullitt met with Potocki in November 1938 to discuss affairs in Europe. Potocki inquired into America's willingness to participate in hostilities if they were to combust in Europe. Bullitt's response was, "Undoubtedly yes, but only after Great Britain and France had let loose first!" Some American diplomats seemed ready, even giddy, for war. However, both Great Britain's Chamberlin and French Prime Minister Edouard Daladier, who arguably had a greater discernment of European affairs, were still content with their policy of appeasement. They certainly did not see a need to start a war with Germany over Poland.

Roosevelt wanted war and decided to play his hand. Using the misleading excuse that a German victory in Europe would be inimical to United States' interests, Roosevelt sent an ultimatum to Chamberlin on March 16, 1939 demanding that he end his policy of appeasement towards Germany on the question of Danzig. If he did not, Roosevelt would withdraw aid, military and otherwise. Chamberlin capitulated the next day in a speech in which he denounced Hitler. On March 31st, because of pressure from the White House, Great Britain and France pledged to enter the conflict against Germany on the side of Poland if hostilities arose over Danzig. This FDR-induced pledge had the effect of placing a spine into the back of Poland, now deciding that it did not have to appease Germany, because it surmised that Hitler wouldn't risk war with Great Britain and France over Danzig. How wrong it was.

On April 25, 1939, imbued with a bellicose spirit, Ambassador Bullitt called American newspaper columnist Karl von Wiegand, chief European correspondent of the International News Service, to the U.S. embassy in Paris and bragged:

> "War in Europe has been decided upon. Poland has the assurance of the support of Britain and France, and will yield to no demands from Germany. America will be in the war soon after Britain and France enter it."

The diary of James Forrestal details a conversation he had with British Ambassador Joe Kennedy (father of President Kennedy) shortly after the war,

> "Kennedy's view: That Hitler would have fought Russia without any later conflict with England if it had not been for Bullitt's urging on Roosevelt in the summer of 1939 that the Germans must be faced down about Poland; neither the French nor the British would have made Poland a cause of war if it had not been for the constant needling from Washington."

This dovetails nicely with Hitler's January 1936 meeting with Lord Londonderry in which he wanted to join forces and invade the Soviet Union in an attempt to wipe out communism. Why was FDR hell bent on starting WWII?

In addition to his bruised ego, the best answer seems to come from Polish Ambassador Potocki on July 6, 1939:

> "In the West, there are all kinds of elements openly pushing for war: the Jews [i.e. the bankers], the super-capitalists, the arms dealers. Today they are all ready for a great business, because they have found a place which can be set on fire: Danzig; and a nation that is ready to fight: Poland. They want to do business on our backs. They are indifferent to the destruction of our country. Indeed, since everything will have to be rebuilt later on, they can profit from that as well."

FDR was the cabal's conduit to war profits.

For sure, not everyone in America was falling for Roosevelt's truculence. Hamilton Fish III, a Republican Congressman from New York did his best to warn his fellow countrymen:

> "The time has come to call a halt to the warmongers of the New Deal, backed by war profiteers, Communists, and hysterical internationalists, who want us to quarantine the world with American blood and money.

> He [Roosevelt] evidently desires to whip up a frenzy of hate and war psychosis as a red herring to take the minds of our people off their own unsolved domestic problems. He visualizes hobgoblins and creates in the public mind a fear of foreign invasions that exists only in his own imagination."

Doesn't this sound hauntingly familiar -- like the world you live in today? [If you still don't understand, substitute "totalitarianism" with "terrorism".]

The war started without the United States, and despite the president's efforts to arouse the American public into war preparedness, FDR had miscalculated its entrenched isolationistic position. When hostilities broke out in Europe, 94% of the American public was against any involvement in the war. The president needed assistance selling the idea of war. Enter the Committee to Defend America by Aiding the Allies (CDAAA), which was formed in May 1940 by the J.P. Morgan, Lazard Freres, Mellon, and Warburg banking interests in conjunction with major media moguls Henry Luce (CFR), William S. Paley (CFR), and Samuel Goldwyn. Its stated aim was to push the 'peace through strength' initiative, arguing for strong support of the British Allies as the United States' best chance to avoid war. Its real aim was to manipulate the American public into war. Despite the efforts of the CDAAA and Roosevelt's rabble rousing, the citizens of the United States were still not biting.

Undeterred, FDR tried to provoke Germany into a declaration of war. He armed the Allies with military equipment through Lend-Lease; he assisted the Allies with aerial reconnaissance. The United States and Britain pooled intelligence, jointly tested military equipment, and participated together in "shoot on sight" naval convoys in the Atlantic. He even told Ambassador Bullitt that war with Germany was a certainty; he was just waiting for an "incident" that the Germans would give him, but Hitler wasn't taking the bait either.

Hitler knew the score as evidenced by a 1944 exchange he had with General Otto Ernst Remer, who was in charge of defense at Hitler's Wolf's Lair, on whether he could have waited to invade Poland:

> "You are mistaken. I knew as early as March 1939 that Roosevelt had determined to bring about a world war, and I knew that the British were cooperating in this, and that Churchill was involved. God knows that I certainly didn't want a world war. That's why I sought to solve the Polish problem in my own way with a kind of punishment expedition, without a declaration of war. After all, there had been thousands of murders of ethnic Germans and 1.2 million ethnic German refugees. [Hitler likely considered every ethnic German in Poland and Danzig a refugee. The actual number was approximately 80,000, due to pre-war pogroms committed by Poland against ethnic Germans.] What should I have done? I had to act. And for that reason, four weeks after this campaign, I made the most generous offer of peace that any victorious leader could ever have made. Unfortunately, it wasn't successful...."

You didn't know about the peace proposal? It took Germany 29 days to run roughshod over Poland. One week later, Hitler offered to back out of Poland, keeping only the Free City of Danzig and the corridor territories connecting it to the Reich. This rather stunning peace offer was rejected by Great Britain and France because they really weren't interested in Poland's well-being; they (and FDR) were interested in the destruction of Germany.

If he couldn't coerce Germany into war, FDR had a backup plan: incite German ally Japan into firing the first shot. He armed the Chinese with military supplies for its war against Japan. Starting in 1939, he waged economic warfare against the Japanese, commencing with the unilateral termination of the 1911 Treaty of Commerce and Navigation between the United States and Japan. In July 1940, he signed the Export Control Act authorizing him to prohibit the export of defense materials, which of

241

course he did to Japan – Standard Oil, of course, didn't obey. In October 1940 an export embargo of scrap iron and steel was implemented. Excepted from this embargo were Great Britain and nations of the Western Hemisphere. The final straw came when he froze Japanese assets in the United States on July 26, 1941. These actions were in blatant violation of the Neutrality Acts of the late 1930s, passed by Congress and signed by FDR. The Japanese did not desire a military showdown with America and attempted to negotiate the unfreezing of its assets. Every time the Japanese made concessions, FDR would demand more. When word returned to FDR from his Japanese Ambassador, Joseph Grew, that Japan would attack Pearl Harbor if talks broke off, he simply broke off negotiations.

To imply that the attack on Pearl Harbor was unprovoked is specious and to imply that it was a surprise is utterly disingenuous. First, American codebreakers solved the Japanese diplomatic code in 1940 giving the United States access to Japanese internal strategic correspondences on a same day basis. In one of those communications, which FDR read daily, Japan told Germany that war was about to break out with America. There is also some evidence that Japan's naval code was also broken with Roosevelt receiving this communique addressed to the Japanese First Air Fleet on November 26, 1941 from Admiral Yamamoto:

> "The task force, keeping its movement strictly secret and maintaining close guard against submarines and aircraft, shall advance into Hawaiian waters, and upon the very opening of hostilities shall attack the main force of the United States fleet and deal it a mortal blow. The first attack is planned for the dawn of x-day -- exact date to be given by later order."

That seems pretty unambiguous. That wasn't all. J. Edgar Hoover had warned the President based on information received from a Yugoslavian double agent Dušan Popov, who was privy to a meeting between Japan and Germany where Japan asked for advice on how to attack Pearl Harbor. Brigadier General Elliot Thorpe, who was stationed in then Dutch-controlled Java, received word from the Dutch, who had also broken the Japanese diplomatic code, that an attack on Pearl Harbor was imminent. He warned Washington four times, but was told by U.S. Army Chief of Staff General Marshall's office to stop with the warnings. Dutch attaché Colonel F.G.L. Weijerman personally warned General Marshall.

Congressman Martin Dies personally warned FDR. He came into possession of a strategic map which detailed the intentions of the Japanese to make an assault on Pearl Harbor. The strategic map was prepared by the Japanese Imperial Military Intelligence Department. You know what happened next.

Shortly after the attack, an investigative body (the Roberts Commission) was convened to investigate Pearl Harbor. This Roosevelt-friendly body concluded that Pacific Fleet Commander Admiral Husband E. Kimmel and General Walter Short were guilty of "dereliction of duty". In short, this commission, like all presidential-appointed commissions investigating mass murders of United States citizens (or assassinations of recent presidents), was a whitewash. Because of the commission's bogus findings, Kimmel and Short were the most hated men in America. Knowing that they were being thrown under the bus, Kimmel and Short requested Court Martials in order to obtain a fair hearing. Roosevelt resisted, but the military men finally prevailed in 1944 when Congress mandated that the Naval Court of Inquiry and the Army Pearl Harbor Board try Kimmel and Short, finally allowing them their day in court. At the hearings, irrefutable evidence was presented that proved that Washington had foreknowledge of the attack on Pearl Harbor. Admiral Kimmel said it best:

> "We needed one thing, which our own resources could not make available to us. That vital need was information available in Washington from the intercepted dispatches which told when and where Japan would probably strike. I did not get this information."

As you can imagine, when proof that Washington knew in advance of the attack was presented at the hearings, the military men conducting the hearings were a bit incensed, to say the least. The conclusion of the Army Pearl Harbor Board:

> "Up to the morning of December 7, 1941, everything that the Japanese were planning to do was known to the United States"

The acquittals of these two officers were covered up by FDR when he declared the results of the trials "top secret" under the guise of securing the interest of the war effort. Remember, anytime the national security card is played, it is to cover up the crimes of your elected officials.

Before the attack on Pearl Harbor, according to a Gallop poll conducted in the fall of 1941, 80% of Americans wanted no involvement in the war. After the attack, one million men volunteered for battle.

One can argue that war in Europe was inevitable, that Hitler's seemingly insatiable land grabs would eventually result in armed conflict. This is true. However, the war was going to be between *debt-free* money Germany and the debt-based money cabal-birthed Soviet Union -- the two major totalitarian governments in the European theatre. Wasn't this FDR's wet dream – two totalitarian governments at war with each other? Or was all his anti-totalitarianism bluster just a smokescreen to start another war for the bankers who put Roosevelt into office? And was it also a distraction from the fact that his policies had failed to pull the United States out of the Great Depression? And was it at the behest of the debt-based money cabal that needed to eliminate Hitler and his *debt-free* money? If you don't believe that Hitler only wanted war with the Soviet Union, ask yourself why he tried to recruit the British in his campaign to stamp out Soviet communism in January 1936. Ask yourself why Hitler offered to back out of Poland and end hostilities one month after he invaded. Ask yourself why he let the 335,000 British and French troops escape at Dunkirk when he could have annihilated them in May 1940.

Ask yourself why the anti-Hitler Nazis reached out with an offer of honorable surrender back in 1943. Did you know about that? Commander George Earle was FDR's personal naval attaché to Istanbul – Turkey was neutral during World War II until joining the Allies on February 23, 1945. Shortly after FDR and Churchill announced their "unconditional surrender" policy for Germany after meeting in Casablanca, Commander Earle was approached by Admiral Wilhelm Canaris, head of the German Secret Service. Canaris indicated to Earle that Germany would accept an honorable surrender, where the Nazi Army would surrender to the American forces. The German Army, if permitted, would move entirely to the Eastern Front where it could halt the advance of the Soviet Union into Europe – the real enemy. Also, Hitler would be removed from power. German Ambassador to Turkey (and former Chancellor) Franz von Papen then met with Earle to reiterate the offer and emphasize its sincerity. Earle promptly dispatched a coded message to FDR in Washington, via the Diplomatic Pouch, detailing the proposal. No response.

Earle would then meet with Baron Kurt von Lersner of Orient Society, which was a German 'cultural organization' in Istanbul. Lersner made the same offer – although he wanted Allied cooperation in keeping the Soviet Union out of Central Europe. Earle dispatched another urgent message to FDR. No response. This was followed by another meeting with Lersner and another urgent message to FDR. Finally an answer arrived: take up any proposals for a negotiated peace with the Field Commander in Europe. [What?] If FDR had accepted this surrender, there would not have been a D-Day, a Berlin Wall, or quite possibly, a Cold War.

The fact of the matter is that Germany (including the anti-Hitler Germans such as von Papen) didn't want war with Britain and France – only with the Communists in the Soviet Union. And Britain and France never wanted war with Germany, with the possible exception of Winston Churchill. FDR wanted that war for his ego, the Communists, along with the banking and military-industrial interests – especially the Rockefellers -- who had bought him the White House. You see, the bankers pulled their support from Hoover in 1932 when he refused to endorse the unconstitutional and fascist National Industrial Recovery Act; FDR promised his backing.

The communists, you ask? Indeed – Lend Lease military officer George Racey Jordan testified to the House Un-American Activities Committee in December 1949 that FDR's good pal Harry Hopkins was secretly providing the Soviets with very rare uranium, heavy water, and technical information needed to construct an atomic bomb *before* the United States had completed construction of its own bomb. He also provided them with money-plates, special paper and ink to print money. Harry Hopkins was Roosevelt's unofficial emissary to British Prime Minister Winston Churchill during the war and his Secretary of Commerce before the war. These "supplies" were loaded into a couple of planes near Great Falls, Montana and sent to Russia. The money plates supplied to the Soviets would eventually cost the U.S. taxpayers $250 million in redemptions. Through Lend-Lease, the United States provided the Soviet Union with $11 billion worth of military resources and humanitarian aid.

The Soviet Union agreed to pay back $722 million in 1972, with the United States only receiving $34 million. You, the American taxpayer, were left holding the bill. You must have the next enemy image well-armed and financed.

If that wasn't criminal enough, FDR was recognizing Stalin's Soviet Union in November 1933, while five to ten million peasants were starving to death in the Ukraine and North Caucasus. Stalin refused to release large grain reserves that could have alleviated the famine, while continuing to export grain. The American public didn't give FDR much grief about it since they weren't in the know because *New York Times* correspondent, Walter Duranty, staunchly denied in print that any famine existed, although he admitted it in private. For lying from Russia to push the elitist agenda, Duranty won a Pulitzer Prize. The *New York Times* later admitted it was "some of the worst reporting to appear in this newspaper." *That* form of totalitarianism was okay with FDR; Hitler's wasn't.

FDR let the CFR's War and Peace Studies group dominate his final six plus years in office – they practically ran the State Department, and were largely responsible (through its Informal Agenda Group) for the creation of the United Nations, the International Monetary Fund (IMF), the World Bank, and the division of Korea and Vietnam. Funding for the project, totaling $350,000, was provided by the Rockefeller Foundation. It was a good investment, considering that the creation of the United Nations was a major advancement towards one-world government, not to mention the fortunes eventually made in the East Asian war theatre. FDR sucked up to the Rockefellers so much that he wouldn't fire Nelson Rockefeller from his South American post when it was known that he was selling fuel to the enemy. He was either another stooge for -- just like Woodrow Wilson -- or a sellout to, the moneyed interests. Either way, coming from one of the wealthiest families in America, he certainly knew the score as evidenced by his message to Wilson puppeteer, Colonel Edward House, dated November 21, 1933: "The real truth of the matter is, as you and I know, that a financial element in the large centers has owned the government ever since the days of Andrew Jackson."

The only time he seemed to stand up to the banking interests was at Bretton Woods in July 1944. Out of Bretton Woods came the aforementioned International Monetary Fund and the International Bank for Reconstruction and Development (now part of the World Bank). Here's the public headline on the IMF: an organization of 188 countries, working to foster global monetary cooperation, secure financial stability, facilitate international trade, promote high employment and sustainable economic growth, and reduce poverty around the world. The reality: it guarantees loans that major banks make after impoverished countries have experienced regime change. The conditions of the loans are generally ridiculous such as the transfer of control of its natural resources to multi-national corporations. If regime change has not yet been actuated, it is sometimes a condition of the loan. How does the IMF get the capital to guarantee these loans? The answer: from "members' quotas". Since the members' quotas are based on a country's wealth, the United States' taxpayers foot the majority of the bill. As British politician and journalist A.K. Chesterton explained,

> "The World Bank and International Monetary Fund were not incubated by hard-pressed governments, but by as Supra-national money power which could afford to look ahead to the shaping of a postwar world that would serve its interest."

What does this have to do with FDR standing up to the banks? He approved the IMF and World Bank and put the United States back on the gold standard at Bretton Woods. The rest of the world would also be on the gold standard since the U.S. Dollar would be the anchor currency for the whole system.

However, FDR also approved the dismantling of the Bank of International Settlements (BIS). The BIS was created under the guise of facilitating money transfers arising from German obligations from the peace treaty after the First World War. During World War II, the BIS -- with IG Farben director Hermann Schmitz and J.H. Stein Bank owner Baron von Schroeder on its board -- with the aid of American, British, and French banks, was used by Hitler to loot assets from occupied countries and prison camp victims. Because of these crimes a resolution was put forth to liquidate the BIS "at the earliest possible moment". The dissolution was approved, but never actuated, thanks in large part to the efforts of John Maynard Keynes and Chase Bank representative (and future Secretary of State) Dean Acheson.

While the conference that put the dollar, and by default the world, back on the gold standard was wrapping up, the selection of the next president was taking place in Chicago. One would figure that the only three-term president -- and soon to be four-term -- would have a say in who his running mate would be. However, instead of incumbent Henry A. Wallace, Roosevelt was force fed Harry Truman. FDR bent to his controller's wishes and the rest is history. FDR was in failing health and everyone knew that the vice-president would be the next president. One of Truman's first acts as president was to suspend the dissolution of the BIS which would be officially reversed in 1948 – how convenient. The BIS is now an ultra-secret central bank for central banks. It is the monetary nerve center for worldwide debt-based banking. In biblical terms, it is Satan.

As an ironic aside, the Soviet Union refused to ratify the Bretton Woods agreements, charging that the institutions they had created were "branches of Wall Street". Talk about the pot calling the kettle black....

About 3% of the world's population died in World War II – FDR must have felt a twinge of empathy for Christopher Columbus, for whom he created a national holiday. [What? A little too soon?]

Chapter 33 (October 2016)

The media sharks smelled blood. Knowing this, Fitz surmised it a good time to introduce Evan Spring, U.S. Vice-Presidential candidate to the world. With the media waiting to ambush Fitz about his bid for the presidency, his "negotiate with terrorists" comment on the Alex Jones show, and his standing in the polls, they would pay little attention to Spring – not that he couldn't handle himself in a pressure packed situation, but a bout of the nerves would be expected in this totally foreign environment. Fitz had become accustomed to the spotlight over the course of the past five months, but he also remembered how he felt when the media first engulfed him at LAX and wanted to be there in case Spring had a "deer in the headlights" moment.

Fitz's appearance on the Alex Jones show was listened to through various forms of media by over ten million people – and it was only Tuesday evening, forty-eight hours after the initial broadcast, not to mention the dozens of articles and blogs commenting on the interview. Polly had arranged a press conference at a Downtown Marriott event room. The space had capacity for 120. When Fitz arrived with Evan, the room was nearly full. When they approached the podium in the front of the room, reporters started shouting questions. Fitz instructed Polly to walk around with a wireless microphone and give it to the questionnaire designated by Fitz. The first question wasn't a surprise:

"Would you really negotiate with terrorists?"

"Yes. They are human beings, however barbaric the press portrays them. Nothing gets accomplished in life if you don't communicate. A better question for the other candidates might be, 'Why are we fighting alongside ISIS in Syria and against them in Iraq?' Since that is the case, then we must already be communicating with terrorists. How else would they get armed? The answer has to do with a natural gas pipeline that we are trying to run from Qatar through Syria and out to Europe so Russia doesn't have as much leverage over Europe. Why isn't that covered in the mainstream press? Getting back to your question, we have caricatured people to such an extent in the Mideast that most Americans probably don't think that Muslims are of the human race. Let's see what they want. If it is as simple as us getting our military bases off of their soil and bringing our troops home, I don't see a problem with that. If their 'religion' is intolerant and calls for the destruction of all people not like them and doesn't allow for freedom of choice, then it is not a religion and will be treated as such. But I will argue that if we have a dialogue and a more comprehensive understanding of what our adversaries look to accomplish, I think we can come to an understanding that will make the world a much safer place, instead of living in fear of Muslims and terrorists on a daily basis."

"Do you think that we can have an understanding with an organization that tapes beheadings?"

"Are you referencing that organization that is funded by our own CIA? As I said on Alex Jones, we kill their people; our methods are just more impersonal. It still results in the same end: death. By the way, this is my running mate, Evan Spring. You should all have a copy of his resume, for lack of a better word." Evan acknowledged the media with a slight raise of his right hand.

"Evan, what is your theory on the law?"

"I'm not sure exactly what you mean, but I follow the precept that you do not harm the harmless. The more harm you inflict and the more harmless the victim, the greater the consequences for the perpetrator."

Fitz chimed in, "To that end, I am for freeing from our prisons all non-violent marijuana related criminals and putting in their place people who commit acts of animal cruelty."

The questions went back to Fitz and his stance on eliminating the debt through the abolition of the current system of money creation – it was clear that many were having a hard time getting their minds around that concept – his new tax system, and his stance on immigration; and of course, whether or not he was participating in the next debate – "No". The press conference lasted two and half hours. Fitz took the position that he would answer every question asked and would not cut the press conference short. He would outlast the press. One hundred fifty minutes later, the press had had enough. Evan had only one other question asked of him – one that he was expecting. "What makes you think that you are qualified to handle this job?" His response: "With a congressional approval rating of 16%, it appears that the American people are looking for real change. That is not going to come from within; it is going to come from without. My greatest qualification is that I have not been corrupted by the system and I am not beholden to the real power structure that is responsible for the sad state of current affairs." Fitz couldn't have said it any better himself.

By not hiding from any question – sixty-seven in total, Fitz earned the respect of the press corps assigned to cover his huggermugger, incognito, yet suddenly and unbelievably realistic campaign for the presidency. Through this performance, he hoped to put Clinton and Bush on the defensive during the next debate. Maybe the question askers at the debate would phrase their questions concerning Fitz's policies differently now that they had a clearer understanding. Instead of, "Please comment on Mr. Cavendish's tax plan," the question may now be phrased, "Why haven't you thought of this plan?" However, knowing that the Council on Foreign Relations was pulling the strings at the puppet show, Fitz expected no mercy, especially after he fried the organization in his closing speech a week ago. However, by shedding light on the true workings of this staged production, he had imbued the American public with a healthy dose of skepticism concerning any future debates.

****

The debate was watched by sixty million Americans – surprisingly strong, given that the main attraction was not in attendance. It was if the public wanted to give the Republican and Democratic candidate one more chance to point out the flaws in Cavendish's logic. What resulted was a very clumsy showing for both as they seemed confused as to whether or not they should be debating each other or the eidolon in the assembly hall who was still registering 54% in the latest poll. It was as if the main show had been relegated to the pre-debate reserved for those who had received less than 5% of the vote in the initial Republican debates of 2015. Their only chance to hurt Cavendish came when the concept of negotiating with terrorists was breached. Instead of tearing down Cavendish's idea, the candidates sparred with each other over one's lack of experience versus one's bad experience in foreign policy. Both dismissed Cavendish's viewpoint as being indicative of why he is not ready for the position of president, but did not elaborate.

Cavendish watched from his couch, declining to do a post-debate rebuttal on Russia Today cable channel, the only network that contacted him. In return for their offer, he said he would sit for a half an hour interview after he was elected, if he was elected. Even though the press came out in droves to his conference and a few pundits poo-pooed his money creation and tax schemes, the mainstream media and the power structure that controlled them were still behaving like "what just happened?" They were lying on the beach in Banda Aceh, sipping on a daiquiri, when out of nowhere the tsunami hit. Oz had been exposed. The power brokers behind the scenes couldn't ascertain if Fitz's showing in the polls was just a temporary guilty pleasure on behalf of a disillusioned republic that would quickly reverse course as the day of reckoning drew near, OR had Fitz's message harmonically and deeply resonated with America? Fitz's mind drifted. He didn't care what the candidates had to say. Fitz's platform/message wouldn't be altered by the staged performance on TV. His mind wondered back to the days of cuddling on that same couch with Annie and Oliver. He missed her madly and wondered what she thought of the entire circus that was unfolding before America. Even though the journey was painful without Annie, the days of summer, and now autumn, had passed with increasing rapidity. He drifted off to sleep.

****

By contrast, the days for Annie were agonizingly slow. Even though watching Fitz's sudden emergence on the political landscape held the excitement of a pennant race, she wanted to know the outcome and her role, if any, in it. She wanted to get on with her life. It was as if her spirit had been racing along in high gear on halcyon seas, when all of sudden the engine was shuttered when the fuel line snapped, setting the boat adrift. A rescue boat was promised, but was nowhere on the horizon. The seas remained still, but there was no guarantee that wouldn't change. If deliverance didn't arrive, she just might drown. As a result, her self-imposed exile couldn't end soon enough. She had considered adopting two Italian Greyhounds as a distraction, but decided that Oliver wasn't terribly good at sharing. She decided to do a little more research on Fitz's father.

****

By the time Fitz awoke the morning after the second debate, three clues foreshadowing the outcome of the election had arrived. The first was a text from Polly stating that the post-debate poll revealed that neither Clinton nor Bush had gained any ground; actually quite the opposite: Cavendish 62%; Clinton 18%; Bush 17%; other or Undecided 3%. Those were staggering numbers. Those were you can't rig the voting machine numbers. Those were hanging chads don't matter type of numbers. Those were you could turn away previously convicted felons at the voting stations and it wouldn't matter type of numbers. Those were landslide in the thirty-six states where you could vote for Fitz numbers. Even though counting write-in votes could be a long and potentially tricky process, all one had to do on election night was count the total votes for the gubernatorial or senatorial candidates in each state and subtract the votes for Clinton and Bush and one could arrive at a rough figure for Cavendish.

The second clue came in an article written by *Zero Hedge*. *Zero Hedge* is a financial blog that has refreshing and controversial editorial opinions on the economic and political landscape around the globe. All of the blogs are written by "Tyler Durden", a pseudonym taken from a character in the movie *Fight Club*. Although accused of being a conspiracy theory site, it has gained a foothold on Wall Street, with over 300,000 unique visitors a month. "Tyler Durden" is used to protect the editors from retaliation for dissident speech while safeguarding the integrity, objectivity, and independence of their reporting. *Zero Hedge* wrote a piece that morning on how there was a plot afoot to create a crisis during the lame duck period after Fitz was elected that would be used as an excuse to suspend the Constitution, keeping Obama in charge with no transfer of power to Cavendish. After the third clue arrived under his door, Cavendish decided to contact *Zero Hedge* through Polly.

The third clue was a royal blue envelope on the floor just inside the door to his residence. It housed an invitation that arrived at some point during the early morning. Given that one had to be "buzzed" into his SoHo building, the formal solicitation's presence was cause for concern. *Could someone have just paid the Chinese delivery man to get into the building, or did they have access?* The invite was for a meeting at the Harold Pratt House on 58 East 68th Street at 8:00pm with the rather ominous request, "Please come alone". A chill shot up Fitz's spine. He knew that he was being observed and he knew who was doing the

253

observing. He had struck a nerve at the power center and they were not happy, to put it mildly.

Fitz showered, checked his clothing thoroughly for any tracking devices, left his wallet hidden in a faux book with cutout pages on his bookshelf, and walked to Preston & Associates.

Polly was over the moon about the latest poll numbers as her normally toothy smile seemed to have adopted a few more Chiclets when she greeted Fitz at her office. She was downright radiant. Fitz, usually happy to see his confidant in crime, was less upbeat than Polly had expected. Before she could say anything, Fitz pointed his index finger upward and placed it on his mouth and directed Polly to her office. Once in the office, Fitz grabbed a pen and paper and started writing messages to Polly.

"I have reason to believe that your office and my apartment are bugged and that our cell phones have been compromised."

Polly seemed confused. She wrote, "How do you know this?"

Fitz produced the invite and wrote, "This was under my door this morning. They want to meet with me tonight. I am going to go, but I suggest that we use pre-paid cell phones – not that they can't tap into them in two seconds, but at least we will make them aware that we are on to them. I would like you to contact someone over at *Zero Hedge*. I would like one of their editors to "follow" me to the meeting. I will give him or her the scoop. Do you know anyone over at *Zero Hedge*?"

The writing continued, "Yes. I will contact them right after I obtain another phone."

"I want you to continue to do what you do, but any communication with me should be by pre-paid phone." Fitz produced two cell phones from his jacket pocket. "I was probably followed here so just beware."

"Do you have any idea who will be at the meeting?"

"I've got a pretty good idea. I would imagine that it is near the top of the pyramid in terms of the real power structure that runs this country, this world. That is why I want you to be aware. I may have to take drastic

254

action to protect you. Do we have any work left to do in the thirty-six states?"

"You're making me nervous. We are good to go in all thirty-six states. All that is left to do is a little campaigning."

"Thanks. You're the best. I will reach out tomorrow after the meeting. Be safe." Fitz then departed the offices of Preston & Associates for the last time.

****

Tyler Durden was hanging out just outside of the Council on Foreign Relations New York headquarters without trying to look too conspicuous. It was a challenge since there was a dearth of bars and restaurants to blend into in the high rent residential neighborhood, coupled with the fact that the first autumn chill had descended upon Manhattan, leaving East 68th Street near Park Avenue relatively abandoned. The Harold Pratt House hosts more than two hundred fifty events annually, including panel discussions, lectures, interviews, symposia, town hall meetings, film screenings, book clubs, and conference calls; the vast majority of which are not for public consumption. It appeared that no event was being conducted that evening as most of the lights were out. The meeting that was to take place in a couple of minutes was definitely not meant for public consumption.

Fitz emerged from a yellow taxi at precisely 8:00 pm and entered the building through the main entrance on 58th Street. Durden was amused by the fact that someone who was likely to become the next POTUS was able to go anywhere undetected. When Obama met in secret with his "real" handlers back in early June 2008, he had to get rid of the press pool that was assigned to him. He accomplished this by having his press pool wait in a plane that he was supposed to board. The plane then suddenly closed its doors and took off for Chicago without Obama. That freed up the future 44th POTUS to meet with Hillary Clinton and their handlers in Chantilly, Virginia. Cavendish didn't have this problem considering his emergence on the political landscape as the runaway candidate literally happened overnight. There was no press pool to follow him around. In fact, the paparazzi practically stopped following him; the logic being that there were no 'exclusive' pictures to snap if the mainstream media was following him around 24/7. However, since the mainstream media took their marching orders from a higher authority and since that higher authority was still in a state of shock as to what just transpired over the past seven days, no one had been assigned to follow Cavendish – partly because no one knew his next move. In fact, he had not been afforded any Secret Service protection. He was, in many ways, still citizen Cavendish. TMZ still managed to do a piece on the man it "birthed" almost daily and the mainstream media still called his policies impractical, delusional, and unrealistic, but the poll numbers were so overwhelming and the shift so dramatic that Fitz found himself in the eye of a self-generated hurricane, which made this "furtive" meeting with the "real" world leaders possible.

Fitz was greeted by a tall, bald-headed gentleman who looked in his mid-50s. When Fitz extended his hand to exchange greetings, the man seemed a bit uncomfortable, but extended his hand in return. Fitz noticed that his hand was enormous and attached to a monster. He obviously performed some sort of security function. "Right this way, sir."

Fitz followed the gentlemen for a few paces and was shown into the Dillon Room. The room was immaculate, yet comfortable, and impeccably detailed. Waiting in the room were three gentlemen, all of whom Fitz recognized. The oldest gentlemen, seated in a wheelchair gestured to Fitz to take a seat on the chair facing the coffee table. The other two men took their place across the coffee table on a couch. No handshakes were exchanged. The room was well lit and there was tea on the coffee table. It wasn't what Fitz had envisioned. He had expected to be seated in a dimly lit, dark paneled office, with voices emerging from the shadows. The youngest man in the group, who appeared to be tall, Jewish, with a blonde receding hairline, and approximately sixty-five opened the discussion, "Thank you for taking time out of your busy schedule."

Fitz replied cautiously, "Certainly, what can I do for you?"

The short man in his late eighties, and also seated on the couch, said with a deep, deliberate, and gruff German accent, "We want you to not run for president."

That was direct. No small talk here. "If you have seen the latest polls, it seems to be the will of the people to have me as their next leader."

The old man in the wheelchair seemed to be very displeased with Fitz's response, although in his condition, the act of living may have displeased him. "There are events that are in motion of which you are ignorant. If you were to prevent these events from happening, humanity could be in jeopardy."

Cavendish surprised them with his grasp of the situation. "Listen, I am a Malthusian just like you three gentlemen. There are too many people on this planet absorbing too many of the remaining natural resources too quickly. Population control is vital. I also agree that we are destroying the environment and that the pH of the ocean is starting to drop to a point that certain life, especially the shellfish, won't be sustainable. If we stand idly by, we will careen down a path towards extinction, destroying most of Earth's spirit along the way." The looks on the other men's' faces turned slightly hopeful. They would quickly be extinguished.

Fitz continued, "However, the disagreement regards your modus operandi. You would rather see a dramatic drop in population through some engineered plague that won't affect you gentlemen personally. Until that has been engineered, you are quite content to keep a lid on life expectancy by allowing the population to be poisoned through the air, water, food supply, and the joke presented as a medical system. If elected, I won't allow that to happen. In fact, I will do everything in my power to reverse it. I will, however, dis-incentivize the population to procreate through taxation."

The tall blonde haired man offered, "Your plan won't work because it will be impossible to implement, and even if you could make it a matter of policy, it will take too long to have any meaningful impact -- the time for action in now. We are going to be at ten billion by 2050. Something drastic must transpire."

Fitz could tell that these three didn't have their grandkids vaccinated, or ever had their help serve them pop tarts for breakfast. "My problem with your plan is twofold. First, you are willfully committing mass murder. That is unacceptable. Second, once you decrease the population to less than a billion, you are going to run it under a communist-styled regime, with you guys running the show and no constitutional freedoms for the masses."

The man in the wheelchair piped in, "Do you really believe that the populace is worthy of self-determination? Look at the mess we have on our hands."

"Winston Churchill once said, 'The best argument against democracy is a five-minute conversation with the average voter.' To a certain extent this is true. But you created that voter with your educational system aimed at creating workers and not thinkers – I believe that is what your grandfather said. You've created that voter by putting poison in their water supply, GMO high-fructose corn syrup in their food supply, industrial filth in the air, and zombie inducing drugs in their medicine. You created, no; you've engineered the mess on our hands by bankrupting the populations of countries through your money creation system, and since that wasn't good enough, you engineered wars to kill the population and to steal from them faster. You financed the woman's lib movement so you could have two members of the household paying taxes to line your pockets more quickly. You steal their right to self-determination through false flag operations and make them cower in fear over the concept of terrorism through your manipulation of the media. It's a mess you've created and now you are going to offer the solution of communism to them after you wipe out the population with some sort of Dan Brown "Inferno" virus. I'm here to interrupt your Hegelian Dialectic."

The old German responded, "Your take on the situation is interesting, but the fact of the matter is that we are at a tipping point. Your presidency could set our plans back forty years, which could have dramatically adverse consequences for this planet."

Wheelchair man added, "Five hundred million dollars to drop out of the race. We can come up with some excuse. We can fake your death."

Blonde-haired man interjected, "Like we did with Kenneth Lay."

Or not fake it.

Wheelchair man continued, "We can fake your death and set you up in a remote location in the world."

"Sorry, but I like the United States."

"We can come up with an illness that won't allow you to run."

The German was losing his patience, "Or you can simply drop out -- five hundred million dollars. What are you worth – about fifteen to twenty?"

Nailed it – you guys have done your homework. Fitz knew how these men operated. If he accepted the terms of the deal, he would be set for life in return for his acquiescence. If he didn't accept the terms of the deal, he was likely a man marked for extermination. It was like winning on a high-stakes game show: "You've figured us out and since you blabbed it to seventy million people who took it to heart, you receive $500 million as a parting gift. If you don't accept the prize, you get what's behind door number two, which is likely a gun pointed at your head."

Fitz surmised, "Since the American public is on to you, it is probably too late to back-pedal out of this mess that *I've* created. Besides, I could never take a bribe from men ultimately representing an organization that killed my father." Fitz stood up and left. None of the men moved. The well-built bald man with the huge hands, Security Man, acting upon a gesture from Wheelchair Man, opened the door for Fitz, allowing his exit.

A taxi all too conveniently pulled up to the Harold Pratt House entrance. Fitz feigned as if he was going to get in, but then told the driver – who pretended not to recognize Fitz -- that he was going to go for a walk. He walked west on 68th towards Central Park where he was followed by Durden. Durden had been instructed to follow far behind Fitz to see if anyone was following him. If no one was following him, Durden and Fitz were to rendezvous at the Red Cat on 10th Avenue between 23rd and 24th Streets within an hour of Fitz departing the meeting, in this case 9:09pm. If Durden wasn't at the bar by 9:09pm that meant that Fitz was being followed, and a meeting would be arranged for the following morning. Fitz walked south along the park and hailed a cab. After approximately ten blocks, the cabbie, a Pakistani named Dihyat Kashani, recognized him.

"Hey you da guy whose running for president?"

"Yes I am. How are you today?"

"I'm well, thank you. Are you going to really going to negotiate with the Muslims?"

"Why not? Let's see what they have to say. What do you think?"

"I think the American media portrays it all wrong."

"So do I. I think most of it is CIA-sponsored."

"Exactly! That's what my friends and family back home say. Are you really going to give out $10,000 to every citizen?"

"As long as I can institute a sales tax of 30% -- are you a citizen?"

"Yes I am. Do you think you can get this done? Many on TV say you can't."

"You already know not to believe what you hear on TV."

The driver chuckled and then said, "I just wanted to say that I am voting for you."

"Thank you very much. I'm glad to see that my message has reach. I hope to make you proud of that vote." Normally, Fitz wouldn't be sure who to trust -- maybe the cabbie was just sucking up for a good tip, which he received when the taxi pulled over in front of Red Cat – but in this instance, he genuinely believed his driver. Besides for the Alex Jones show, which consisted of listeners calling into the show, Fitz had had next to no personal contact with the population during his meteoric ascension from unknown to media darling to front-running presidential candidate. Only in this Facebook generation where people would "friend" complete strangers was this dynamic possible. Fitz had won the voters over by defining what they perceived: that their politicians were corrupted and compromised by something behind the scenes. The choices offered always seemed inadequate; and the avenues to express their displeasure seemed insubstantial – a sub-twenty percent congressional approval rating? *What was that going to change?* Fitz's identification of the plotters, the outing of their scheme, and his plans to reverse the perversion of the globalists presented at the debate delineated a heretofore unsubstantiated intuition of political intellectual incarceration due to an institutionally orchestrated suppression of meaningful alternatives. Fitz's bloodless coup succeeded because of a previously unattainable symbiosis: he was able to pull back the curtain and the citizens were fed up to the point where they were willing to believe – they didn't avert their eyes in denial. They did not need to touch Fitz; they just needed to trust someone – anyone. This trust could be engendered with a well-reasoned tweet.

Durden arrived a little before 9:00pm. Fitz complemented the editor for his blog and gave him the scoop for the story – Fitz would not be quoted, only a "source familiar with the discussion." Fitz only mentioned the bribe offer, their goal to reduce the world's population, and his belief that his privacy had been compromised. Fitz did not discuss his belief that the organization, *ultimately* fronted by the men in the room, was responsible for his father's death.

Fitz did not sleep well that evening. Adrenaline was still coursing through his veins from his declaration of war on the now slightly less invisible power structure. When he finally awoke for good at 8:00am, another envelope with another royal blue invitation was waiting on the floor. Except this time, it wasn't an invitation, just a message, "And your mother as well." Fitz's foggy disposition owed to his lack of sleep lifted immediately. His being filled with rapid fire blasts of emotion: shock, then rage, then confusion; then serenity, then uncertainty. This confusion reengaged his mind. *Are they telling me that they were responsible for my mother's death? Are they telling me that they are omniscient and omnipotent? Or is this a sweetening of the offering: $500 million and the real story behind your mother's "accident"?*

Fitz had never given much thought to the circumstances surrounding his mother's death. He had received a call at his San Francisco office from a state trooper barracks in Holmdel, New Jersey stating that his mother had been in a serious auto accident on the Garden State Parkway that morning and that he better book a flight back east. At the time, he was splitting time between Silicon Valley and New York for Volpe Brown. By the time he had arrived at the hospital, his mother had been pronounced dead. En route to the hospital Fitz had tried to contact

Gertrude, but to no avail. He ran into her at the hospital after his discussion with the ER doctor. He blocked out the litany of trauma described by the doctor and took comfort in the fact that she had died instantly – the phone call from the trooper was disingenuous as he already knew she was dead, but well intended. The viewing was closed casket – just as well. He couldn't bear the sight of her dead. He wanted to remember her as she was, alive. The investigation revealed that she had slammed into massive concrete overpass support after "drifting" into the median of the Garden State Parkway. Fitz found this very odd as his mother almost exclusively remained in the slower lanes which were furthest from the median. However, with the post-funeral deterioration of Grandma Gert, his busy work schedule that he was trying to operate exclusively from New York in deference to Grandma Gert, and the affairs of his mother's estate, Fitz never investigated the matter of his mother's accident any further. The more recent "message" just clarified that pause of curiosity a mistake.

Deciding it was too late to do anything about his mother's death, Fitz chose to compartmentalize and focus on what was in front of him. He was likely three plus weeks away from being the President-Elect and he needed to recruit some help. He made two calls that morning. The first was to the Ambassador to Japan. He used his "old" cell phone for this call. He had no idea where Caroline Kennedy was at this time – Tokyo – or what time it was where she was, but he needed to talk to her. She picked up on the second ring. It was 9:30pm in Tokyo.

"Fitz?"

"Yes. Caroline?"

"Yes. How are you doing? I don't even know how to describe what you've done. I thought you were smart, but you've turned the world -- or at least the United States -- completely upside down since we last spoke. Incredible!"

"Thanks. I apologize for not getting back to you sooner, but this was my hope."

"Can I stay on as ambassador?" Caroline joked.

"I've got bigger plans for you. I want you as my Secretary of State. That is why I called – and to catch up with my Sis."

Caroline paused, assuming the gravity of the request, "I'd be honored. Do you think the Senate will confirm me?"

"As I foresee it, you will be the only appointment that will be approved. It will be just like the old days when our father was the president and our uncle was the Attorney General – keeping it in the family."

"I'd be honored!"

"When are you back in New York?"

"Just before the election."

"Perfect. We will meet up then. Just reach out to me or to Evan."

"Oh my God! That's right! I almost forgot about Evan. I did speak to him a few days ago. He's still in a state of bewilderment."

"He'll be fine. Anyway, he's the smart one of the bunch. He'll figure it out. And you'll be there to coach him. I apologize again as I'm going to cut this short now. As you can imagine, things are starting to get a bit crazy around here -- time to organize."

"No need to apologize Fitz. Can I call you that instead of Mr. President?"

"Indeed. Be well, Caroline."

"Take care."

Fitz's next call was to Polly on the "new" phone. He wanted her to reach out to Evan Spring and Mafia Mike, give them his "new" number and have them contact him at their earliest conveniences. He reminded Polly that Mike was on the West Coast and not to call until after noon. By the end of the day, he had a face to face with Evan, where notes were passed, informing him to be cautious in his communications. He also detailed a two week bus trip across America on which Evan would be dropping into twice to "support the cause". Evan called the bus trip a "victory lap". Also by day's end, Mafia Mike had agreed to move out east and become Fitz's "personal assistant", after Fitz clarified to Mike that he was not going to be the next Chief of Staff.

Chapter 34 (The Lies of Wars)

The war on terrorism is based on false pretenses. It is simply another example of the debt-based money cabal implementing the Hegelian Dialectic: problem (terrorist attack), reaction (perpetual war), and solution (Patriot Act and Department of Homeland Security). If it isn't, it would be the first armed conflict in some time in which a blatant deception or lie didn't usher the United States into predetermined combat action. The U.S. Constitution doesn't allow America to wage pre-emptive wars, so the only way Congress is going to declare war is if it is provoked. As a result, no war is ever declared when U.S. business or banking interests need to actuate regime change to make a buck. Consider United States Marine Corps Major General Smedley Butler's quote:

> "I spent 33 years and four months in active military service and during that period I spent most of my time as a high class muscle man for Big Business, for Wall Street and the bankers. In short, I was a racketeer, a gangster for capitalism. I helped make Mexico and especially Tampico safe for American oil interests in 1914. I helped make Haiti and Cuba a decent place for the National City Bank boys to collect revenues in. I helped in the raping of half a dozen Central American republics for the benefit of Wall Street. I helped purify Nicaragua for the International Banking House of Brown Brothers in 1902-1912. I brought light to the Dominican Republic for the American sugar interests in 1916. I helped make Honduras right for the American fruit companies in 1903. In China in 1927 I helped see to it that Standard Oil went on its way unmolested."

The Spanish-American war was sparked by the sinking of the *USS Maine* on February 15, 1898. The only problem was that the conclusion of a subsequent U.S. Naval investigation, stating that the internal explosion was created by an external explosion under the *Maine's* hull, was incorrect. Despite vigorous denials of any involvement from the Spanish government, the United States used this flawed investigation as a pretense for declaring war on Spain, so it could take over the Caribbean and some of the Pacific – a war that was prepared for well in advance by then Secretary of War Teddy Roosevelt. As it turns out, the *Maine's* destruction was the result of its own explosives that were stored too close to the steam room. It took until 1980 for the United States to 'fess up to Spain that it wasn't really responsible for the explosion inside the *Maine*; the subsequent overreaction to which resulted in the annihilation of the Spanish armada.

You have already received your history lesson on World War I and World War II.

****

The Korean War is a lie on several fronts. At the Yalta Conference, Stalin agreed to enter the war against Japan within three months of Germany's surrender on the conditions of East Asian territorial concessions as well as *600 shiploads* of Lend Lease supplies being shipped to Stalin for conduct of the campaign. By the time the Soviets had entered the war against Japan (August 9, 1945) the United States had already dropped the atomic bomb on Hiroshima with the annihilation of Nagasaki only hours away. This still gave the Soviets (and Chinese) time to commit atrocities at Gegenmiao. Three days after the Japanese surrender on August 15, 1945, the Soviet Army occupied North Korea. A trusteeship was set up with the Soviets controlling North Korea and the United States in charge of South Korea -- as the CFR had wished under its "containment" policy. This was agreed to between Stalin and Harry Hopkins, the same person responsible for supplying the Soviets with materials for its first nuclear bomb.

The Soviet Union left North Korea in 1948, but left behind a well-armed North Korean force under Kim Il-sung – equipped with some American-made or reverse engineered war materials. [You can guess that some of the 600 shiploads of goods provided by the United States for the Soviet Union's six day campaign against Japan made its way into North Korea.] The United States left South Korea in 1949, just as Mao Zedong was wrapping up his victorious campaign in the Chinese civil war, making North Korea's border Communist. The United States invited invasion of the South by leaving the South Koreans relatively unarmed; and by declaring South Korea not part of its strategic Asian Defense Perimeter outlined by Secretary of State Dean Acheson. Predictably, Kim Il-sung invaded the South on June 25, 1950, wiping out most of the South Korean army in five days and occupying most of the southern territory by September 1950.

Enter the U.N. forces – really United States forces – led by General MacArthur. In the span of a month (beginning with the landing at Inchon on September 15, 1950), U.N. forces had forced the North Koreans back, past the 38th parallel, and near its border with China, at the Yalu River. The Chinese decided to come to the aid of the North Koreans by sending 200,000 troops across the Yalu River.

Deception #1: MacArthur planned to bomb the river crossings so the Chinese couldn't advance into North Korea. However, he was overruled by Secretary of Defense General George Marshall, allowing the Chinese invasion. Deception #2: Even though Mao had won the civil war, former Chinese leader Chiang Kai-shek had an army nearly a million men strong that was still harassing the communists from the island of Formosa (Taiwan). With China invading North Korea, you would think that Truman would want to help Kai-shek in any way possible. He ordered the 7th Fleet to protect Formosa, but at the same time he called "upon the Chinese Government on Formosa to cease all air and sea operations against the mainland. The 7th Fleet will see that this is done." Truman and Marshall were essentially freeing up Mao to attack American troops in the Korean theatre. [What?] MacArthur was rightfully angry and was relieved of his duty in 1951 for wanting to win the war. The war wasn't supposed to be won, only "contained" as laid out by the CFR. The conflict dragged on for another three years. This episode is yet another example of the United States generating its own enemies on behalf of the debt-based banking cabal and the military industrial complex.

****

The Vietnam story is almost too ridiculous to believe. Kennedy committed 10,000 military advisors to Vietnam in 1961, based largely on the advice of the first ever United States Deputy National Security Advisor, Water Rostow (CFR). Rostow went on to serve as LBJ's National Security Advisor from April 1966 to January 1969. Previously, he served in the Office of Strategic Services (precursor to the CIA) under William Joseph Donovan during World War II. Rostow's three attempts to enter the CFR-dominated State Department were rejected because he was deemed a security risk by security head Otto Otepka. This was due in large part to a communist and socialist family background and his blatant one-world government leanings, which fit hand in glove with the CFR's true philosophy. Rostow's fourth attempt was successful, but only after Kennedy's Secretary of State Dean Rusk (CFR) had Otepka fired. Even though Rostow declared in 1960 that it should be "an American interest to see an end to nationhood as it is historically defined", he was advising Kennedy to put troops in Vietnam.

Kennedy was going to pull the United States completely out of Vietnam after he was re-elected to a second term in 1964. He had already signed National Security Action Memorandum 263 on October 11, 1963 which ordered the withdrawal of 1,000 US military personnel from Vietnam by the end of 1963. Not surprisingly, National Security Advisor McGeorge Bundy (CFR) drafted a National Security Action Memo (273) while Kennedy was campaigning in the south, his final stop being in Dallas. McGeorge Bundy's NSAM, which reversed NSAM 263, was signed by President Johnson, shortly after Kennedy was assassinated. [The strong suggestion here is that McGeorge Bundy had foreknowledge of the events in Dallas. McGeorge also informed the rest of Kennedy's cabinet, who were airborne over the Pacific, of his assassination. McGeorge told them it was the act of a lone nut. How did he know this only an hour after Kennedy had been declared dead?]

With Kennedy out of the way, the military industrial complex was in a position to profit from conflict. Assistant Secretary of State for East Asian and Pacific Affairs, William P. Bundy (CFR), McGeorge's brother, drafted the infamous Gulf of Tonkin Resolution. William became Honorary American Secretary General of the Bilderberg Meetings from 1975 to 1980. [You will learn more concerning that group later.] The only problem was that the Gulf of Tonkin incidents hadn't yet occurred. In fact, the second incident actually never happened and the events surrounding the first episode are a lie.

On May 25, 1964 McGeorge Bundy sent LBJ a memo stating:

"It is recommended that you make a Presidential decision that the U.S. will use selected and carefully graduated military force against North Vietnam. . .

'This basic Presidential decision is recommended on these premises:

(1) that the U.S. cannot tolerate the loss of Southeast Asia to Communism;

(2) that without a decision to resort to military action if necessary the present prospect is not hopeful, in South Vietnam or in Laos;

(3) that a decision to use force if necessary, backed by resolute and extensive deployment, and conveyed by every possible means to our adversaries (enemies), gives the best present chance of avoiding the actual use of such force."

The cabal was itching for action. Johnson likely wanted escalation, but was facing re-election in a few months. It was his good fortune that he was opposed by Republican candidate Barry Goldwater, whose aggressive stance on Vietnam made LBJ's Southeast Asian policy seem dovish by comparison. His peaceful posturing was a ruse to get re-elected. However, if an incident could be instigated and the North Vietnamese could be baited into firing the first shot (just like the Japanese at Pearl Harbor), LBJ could present a case to Congress allowing him the latitude to take all necessary steps, including the use of armed forces to protect American interests in Southeast Asia.

Enter the Gulf of Tonkin incident. The story presented to Congress was that on August 2, 1964, the destroyer *USS Maddox*, while performing a signals intelligence patrol was attacked by three North Vietnamese Navy (NVN) torpedo boats. The *USS Maddox* returned fire. Four USN F-8 Crusader jets launched from the aircraft carrier *USS Ticonderoga* attacked the retiring NVN torpedo boats. The result of the skirmish was one damaged US aircraft, one bullet hitting the *USS Maddox*, three NVN torpedo boats damaged, four North Vietnamese sailors killed, with six more wounded. There were no U.S. casualties. On August 4th, the *USS Maddox* and *USS Turner Joy* began firing at radar, sonar, and radio signals that were believed to represent another attack by the North Vietnamese navy. A torpedo was fired from a North Vietnamese vessel. The *Maddox* and *Turner Joy* fired for approximately four hours, eventually claiming to have sunk two North Vietnamese torpedo boats. Later that evening, LBJ presented the incident to the American public in a television address, stating that U.S. naval forces had been attacked and that he would be asking Congress for broader authority to conduct hostilities. Based on this information, the Gulf of Tonkin Resolution was passed 416-0 by the House and 88-2 by the Senate on August 7th. LBJ signed it into law on August 10th.

What follows is what actually happened. According to a NSA assessment, after playing a cat and mouse game with North Vietnamese torpedo boats,

"...the *Maddox* fired off three rounds to warn off the communist boats. This initial action was never reported by the Johnson administration, which insisted that the Vietnamese boats fired first. A few minutes later the *Maddox* resumed fire."

According to North Vietnamese General Phung The Tai, "On August 2 the ship [Maddox] continued to attack a number of our fishing boats. Our patrol boats were therefore forced to fight back."

As far as the attack on August 4th, the *Maddox* and *Turner Joy* were shooting at radar blip abnormalities that were probably the result of high seas and bad weather as no North Vietnamese patrol boats were in the area. Captain Herrick's (commander of the *Maddox*) initial messages of a single torpedo attack by North Vietnamese were followed by confessions that there was confusion about what was really transpiring. In 1981, Herrick admitted that the first torpedo report was in fact, "unfounded". Squadron commander James Stockdale was one of the U.S. pilots flying overhead during the second alleged attack and he reported that, "...our destroyers were just shooting at phantom targets—there were no PT boats there...." In 1997, retired Vietnamese defense minister, Vo Nguyen Giap, meeting with former Secretary of Defense McNamara, denied that Vietnamese naval sorties occurred on August 4th. Secretary of Defense Robert McNamara (CFR) neglected to tell LBJ – or so the story goes – about Herrick's subsequent messages that essentially retracted his original transmissions concerning the attack. LBJ, most likely complicit in the deception, would later remark about the dustup on August 4th, "For all I know, our navy was shooting at whales out there."

The fact of the matter is that the real mission of the *Maddux* was to provoke the North Vietnamese into the first shot – which, as it turns out, wasn't successfully accomplished – which would then provide an excuse for escalation. This pack of lies was used as the excuse to send 58,000 young American men off to their deaths, not to mention the 303,000 wounded. It seems almost incomprehensible at the time that a superpower that had won World War II couldn't defeat a relatively small third world country in a couple of months. However, small brief conflicts aren't very profitable endeavors for the bankers and its war machine. In order to make it a fair fight – and thus a longer conflict – restrictions needed to be placed on the American superpower.

This was accomplished by hiding behind the technicality that Vietnam was a "police action" and not a formal "war". In 1985, the rules of engagement for the Vietnam War were declassified. They contained mindboggling illogicalities such as not being allowed to bomb enemy aircraft on the ground or anti-aircraft missile systems until they were known to be operational; no enemy could be pursued once they crossed the border of Laos or Cambodia; and the most critical strategic targets were not allowed to be attacked unless initiated via high military officials – very significant considering McNamara only allowed 6% of these strategic targets to be bombed. Couple those restrictions, with strategic absurdities such as not blockading the port of Haiphong or the Ho Chi Minh Trail and you have the formula for a protracted, unwinnable fight.

$111 billion was borrowed for the conduct of the conflict that was done in the name of keeping the communist dominos from falling in Southeast Asia. This number really understates the money made by the military-industrial-banking complex when you consider that David Rockefeller was financing the Soviets and had lobbied the White House to provide them with scrap metal, synthetic rubber, radar, explosive materials, computers, rocket engines, fuel, auto parts, etc. [really?!] which were then passed on to Hanoi to fight the Americans. Johnson agreed to this easing of trade restrictions with the Soviets and Eastern Bloc nations in October 1966. Johnson also put into motion the welfare state, which is the inevitable result of a debt-based money creation system. The only reason this sorry state of affairs wasn't actualized sooner – remember the Great Depression wasn't "solved" -- was the fact that the United States won World War II, which wasn't fought on its own soil. Its unaffected industries provided many of the supplies for the rebuild of Europe, creating an enormous trade surplus. Wealth was merely shifted back to the United States.

For their roles in Vietnam, Robert McNamara was named head of the World Bank and William Bundy became editor of the CFR's journal, *Foreign Affairs*. But that's not all. The real escalation took place after Johnson was re-elected. In 1965, a group of policy advisors known as "The Wise Men" held a secret meeting with LBJ during which they urged Johnson to send more troops into Vietnam under the CFR-devised scheme of "containment". LBJ was persuaded and the rest is history. This advisory group consisted of CFR members Dean Acheson, Secretary of State under President Harry Truman; Charles E. Bohlen, U.S. ambassador to the Soviet Union, the Philippines, and France; W. Averell Harriman, special envoy for President Franklin Delano Roosevelt; George F. Kennan, ambassador to the Soviet Union and Yugoslavia; Robert A. Lovett, Truman's Secretary of Defense; and John J. McCloy, U.S. High Commissioner for Germany, chairman of the CFR, chairman of the Ford Foundation, trustee of the Rockefeller Foundation, and chairman of Rockefeller-dominated Chase Manhattan Bank. [All of this is detailed in the adulatory book, *The Wise Men*, by Walter Isaacson (CFR) and Evan Thomas (CFR), which of course received a glowing review from *Foreign Affairs*.] Acheson, the leader of the Wise Men, and most vocal hawk on Vietnam, was a lawyer in the 1920s representing Bolshevik interests in the United States. His law partner was Donald Hiss, brother of convicted Soviet spy, Alger Hiss. His actions help block the dismantling of the BIS at Bretton Woods in 1944. Acheson surrounded himself with communists in the State Department, including John Stewart Service, who was subjected to loyalty and security hearings every year from 1946 to 1951, with the exception of 1948, because he was accused of passing confidential U.S. materials from his time in China to the editors of the *Amerasia* magazine. So why is Acheson – just like the communist leaning Walt Rostow advising Kennedy -- so vocal on containing communism, you ask? You see, he really isn't. The real interest of the "Wise Men" was making their cabal more money while weakening the United States in an unwinnable war – hell, this group even wrote the rules of engagement. They didn't stop the spread of communism, but they made the Rockefeller interests rich. Are you beginning to see a pattern here? Hint: Rockefeller and the Council on Foreign Relations.

****

272

The Gulf War was based on lies and a little misdirection by President George H.W. Bush's Ambassador to Iraq, April Glaspie. After Iraqi forces had amassed on its southern border with Kuwait, Glaspie met with Saddam Hussein on July 25, 1990 and stated that the United States had "no opinion on the Arab–Arab conflicts, like your border disagreement with Kuwait." Couple that passive remark with an earlier communique from the State Department stating that it had "no special defense or security commitments to Kuwait" and Saddam may have interpreted the U.S. position as a green light to invade its tiny neighbor, which he did one week later.

What is not up for interpretation was the perjured testimony of Nayirah al-Ṣabaḥ, a fifteen year old, who was later revealed to be the daughter of the Kuwaiti Ambassador to the United States, Saud Nasir al-Sabah. Her testimony given before the Congressional Human Rights Caucus on October 10, 1990 was cited numerous times by United States senators and President George H.W. Bush in their rationale to back Kuwait in the Gulf War. The money shot of her testimony was as follows:

> "I volunteered at the al-Addan hospital with twelve other women who wanted to help as well...While I was there I saw the Iraqi soldiers come into the hospital with guns. They took the babies out of the incubators, took the incubators and left the children to die on the cold floor. [Crying] It was horrifying."

It turned out she was coached into this false statement by the public relations firm, Hill & Knowlton, who taped the her unsworn performance and sent it to media outlets reaching an estimated audience between 35 and 53 million Americans. This testimony helped sway not only Congressional opinion but, just as importantly, public opinion, much in the same way the *Lusitania* sinking, Pearl Harbor, and the Gulf of Tonkin Incident helped galvanize bellicose attitudes towards a target country.

While Ms. Al-Sabah was moving the needle of worldwide opinion against Saddam Hussein, Secretary of Defense Dick Cheney was meeting with the Saudis, showing them "top secret" satellite images of 250,000 Iraqi forces and 1,500 tanks amassing at the Saudi Arabian border. Fearful of an Iraqi invasion, the Saudis took the extraordinary step of allowing American military installations on their soil.

This American armed occupation of Saudi Arabia infuriated one Osama bin Laden, who had argued in a meeting with King Fahd and Saudi Defense Minister Sultan that only Muslims should defend the two holiest shrines of Islam, Mecca and Medina, the cities in which the Prophet Mohamed received and recited Allah's message. To back up his argument, he offered his services and fighters. His offer was rejected, and Osama bin Laden has hated America ever since.

There is only one problem with this entire episode: the top secret photos of Iraqi troops on the Saudi border, used as an excuse for U.S. military occupation of Saudi Arabia, were fictitious. An enterprising journalist at the *St. Petersburg Times*, Jean Heller, acquired two commercial Soviet satellite images of the same area, taken in mid-September 1990. These images coincided with the dates of the satellite reconnaissance that Cheney presented to the Saudis. These images showed that no Iraqi troops were visible near the Saudi border, just empty desert, contradicting Cheney's claim to the Saudis. This was not just Heller's judgement, but that of experts, including a former Defense Intelligence Agency analyst who specialized in desert warfare. Cheney, when questioned about this contradiction, refused to release the Pentagon photos shown to the Saudis.

To summarize, you were led to believe that Saddam Hussein invaded Kuwait as a pretext to invading Saudi Arabia, and that while in Kuwait, his troops committed "ghastly atrocities" as stated by President George H.W. Bush, backed up by the testimony of a fifteen year old nurse. The truth of the matter is that the United States duped Saddam into believing that it was copacetic with his invasion/occupation of a disputed oil producing territory in Kuwait. Iraq had accused Kuwait of slant-drilling across the border into Iraq's Rumaila oil field. Once the area in question was occupied, the United States lied about the nature of the invasion to the world, specifically to the Saudis, as an excuse to put military bases in Saudi Arabia. Indiana Congressman Lee Hamilton said it best, describing it as a case of "intelligence [being] driven by...policy, rather than the policy being driven by the intelligence". 35,000 members of the Iraq army were obliterated while in retreat; another 75,000 were wounded. The oil companies had their interests protected with the introduction of U.S. military bases.

****

The United States' second spat with Iraq, the largest period being the Iraq War, was based on three lies: 1. the forged documents claiming that Saddam Hussein was attempting to purchase yellowcake uranium from Niger. 2. Secretary of State Colin Powell's February 2003 bogus testimony to the UN Security Council, which contained computer generated celluloid images of Iraqi mobile biological weapons labs. 3. Phony Iraqi ties to the terrorist group Al Qaeda. You don't need any evidence of this; it is a matter of public record. The United States borrowed $1.1 trillion that it didn't have to finance that war based on lies. The bankers and the military-industrial complex win again. And the beat goes on....

Chapter 35 (October – November 2016)

The bus tour that started in Portland, Maine and finished in Los Angeles became -- as the soon to be Vice-President Elect Evan Spring predicted – a victory lap. Polly and Fitz knew the route, but only tweeted out a campaign stop a day, or in some cases, a couple hours in advance. This was done to give the tour some flexibility. If the ride across America experienced an unexpected setback, a campaign stop along the way could be skipped with no one being disappointed. Despite the stealthy nature of the excursion, turnouts were huge. An excited anticipation had swept across the country. It was as if everybody knew who the next American Idol was going to be and was now curious to see what his recording contract would produce. Where a true sense of change had engulfed the populace, the Republican and Democratic parties were in a state of shock and resignation. Less than ten million people bothered to tune into the last debate – who wanted to watch the losers? Everyone loves a winner, and that maxim was certainly on display during Fitz's two week road trip.

The press had finally turned its full attention towards the biggest story in the world: Fitzgerald Cavendish's presidential coup. Remarkably, the *Zero Hedge* piece on the half a billion dollar offer to drop out of the campaign, was eventually picked up by all the major media. They really didn't have a choice. It was a question that was asked of Fitz at every one of his stops which he answered succinctly and honestly. *Those guys must be pissed.* Fitz had decided not to give speeches along the way, but rather answer questions and concerns that the population had regarding his platform. He certainly would be unintentionally harming certain segments of the population – accountants and bond traders to name a few -- with his radical platform. His "listening campaign" as Polly had coined it would provide an opportunity to nip unforeseen problems in the bud before he became the president.

"I have a private pension for a vast majority of my retirement income. Is the buying power of that money going to drop by 30%?" That question was asked a lot around the country. Fitz would answer "No, because your pension income will no longer be taxed and it will be supplemented by the $10,000 check."

"What if Congress doesn't approve of your tax plan or your plan to kill the Fed?" That was also a frequently asked question. Fitz would answer, "If I am voted into office, I will take that as a mandate, especially under these circumstances. If problems arise I will appeal to the people to pressure your congressmen into passage of these reforms. You are voting for me because of my platform. It is too late to find four hundred plus congressmen that are going to run on my platform so it is incumbent upon the voters to make sure you express your wishes to your representatives." Fitz knew that answer was empty, but he did not want to reveal his actual plan for implementation. The element of surprise would be necessary.

"Can you promise what the debt will be in four years?" Fitz would answer, "Yes I can – to the penny. It is simply a function of what part of the debt comes due in four years. Approximately 58% of the debt is due in four years. Instead of rolling it over, it will be paid off with United States Money. At its core, it is really a simple mechanism. It is hard to grasp because we were never taught to think about money in this manner – as an aid in the conduct of commerce, not a lien on it."

"My farm isn't certified as organic. Are you going to put me out of business?" Fitz would answer, "It is not my intention to put any farmer out of business. It is my intention to purify the food supply so we don't develop degenerative diseases from it. Food can be part of the healing and restoration process. It shouldn't be part of the poisoning process. Getting back to your question, because there are going to be dislocations as part of the switch, food that contains GMOs or artificial hormones, etc. – in short, food that it isn't at least all natural, with some exceptions – will initially be taxed at 30% like everything else, but each month, the tax will be increased 10% until it reaches 150% a year later. This will give farmers and big food producers a chance to adjust to the change in tax policy as it relates to their crops and their consumer products. If you think that I am going to be elected the next president, my advice to you is to start making preparations now as it relates to your farm. For example, stop feeding your cows GMO corn, stop injecting them with bovine growth hormone, and if you are, stop keeping them in inhumane conditions. Those changes will mean the difference between a 30% and a 150% tax on the goods you bring to market."

"I saw you on the Dr. Oz show. You seem awfully self-righteous about health and wellness." Fitz would respond, "I don't know if that is a question or a critique, but I can answer it by saying that I want every citizen to become self-righteous about his or her health. You can have everything in the world, but it isn't worth anything if you are lying in bed sick all the time. Stop listening to these talk show hosts who tell you that it is okay to be overweight and that those skinny supermodels aren't normal. Actually, that is what we should aspire to – I'm not talking about the stick figures, but the slimmed, toned people. Generally speaking, they are the epitome of good health. If you look at pictures from seventy years ago, heck, even my high school class photos of thirty-five years ago, very few people were overweight. Nobody had allergies and earaches. What has changed over this time? The bombardment of our bodies with artificial sweeteners, processed garbage passed off as food, GMOs, and prescription drugs that do our bodies more harm than good. The answer to reversing this disturbing degenerative disease trend is to stop this bombardment of insults to our bodies and to cleanse out the toxins that currently reside in them. That is one of the goals of my sales tax system."

When Fitz arrived in Los Angeles, the election was four days away. It seemed that more people were climbing onto the bandwagon. Some polls showed that Fitz had as much as 65% of the popular vote. His twitter followers were nearing fifty million. The disenchanted Democratic and Republican voters decided that the two-party system had polarized and paralyzed the country. It was time to take a bold step in a new direction. They had *finally* agreed on something: Fitzgerald Cavendish.

Mafia Mike loaded his belongings onto the RV that performed the roll of bus on Fitz's "listening tour" and drove to Washington D.C. He apologized to Fitz about not being around on Election Day to write in his name for the presidency. Fitz joked that he hoped that wasn't the vote that would tip the election and wished him a safe journey. Polly and Fitz flew back to New York with Evan who met up with them in Las Vegas. It was time to make history.

****

November 8, 2016, Election Day, was anti-climactic. Despite some concerns about voters being confused about the write-in process in each state that allowed it, the results were never in doubt. Fitz won every state that he was registered as a candidate. It would take time to count all of the write-in votes and make things official, but concession speeches were made by Hillary and Jeb after polling stations closed on the West Coast. In fact, protest 'non-votes' were made in the fourteen states where Fitz wasn't on the ballot. If you counted the total voters and subtracted out the votes made for Clinton and Bush, the 'non-votes' for Cavendish would have given him the plurality in all fifty states – an absolute stunning turn of events in one month. He was congratulated by world leaders and celebrities, including all of the talk show hosts – Stephen Colbert, of course, took all of the credit. Terrorist organizations sent out messages, not of congratulations, but of hope that Cavendish would keep his promise to come to the table to hear their grievances. From the time he walked into Polly Preston's office until his victory speech, Fitzgerald Cavendish had spent just slightly over $2 million, the largest part going for Polly's services. He did not place one advertisement on TV or radio, and only communicated through the internet, social media, Alex Jones' radio show, the two-week bus tour, and an occasional press conference. The only honest televised coverage of his platform for America came at the first presidential debate.

His victory speech was short – it was at the same downtown New York Marriott where his vice-presidential press conference was conducted -- and mostly of thanks. He spoke of the "change" promised in other speeches from Jimmy Carter to Barrack Obama. He promised that his change would be different as he would not be captive to the Council on Foreign Relations or other behind-the-scenes organizations and secret societies that had been the real seat of power in the United States. For starters, his administration would have no high ranking officials who were members of these one-world government organizations. The conservative and liberal voters had spoken. The message was loud. The message was clear. It was time for sweeping change.

When he stepped away from the podium, Polly Preston gave him a big hug and a kiss while the cameras were still rolling as network commentators speculated as to what was in store for the United States. Fitz smiled ear to ear and said to Polly, "We did it!" Annie Van, who was watching in her apartment only blocks away, threw a shoe at the TV set. Oliver whimpered.

****

The Old German, Wheelchair Man, and the Blonde Jew all watched from Wheelchair Man's residence in upstate New York overlooking the Hudson River. They had been staring at the TV screen for hours in contemplative silence. The Blonde Jew broke the reticence referencing the hug and kiss between Fitz and Polly, "I thought that they weren't a couple?"

The Old German replied, "They aren't. We monitored his bus tour. The best we can tell, unlike his old man, Mr. Cavendish hasn't gotten laid in months."

The Blonde Jew inquired, "Is he gay?"

"No. We checked into his background thoroughly. He seems to be a playboy, but a loner. He has spent some summers on the French Riviera with friends. He likes very attractive women – who doesn't -- but has never settled down. Either way, it's too late for that line of tact now, with the Secret Service protection and what not."

The Blonde Jew seemed unhappy, "So this guy has no family and no one that he is close to – no buttons to push? Does he have a fucking dog for Christ's sake?"

Wheelchair Man entered the conversation, "You know it's always funny hearing a Jew use the Lord's name in vain. Listen, as Hank said, it is too late for that tact now. Remember, just because this guy thinks he has a mandate from the people, we still control Congress. He doesn't take office for another ten weeks. It's going to be tough for him to run a government if he doesn't have any Cabinet appointments approved."

Blonde Jew: "But this guy is different. This coup he engineered was genius. He has outed our plans to the population. He has me gravely concerned."

Old German: "He hasn't made any public proclamations about population control. He agrees with us on this point – or at least he told us as much. If he becomes a problem, the vice-president looks to be malleable."

280

Chapter 36 (Iran – Contra)

Gene "Chip" Tatum has a story to tell. It involves Iran-Contra and it involves the 1992 election and it's a doozy. Chip started his service to his country by joining the Air Force in February 1970. After extensive training, he was recruited into "Team Red Rock" at the end of 1970. Shifty President Richard Nixon and his shiftier Secretary of State Henry Kissinger were running a secret war in Cambodia and Laos. The Cambodian leader, Lon Nol, was only interested in continuing the fight as long as the United States did the fighting. Nixon wanted Lon Nol to have his forces more engaged in the conflict so the United States could remove its forces before anyone found out about these illegal wars.

To that end, the members of Team Red Rock – consisting of eight US Army Green Berets, three US Navy Seals, two CIA paramilitary specialists, and Chip -- were employed on a secret mission. They would parachute into the Cambodian capital of Phnom Penh, and attack the airport, military and civil installations – essentially waging war against their ally. Team Red Rock would also parachute in unarmed and previously captured North Vietnamese soldiers who would be shot once they touched ground in Phnom Penh. The plan was to create the illusion that the attacks were carried out by the NVA soldiers, which would enrage Lon Nol, inducing him to commit more of his soldiers in the cause against the communist forces of North Vietnam. The real mission was to convince Congress to authorize more money to finance new and improved aircraft in support of the pro-U.S. and anti-communist Lon Nol regime. This was a classic "false flag" operation, and an attempt at employing the Hegelian Dialectic.

Unknown to Team Red Rock was the caveat that Nixon had arranged to have them liquidated as well – by Vietnamese tribesman (the Degar), who were on the CIA payroll -- so word of the operation would never get out. Team Red Rock sensed that they were in for the double cross, and after a successful mission in Phnom Penh, did their best to foil the Degar assigned to kill them. To make a long story short, after ninety-two days in captivity as a prisoner of war, during which Chip and other members of his team were tortured, he was accidently rescued by U.S. Marines. He was one of only two of the original fourteen who survived. In a Philippine hospital, he was debriefed by CIA Saigon Chief, William

Colby, and immediately assigned to the CIA, where he would serve the agency for twenty-five years.

Fast forward to 1983: Tatum gets a call from then former CIA Director Colby that he is going to be receiving a call from a man named "North". He was stationed at Fort Campbell, Kentucky, as a Special Operations Pilot. Part of his duty involved flying white coolers marked "Medical Supplies" to Little Rock Air Base and Mena Airport, both located in Arkansas. On two occasions at Mena, Tatum delivered the coolers to Dr. Dan Lasater, friend of then Arkansas Governor Bill Clinton.

The balance of this paragraph is a Cliff Notes version of the horse manure you were fed about the Iran-Contra Affair. In an attempt to secure the release of seven American hostages held in Lebanon by a group with Iranian ties, the United States agreed to sell arms to Iran using Israel as a conduit, which was counter to its advertised arms embargo. The proceeds from those sales were then used to fund the Contras in Nicaragua, in violation of the Borland Amendment in which the United States was forbidden from providing any non-humanitarian support to the anti-communist rebels. This operation was orchestrated by Col. Oliver North at the behest of Admiral John Poindexter and CIA Director William Casey, amongst others.

The real story is much more interesting. The whole notion of arms for hostages started back in 1980 when the Reagan camp secretly negotiated a better deal with Iran for the release of fifty-two American hostages, the ones that were held for 444 days at the U.S. Embassy in Tehran. With the outcome of the election still in the balance, Carter believed that if he could negotiate the release of the hostages on favorable terms to the United States, it might inspire the electorate to give him four more years in the White House. He was secretly offering the unfreezing of $4 billion out of the $12 billion in Iranian assets that were domiciled in U.S. bank accounts. Even though they were not yet elected officials, Reagan and Bush were in contact with the Iranians offering a deal – negotiated in Paris and Washington D.C. by Bush along with soon to be CIA Director William Casey. Their proposal included not only the unfreezing of all Iranian assets, but also unclogging the pipeline of military equipment that was earmarked for Iran before the embargo was issued. The Iranians, making sure they had their entire base covered, reached out to third party candidate John Bayard Anderson to see what deal he would offer. Anderson, for his part, reported the matter to the FBI.

One might ask: What did the Israelis have to gain from being the middle man in a deal that would arm their sworn enemy? The answer is two-fold. First, they could help maintain a balance of power in the new Iran-Iraq conflict. If each side was equally armed, it could be reasoned that the war would last longer and both enemies of Israel would suffer more casualties. More dead Muslim soldiers represented victory for Israel. Second, the Israelis could use their knowledge of the Reagan administration's covert activities (before they were elected into office – in essence, treason) as blackmail/leverage in any other Mideast situations involving Israel.

With Carter unable to bring the hostages home, Reagan and Bush were elected in a landslide. A small shipment of airplane parts was sent from Israel to Iran in October 1980 – before the election -- as a good faith gesture by Reagan and Bush. In return, Iran held the hostages for a few extra months, and released them as Reagan was being sworn in as the 40th President of the United States – Iran's signal to the Reagan administration that they were holding up their end of the bargain. Arms continued to flow into Iran via Israel for years, well in advance of the Iran-Contra scandal. Some of the money that was made on the inflated sales of these weapons was deposited in Swiss accounts for use by the Contras.

Meanwhile, Col. North was busy running an enterprise that was making himself and his partners wealthy using the Contras as cover. He was running the biggest cocaine operation in the Western Hemisphere, and quite possibly, the world. The raw product in the form of coca leaves was supplied by the Colombians and pressed into large cube-shaped bales and then shipped to Nicaragua and Honduras. In return for money deposited in Swiss bank accounts and weapons that were being supplied to the Contras, North's operation received cocaine. That cocaine was then shipped into the United States at multiple locations, including Mena Airport in Arkansas. Keep in mind that this is only one tentacle of a larger operation.

On February 15, 1985, Tatum -- in addition to his new duties as a U.S. Army Medevac pilot out of Palmerola Air Base, Honduras -- was assigned to Major Felix Rodriguez, where he would support Pegasus missions – allegedly the same Pegasus organization set up by President Harry S. Truman that reported to the president until Kennedy was assassinated. Afterwards, Pegasus became a shadow CIA operation with other nations like Israel, UK, and other foreign government and foreign intelligence services as members. Pegasus reported to the National Security Council, which developed three sub-groups (the Special Situation Group, the Terrorist Incident Working Group, and then the Operational Sub-Groups) which did not answer to Congress. In 1981, President Reagan signed a National Security Decision Directive #3 that placed the Special Situation Group (and eventually the other sub-groups), and all intelligence assets under Vice President George H. W. Bush. This was the group that was running drugs for their own personal profit.

On February 26, 1985, Tatum and his crew were instructed to fly two employees of Corporate Air Services (a.k.a. CIA Air) to a Contra camp on the Honduran border. Following a meeting between the CIA agents and Contra leaders, Tatum was given a sealed cooler marked "Vaccine" weighing approximately 200 lbs. and was instructed to deliver it to a USAF C 130 transport plane at La Mesa airport, Honduras. Two crew members off-loading the cooler accidentally dropped it breaking the seal. Inside was over 100 bags of cocaine. Tatum resealed the cooler and later watched as it was transferred aboard the C-130 outward bound for Panama. He reported this incident to Col. North who claimed that the cocaine was bound for a world court to be used as evidence against the Sandinistas, proving that they were funding their military operations through illegal drug sales. Tatum, not being born yesterday, and remembering all of the "Medical Supplies" shipments he made into Arkansas, decided to keep a diary of all his Pegasus activities on the back of his flight logs. He figured this information might keep him alive at some point down the road.

As it turns out he would do one better. On March 16th, he was flying two members of the operation, an Israeli intelligence officer in the Mossad named Mike Harari and Bill Clinton associate Buddy Young, from a meeting at the U.S. Embassy in Tegucigalpa to Palmerola Air Base, both in Honduras. He taped part of their conversation regarding the operation. The conversation (and Tatum's observations) follows:

Buddy: "Arkansas has the capability to manufacture anything in the area of weapons - and if we don't have it - we'll get it!"

284

Mike: "How about government controls?"

Buddy: "The Governor's on top of it, and if the feds get nosey - we hear about it and make a call. Then they're called off." (He was looking around the countryside and continued), "Why the hell would anyone want to fight for a shit-hole like this?"

Mike: (Shaking his head in awe, answered), "What we do has nothing to do with preserving a country's integrity - it's just business, and third world countries see their destiny as defeating borders and expanding. The more of this mentality we can produce -- the greater our wealth. We train and we arm - that's our job. And, in return, we get a product far more valuable than the money for a gun. We're paid with product. And we credit top dollar for product."

Buddy: (Still looked confused.)

Mike: "Look - one gun and 3,000 rounds of ammo is $1,200. A kilo of product is about $1,000. We credit the Contras $1,500 for every kilo. That's top dollar for a kilo of cocaine. It's equivalent to the American K-Mart special - buy four, get one free. On our side - we spend $1,200 for a kilo and sell it for $12,000 to $15,000. Now, that's a profit center. And the market is much greater for the product than for weapons. It's just good business sense - understand?"

Buddy: "Damn! So you guys promote wars and revolutions to provide weapons for drugs - we provide the non-numbered parts to change out and we all win. Damn that's good!"

Mike: "It's good when it works - but someone is, how do you say, has his hand in the coffer."

Buddy: (Responding on the defensive), "Well, we get our ten percent right off the top and that's plenty. GOFUS can make it go a long way."

Mike: "Who is GOFUS?"

Buddy: "Governor Clinton! That's our pet word for him. You know they call the President 'POTUS' for 'President of the United States'. Well, we call Clinton 'GOFUS' for 'Governor of the United States'. He thinks he is anyhow."

Mike: "That's your problem in America. You have no respect for your elected officials. They are more powerful than you think and have ears everywhere. You should heed my words and be loyal to your leaders. Especially when speaking to persons like me. Your remarks indicate a weakness - something our intelligence analysts look for."

Buddy: "Aw hell, Mike. Everybody knows the Clinton's want the White House and will do anything to get it. That's why I'm here instead of someone else. We know about the cocaine - hell! I've picked it up before with Lasater when he was worried about going on Little Rock Air Base to get it."

A new line of conversation ensued. Harari questioned Young about his knowledge of who the "players" were. He went down a list. He started with "The Boss – Clinton". Here's a synopsis of the players according to Young.

Buddy: "Clinton - thinks he's in charge, but he'll only go as far as [CIA Director] Casey allows. Me and my staff - we keep the lid on things you know - complaints about night flying - Arkansas people are private folks - they don't like a lot of commotion and Mena just isn't the right place for the operation. It keeps us busy at the shredder - if you know what I mean. Dan the Man [Lasater] - He does magic with the money - between him and Jack Stevens we don't have to worry a bit. Then we got Parks - if there's a problem - he's the man. We call him the Archer - that's the codename that Casey and Colby told us to assign to that position. Finnis [unknown] oversees our drop zone. Nash [unknown] - he's just the boss' 'yes' man. Personally I think he's a mistake! [Barry] Seal and his guys - I like his attitude 'and leave the driving to us!'" (he said, quoting one of Seal's good ole boy sayings.)

Mike: "You like Seal?"

Buddy: "Hell! He's the only one I trust - respect is the word."

Mike: "Do you see much of him?"

Buddy: "Hell, yea. We test drive Clinton's rides before we send 'em on, ya know? (He laughed, grinding his hips.) Say - how much coke do you recon [sic] you can make in a week?"

Mike: "One camp can produce 400 keys a week. The others are about half that. But that's just our operation here. We have other sources in various parts of the world. Why do you ask?"

Buddy: 'What? Oh, the Governor wanted to know our capacity."

The conversation continues uneventfully from there. Barry Seal, who flew weapons out of and drugs into Mena Airport, befriended Chip Tatum. Barry provided Chip with a list of the American kingpins in the operation. The list included Vice-President George Bush (CFR); CIA Director William Casey (CFR); Governor of Arkansas Bill Clinton (CFR); Col. Oliver North; Head of CIA's Central American Task Force Clair Elroy George; Henry Kissinger (CFR); Secretary of State General Alexander Haig (CFR); National Security Advisor Donald Gregg (CFR); CIA Costa Rican Station Chief Joseph Fernandez; former Director of Central Intelligence William Colby (CFR); head of the Criminal Division at the US Justice Department William Weld (CFR); CIA operatives Felix Rodriguez, John Singlaub, Richard V. Secord, and Duane "Dewey" Clarridge; and General Peroot of the Defense Intelligence Agency. Through his own investigation while he was involved, Tatum compiled an impressive (and very long) list of international involvement that included Panamanian Dictator General Manuel Noriega; Mossad officer Mike Harari; former Mossad agent, Pegasus officer, and Advisor to Vice President Bush Amiram Nir (a.k.a. Pat Weber); two-time Israeli Prime Minister Yitzhak Rabin; Iranian arms dealer Manucher Ghorbanifar; leader of the Contras Enrique Bermudez; Former Chief of Staff of the Honduran Military General Gustavo Alverez; Medellin drug trafficker Lt. Col. Ramon Navarro; and politicians, military, and intelligence officers from Saudi Arabia, Columbia, Honduras, El Salvador, Mexico, and Nicaragua. Barry Seal was later arrested and became a Drug Enforcement Agency (DEA) informer – not an occupation with a long life expectancy considering the power at the top of the world wide drug network, especially with no government protection. Seal's work for the DEA included taking pictures during an operation that showed Pablo Escobar, Jorge Luis Ochoa Vásquez, and other members of the Medellin Cartel loading kilos of cocaine onto a C-123 transport plane; however, this cocaine was allegedly brokered by the Sandinistas – or so the story was supposed to go. Tatum was at a meeting with Oliver North, Felix Rodriguez, Amiram Nir and General Alverez from Honduras, when the Barry Seal "issue" was discussed. According to Tatum, North said that VP Bush was going to have his son Jeb arrange "something out of Columbia." That "something" was a hit on Barry Seal by the Medellin Cartel -- Colombian hitman Luis Quintero was the trigger -- on February 19, 1986. With Seal's death the DEA ended its investigation.

If you think Tatum's story is a drug-induced fantasy, Al Martin, former Lt. Commander from the U.S. Naval Reserves and black ops specialist in the Office of Naval Intelligence, corroborates it. In his book, *The Conspirators: Secrets of an Iran-Contra Insider*, Martin relays a conversation he had with Jeb Bush shortly after Barry Seal was "removed" where he threatened to chirp to authorities about Jeb's (and others') role in the Barry Seal and Iran-Contra affair.

> "I had told Jeb that I had substantial corroboration of that meeting [with Jeb, Oliver North, Richard Secord and Dewey Clarridge where the Seal "issue" was discussed]. And I think Jeb understood what I meant. It would certainly place him into a conspiracy to assassinate a CIA drug runner for the sake of political expediency. When I was through speaking, Jeb became quiet and his demeanor became serious and changed. He became flushed, as he often does when he's frightened. Jeb responded by telling me that it would be most unfortunate if I were to do that, since I might wind up like George Morales or Johnny Molina."

Molina was killed later that day. Morales was already in jail, but according to Martin, Jeb said, "Of course, Morales will never leave prison alive." Sure enough, he was "accidented" the day before he was to be released from prison. According to Martin,

"The following day [the day of his scheduled release], Morales was due to be picked up at the Miami International Airport by a Congressional charter flight arranged for him by Congressmen Alexander, Rose, Brooks and Gonzalez. He was to be taken to Washington to have a detailed discussion with them and their investigators about his knowledge of Iran-Contra."

Louisiana Attorney General, William J. Guste, Jr. sent a strongly worded letter to Attorney General Edwin Meese on March 3, 1986 decrying the lack of government protection for Barry Seal. Guste stated, "WHY WAS SUCH AN IMPORTANT WITNESS NOT GIVEN PROTECTION WHETHER HE WANTED IT OR NOT?" [Emphasis not added.] Guste was obviously not part of Iran-Contra.

Getting back to the operation, as the cocaine entered different parts of the country, the money received for it had to be laundered. In Arkansas that was accomplished by Jackson Stevens, owner of Worthen Bank & Trust Company that was closely aligned with Governor Bill Clinton, and by the aforementioned Dan Lasater. Dan's company, Collins, Locke & Lasater was "allowed" 15% participation as an underwriter in $637 million of Arkansas Housing Development Agency and Arkansas Development Finance Authority bond offerings between 1983 and 1986. These agencies were a creation of Bill Clinton and sold under the guise of creating jobs, while assisting churches and schools. However, its decision making procedures were made a secret so it could funnel money elsewhere. Pressure was put on these agencies from the Governor's office to allow Lasater's participation. Lasater's cocaine money was used to purchase these bonds. For example, the money was sent to ADFA bank accounts in Florida, Georgia, New York, and Illinois, according to once good friend of Bill Clinton's, Larry Nichols. Those accounts would eventually zero out with the money returning to Lasater minus the laundering fee. Again, this was just one tentacle in the drug and money laundering operation.

Tatum was recruited into Pegasus in 1986 by William Colby. He was assigned to be the head of several construction companies in upstate New York that were nothing more than money laundering and arms smuggling operations. The money laundering became necessary as the outfits in Arkansas, Colorado, and Ohio could not handle the influx of money.

As the Iran-Contra Affair unfolded in front of America with North giving riveting, yet specious testimony, Vice President Bush grew concerned. He was fearful that people would talk, resulting in a lost bid for the White House, or worse yet, jail time. As it turned out Secretary of Defense Casper Weinberger, National Security Advisor Robert McFarland, Asst. Secretary of State Elliot Abrams, Chief of the CIA's Central American Task Force Alan D. Fiers, businessman Albert Hakim, CIA Chief of Covert Operations Clair George, Oliver North, John Poindexter, Duane Clarridge, and Richard Secord all were indicted as a result of the scandal. More people than just Barry Seal had to be silenced. To that end, Amiram Nir was scheduled to testify to the Senate subcommittee and it was feared he would reveal the truth. He perished following the shoot down of his aircraft with missiles from Tatum's helicopter in Mexico during December 1988. General Alverez was assassinated by Pegasus in 1989, following his demand for a bigger split of the Cocaine profits. Contras leader Enrique Bermudez tried to pressure Bush into coercing the Nicaraguan government into giving Bermudez a prominent post, by threatening to expose Bush's role in the scandal. Bush ordered his disposal. He was assassinated by Pegasus in 1991. Chip Tatum was involved in all three of these murders. Thanks to some well-placed pressure and President Bush pardons, not one of those indicted ever served any jail time.

There was one other person that Bush needed to silence: Manuel Noriega. Noriega was extradited to the United States after it invaded Panama. His trial was a complete joke as he was not allowed to reveal that he had received $10 million from the CIA in return for some "services". Remarkably, the district court held that the "information about the content of the discrete operations in which Noriega had engaged in exchange for the alleged payments was irrelevant to his defense." It ruled that the introduction of evidence about Noriega's role in the CIA would "confuse the jury." What exactly were these services? You see, sometime in the late 1960s or early 1970s the CIA had secretly provided to the Shah of Iran a set of printing plates that could reproduce US$100 bills. After the Shah's overthrow, $8 billion of these counterfeit bills were sitting shrink wrapped on two pallets in Iran. Bush cut a deal with Noriega and the Iranian leadership. Bush, with Noriega overseeing the Panamanian side of this operation, withdrew $8 billion from Pablo Escobar's account at Panama's central bank. $4 billion was given to the Iranians in exchange for the $8 billion of counterfeit bills. The $8 billion in counterfeit bills were then flown to Panama and placed into the Panama central bank, replacing Escobar's real money. Remember, this was pre-internet and practically pre-personal computer time in Panama: instead of operating digitally, the Panamanian central bank was probably operating by abacus. That $4 billion was then used by the Iranians to buy weapons from the CIA. The CIA now possessed $4 billion for its black operations without having to get funding approval from Congress. The other $4 billion went into an account that was co-owned by Vice President Bush and CIA Director William Casey. When Casey passed away in 1987, Bush had sole control of the money. Casey had hired Nana DeBusia to launder the money through various banks. DeBusia cut was $200 million and thirty-two trumped up charges of bank fraud, on which he was later acquitted. These charges were brought and then dropped with the effect of discrediting and silencing DeBusia. Noriega's trial in the United States was a complete whitewash resulting in his conviction on September 16, 1992 on eight counts of drug trafficking, racketeering, and money laundering. He served seventeen years in prison, never being allowed to tell his role in Oliver North's drug enterprise or in the fleecing of Pablo Escobar's drug money. Escobar was eventually hunted down and killed on December 2, 1993.

The Reagan administration was perfectly fine having a few hostages in the Mideast as it provided a cover for the CIA funding its black ops. If they were ever caught, the excuse of trading weapons for hostages provided a sympathetic alibi. A government not negotiating with terrorists might be the stated policy, but if it was your son or daughter, you would exhaust all means to return him or her home safely. Even though your government is violating policy, the human condition of the situation might give them a compassionate rationalization. This line of reasoning may seem half-baked until you consider the experience of Sis Levin, wife of kidnapped CNN Bureau Chief Jerry Levin. Despite Reagan's public rhetoric to do everything to get the hostages back, Sis Levin had no access to the administration and was "simply told to stay home, to be quiet, to trust, and the agenda would be fulfilled." Frustrated with seven months of inaction by the Reagan Administration, Sis went to the Mideast and negotiated the release of her husband – more like an authorized escaped –

from the Syrian government. Sis said, "Now we know the agenda was to Iran." Looking back at it, Sis says,

> "...if there had not been hostages, they would have had to have been created, because if the agenda to get arms to Iran were discovered, the only thing the American people would take as an excuse would be the very human element of a very human president weeping over hostages."

In 1992, President George H.W. Bush was running against Governor of Arkansas William Jefferson Clinton. Whoever won, their secrets would be safe; except that some guy named Ross Perot led in the Gallop poll with a 39 percent rating in June of the election year. Perot had to be stopped. Perot also had a pretty good inkling what was going on with Iran-Contra, stating when asked about CIA drug smuggling, "What I have found is a snake pit without a bottom. They will do anything to keep this covered up." Perot was correct. Bush sent a memo to his assassin Chip Tatum expressing his desire to see Perot "neutralized" because he allegedly "illegally obtained documents which are of vital concern to the security of the United States...You are authorized to use whatever means necessary to recover said documents...." And "If loss of life occurs as a result of the performance of your duties, you shall be exempt and protected from prosecution." This is where Tatum drew the line. He told Bush that he was not going to "neutralize" American citizens on behalf of Bush.

For the avoidance of doubt, "neutralization" does not necessarily mean assassination. There are three phases of the "neutralization" process. Step One is intimidation or coercion (e.g. issue a threat). Step Two is compromise (e.g. create a scandal such as Gary Hart – Donna Rice). Step Three is assassination. Tatum had refused the Gary Hart job on the grounds that he was an American citizen. Perot was Tatum's second refusal of Bush.

Bush admonished Tatum that he didn't have a choice in the matter. Tatum countered that he had documentation detailing the illegal activities of the past six years and these documents were copied six fold and secreted away in six locations throughout the world. If the possessors of these documents didn't receive a call from Tatum on a certain date (or were told to return them to Tatum), the documents would be mailed to the address written on the envelopes. This is how Tatum "retired" from Pegasus and protected Perot by contacting him through a trusted FBI agent at the Saddlebrook Resort in Florida. Because of subsequent strong harassment from Bush and North, Tatum began releasing *some* of what he knows to the world. His story is incredible. Perot was ostensibly "neutralized" when he received threats that digitally altered photographs would be released by the Bush campaign to sabotage his daughter's wedding. The leading candidate in the polls temporarily dropped out of the campaign, negating any chance at the White House.

You might be asking at this point, "What happened to the $3.8 billion under Bush's control?" Answer: good question. According to Tatum, it would serve many purposes; the most important was furthering the cause of one-world government. Democratic House Representative Jack Brooks from Texas obviously hit on a nerve at the Iran-Contra hearings when he asked Col. Oliver North about his role in Readiness Exercise 1984 (Rex 84), which was a program that suspended Constitutional rights in the event of a national emergency. Housed under FEMA, it was a program that could quell political dissent – the line between political dissent and terrorists can become quite blurred contingent upon the paranoia level of the decision maker. FEMA head Louis Giuffrida, George Bush, and Oliver North turned FEMA – initially put into place to coordinate resources in the event of a natural disaster -- into an "anti-terrorist" organization. Rex 84 was essentially similar to a plan authored by Giuffrida in 1970, while at the Army War College, which proposed the detention of up to 21 million "American Negroes", if there were a black militant uprising in the United States. On initial questioning of North regarding this program, Chairman of the Senate Select Committee on Secret Military Assistance to Iran and the Nicaraguan Opposition Hearings Senator Daniel Inouye interrupted Brooks telling him that the matter was "sensitive" and not appropriate in a public inquiry. Brooks responded,

> "I was particularly concerned, Mr. Chairman, because I read in Miami papers [by reporter Alfonso Chardy in the July 5, 1987 edition of the *Miami Herald*] and several others that there had been a plan developed by that same agency [National Security Council], a contingency plan in the event of an emergency that would suspend the American Constitution, and I was deeply concerned

about that and wondered if that was an area in which he [Oliver North] had worked."

Inouye: "May I most respectfully request that that matter not be touched upon at this stage."

Tatum knew the game:

> "I can see that everything that we were doing from 1986 in the OSGs [Operational Sub-Groups] until I left... in 1992 were designed to align countries into a one-world government. There is no doubt in my mind that that's what we were doing...As a matter of fact, having seen certain time schedules for things to happen [for one-world government], [at the time] not understanding what it was designed for, I can say that they are ahead of schedule."

All of the files relating to Clinton's involvement in Whitewater and Iran-Contra were shipped to Oklahoma City and stored in the Alfred P. Murrah Federal Building. You know what happened to that building. What you don't know is that the rescue operation was completely suspended shortly after the bombing so a group of federal agents in unmarked blue jackets could remove boxes of records/files for "national security reasons."

There are two lessons to be learned from this story: 1. to repeat, any time you hear a government official use "national security" as a reason for not disclosing information to the American public, it is being employed as a shield to hide illegal activities. National security was the excuse given in the Kennedy assassination: if anyone knew about Oswald's (sheep-dipped) Communist connections, World War III could result, wiping out most of the planet, so the investigation can't be thorough, or so the logic goes. In truth, a real investigation would actually point to the real killers. 2. Do not make the mistake of projecting your ethos onto your political leaders. They don't think or act like ninety-nine point nine-nine percent of the population. They don't care about you. Some are extraordinarily evil – as you will come to see.

Two more observations: 1. Why is this not the top story in the news? 2. Purchase copies of *Chip Tatum Chronicles; Compromised: Clinton, Bush and the CIA; Barry & 'the Boys': The CIA, the Mob and*

America's Secret History; Bushwhacked: Inside Stories of True Conspiracy; and *The Conspirators: Secrets of an Iran-Contra Insider,* if you need further convincing.

Chapter 37 (January 20, 2017)

Where is she? This question at that moment, occupying Fitz's mind, applied to two women, actually three. Fitz had sent an invitation to Annie and her mother to attend the inauguration, along with all of the subsequent pomp and circumstance. It was to be her coming out party. He had not spoken to Annie. The invitation was his first act of correspondence with her in eight months. He had secured a room for them at The Jefferson, a room he was hoping that Annie wasn't going to need by the end of the inaugural evening. He had written a corny note with a little puzzle inside instructing her how to respond. It was sent via Federal Express and it had been signed for by someone at the front desk of her building six days ago – yet, there was no response. *Is she not coming? Has she moved on?* She couldn't be on vacation from teaching as Fitz had checked into the schedule at the United Nations School. Neither Annie nor her mother checked into The Jefferson last night. *Maybe she thought that I had moved on based on all of the rumor and innuendo surrounding Polly and me.*

Speaking of which, Polly was nowhere to be found. It was only minutes before Fitz was to head to the White House from where he and Barack Obama would proceed to the inaugural grounds at the United States Capitol. This was odd. Polly Preston was perfectly punctual. Unlike Annie, she had checked into The Jefferson yesterday afternoon. Even though communication became challenging once Fitz became the President-Elect – the Secret Service detail provided Fitz with a new phone, more or less a military grade communications device that looked like a smart phone – Polly was in regular communication with Fitz and had checked in with him when she arrived at the hotel. She was meeting an associate for a cocktail to discuss a business lead and then she was meeting some of the girls from her office that she invited down and put up in another hotel as a thank you for the successful conclusion to Fitz's campaign. Fitz spent the evening out celebrating with some friends that concluded with a drunken game of Hearts back at his hotel room. Fitz tried to reach Polly on both of her devices, but no one answered. Fitz realized that this was the first time that Polly didn't pick up the phone when he had called her since their relationship started eight months ago. Her absence was very troubling.

Given the highly unlikely circumstances surrounding his election, Fitz viewed his Secret Service detail with caution, but not suspicion. It was for this reason that he hired Mafia Mike as his personal assistant. Mike could handle himself and was adroit at getting things "done", like Winston Wolfe in *Pulp Fiction*. Fitz placed a call to Mike concerning his missing ladies and armed with requests and phone numbers, he sprang into action.

Fitz had plenty on his mind: two missing women; an inauguration speech; and a stock market on the brink of freefall that was somehow his fault. Since the evening of the debate, the wisdom of his economic platform had been called into question. Once he became the President-Elect, the negative rhetoric ratcheted up even more. Some said it made no sense; some said its implementation was impossible; some said that if his platform was carried out, it would lead to economic collapse; and others said that his new *debt-free* currency would not be accepted by foreign countries. Meanwhile these same pundits said nothing of the fact that the debt ceiling was raised annually by Congress or why that had to happen for government to function in a debt-based money system. It was enough criticism to make some Americans question why they had elected a political neophyte to the highest office in the land. It was the kind of animadversion that would have scared off enough would be voters if the cynics and the critics had more time to organize and assail Fitz's policies – but they didn't. The Blonde Jew, the Old German, and Wheelchair Man had made calls after the election, prompting the habitual skepticism machine into overdrive. The goal was to whittle away at Fitz's popularity and credibility before he entered office, making his claim of a mandate less certain. The stock market, as measured by the Dow Jones Industrial Average, reached an all-time closing high of 18,312.39 on May 19, 2015. When Fitz made his brief summer appearance on CNBC the market was at 16,500. When he was elected, the average stood at 15,400. On inauguration day, the Dow was hovering at 14,700, just above bear market (or down 20% from the previous high) levels.

The tone of his upcoming inauguration address was dour. Fitz had shared its contents the night before with a group of his friends that would comprise most of his cabinet members, and Chuck Schilling, who he had asked to be his Press Secretary, one of the few appointments not subject to Senate approval. The appointment smoothed over any awkwardness related to the choice of Polly Preston as his public relations manager. His future cabinet staff ribbed him over a few beers that he was going to be hammered by the press for the speech's timbre. They also needled each other about their odds of being approved by the Senate. Fitz knew that the transition process was laborious with potentially nine thousand appointments to be made. The series of actions required to fill just the top level Cabinet posts was likely a three month process. Fitz didn't have that kind of time.

With no sign of Polly or Annie, Fitz made his way over to the White House, where President Obama greeted Fitz warmly. He praised his choice of Caroline Kennedy for Secretary of State, and said that he would do his best to see to it that she was approved. After he briefed Fitz on all of the sensitive situations transpiring in the world that were unknown to the public, the two made their way over to the west front of the Capitol Building. Cavendish sensed that Obama was looking forward to relative obscurity for a while; and though he felt that Obama was part of the problem, and not part of the solution, he felt a smattering of sympathy for the man. *It must be difficult to reach the highest office in the land and find out that you are merely a puppet of the elite.* Then Fitz re-rationalized, *he knew the deal going in. He's one of them. That's how he got to where he is.*

On January 20, 2017, a cold, sunny Friday, with only Caroline Kennedy at his side, Fitzgerald Cavendish was sworn in as the 45th President of the United States. After making a quick joke about the transition of power taking place outdoors in the winter to keep the inaugural speeches short, Fitz said,

> "My fellow Americans, fifty-six years ago, my father stood right here and said, 'ask not what your country can do for you -- ask what you can do for your country.' Fifty-six years later, with more than fifty million citizens receiving food stamps, more than twenty million in the Women, Infants and Children program, more than twenty million receiving Supplemental Security Income, more than ten million in public housing or receiving housing subsidies, more than five million receiving Temporary Assistance to Needy Families, and nearly five million needing other Federal cash assistance, it is time that your country -- your government --

do something for you. You see, these government programs are the symptoms of a broken system. They are patches to leaks in a dam; a dam which is about to burst. When wealth is transferred discreetly through a debt-based money creation system, from the populace to the originators of that money, there is less money per capita for the population. You get poorer and your government goes deeper into debt, to a mind-boggling extent. As the population gets poorer, the need for assistance becomes greater. Once you are dependent upon your government for subsistence, you are willing to give up certain rights and privileges in order to maintain your assistance. This is a very sad state of affairs. This government-sponsored wealth transfer is simply a smokescreen, hiding the fact that per capita, on an inflation-adjusted basis, you are getting poorer by the day. The government is in an inevitable perpetual upward spiral of debt; and with the level of debt always greater than the level of money, retiring the debt is impossible, at least so it seems. With Congress facing nearly a half a trillion dollar interest payment on the debt every year, how would any reasonable person expect them to balance the budget? This is all by design. Once the central bankers have bankrupted enough of the population, and that tipping point is near, you will be willing to give up certain Constitutional rights to maintain this socialistic state that a great many of you have become dependent upon; a socialist state that has befallen this once great and fiercely independent country – a country founded on the concept of rugged individualism. Amongst those rights you have already surrendered is the Bill of Rights through the Patriot Act. Those who are willing to surrender their individual rights for security deserve neither. The next surrender will be the submission of the sovereignty of the United States of America to a regional government concept, a precursor to a one-world government, which will not be run on the principles of rugged individualism, not on a U.S.-styled Constitution, but rather on a Soviet-styled corporate socialistic lie run by the moneyed and corporate elite. Is this what you want? [The audience, like a church congregation, cries out sporadically "no".] I think not. The root cause of this trouble is the Federal Reserve and its debt-based money system. These are the secret rulers of you. You have elected me to make

299

the men behind the curtain disappear – forever. I will work tirelessly to repeal the Federal Reserve Act of 1913, and get the country on *debt-free* fiat money. I will also work to create a simpler and fairer method of taxation that will solve this country's healthcare and immigration crises. The end result of these measures will be to remove people from government assistance and make them a productive part of the economy. Broadly speaking, people who are not on government assistance are contributing more to the betterment of the overall standard of living versus people who are.

"Fifty-six years ago, my father said, 'my fellow citizens of the world: ask not what America will do for you, but what together we can do for the freedom of man.' Since my father put forth that challenge, the world is freer, not because we toppled democratically elected regimes for multi-national corporate interests under the smokescreen of defending freedom, but because communism is a lie. Lies eventually collapse under the weight of scrutiny. They are not tough and rigid like the truth. The war on terror is a lie – a myth perpetuated by our military-industrial complex and the media. Your brave sons, daughters, mothers, and fathers will be coming home. The never ending war on terror can only be won when we don't give the "terrorists" a reason to hate us. This is not a stance born out of fear or weakness. This is a stance born out of common sense. They don't "hate our freedoms". They just want some of their own. And if you haven't noticed, the war on terror has been used a red herring to take away our freedoms. If you really think that Muslims are trying to take over the world, just give them what they have desired for a century, since the Ottoman Empire fell: a caliphate – and see what happens. If they get their desired caliphate, it would be a magnet for those who desire such a system of rule – the media dubs them 'radicals'. You might see an outflow of 'radicals' from the United States and other countries to the caliphate. The establishment of a recognized caliphate would also provide the world a nation-state; thus a channel for diplomatic correspondences, as opposed to the current system of unapproachable, CIA-sponsored privateers known as terrorists whom we are not supposed to negotiate with because of some unwritten doctrine that states that by maintaining a dialogue with them we will only foster similar behavior. Since we have employed this illogical dogma, terrorist groups and terrorist activity have sprouted up like a weed, turning our war on terror into a game of whack-a-mole.

"Back to our defenses – when this country is spending more on defense than China, Saudi Arabia, Russia, the UK, France, Japan, India, Germany, and South Korea combined, we have a problem. Throughout the course of history, great empires and great nation-states fail for the same reason: they bankrupt themselves. Close to $20 trillion in debt, this country is in the course of realizing the same fate with its debt-based money system and its ridiculous outlays for defense. This must end.

"I did not come here to make you feel good about yourself, like prior presidents Ronald Reagan and Bill Clinton; or proud, like Barack Obama. I have come here to solve the problems at their root. That is why you elected me. Those puzzles that need immediate disentanglement are as follows:

1. The loss of your Constitutional rights.

2. A money system whose only end is perpetual debt.

3. A broken healthcare system, which is the result of governments poisoning the water supplies, injecting your children with contaminated vaccinations; and Big Food companies slowly eroding your health with crap that really isn't food, while Big Pharma, the FDA, and the AMA suppress any cure that can't make them money.

4. A welfare state that makes almost half of Americans dependent on their government for subsistence.

5. An outmoded and complicated system of taxation.

6. A massive illegal immigration problem.

7. A fundamental lack of choice under the illusion of choice.

All of these issues add up to a subtle erosion of this country's sovereignty, which is being engineered by the secret powers that exist. To that end, as I have said before, no one will serve in my cabinet who is a member of the Council on Foreign Relations, the Trilateral Commission, and any other organization or think tank whose goal is one-world government. The central banking interests and their friends, the military industrial complex and the corporate elite, have been working behind the scenes to destroy this country for nearly a century. This is done while they enrich themselves. They are inimical to your interests. The remedy of these issues will advance pride and goodwill much more than any well-meaning, pleasing rhetoric.

"For the avoidance of doubt, there are other pressing issues that need to be addressed – debated down to an understanding, more so than solved. The seven issues outlined above are the ones that I will get to work on immediately. And in the words of President George Washington, 'When the occasion proper for it shall arrive, I shall endeavor to express the high sense I entertain of this distinguished honor, and of the confidence which has been reposed in me by the people of united America.' I will report back to you in approximately one month at the State of the Union.

"Be well."

****

Annie Van watched the inauguration with her class. A tear escaped from its duct and slid slowly down over her cheek at which point the sensation pierced the numbness that had enveloped her slender, athletic body. She quickly snapped to and wiped the melancholy excretion away. It had been eight months. Her boyfriend – her love – was now the President of the United States and she was so alone in a classroom full of students. She felt terribly insignificant, something that wasn't possible until she had met Fitz. *Why was I so stupid to believe that he wasn't having an affair with Polly Preston? After all, he is a Kennedy!* She didn't know who to hate more: Fitz, or herself for allowing this to happen. Just as she was contemplating that question, her students charged out the door for lunch. She followed them out the door and down the hall to the teacher's lounge. She grabbed her smart phone and saw a text from a number she did not recognize. It read,

> "The President of the United States, Fitz, invited you to the inauguration. If you did not receive the invite and would like to come, please let me know and I will arrange for transportation immediately. Your presence is requested at the inaugural balls. He really wants to see you. Call or text me as soon as it is convenient. Mike Martelli."

A thunderbolt shot through Annie with such force, it suspended her ability to think. She was experiencing an inverted anxiety attack; the result was the same, but the emotion was the opposite. She went to reply by text, but found it too difficult – she couldn't calm her nerves. She finally tapped the phone number accompanying the text and waited for the pick-up. Mafia Mike picked up on the first ring, "This is Mike."

"Hi. Yes this is Annie. This isn't some practical joke or anything?"

"No. My name is Mike Martelli. I am Fitz's assistant. He sent you an invite to the inauguration that was received by your front desk six days ago. Did you not get it?"

"No." She didn't care about the invite, only that she was invited. "What do you want me to do?"

"I can come get you. I am already in transit to New York."

"Great! When can you be here?" Her head was starting to clear. "Do you want me to meet you in New Jersey -- with Friday traffic being what it is?"

"Sure. Just tell me where you want me to pick you up. I should be there by 3:30pm."

"466 Liberty Avenue, Jersey City. I will text it to you. Also, I will call you if there are any problems."

"I will do the same."

Annie ran down the hall to another teacher who would have her lunch break after Annie's and begged her to watch her kids for the last part of the day. The teacher agreed to the request and asked Annie if she was okay. By the time she could get the words of concern out of her mouth, Annie was running for the exit. Another text came from Mike reminding her to dress for the Inaugural Ball. She hadn't felt this energized in months. She hailed a cab to her apartment, didn't bother confronting anyone at the front desk about the invite, packed up her belongings along with Oliver, hopped into another taxi and headed for Jersey City.

****

Polly Preston was still missing. Her room was searched. It did not appear that she had returned to the hotel after heading out for drinks and dinner around 6:18pm, as far as the surveillance tapes indicated. Given that Cavendish was at a luncheon and then would be leading a procession (alone) down to the White House, it was not the time to get him involved. Instructions had come from the Secret Service to relay all news regarding Polly to Special Agent Quint Dravis, who would communicate it to Mafia Mike.

The suspense was killing Fitz. He deemed it poor etiquette to use a mobile device at the Congressional luncheon or during the subsequent parade. There were empty seats at the event thanks to absence of Polly, Annie, and Mrs. Van. Fitz's other guests included eight friends from school and work who would be subjected to Senate approval once Fitz officially nominated them to Cabinet positions. Fitz didn't know if this gesture was inappropriate, but he figured a little social interaction before the approval hearings could break the ice – put a more human face on the proceedings. It didn't. The whole affair was pleasant, but awkward as most of the leaders from both houses of Congress knew that Fitz and his landslide election victory changed the game. They couldn't hide behind partisan politics – Fitz wasn't from either side of the aisle. They ran the risk of being voted out if they didn't listen to Fitz. But these men and women took their marching orders not from their constituency, but from special interests and the debt-based money cabal. At the end of the day, they were the ones who had compromised the lawmakers with campaign donations, favors for family members, lucrative business deals, and simple blackmail. It was okay to debate gun control – especially since the cabal wanted guns removed. It was okay to debate healthcare. It was okay to debate immigration – as long as nothing was accomplished. It was *not* okay to repeal the Federal Reserve Act of 1913. It was *not* okay to repeal the 16th Amendment to the Constitution: Income Tax -- the cabals' blessed tax-free foundations would no longer be free from tax. It wasn't that the battle lines hadn't been drawn; it was that the Congressmen weren't sure where to stand. For now, they wandered in a philosophical and political de-militarized zone.

The walk to the White House for the viewing of the Inaugural Parade was also awkward. Fitz walked alone. He hadn't anticipated Annie's absence (or Polly's for that matter) and even though Caroline was family, the look of the President and the future Secretary of State, half-brother and half-sister, a portrait in nepotism, walking down Pennsylvania Avenue might send the wrong message to the American public. Besides, Caroline wasn't moving into the White House with Fitz. The walk to the viewing stand was packed with well-wishers and the event was must see TV – Fitz was still a celebrity first – as much as observing someone walk down a street could be. Fitz, in a rare moment of insecurity, was curious as to what people inspecting his every step down Pennsylvania Avenue thought about the fact that he had no one escorting him to his home for the next four years. It wasn't supposed to be this way. In fact, that was one of the tasks that he had paid Polly to perform: worry about what other people were thinking. He desperately wanted to run to the White House and get an update from Mike regarding Polly and Annie. But that wasn't going to happen until he reviewed a parade from an enclosed stand at the edge of the White House's North Lawn. He also thought about his mother.

****

A very sleek black Lincoln Town Car turned onto Liberty Avenue in Jersey City and parked on the street at 466, effectively blocking the driveway entrance at 3:20pm. Mafia Mike got out and proceeded to the entrance which was on the side of the house up a concrete stairway. He knocked on the door and was greeted by a barking Jack Russell Terrier and Annie.

"Shush. Oliver." Oliver obeyed as Annie opened the door from the kitchen.

"Hi. I'm Michael Martelli. Are you Annie?"

"Yes. Come on in." Mrs. Van was also in the kitchen.

Mike was taken aback by all the beauty in the room. "Hi. Are you Annie's sister?"

Mrs. Van got out an "Oh, please. Are you kidding me? I'm her mother."

Mike replied, "You know I apologize. The invitation was not only for you Annie, but for your mother as well."

Mrs. Van instinctually replied, "Oh no."

Before she had a chance to reconsider, Annie, anxious to get on the road, replied, "By the time she finds a dress.... She's going to watch Oliver. Should we be going?"

"If that is your wish, I am here to make it come true."

Mike gathered up her duffel and garment bags and off to Washington DC they went. Mike texted Fitz that the two of them were en route to the Jefferson Hotel in DC. He still had no updates on Polly. Along the way, the two chatted incessantly about Hoboken and Jersey City. Mike was originally from Hoboken and knew some of the same people as Annie. They were becoming fast friends. Mike finally felt comfortable enough inquiring, "Annie, this is none of my business so don't feel obligated to say anything if you don't want to, but what is your relationship to Fitz?"

Annie felt that she no longer had to keep it a secret anymore, "Fitz was my boyfriend before he announced to the world that he was President Kennedy's son. He told me that he would come back for me in eight months and lo and behold, I think he has."

"Marone! That explains everything! When I first met Fitz in Los Angeles, right when he made the announcement, I just assumed that he and Polly were dating. But having been around the two of them – and Polly is a wonderful person – as much as I have, I came to believe what Fitz was telling me was true about their relationship being strictly professional. But it made me wonder sometimes -- he being such an eligible bachelor and all.

You explain everything. And by the way, I don't mean no disrespect, but you are a stunningly beautiful lady."

"Thank you very much. That is very sweet – not only the compliment, but also the observation about Fitz. I really thought we had something special and he seemed so sincere when he left me that I blocked out all of this noise about Polly. Admittedly, I was starting to give up hope, but that text you sent me meant the world. I'm still having a hard time wrapping my brain around the fact that he is the President of the United States."

Mafia Mike thought about making an allusion to her being the First Lady, but that wouldn't be appropriate. Plus it just occurred to him that he had dropped off Fitz at a fine jeweler a few weeks ago. He said that he was purchasing some diamond cuff links for the Inaugural Ball, but now that visit seemed to take on a different meaning for Mike. He changed the subject back to Hoboken.

****

While in the reviewing stand, Fitz, the leader of the free world, couldn't help but feel imprisoned. There were much more pressing matters that needed his attention, but he had to extend a veneer of strength and calm during the procession that he pretended to notice in front of him. He fought the urge to bolt his perch by conversing with some of the military personnel. Fitz was invited to witness a demonstration of the latest non-nuclear weapons of mass destruction and drone technology. He feigned interest and agreed to attend once he had more visibility with his schedule. Air Force Lieutenant General Charles "Chaz" Wyckoff, situated a couple bodies from Fitz, waited for the perfect moment to approach the new President, introduce himself, and then discreetly informed him, "Mr. Jones said that we should talk."

Fitz snapped out of his malaise. "Do you have time early next week?"

"I do." With those words, Wyckoff presented his business card – *I didn't know military personnel carried business cards* – to Fitz.

After Wyckoff returned to his position, Fitz's mind drifted to Polly. He just realized that he had no idea what was on the itinerary for the balance of the day. Polly would just tell him what to do and he would follow her lead unconditionally. They had two weeks apart over the holidays. Polly invited Fitz to her parents for Christmas, but Fitz declined. Even during that time away, Polly and Fitz were in contact every day. He had asked her to be his Chief of Staff. She had not given him a firm answer, citing her burgeoning PR business. In fact, Inauguration Day was the final day of their retainer agreement. Now she was missing. He knew the news couldn't be good. Even if there was an emergency, she would have gotten word to him, if not directly, through an intermediary like Mafia Mike.

At last! The parade was over. He could get back to the White House and get an update on the fates of Polly and Annie. The second he was out of public view, Fitz grabbed his communications device in search of news. His eyes immediately focused on the message from Mike. Annie was en route – *awesome* – no word on Polly – *awful*. Chuck Schilling met Fitz at the White House and briefed him that Polly's parents were informed of her disappearance. They had declined her invitation to attend the inauguration, opting for the warmth and laid back lifestyle of their home in La Jolla, California. Now their daughter was going to be the biggest news story on this historic day.

Chuck did his best to take over for Polly. He had contacted one of her lieutenants who was in town and was part of the dinner celebration the night prior. Dana Gordon had spent a good part of her day communicating with police once word returned to her that Polly hadn't made it back to The Jefferson after they left the restaurant. She was able to track down Fitz's schedule of events for the evening and relay them to Chuck.

"Ten freaking inaugural balls -- are you kidding me?" Fitz's normally cool demeanor was starting to melt.

"Six of them are at one location. Do you want me to regretfully inform any of them of your non-attendance?"

"No." Fitz quickly calmed down. He really didn't know what to do. His close confidant -- the woman the public assumed he was in a relationship with -- was still missing. Fitz surmised that Polly was probably gossip fodder right now. The lovers probably had a falling out and that is why she didn't attend the swearing in ceremonies, or so the assumptions went. Some were probably speculating that Fitz was back on the market. Even though authorities had been looking for Polly since this morning when attempts to contact her had failed, nothing had been leaked to the press. The public had no idea as to the seriousness of her absence. That would change shortly. Meanwhile, Fitz's true love, whom he hadn't seen in eight months, was finally coming back into his life, hopefully forever. Emotional cohesion was not a term to describe the conditions inside Fitzgerald Cavendish's brain five hours into his presidency.

He decided to call Polly's parents as Chuck Schilling was able to obtain the number from Ms. Gordon. He told them that he didn't know much, but he was making sure that every available resource was being deployed to find her. He also told them how wonderful a person she was and how he really owed this day to her. Polly's parents, still in a state of shock from just learning that their only child was missing, were further anesthetized from Fitz's gesture – it's not every day that the President of the United States calls.

After a quick shower, Fitz put on his penguin suit, hopped in the Presidential Limousine with Chuck, and started the rota of inaugural ball appearances. Inside the car, Fitz confided to Chuck, "I don't mean to offend your sense of masculinity, but this is one of the two reasons that I hired Polly. I knew that if my scheme was successful, I, and everyone who surrounded me would become a target. Now I feel just utterly terrible."

Chuck, not fully digesting everything Fitz just served, responded, "Just because she is missing doesn't mean that it has anything to do with you pissing off people in high places."

"How could it not? These people have the means to do just about anything. Remember, I was offered a half a billion to drop out – that's with a 'B'. If it wasn't for Annie, I think I would have had feelings for Polly. Oh yeah, that reminds me." Fitz tapped his device to get an ETA on Annie. "I may not have told you, but that is why I broke up with Annie. I didn't want them using her to get to me. By the way, Annie is en route."

"How did you know about these people before you hatched your bid?"

"When I discovered who my father was, I started researching the circumstances surrounding his assassination and realized what he was up against. It did help that a note he had sent my mother before his death pointed me in the right direction. If they killed my father, they'll do anything to stop me. The difference is that they weren't prepared for me. I ambushed the whole process – well, actually Polly and I ambushed the whole process."

"What was the second reason?"

"I took one look at Polly and realized that her looks would make good copy for my 'coming out' tour. People like a good story. I could see that the story of her and me as a couple might keep me more relevant. I can't say that I knew how it would all play out, but I just had an instinct that she was the right person to get the whole "Fitzgerald Cavendish, celebrity" campaign into high gear. I hope you don't take any offense…"

Chuck cut him off right there. "You don't have to explain any further. No offense taken. Your plan worked, brilliantly." And then with a slightly sarcastic and playful tone of voice, "And I got a job out of it – leaking stories to the press and fending off questions from journalists."

"And you're going to be in a lot of boiling water, starting tomorrow – unless, of course, something miraculous happens with Polly."

A text came back from Mike, "Traffic. 8:30pm ETA into The Jefferson". Fitz consulted his schedule with Chuck and texted back, "Bring her to the Commander-in-Chief's Ball at the National Building Museum around 10:30pm. Any problems let me know. I assume nothing on Polly?"

A text immediately came back: "Sorry Boss -- nothing."

****

Polly Preston's "old" phone emitted its last signal from just off the road on Interstate 95 South at the exit (56) for Fayetteville/Fort

Bragg/Pope AAF in North Carolina right underneath a "Reduce Speed" sign on the exit ramp.

****

By 10:15pm Fitz was running on fumes. He, Chuck, Vice-President Spring, and his wife Tracy had managed to knock out nine balls without looking too disinterested. The Commander-in-Chief's Ball was all that remained. On the way over to their final commitment he imbibed an I Am Energized shot which contained 8000% of the recommended daily allowance of vitamin B12 and 2000% of B6 to get him to the finish line. The entertainment at the Commander-in-Chief's was impressive: Taylor Swift and Tom DeLonge. Evan and Tracy Spring spared no time cutting up the stage. Fitz alerted the Secret Service that a woman would be arriving shortly by the name of Ann Van. Fitz was more nervous than he had ever been in his life. His back was starting to perspire even though the temperature inside the National Building Museum was cool and the temperature outside was frigid.

Before he could get any more anxious, Annie Van entered the room wearing a Palatinate blue sheathed silhouetted dress with a Queen Anne neckline and an open back, diamond stud earrings – a gift from Fitz – and sparkling Palatinate blue and platinum heels. It was all a waste, as everyone could plainly see that she would have shimmered in a potato sack. Fitz's knees buckled just for a split second. Their second first encounter had the same effect on him as the first. She was a truly dazzling phenomenon. Her eyes caught his as he headed towards the Presidential Seal on the stage. She hurriedly made her way through the people towards the stage. They met at the Presidential Seal where they engaged in a long overdue everlasting kiss. They hugged and Fitz lifted her so that her shoes dangled inches above the stage like he did every time they met and whispered, "My shining joy." Breathless, she was able to let out a carefree "whoa" at the pitch of a six year old girl. Completely consumed by the moment, Fitz gently brought her back to terra firma by bending slowly at the knees. When her feet touched the stage, he reached into his jacket pocket, continued to descend until he was perched on one wobbly knee, pulled out a diamond ring, and before he could say anything to her in front of the gala attendees – all snapping pictures with their smart phones – Annie lunged at him, knocking him over. Annie lost her balance and fell right onto Fitz. They hugged liked two kids wrestling on the playground. She started crying tears of joy and relief. Her belief in him had paid off. Fitz held back tears and said to Annie as the crowd roared with approval, "I don't think this looks very presidential." Annie laughed and cried. Fitz let go of Annie long enough to stand up, at which point he offered his hands to her. With Fitz's help she popped back up quite athletically, especially considering she was wearing three inch heels. Both now fully erect, Fitz slipped the ring on her finger. Taylor Swift and Tom DeLonge broke into Sonny & Cher's "I've Got You Babe" while Annie and Fitz shared the happiest moment of their lives in each other's' arms, swaying to the serenade.

Evan and Tracy were in a joyous state of shock. Annie's mother, who was glued to the TV, cried out "Oh my God! Oh my God!" and gave Oliver a big hug. Oliver just wanted to go back to sleep, but Mrs. Van was in a playful state, keeping him up with repeated, "You're going to be the First Dog" chants. Newspaper editors were in a panic. In the span of fifteen minutes, events coerced them to change the day's narrative: an out of nowhere celebrity president assumes power, proposes to his girlfriend that absolutely no one knew anything about – even TMZ didn't know her name – while it has been disseminated that a missing person's report has been filed on the woman who has been the president's closest companion, assumed girlfriend, and mastermind of his campaign. Who's writing this cheesy novel?

Chapter 38 (The Assassination of JFK)

If eBay could auction off the opportunity to go back in time and be a fly on the wall in Clint Murchison Jr.'s Dallas mansion conference room the evening of November 21, 1963, it would fetch more than a trip to outer space. Certain attendees were corralled into the powerful oil magnate's son's conference room and were "asked" to sign a document (and a duplicate) produced by J. Edgar Hoover that in essence stated, "The undersigned agrees that John F. Kennedy should be killed tomorrow." According to eyewitness accounts, the signatories in the room included host, owner of the Dallas Cowboys, and son of oil magnate Clint Murchison Sr., Clint Murchison Jr. ; fellow oil tycoon and owner of the Kansas City Chiefs H.L. Hunt; H.L. Hunt aide John Currington; George Brown of oil concern Brown & Root; U.S. Vice President Lyndon Baines Johnson; LBJ aide Cliff Carter; LBJ hitman Malcolm "Mac" Wallace; FBI Associate Director Clyde Tolson; mob bosses Carlos Marcello, Sam Giancana, Joseph Civello, and Johnny Roselli; Dallas Sheriff Bill Decker; former Dallas Mayor Robert Lee Thornton; Dallas Mayor Earle Cabell; Texas Governor John Connally; CIA's Western Hemisphere Division Head David Atlee Philips a.k.a. Maurice Bishop; mob associates Jack Ruby and David Ferrie; creator and publisher of the Fort Worth Star-Telegram Amon Carter; and former chairman of the Rockefeller-dominated Chase Manhattan Bank, former trustee of the Rockefeller Foundation, and at the time Chairman of the Council on Foreign Relations John J. McCloy. One copy of the executed document went to Hoover's right hand man Clyde Tolson and the other copy went to LBJ. That is some lineup. All of the people in that room had something to gain from JFK's death – no cut in the oil depletion allowance for the oilmen, no more heat on the Mob from (JFK's brother) Attorney General Bobby Kennedy, money and pleasing one's bosses for Jack Ruby, David Ferrie, and Malcolm Wallace, staying out of prison for LBJ, etc. There was one other person alleged to be in the conference room: Richard Milhous Nixon.

Former U.S. Vice President Nixon likely missed the conference room meeting by a few hours. He was invited to the party at the mansion, which he attended, but had to leave for a social engagement with Joan Crawford before current U.S. Vice President Lyndon Johnson arrived and convened the meeting in his conference room. Tricky Dick no longer had any political skin in the game. After losing the 1962 California gubernatorial election, he declared, "You don't have Nixon to kick around anymore." Working for a New York law firm, Nixon was ostensibly in Dallas for the annual meeting of the American Bottlers of Carbonated Beverages at Market Hall to meet his client, PepsiCo. Against this backdrop, he attended a party honoring J. Edgar Hoover the night before JFK's assassination. You could argue that he wanted revenge for having the 1960 election stolen from him. If he had a beef, the guy who pulled it off for Kennedy (Sam Giancana) was also in attendance at the celebration. For sure, some of Nixon's Operation 40 crowd – remember the Bay of Pigs was his brainchild, not Kennedy's, who inherited it from Nixon when he assumed office -- were in Dallas that evening and played a role in the assassination, but the former vice-president's presence at the party and not at the LBJ-led conference room meeting almost seems like an unhappy accident. Nixon was paranoid, but he was also intelligent. He probably put two and two together with the help of his Operation 40 crew. Could he have been aware of the executed documents and could that have been the focus of the Watergate break-in? Could the missing 18 minutes of tape recordings be related to this matter? Keep this extraordinarily powerful group in mind when someone tells you that there couldn't be a conspiracy, because eventually word would get out -- yeah, right.

Other people (by some accounts) at the social included KLIF radio station owner Gordon McClendon; UPI reporters Helen Thomas, Phillip K. Elliot, Ted Powers, and Dave Blair; AP reporters Frank Cormier and Les Dale Owens; KTBC TV's Ned Spelce and Richard "Cactus" Prior; and Val Imm of the Fort Worth Star-Telegram. They were not in the conference room. Funny how this party never made the news. Some people will tell you this meeting was a fantasy because it would have been impossible for Nixon and Johnson to have been at the party – rubbish. Madeline Brown, Malcolm Wallace, and Jack O'Halloran (who was trying out for the Cowboys and whose father was crime boss Albert Anastasia) must have all experienced the same hallucination. They all mention the presence of Nixon and the late arrival of Vice President Johnson. As O'Halloran said, "There were people from the FBI that swore J. Edgar Hoover was nowhere near Dallas that night. But [Hoover was] sitting as close to me as you [interviewer Sean Stone] are, so you can't tell me the man wasn't there." For what it is worth, O'Halloran also claims that Allen Dulles, members of the Rockefeller family (and other banking interests), and future U.S. presidents Gerald Ford and George H. W. Bush were also in attendance. In that room were the motives and the means to kill the president. The reason for the meeting in Clint Murchison's conference room that evening was to discuss the cover-up of the next day's murder.

Trenton Parker, who worked for the then ultra-secret CIA counter-intelligence unit Pegasus, said as much. Pegasus was initially set up by President Truman to "monitor" the activities of the CIA. He was fearful that an organization like the CIA, without proper controls, could become a criminal organization – how right he was. Pegasus answered to presidents Truman, Eisenhower, and Kennedy. That chain of command would change after Kennedy was assassinated. Pegasus had bugged J. Edgar Hoover's office phone and learned of the plot to kill Kennedy. Trenton Parker had possession of and listened to these tape recordings. Trenton says that Kennedy was warned on numerous occasions about the plot several weeks before it happened, including the three target cities – presumably Chicago, Miami, and Dallas – and the names of the plotters. When Parker was questioned by author Rodney Stitch as to the identity of the plotters he said, "Rockefeller, Allen Dulles, Johnson of Texas, George Bush, and J. Edgar Hoover." Parker also recounted one of the conversations he had heard between Nelson Rockefeller and J. Edgar Hoover in which Nelson asks, "Are we going to have any problems?" Hoover responds, "No, we aren't going to have any problems. I checked with Dulles [ironically, the man Hoover was spying on for treasonous activities during World War II and communist activities post-World War II]. If they do their job we'll do our job."

Many years later these tapes, along with other incriminating documentation, were turned over by Parker to U.S. Congressman Larry McDonald in the Caribbean. McDonald was the cousin of General George S. Patton of World War II fame from whom he inherited a trove of anti-Soviet intelligence records. With these records as a starting point, McDonald formed his own private intelligence network. Shortly after taking custody of the box containing Pegasus documentation from Parker, Larry McDonald was killed when Korean Air Flight 007 was "allegedly" shot down by Soviet interceptors on September 1, 1983. What became of the tapes is anyone's guess. As far as a guess, keep in mind that Larry McDonald, despite being a Democrat, was considered the most conservative member of Congress by some measures. At the time of his death, he was the president of the ultra-conservative John Birch Society and an outspoken critic of the Rockefellers. In 1980, he introduced a resolution to the House of Representatives calling for a comprehensive congressional investigation into the Rockefeller dominated Council on Foreign Relations and the Rockefeller founded and funded Trilateral Commission. McDonald said,

> "The drive of the Rockefellers and their allies is to create a one-world government, combining super-capitalism [corporate socialism] and Communism under the same tent; all under their control ... Do I mean conspiracy? Yes I do. I am convinced there is such a plot, international in scope, generations old in planning, and incredibly evil in intent."

David Rockefeller admitted as much in his autobiography:

> "For more than a century ideological extremists at either end of the political spectrum have seized upon well-publicized incidents...to attack the Rockefeller family for the inordinate influence they claim we wield over American political and economic institutions. Some even believe we are part of a secret cabal working against the best interests of the United States, characterizing my family and me as 'internationalists' and of conspiring with others around the world to build a more integrated global political and economic structure – one-world, if you will. If that's the charge, I stand guilty, and I am proud of it."

What American family controlled the Soviet Union since its inception? There are no coincidences. If you think that the Rockefellers lost their grip on the Soviet Union after World War II, consider this: after Kennedy was "removed" from office, the other peacenik problem was Khrushchev. The North Vietnamese would need Soviet military support to fight the upcoming war against the United States. That issue was solved when David Rockefeller "vacationed" in the Soviet Union in 1964. [After all, it was a *huge* American tourist destination back then.] Upon Rockefeller's return from his October respite, Khrushchev was peacefully "removed" from office. You might find this fantastical, but David Rockefeller was a rock star in the former Soviet Union. He would be greeted by crowds at the airport. The streets would be lined with well-wishers chanting his name as his limo passed by. American investor, Nelson Rockefeller speechwriter, and economist George Gilder commented that no one knows how to revere, blandish, and exalt a Rockefeller half as well as the Marxist.

For those of you in the "Oswald acted alone" camp, you: 1- don't care that much about the subject, consumed too much fluoride in the drinking water, and blissfully believe what comes through your television set, which certainly is not a crime; 2- are part of the cover-up (which technically means that you believe Oswald didn't act alone); 3- have done meaningful research and have the IQ of a houseplant. If instead of the Allen Dulles-controlled Warren Commission producing a report of its findings that is then presented as the final word on the matter, assume that members of the press, academia, local law enforcement, etc. were to conduct three concurrent, independent investigations along with the Warren Commission, and then all four of the investigations each anonymously produced a report of its findings at the same exact time and the American public voted on which one they believed was closest to the truth. Under this scenario, the Warren Commission report would receive zero votes from the entire population. Of the 266 known witnesses to the assassination, the commission questioned 126, not the 140 who could contradict its conclusions. When the most powerful men in America are plotting the cover-up of the crime of the century, you are only going to hear what they want you to hear. Allen Dulles (CFR), future president Gerald Ford (CFR), and John J. McCloy (CFR) were the driving force of the seven member-Warren Commission. Remember, history is a big lie – a lie of omission.

The only exhibit of fact that you need to prove that the assassination was the result of a conspiracy is that the plume of blood and brain matter from the fatal head shot ended up on Dallas Motorcycle Police escort Bobby Hargis, who was riding slightly behind Kennedy on the driver's side. He is the person you would expect to be hit by brain matter if a shot came from the grassy knoll, using simple physics and geometry. But of course you are told by the apologists and the liars that you don't know anything about ballistics and that it was an extremely windy day. A headshot from above and behind Kennedy wouldn't get any brain matter on Governor John Connally, sitting directly in front of Kennedy. No! It would create a plume around the impact that would predominantly blow backwards – the car was, after all, speeding along at eleven miles an hour [sarcasm], and by many accounts, a lot less, versus the speed of a bullet. That plume would also blow about eight feet to the left. Geez, it must have been really windy that day in Dallas for the brain matter to end up on the driver side motorcycle escort as oppose to the passenger side escort –the side of the car in which Kennedy was situated. And what was Jackie Kennedy climbing towards on to the back side of the limo directly behind her? Was that a piece of her husband's skull – right where you'd expect it to be if he was shot from the grassy knoll? But you don't know anything about ballistics.

How about the testimony of Sam M. Holland, track and signal supervisor for the Union Terminal Railroad? He probably had the best view of the assassination from atop the Triple Underpass, under which Kennedy's limo was headed when he was shot. Holland claimed there were four shots. He said that the first one hit Kennedy. The second one hit Connally [implication, no magic bullet that hit Kennedy and Connally]. The third shot came from the grassy knoll that killed Kennedy – it did not have as loud a report as the first two shots. This was followed immediately by a fourth shot, possibly the one that missed and hit James Teague. Either way, he saw a puff of smoke emanating from the picket fence on the grassy knoll, which is consistent with a short barreled weapon shooting a high powered cartridge, as the excess propellant would generate smoke from burning at a lower temperature as it left the muzzle.

Sam saw two police officers, one on a motorcycle, ascend the grassy knoll to investigate the source of the third report. Sam and his colleagues left the Triple Underpass and ran over to the area behind the picket fence on the grassy knoll to see if they could find the shooter. By the time they made it over, no one was found. He said that he and his colleagues found muddy footprints in the area where the smoke originated along with mud on the bumpers of some nearby cars and on the 2 x 4 railing on the picket fence. There were also some fresh cigarette butts. Sam's testimony went down in the Warren Report as proof that there wasn't a shooter over in the grassy knoll area. Even though Sam and some of his colleagues witnessed the same scene – i.e. Kennedy and Connally being hit with three different shots, not two and the report and subsequent plume of smoke from behind the picket fence – only Sam was called to testify in front of the Warren Commission. Fellow employees James L.

318

Simmons and Richard Dodd, who were with Holland and corroborated his account, were questioned by the Dallas police and/or the FBI, but they were never called to testify in front of the Warren Commission. Dodd and Simmons statements are mentioned in the Warren Commission Report and/or its supplemental volumes, but the FBI accounts of their statements (in the report) strongly contradict what they claimed to have told the authorities in subsequent interviews with Mark Lane. Simmons and Dodd were two of many witnesses whose experience of the JFK assassination was for some reason not fully or accurately reflected in their official statements. Holland, Simmons, and Dodd's recollection matches with Governor Connally, who was hit with the second shot:

[Warren Commission attorney] Arlen Specter: In your view, which bullet caused the injury to your chest, Governor Connally?

Gov. Connally: The second one.

Mr. Specter: And what is your reason for that conclusion, sir?

Gov. Connally: Well, in my judgment, it just couldn't conceivably have been the first one because I heard the sound of the shot … and after I heard that shot, I had the time to turn to my right, and start to turn to my left before I felt anything. It is not conceivable to me that I could have been hit by the first bullet.

If Connally wasn't hit with the first shot, the Warren Commission's "magic bullet" fantasy – where Kennedy's throat/back wounds and all of Connally's injuries were the result of the first shot – falls to pieces as does its assertion that lone nut Lee Harvey Oswald killed JFK with three shots from the sixth floor of the Texas School Book Depository. Sam Holland's corroborating account was ignored. In fact, as far as the Warren Commission was concerned, Sam Holland's and Governor Connally's testimonies were incorrect, and the fact that Holland -- and nobody else -- found the shooter behind the picket fence, lent credence to the lone gunman hypothesis. As far as Simmons and Dodd were concerned, the FBI and the Warren Commission didn't want any additional contradictory evidence to its lone gunman story.

If your fantasy involves the first shot missing and hitting James Teague and the second shot being the "magic bullet" that did all of the damage, you lose because the Zapruder film clearly shows Kennedy reacting to being struck a full second before Connally shows any signs of discomfort, also corroborating Holland, Simmons, and Dodd's accounts. Either way, you need a fourth bullet.

Maybe Jesse C. Price would have been an interesting witness to call in front of the Warren Commission? The engineer in charge of the Terminal Annex Building decided to watch the motorcade from the roof of his building, giving him a commanding view from above, of Dealey Plaza and the parking lot behind the picket fence. After the shots rang out, Price said in a filmed interview with Mark Lane, that he saw a man running "over behind that wooden fence [on the grassy knoll], pass the cars, and over behind the Texas [School Book] Depository building." Price described the man as

> "....about 25 years of age with long, dark hair. He was wearing a white dress shirt with no tie and khaki-colored trousers...The man was carrying something in his hand and that it may have been a 'head piece'."

Funny how presidential assassins and their spotters don't hang around to get caught after the job has been completed. Price gave that information to the Dallas Sheriff's Department thirty minutes after the shooting, but was never called to testify in front of the Warren Commission. To be sure, there was a FBI document in the supplement to the Warren Commission Report that states that Price saw Kennedy slumped over in his car after he heard some shots [not exactly ground shaking testimony]. It also says he "saw nothing pertinent". [Really?] It seems that the FBI changed the account of every witness that didn't fit with the lone gunman from the sixth floor tale.

Even if you think that eyewitness accounts are unreliable and you don't believe that the FBI altered witnesses' testimony to suit an already agreed upon narrative, what seems in no dispute is that Lee Harvey Oswald didn't fire a rifle that day. In addition to that minor detail, the rifle that he was claimed to have employed in the execution of the president, was a piece of garbage – and that is putting it mildly. When a person fires a gun, gunpowder residue (more specifically, barium and antimony) will be deposited on the shooter's skin that is closest to the gun. In the case of a rifle, that would be the cheek and the hands. A paraffin test would extract from deep in the pores of the shooter's skin any fine residues given off by the firing of a gun. Oswald was subjected to a paraffin test after being taken into custody. The spectrographic analysis of that test showed evidence of barium and antimony on Oswald's hands, but not on his cheek. This would probably be the result of handling books, which was Oswald's job at the depository -- or James Files' shell casings from the day before when Files was citing up his scope on a makeshift range. James Files claims to be the grassy knoll shooter and claims that Oswald retrieved his spent casings at the range the day before the assassination. Neutron activation analysis, which is capable of identifying the presence of substances in quantities much too small to be captured by spectrographic analysis, also showed no incriminating quantities of residues on Oswald's cheek. In an internal Warren Commission memo to Allen Dulles, staff lawyer Norman Redlich concluded: "At best, the analysis shows that Oswald may have fired a pistol, although this is by no means certain. ... There is no basis for concluding that he also fired a rifle." That still wasn't good enough. The FBI conducted its own controlled test in which seven marksmen fired the rifle alleged to be used by Oswald. All seven showed large quantities of barium and antimony on their hands, and more importantly, on their cheeks. But since it was agreed upon in advance that "the dissemination of the results will be under complete FBI control", the results were not released for two decades, and only as the result of a lawsuit filed by Harold Weisberg. Are you beginning to see a pattern here? It appears that J. Edgar Hoover was holding up his end of the "we'll do our job" part of the agreement.

The weapon itself is laughable. Initially, the weapon authorities found in the sniper's nest on the sixth floor of the Texas Book Depository was a 7.65 Mauser. According to Deputy Sheriff Roger Craig, who was present when the rifle was found, "7.65 Mauser" was stamped right on the barrel. Additionally, Craig said that Officer Seymour Weitzman, gun enthusiast and former sporting goods store owner, who was with him at the time the weapon was located, identified it as a 7.65 Mauser. Weitzman made a sworn affidavit to that effect. Initial news reports also identified the weapon that way. The problem started when the three shell cartridges found in the southeast corner of the sixth floor came from a 6.5 Italian Mannlicher Carcano bolt action rifle. So the Mannlicher Carcano bolt action rifle was now Oswald's weapon – the one they allegedly found in his garage. Weitzman retracted his Mauser story to reflect a 6.5 Italian Mannlicher Carcano in his testimony to the Warren Commission after he was "visited" by two Cuban men. Roger Craig's story never changed -- more on him shortly.

This "discovery" created another problem for the Warren Commission, which was doing everything in its power to prove that Hoover's FBI report on the assassination – released in December 1963, stating that Oswald acted alone by firing three shots from the Texas School Book Depository – was correct: the weapon was not operable. When experts from the FBI and the U.S. Army were brought in to test the rifle, two shims had to be added -- one which adjusted the azimuth, and one which adjusted the elevation -- to the telescopic site before it could be aimed. Once the telescopic site was adjusted, the weapon still proved to be highly unreliable and inaccurate, with the bolt and trigger in such poor condition that the rifle could not be aimed accurately after each firing. These were the findings of the Warren Commission. But don't worry citizens; Oswald was able to get those three shots off in less than six seconds from the sixth floor -- while having lunch on the first floor.

Then there is the famous backyard photo of Oswald holding his Mannlicher Carcano rifle that was published in Time Life's *LIFE* magazine in its February 21, 1964 issue. The only problem is that the gun in the photo isn't the same as the Mannlicher Carcano allegedly found in the Texas School Book Depository. The one in the backyard photo has a sling mount on the underside of the rifle – it is part of the rifle. The weapon found on the sixth floor has side sling mounts. The rifle that Oswald allegedly ordered under the alias "Alek J. Hidell" and according to the Warren Commission was used to assassinate JFK has the sling mount on the underside of the rifle. Sorry, Warren Commission: you can't have it both ways.

As for Roger Craig, Dallas Traffic Commission's 1960 "Officer of the Year" was fired from the police department in 1967 after he was found to have discussed his evidence with a journalist. Later that year he was shot at while walking to a car park. Lucky for Roger, the bullet only grazed his head. In 1971, Craig wrote *When They Kill a President* which detailed some of the many changes the Warren Commission had made to his testimony. After two more attempts on his life in 1973 and 1974, one resulting in a gunshot wound to his shoulder, Craig was found dead on May 15, 1975. It was later decided he had died as a result of self-inflicted rifle wound.

Lee Harvey Oswald was actually having lunch on the first floor when Kennedy was shot. However, as you will see, the Warren Commission was quite good at taking evidence proving that he was on the first floor and turning it against a dead man. According to the Warren Commission Report, in an interview with FBI agent James Bookhout,

> "OSWALD stated that on November 22, 1963, he had eaten lunch in the lunch room at the Texas School Book Depository, *alone*, but recalled possibly two Negro employees walking through the room during this period. He stated possibly one of these employees was called 'Junior' and the other was a short individual whose name he could not recall but whom he would be able to recognize." [Italics emphasis added]

This version of Oswald's account was corroborated by the notes of Captain Will Fritz, head of the Dallas Police investigation into the assassination of JFK, who spent more time with Oswald after his incarceration than any other person in authority. The two Negro employees in question were James "Junior" Jarman and Harold Norman. These gentlemen were watching the proceedings, but decided when the motorcade reached Main Street, because of the crowds, that they could obtain a better view of the president from inside the building. Since the front entrance to the Texas School Book Depository was cramped with spectators, Jarman and Norman used the building's rear entrance, which would have brought them past the room in which Oswald was having his lunch. The time was between 12:23 and 12:25pm, confirmed by police logs of the location of the motorcade. Jarman and Norman's story corroborates Oswald's claim that he was having lunch on the first floor just before the assassination (which took place at 12:29pm). How else would he know about the presence of these two gentlemen walking past the room in which he was having lunch if he was not indeed on the first floor? You might think that this seems fairly persuasive.

However, Thomas Kelley, a Secret Service agent who attended the same interview, gave a slightly different, inaccurate, and less detailed account of this incident: "He said he *ate his lunch with the colored boys* who worked with him. He described one of them as 'Junior', a colored boy, and the other was a little short Negro boy." [Emphasis added] Warren Commission attorney George Ball used this version of events when questioning Junior:

> Mr. Ball: After his arrest, he [Oswald] stated to a police officer that he had had lunch with you. Did you have lunch with him?
>
> Mr. Jarman: No; I didn't.

That testimony proves Secret Service agent Kelley's recollection of the Oswald interview as incorrect.   However, the Warren Commission concludes:

> "[Oswald] stated that at the time the President was shot he was having lunch with "Junior" but he did not give Junior's last name. The only employee at the Depository Building named "Junior" was James Jarman, Jr. Jarman testified that he ate his lunch on the first floor around 5 minutes to 12, and that he neither ate lunch with nor saw Oswald."

The Warren Commission conveniently ignores the more plausible version of events – that claims Oswald only saw the two gentlemen pass through, not sit down with him for lunch – which exonerates Oswald. Instead the Commission turns him into a liar.

Texas School Book Depository secretary Carolyn Arnold saw Oswald in the lunchroom between 12:15 and 12:25pm. Remarkably, she was never called to testify. She was not called to testify because her statement would contradict the Warren Commission's conclusions. Arnold Rowland saw a man on the sixth floor, holding a rifle, at 12:15pm or very shortly afterwards. That man obviously wasn't Lee Harvey Oswald. It appears that Warren Commission member Allen Dulles, forced to resign as CIA Director by Kennedy after the Bay of Pigs fiasco, was also holding up his end of the bargain with J. Edgar Hoover by "doing his job".

For his part, Oswald was aware of "The Big Event" – as those who were part of the operation called it -- and the possibility that he might be used as the patsy as early as July 29, 1963. Oswald was enlisted as a marine in 1956 and spent part of his service before a hardship discharge in 1959 assigned to Atsugi Naval Air Station in Japan, which housed a large CIA facility. The evidence is quite strong that Oswald worked for the CIA. Oswald's nonbinding "defection" to Russia fits perfectly the profile of an Office of Naval Intelligence program to infiltrate American servicemen into the Soviet Union during the late 1950's. How else could this "defector" so easily obtain passports in 1959 and 1963? How could he have obtained a small Minox camera that was not available to the public in 1963 which the Dallas Police found amongst his possessions? The United States Armed Forces taught him Russian. Upon return from the Soviet Union, Oswald worked for the F.B.I. as an informer and was paid $200.00 a month. His code number was S 172. He was also paid $200.00 a month from the CIA. Jim and Elsie Wilcott, former husband and wife employees of the Tokyo CIA Station said,

> "It was common knowledge in the Tokyo CIA station that Oswald worked for the agency.... Right after the President was killed, people in the Tokyo station were talking openly about Oswald having gone to Russia for the CIA. Everyone was wondering how the agency was going to be able to keep the lid on Oswald. But I guess they did."

As part of his CIA work in the summer of 1963, Oswald was helping out a researcher – who would become his mistress -- Judith Vary Baker, on a top secret cancer bio-weapon project in New Orleans. Baker was a precocious medical researcher who was recruited by Dr. Alton Ochsner to assist Dr. Mary Sherman on this CIA project. David Ferrie, who ended up at Clint Murchison's conference room with Lyndon Johnson and others, also worked on this project. The goal of this enterprise, which took place over the summer of 1963, was to create a substance, disguised as a vaccine that could be injected into an unsuspecting individual causing that person to die from cancer in a very short period of time. The ultimate goal of the project was to deliver this weapon to Cuba's Fidel Castro. At first, hundreds of lab rats were tested; then marmosets; and then African green monkeys. Soon after, unsuspecting, healthy Louisiana state felons became the lab rats. Horrified by the modus operandi of the project, Baker complained in writing to Ochsner – not the smartest thing to do as part of a top secret project – and was subsequently removed. Baker's removal was relatively meaningless as the weapon proved operational as the once healthy prisoners were becoming terminally ill shortly after injection. Her work was complete.

The weapon now needed to be transported to Cuba where it would be used on Castro. Enter Lee Harvey Oswald. In early September, Oswald met up with his CIA handler, Maurice Bishop (also from Clint Murchison's conference room), who he knew as "Mr. B", in Dallas. Also present at this meeting was the anti-Castro Cuban (likely Antonio Veciana) to whom Oswald would drop off the bioweapon to in Mexico City. Once the first prisoner died as a consequence of the bio-bomb, Lee would be sent to Mexico City. He received notice that he would be traveling on September 23, 1963 and on September 25th he boarded a plane from Houma, Louisiana to Austin, Texas. After a brief stopover, he was onto Dallas to meet with Jack Ruby – yes that Jack Ruby, also present at Murchison's conference room -- who wanted Lee to pick up some laetrile, a cancer drug that was legal in Mexico, but illegal in the United States. The irony of that request should not be lost on you.

Oswald then flew to Houston, where he boarded a bus for Mexico City. He arrived in Mexico City on September 27th and checked into a Quaker house. However, his contact failed to show, and his attempts to contact Mr. B also failed. He reached out to his emergency contact in Mexico City, who accompanied him to the Cuban Consulate – that is why there are no pictures of Lee entering the Cuban Consulate: his 'friend' accompanying him in the actual pictures could potentially implicate the CIA. While at the Consulate, Lee applied for a transit visa to enter Cuba so that he could deliver the weapon into Cuba. You see, bio-weapons come with an expiration date and Oswald's thinking was if he could get the weapon into Cuba so it could kill Castro, it might save Kennedy's life, and by extension, his own. Oswald was well aware of the plot afoot to assassinate Kennedy and he was also smart enough to realize that he would make an excellent patsy. His CIA-sponsored work with not only the bio-weapon, but also with the pro-Castro leafleting in August, made him an expendable asset who knew too much, while at the same time proving a plausible cover for an American invasion of Cuba. If it was decided that an invasion of Cuba was no longer in the cards, Oswald could be portrayed

326

as a lone nut. The actual plotters could always lie to investigators that a cover-up was necessary to prevent World War III. Ironically, the transit visa was ultimately approved on October 18th, less than a month later, but that was too late for the bio-weapon, John F. Kennedy, and Lee.

Unlike the men meeting in Murchison's conference room, Oswald was a fan of Kennedy's, as was Dr. Mary Sherman. Upon his return to the United States from Mexico City, Lee was invited to be a participant in the assassination plans against JFK. The plot revolved around three cities, the third one being Dallas. Oswald's activities were confined to the plot in Dallas; however he is very likely the source of the teletype from the FBI into the Chicago Secret Service office (received by agent Abraham Bolden) warning of an imminent (November 2nd) attack on the president at Soldier Field. The source of the call into the FBI was a man named "Lee". Because of this call, Kennedy's trip to Chicago was cancelled and his life was spared for a few more weeks. The trusted FBI contact in Chicago was supplied to Oswald by Dr. Mary Sherman. On July 21, 1964, hours before Dr. Sherman was likely to meet with the Warren Commission, she was murdered. The irony of this story should not be lost on you either.

For the avoidance of doubt, there are a few publications that purport the fantasy that Oswald acted alone. These books, like the Warren Commission Report, always leave out important testimony, leaving the impression of an Operation Mockingbird farce. For example, twenty-one out of twenty-two employees of Parkland Hospital who had the opportunity to see John F. Kennedy, described a massive head wound toward the temporal and occipital regions (i.e. the side and rear of Kennedy's head), which is where you would expect a wound to occur if a shot originated from the grassy knoll. However, Gerald Posner, in his fantastical work, *Case Closed*, portrays the doctors at Parkland Hospital as having changed their minds. For example, according to Gerald Posner, Dr. Malcolm Perry said to him in an interview that he conducted on March 2, 1992: "I never even saw the back of his head. The wound was on the right side, not the back." To continue, Posner says he conducted another interview on April 2, 1992 in which Perry stated: "I did not see any cerebellum." That is borderline hilarious when you contrast it with the statement that Dr. Perry told the House Select Committee on Assassinations "I looked at the head wound briefly by leaning over the table and noticed that the parietal occipital head wound was largely avulsive and there was visible brain tissue in the macard and some cerebellum seen..." He is one of six doctors whose testimony magically changed for Posner's book.

Not to go into all six, but to further the point, examine the before and after testimony of Dr. Charles Baxter: after, in Gerald Posner's book: "I never even saw the back of his head. The wound was on the right side, not the back." and before: "The right temporal and occipital bones were missing and the brain was lying on the table." Parkland Hospital staff Nurse Audrey Bell, Dr. Gene Aiken, Dr. Baxter, Nurse Diana Bowron, Dr. Kemp Clark, Dr. Charles Carrico, Dr. Charles Crenshaw, Dr. Don T. Curtis, Dr. Richard Dulaney, Dr. Robert Grossman, Nurse Pat Hutton, Dr. Marion Jenkins, Ronald Coy Jones, Dr. Robert McClelland, Dr. Perry, and Dr. Paul Peters all describe the back of the head being blown out – all consistent with a shot from the grassy knoll. The only reason for the change in some of their stories for a book that was written nearly 30 years after the assassination is intimidation or fear of facing the same fate as Dr. Mary Sherman or dozens of others whose accounts of JFK's assassination didn't fit the official fairy tale.

You don't believe this to be the case? Secret Service agent Elmer Moore admitted to intimidating Dr. Perry into retracting his statement of an entrance wound in the throat. Moore didn't do this on his own initiative. He was ordered to intimidate Perry. Dr. Crenshaw also saw the entry wound in the throat but was not called to testify. Crenshaw and the other Parkland doctors knew the cover-up was on, but were afraid to say anything. Crenshaw put it best,

> "I believe there was a common denominator in our silence – a fearful perception that to come forward with what we believed to be the medical truth would be asking for trouble. Although we never admitted it to one another, we realized that the inertia of the established story was so powerful, so thoroughly presented, so adamantly accepted, that it would bury anyone who stood in its path."

Crenshaw statement proved prophetic when he broke his silence with the authorship of *JFK: Conspiracy of Silence.* The book was libelously slandered by the *Journal of the American Medical Association (JAMA)*, which accused him of being a liar. He had to file (and win) a lawsuit against *JAMA* to regain his credibility.

You still don't believe that this type of witness intimidation can occur in the United States of America? When the most powerful men in the country decide that the president must die, they certainly aren't going to let anyone else get in their way, especially not Lieutenant Commander William Bruce Pitzer, who had in his possession documents and film that refuted the conclusions of JFK's official autopsy. JFK's official autopsy was a joke in which three pathologists were ordered by senior ranking military officials as to what they could and couldn't examine. (Throat wound examinations were strictly off limits. Probing for a slug in Kennedy's back was forbidden. Burning the first draft of the autopsy report and "disappearing" the lead pathologist's autopsy notes were permitted.)

Pitzer worked at the National Naval Medical Center (NNMC) where Kennedy's autopsy took place and was apparently present at the autopsy of JFK although his presence was not noted in the official records. Either way, as head of the Audio-Visual Department of the NNMC, Pitzer examined photographs and x-rays of the dead president that were contradictory to the ones shown in the Warren Commission Report. He confided as much to his underling Dennis David, who also saw photos and film of the autopsy that would repudiate the official version, showing a small entry wound near the right temple and massive exit wound in the right rear of Kennedy's head. Pitzer was about ready to retire and was preparing to release to the public the real autopsy photos of JFK. Once word got back to the people in power that he was going to be a problem, the CIA set out to silence Pitzer.

Lieutenant Colonel Daniel Marvin was an assassin in the U.S. Army Special Forces. Marvin received training in assassinations and terrorism at the Fort Bragg's Special Warfare School where he witnessed film of the Kennedy assassination (years before the public release of the Zapruder film). He was taught that JFK's assassination was "a classic example of the way to organize a complete program to eliminate a nation's leader, while pointing the finger at a lone assassin." The CIA approached him in the summer of 1965, requesting that he terminate Pitzer because he was about to "reveal state secrets". Marvin declined, but another member of his team "suicided" Pitzer on October 29, 1966. Despite not finding any fingerprints on the alleged suicide weapon (a revolver) and no one witnessing any awkward behavior, Pitzer's death was deemed a suicide. None of his family or friends believed the travesty. In fact, he even wrote himself a note to return the revolver to the security office – an impossible task for someone allegedly bent on killing himself. Pitzer's belief that the autopsy photos in the Warren Commission report were bogus was corroborated by the testimony of Saundra Kay Spencer, who worked at the Naval Photographic Center as the Petty Officer in Charge of the White House Lab. She claimed that the autopsy photos she developed were not the ones in the National Archives. Autopsy photographer John T. Stringer also testified as much to the Assassinations Records Review Board in 1996.

As for the actual shooters of JFK, Malcom Wallace (from Clint Murchison's conference room) was on the sixth floor of the Texas School Book Depository. He was with a sharpshooter of Native American descent named Loy Factor, who did not fire a shot, Ruth Ann Martinez, who was operating a walkie-talkie, and curiously enough, with a man he called Lee Harvey Oswald – more on this peculiar dynamic later. Central command was on the 2nd floor of the Dal-Tex building next door, which was operated by Murchison party attendee Cliff Carter. There were other shooters on top of the Dallas County Records building, in the Dal-Tex building, behind the picket fence on the grassy knoll, across Commerce Street on the "south knoll", and along the sewer line behind the grassy knoll, closer to the triple overpass. A gunman – likely from the Dallas County Records or the Dal-Tex building and likely Charles Nicoletti -- shot JFK in his upper back, about six inches below his neck wound. That slug did not go all of the way through Kennedy. Charles Harrelson or Richard Montoya, from behind the picket fence on the south knoll along Commerce Street and near the triple underpass, shot JFK in the throat, causing what appears to be an involuntary rising of JFK's arms to his neck with his elbows pointing outward. This may have been the shot that went through the front windshield of the limousine.

Shot through the windshield? Richard Dudman from the *St. Louis Post-Dispatch* wrote, "Some of us noticed the hole in the front window [of JFK's limo at Parkland Hospital]. We were pushed away by Secret

Service agents, when we wanted to examine the hole." Patrolman Stavis Ellis: "There was a hole in the left front windshield...You could put a pencil through it...you could take a regular standard writing pencil...and stick [it] through there." Harold R. Freeman: "[I was] right beside it. I could of [sic] touched it...it was a bullet hole. You could tell what it was." Second year medical student, Evalea Glanges: "it was a through-and-through bullet hole through the windshield of the car, from the front to the back...it seemed like a high-velocity bullet that had penetrated from front-to-back in that glass pane." At the time of her statement, Dr. Glanges was the Chairperson of the Department of Surgery at John Peter Smith Hospital, in Fort Worth. She had been a firearms expert all her adult life. Even Secret Service Agent Charles Taylor reported: "Saw hole in front window. Bullet fragments were removed." Shockingly, he later recanted: "my use of the word 'hole' to describe the flaw in the windshield was incorrect." None of these Parkland eyewitnesses appear in the Warren Commission Report.

The limo was cleaned, sent back to the White House Garage in Washington D.C. where it was surreptitiously loaded on a plane to the Ford Rouge Factory B building in Dearborn, MI on November 25th. There, the windshield was replaced and the interior was stripped and reupholstered. While there, the limo and its windshield were witnessed by Ford employee and glass specialist George Whitaker Sr. He also witnessed the bullet hole: "It was a good clean bullet hole right through the screen from the front." Whitaker's subordinates were in charge of constructing a new windshield. The bullet-ridden one was destroyed. The refurbished limo was then sent back to the White House Garage, where it was inspected by the Warren Commission and later "released" back to Dearborn, MI to be redesigned. [That's the way to preserve a crime scene.]

Back to the shooters, Malcolm Wallace then shot Governor Connally in the back, causing a shattered rib, a shattered wrist, and puncture in his left thigh, prompting him to say, "My God, they are going to kill us all." This is an interesting comment from a man who was in Murchison's conference room the evening before. Lee Harvey Oswald of the sixth floor either hit Kennedy in the back or missed.

The man on the grassy knoll, mob hitman and CIA asset James Files, administered the kill shot, blowing out the back and right side of

Kennedy's head. There was also at least one shot that missed, struck a curb, and wounded James Teague. If all of these shots contradict the two, three, or four shots that many heard, think silencers. They were available in 1963.

The Warren Commission asserts the bullet that struck Kennedy in the back, the one that entered through the front of his neck, and the Connally injuries were all actually the result of one shot. This was accomplished when future president Gerald Ford relocated Kennedy's back wound several inches up until it became a base of the neck wound. Then Arlen Specter could concoct that the entry wound in Kennedy's throat was actually an exit wound and when the bullet left Kennedy, it made a slight mid-air turn and did all the damage to Connally.

The crew on the sixth floor immediately ran down the stairs, unseen, as everyone was still out in the street watching the motorcade. They escaped out the back on the first floor through a loading dock. Ruth Ann and Loy Factor got into a car on Houston Street and drove to the bus depot where Ruth Ann dropped off Loy. Mac Wallace was seen fleeing the scene on foot by witnesses Richard Carr (who also saw him on the sixth floor of the TSBD) and James Worrell Jr. Over an hour later, Ruth Ann returned with Malcolm Wallace to the bus depot. They decided that it wasn't a good idea for Factor to be hanging around a bus depot and drove him out of town.

Some of the men behind the grassy knoll, like spotter Aldo Vera ran away behind the Texas School Book Depository. James Files -- whose CIA controller, like Oswald, was David Atlee Phillips a.k.a. Maurice Bishop from Murchison's -- dressed like a railroad worker, walked away with his gun in a briefcase, and rendezvoused with Charles Nicoletti and Johnny Roselli at a car near Houston Street. Others, like CIA asset and future Watergate burglar Bernard Barker, posed as a Secret Service agent with fake ID. Others, like gunmen Harrelson and Montoya, hid in train cars in the rail yard behind the parking lot which was behind the grassy knoll. Chauncey Holt, who delivered the fake Secret Service IDs to people like Barker, and weapons to Harrelson and Montoya, also hid in a railroad car.

As for the "first floor Oswald", he walked seven blocks to a bus stop, boarded a bus that got stuck in traffic, disembarked, walked a few more blocks and hailed a yellow cab, offered to give up the taxi to an old lady (she declined), rode 2.4 miles in the taxi that dropped him off five blocks from his residence, and walked five blocks to his boarding house where he arrived around 1:00pm. He left his boarding house three or four minutes later and hitched a ride in a police car to the Texas Theatre. Warren H. "Butch" Burroughs sold first floor Oswald popcorn at 1:15pm and saw him in the theatre between 1:00 and 1:07pm. This Oswald was moving around the theatre when he first arrived, sitting next to different people, as if he was meeting a contact. He then went out to the concession stand, made the aforementioned popcorn purchase, and returned to the lower section of the theatre (orchestra), where he sat next to a pregnant woman who, after a few minutes, got up and went to the bathroom.

"Sixth floor Oswald" got into a Rambler station wagon at 12:40pm that was likely driven by Antonio Veciana or David Morales, or some other "husky looking Latin". Sixth floor Oswald may have killed Officer J.D. Tippit – or possibly Tippit was killed by mobster Gary Marlow – but either way, he ended up outside the Texas Theatre around 1:45pm to meet his yet arrived rendezvous. He was noticed by Johnny Brewer, a shoe store manager. Brewer decided that sixth floor Oswald matched the description of a man wanted for the murder of Dallas Police Officer J.D. Tippit and alerted the authorities. For what it is worth, Tippit, based on his actions after the assassination, was likely supposed to kill Oswald, but because first floor Oswald got off the bus and hailed a taxi, Tippit lost his mark.

Sixth floor Oswald headed into the theater and up to the balcony. The Dallas police rushed into the theatre and arrested first floor Oswald at 1:50pm in the *orchestra*. He was taken out through the *front* of the theatre as seen in many photographs of the arrest. However, according to Burroughs, another arrest (of sixth floor Oswald) occurred in the *balcony* area three or four minutes later. That suspect was sent out the *back* of the theatre by police and put into a car in an alleyway as also seen by Bernard J. Haire, owner of hobby store just two establishments away, who had come out to see what the commotion was all about. The official Homicide Report on J.D. Tippit also states that the suspect was arrested in the *balcony*. First floor Oswald was transferred to the Dallas Police Station and was shot by Jack Ruby two days later.   Sixth floor Oswald was released a few blocks away from where he was arrested and got into a red 1961 Falcon, which he drove to the parking lot of El Chico restaurant, where he was seen by auto mechanic T.F. White at approximately 2:00pm.

Sixth floor Oswald eventually made his way to a makeshift runway alongside the Trinity River Flood Plain just south of downtown Dallas, where he boarded an unmarked C-54 – unmarked except for the tail, which displayed the CIA rust-brown graphic of an egg-shaped earth, crossed by white grid marks -- with another dark-complected man (likely the same one who picked him up outside the TSBD).   The time was approximately 3:30pm Central time.   The C-54 had just landed and never turned off its engine before it took back off with its new passengers.   It was also carrying one other passenger, U.S. Air Force sergeant Robert G. Vinson of the North American Air Defense Command.   Vinson was hitching a ride back from Andrews Air Force base.   The plane was initially en route to Lowry Air Force Base in Denver, but made a detour into the dusty piece of land near Dallas to pick up sixth floor Oswald and his associate.   The plane then made its way to Roswell Air Force Base in New Mexico, where all passengers disembarked.

Vinson ended up having to take a bus to make the final leg of his journey back to Colorado.   To his wife, Vinson identified the sixth floor Oswald who he flew with from Dallas to Roswell as being identical to the first floor Oswald who was shot and killed by Jack Ruby on live television two days later.   You may think that this was just a coincidence and a case of mistaken identity.   If you do, then ask yourself why were Vinson and his wife subsequently ordered by his commanding officer to sign a secrecy agreement?   Why was he (an administrative supervisor of the electronics division at NORAD) ordered to CIA Headquarters in Langley, VA for five days of evaluation in November 1964, after which he received an enticing job offer?   Why was he reassigned to a top-secret CIA project in Nevada after he rejected the initial CIA job offer to a position for which he was not uniquely qualified?   Answer: he was not supposed to be on that plane with the Oswald doppelganger and was being monitored by the CIA and paid for his silence which he ended on November 23, 1993 by telling the story of his flight to Wichita's KAKE-TV Channel 10 News.

As for the media's role, with the CIA having already infiltrated the top echelons of the mainstream media through Operation Mockingbird, it is fascinating to observe the non-existent independent investigations performed by your illusory free press such as the *New York Times* or the *Washington Post* or the network news outlets. It was only the crime of the century! One of the Council on Foreign Relations main tasks – remember CFR chief McCloy was in Murchison's conference room – through the media and through its military arm (the CIA), has been to perpetuate the cover-up of the assassination of John F. Kennedy.

As for the people in Murchison's room, Jack Ruby was killed in jail on January 3, 1967 by the same cancer bio-weapon that Judith Vary Baker, David Ferrie, Dr. Mary Sherman, and Lee Harvey Oswald had helped develop. He had chirped to journalist Dorothy Kilgallen what he knew about the assassination. Having been in Murchison's conference room, he knew a lot. Before Kilgallen could break the story wide open, she was murdered on November 8, 1965. Two days later, her confidant Mrs. Earl T. Smith also conveniently turned up dead. All her notes regarding the assassination disappeared. David Ferrie was murdered ("suicided") by James Files – the same one who executed the kill shot on Kennedy – on orders from his superiors. Ferrie had been subpoenaed to testify at the Jim Garrison trial of Clay Shaw for the murder of JFK. He had to be silenced.

Lyndon Johnson became the 36th President of the United States and never went to jail for his many crimes. He was a puppet of the cabal and its Round Table groups that reversed NSAM 263 with NSAM 273 (drafted by McGeorge Bundy (CFR and CIA) the night before the assassination), which led to the Vietnam War. Again, McGeorge Bundy was operating the Situation Room in the White House while the rest of the Kennedy's cabinet was over the Pacific en route to Tokyo on the day of the assassination. He reassured everyone within hours of the murder that it was a lone nut that killed Kennedy (how did he know?) Two more interesting side notes on McGeorge Bundy: 1- He was the reason that the Bay of Pigs failed. He called off the airstrikes that would have wiped out what was left of the Cuban Air Force (three planes) before the invasion. No explanation has ever been forwarded. If those three planes were neutralized, the outcome of the invasion would have been markedly different. Kennedy, for his part, never pledged air support for the actual invasion. But the lie that he did permeated the CIA and anti-Castro community, helping to bolster their hatred of Kennedy. 2- To repeat, McGeorge's brother, William (CFR and CIA), authored the Gulf of Tonkin Resolution which gave LBJ broad powers to escalate the war in Vietnam.

Getting back to LBJ, he presided over one the most acrimonious periods in United States history. His tenure wore him down so greatly that he did not seek re-election in 1968, in which he secretly backed Nelson Rockefeller. When it became apparent that Jack Kennedy's brother, Bobby, had a legitimate shot at being elected president – and you can bet he was going to reopen the investigation into the death of his brother – the cabal went into action and Robert Kennedy was assassinated on June 6, 1968. Curiously, Ruth Ann Martinez from the sixth floor of the TSBD was on the scene for that hit as well. Johnson died January 22, 1973.

Malcolm Wallace, who killed at least a dozen people on behalf of Lyndon Johnson, was killed in a single car accident just south of Pittsburg, Texas on January 7, 1971 – rumor had it that he was coming back to blackmail Johnson for more money. Johnson aide Clifton Carter, who was the cutout between Malcolm Wallace and LBJ, died on September 22, 1971.

J. Edgar Hoover, who was beholden to the Mafia (specifically Meyer Lansky) because it possessed lurid photos of him with Clyde Tolson – being gay was a big deal back then – was named FBI Director for Life by LBJ. Because of his compromised situation, Hoover rarely admitted that organized crime even existed, let alone pursue it; his passion was stamping out communism. With Johnson in charge and Bobby Kennedy neutered, the mafia bosses were free to continue their illegalities without fear of prosecution. The CIA got its revenge on Kennedy for firing Director Allen Dulles and Dallas Mayor's brother Deputy Director Charles Cabell. The agency continued its shadow government practices unabated and without interference or protest from the new Commander-in-Chief.

Texas oil barrens kept their depletion allowance. Brown & Root, the embodiment of the military industrial complex, received many construction contracts from Johnson and was part of a consortium that received a $380 million contract to build airports, bases, hospitals, etc. in Southeast Asia.

Sam Giancana was to testify before Frank Church's Senate Committee investigating CIA and Mob collusion in the plot to assassinate President John F. Kennedy. He never made it as he was killed in his own home, most likely by mobster, CIA asset, and fellow Murchison conference room attendee Johnny Roselli, on orders from the Agency. Roselli did not fare any better. He testified before the Church Committee on April 23, 1976. Before he had a chance to come back for further questioning, Roselli went missing on July 28, 1976. His decomposing body was found in a 55-gallon steel fuel drum floating in Dumfoundling Bay near Miami, Florida two weeks later on August 9th.

As for the debt-based banking cabal represented by CFR head John J. McCloy – and possibly the Rockefellers and Allen Dulles if O'Halloran's account is correct -- they gained greatly from JFK's death. McCloy, David Rockefeller, and Allen Dulles weren't just members of the CFR; they were on its Board of Directors. In order for one-world government to form, the populace of all countries has to be convinced or coerced into believing that the situation in its own nation state is so deficient that one-world government -- under any political philosophy -- sounds appealing. The two methods of getting to that unacceptable state are through 1. Bankrupting the population and then making it dependent on the government for subsistence. 2. By dividing the people on economic, political, racial, generational, and/or philosophical grounds. Kennedy was an impediment to these plans because he was a uniter. He was supportive of democratically elected governments in the third world, irrespective of the populations' political leanings. By contrast, the CFR only wanted puppet governments that would submit to IMF loans and their accompanying ruinous conditions. The CFR was neo-colonialist, simply looking to plunder the natural resources of the third world, whereas Kennedy aided the third world in the development of its native bounty, supporting ontogenesis from within. After JFK was assassinated, American policy about-faced toward the CFR position in the Dominican Republic, Brazil, and Indochina. The lie that was the Vietnam War – a war that never would have occurred if Kennedy lived -- and concomitant draft tore the country apart.

On the domestic front, the CFR always takes a position through its publication *Foreign Affairs* that the solution to any economic problem is through less consumption, less government spending, and sacrifice from

337

the citizens of the United States. The group usually advocates higher taxes on individuals, but incentives for corporations. In short, the CFR supports corporate socialism. Kennedy thought the way to long-term prosperity was through a strong middle class. His economic platform was anathema to the policies vigorously promoted by the CFR. A strong middle class means a strong country that is not subservient to the wishes of a one-world government organization. Economic boundaries that define the middle class vary, but since Kennedy's death the middle 60 percent's share of the national income had dropped from around 55% to 45.8% in 2013 . Credit Suisse produced a report depicting median wealth per citizen by country in 2014. America ranked twenty-first. Continued ignorance of money creation will sap the wealth of this productive nation.

Kennedy also produced *debt-free* money in 1963.

As for Nixon, his ability to piece the guests back at Murchison's and the events of the following day likely made him paranoid when he re-entered presidential politics with his successful 1968 presidential campaign. He was a willing tool of the cabal, which, unlike Johnson, he secretly despised. He knew the game – he was the Vice-President for eight years. However, the realization of the consequences for not toeing the line were likely not lost on him, or other futures presidents (Bush Sr. and Ford) involved in JFK's assassination and/or subsequent cover-up. The United States was looted of its gold after it was put back on the gold standard at Bretton Woods, which is the inevitable eventuality of a debt-based precious metal-backed currency: all the gold goes to the money creators. Nixon had no other option but to shut the gold window; there was a run on the U.S. Treasury. Since then, the United States dollar hasn't imploded because most commodity transactions still take place in dollars, creating an artificial demand for your currency. This was done through an agreement with Saudi Arabia in return for weapon sales and a tacit agreement of American protection. This is the main reason why you are fighting wars in places that you don't really care about: to protect the petrodollar. If a country like Iraq started selling its oil for Euros or yen, demand for the dollar would plummet, interest rates would skyrocket, and inflation would result. The United States can't have that. As a result, regime change in "uncooperative" countries is the ultimate outcome. Nixon told political operative and author Roger Stone that unlike LBJ, "I wasn't willing to kill for it [the presidency]." But his geopolitical and economic strategy of "kicking the can down the road" has resulted in untold wars and unnecessary killings.

The gathering at Murchison's conference room projected the appearance of a rare coming together of the far right, communist hating, peace through strength, profit from war, Texas cowboys and the far left, corporate socialistic, one-world government seeking, debt-based money, profit from war, Eastern Establishment. This assumption would be false. LBJ, in the 1950s, was one of only a handful of congressmen who oversaw the CIA. At the same time he was a neighbor and good friend of FBI chief J. Edgar Hoover. John McCloy, the embodiment of the Eastern Establishment, and Clint Murchison, the symbol of right-wing Texas Oil, were good pals who went dove hunting in the summer of 1963. The Hunts, the Murchisons, and the Rockefellers were the wealthiest families in the United States during the 1960s and LBJ was good friends with all three. They had three things in common: they benefited immensely from conflict, sought total control, and hated Kennedy because his policies were inimical to them. Murchison's conference room represented two ends of the political spectrum coming together to remove an obstacle so they could continue to benefit from mankind's suffering– it was no different than a Council on Foreign Relations meeting.

On the 50th anniversary of the assassination, 61% of Americans believed that there was a conspiracy to kill the president (30% said Oswald acted alone; and sadly, 9% probably don't know who President Kennedy was). This is a significant drop-off from a thirty year period from 1973 to 2003 when at least 74% of the population knew there was more to the story than what the Warren Commission was reporting. As people from that era die off and are replaced with a generation that is decades removed from the assassination, the lie that is perpetuated in your children's' history books begins to take hold, with more and more people believing in the fable. This is how the fiction that is your history becomes ingrained in your conscious. This is why you still believe your doctor, your government officials, and your TV set: because you are trained from cradle to grave. As the caretakers of this libelous fiction, you would have been hard pressed to find ONE member of the Council on Foreign Relations in the 70s or 80s who (publically) believed that there was a conspiracy to assassinate JFK. Please remember, the past haunts the present.

Chapter 39 (January 21 – 22, 2017)

Annie Van was in an uncharacteristically frisky mood for the morning, especially considering the exhausting and wondrous events of the night prior. Normally, daybreak greeted her like a ravenous predator. Her first instinct was to hide from the sunlight while employing her pillows as earmuffs in an attempt to block out any audible indication that the world around her had awakened. She would then assume a fetal position under the sheets. Watching this morning ritual for three months in New York, Fitz surmised that Annie, through these childlike machinations, was trying to make herself invisible to the day. If she succeeded she wouldn't have to rise and shine – victory. But surrender was the inevitable denouement, usually on the condition of a cup of coffee. Fitz actually wondered how she ever got out of bed without his barista-like assistance or Oliver's prodding. However, this morning -- the first morning of the Cavendish presidency -- was different. She hadn't seen Fitz in eight months and couldn't get enough of him. Fitz was more than happy to oblige her atypical pre-breakfast appetite. He wanted nothing more than to stay in bed with her all day -- John Lennon-esque – but he had a country to run and best he knew, Polly was still missing. His first meeting was at 10:00am with his would-be cabinet, followed by a more brass tacks conversation with some of the Congressional leaders who hosted yesterday's post swearing-in luncheon. Before she let him go to the shower, Annie had a few unanswered questions that needed resolving.

"Why didn't you tell me about your father?"

"I only discovered that he was my father a few months before I met you. I didn't know if I was ever going to tell anyone. If I decided not to run for office, I would have been happy just being your husband. In fact, if you hadn't solved those riddles, I probably would have stayed silent about it forever."

"You mean the ones that related to your father?"

"Yes. I couldn't solve them for months, and then you come along and solve them in under a minute. The answers were clues to who killed my father and why he was killed. I apologize. I lied to you. Evan did not give me that riddle. The riddle was in a note from my father to my mother."

"Really?"

Fitz wasn't sure if she was responding to the cryptic letter remark or to the fact that he had lied to her. Fitz chose the former. "Yes. You are the reason that I am waking up with you in the White House and not in SoHo. Mafia Mike is overseeing the move of some of my stuff which should be arriving today. I will show you the letter tonight when everything is unpacked."

"Why did you go on the campaign without me?"

A little incredulous, Fitz replied, "Honey, if any of the people who actually run this planet knew about you, they could compromise me by threatening your well-being. If my plan to become the president was successful, I didn't want you known to them until I was the president and you were under Secret Service protection. You are aware of the fact that Polly Preston is missing?"

"What? No. I had no idea. When did this happen?"

"Yesterday – she was supposed to accompany me at the swearing-in ceremony. The last time anyone saw her was the night before. Actually, you were supposed to accompany me as well. Did you not get the invite?"

"No. I didn't. The invite may have been put in the wrong mailbox. At least a Romeo and Juliet scenario didn't play out. More importantly, tell me about Polly."

"I'm going to find out more when I speak to the Secret Service and Mike."

"I really like Mafia Mike. And I think my mother does as well. She texted me that she thought that he was very handsome." Realizing the inappropriateness of her comment under the circumstances, Annie switched back to the more pressing issue, "Is there anything I can do to help? Aren't you worried that the Secret Service is controlled by these people?"

"I am, but I trust that they will perform their duties – as far as my experience, the agents are wonderful. But that is one of the reasons I hired Mike. He can be my eyes and ears. Regarding Polly, the press is going to have a field day with this one: you enter as she disappears. She wasn't under Secret Service protection. Let me go shower so I can get on my way."

Annie wanted to say, "Need help showering?" but the news of Polly's disappearance made it bad form. The irony was not lost on her: she was concerned for someone she subconsciously loathed for eight months.

****

Fitz's first unofficial Saturday meeting with his staff completely revolved around the Polly Preston situation. Authorities found her phone near the exit for Fort Bragg, North Carolina on Interstate 95 South. Fitz decided that he would hold a press conference, instead of subjecting brand new Press Secretary Schilling to the media frenzy, after his second luncheon with Congressional leaders in as many days.

The tone of the Saturday meeting with senior lawmakers wasn't what Fitz expected. They agreed Fitz's policies had merit, but indicated that implementation was hopeless. It wasn't the words that surprised Fitz; it was the manner in which they were delivered. If was as if they were informing Fitz that the thirty-three day search at sea for his loved one was being called off. His proposed legislation wouldn't be able to survive that long, in those conditions. He was told that he didn't understand what he was up against. The views were unanimous and bipartisan. It was as if the legislative agenda was circumscribed by a higher authority and Congress was powerless to introduce any bill that was outside the predetermined playbook. They also politely informed him that there would be a *quid pro quo* regarding his cabinet members being approved by the Senate: drop the campaign platform that got you into the White House and your top-level cabinet members would be approved; otherwise there would be endless delays and rejections. They also conveyed to Fitz that negotiating with terrorists was political suicide.   Fitz thought about reminding the congressmen that he received more than 60% of the popular vote and that their approval rating was 16%, but he thought better of it. He expected Congress to be useless anyway. No good could come from a pissing match

342

with them before his administration incubated. It was better to appear as a deer in the headlights, than to tip his hand. At meeting's end, he thanked them individually for their input. A few of them told him in hushed tones that they thought what he did was remarkable. All of them wished him luck. Fitz felt the warm wishes (coupled with no support) were in the same tenor of Chamberlain's dignitaries to Hitler in his quest to wipe out Soviet Communism back in 1936. *Great! Day two and I feel like Hitler.*

The James S Brady Press Briefing Room was full. Fitz initially thought about restricting the press conference to the Polly Preston situation, but then decided that he best answer everything: Annie Van, Polly Preston, the tone of his inauguration address, his meeting with the congressional VIPs, etc. None of the questions seemed very pointed – only one contested the decorum of proposing to Annie while Polly was missing "I was swept up in the moment" was his response. And remarkably, none said anything about his proposal for a caliphate in the Mideast. He was not caught off guard by any of their questions – most involved Annie and Polly -- and lied only once, when asked why he didn't campaign with Annie. "I didn't really campaign, except for two weeks and I did not want to subject her to the initial 'I'm JFK's son' media blitz" was his slightly misleading response. He asked for assistance from the press pool regarding Polly's whereabouts and reiterated his inauguration speech's promise to address the populace in a month at the State of the Union, which he had delayed until the third week in February.

****

Back in his bedroom, Fitz saw that Annie had arranged most of his belongings. Annie didn't have a staff of a dozen and half employees yet, nor did she want them. Annie and Mafia Mike were heading up to Jersey City Sunday morning to not only pick up Oliver and her mother, but also to sort out her resignation from the U.N. School and her move from Tribeca. Mafia Mike insisted on driving back up to Jersey City with Annie with the Secret Service escorting. They would return on Tuesday.

Curious as to what she had missed during her own JFK research, Annie reminded Fitz of his promise to show her the letters from JFK to his mother. Fitz found the envelopes in a moving box and chastised his own carelessness with these artifacts as they easily could have been accidentally

343

destroyed or misplaced. Fortunately, there were no consequences of his inattention. He handed the envelopes over to Annie, who was sitting at the edge of the bed. She was immediately drawn to the pearls.

"I was going to give them to you as a wedding gift, but I totally forgot they were in the envelope. I'm sorry I spoiled the surprise."

"Were these your mother's?" asked an enraptured Annie.

"Not only were they hers; they were given to her by my father. They are yours now. Again I apologize about spoiling the surprise."

"Oh my God – they're beautiful." Annie was still trying to come to grips with the fact that thirty hours ago she was on the verge of neurasthenia in a classroom full of children and now she was engaged to the President of the United States. Now she was receiving pearls that were purchased by arguably the most popular American figure of the twentieth century. It was a lot to process. She stood up, grabbed Fitz by the hand with her one hand that wasn't holding the pearls and started tearing up. She then immediately laughed at herself for crying. Besides for the ritual morning snuggle with Oliver, it was the endearing idiosyncrasy that Fitz loved most about her. He grabbed the embarrassingly long strand of nacre, folded it up so it formed four circular layers, and placed them over Annie's head and around her neck. They shared a long embrace and kiss. Just when it was turning into a Viagra moment, Annie's curiosity snapped her attention back to the letters. Fitz would have to wait.

She examined the lock of hair, "We should get a glass casing for this and hang it on the wall or put in my curio cabinet." Fitz said nothing. Annie examined the letter Fitz's mother had written to him and the first two letters that JFK had sent Fitz's mother and decided, "Actually, all of this should be displayed." Annie's consideration turned to the third letter.

2^2

3^3

10,91,529____

Nov 19

Dear Mary:

I spoke of my killer
and they are near.

.—— Bye Nary 30

As she inspected it, she noticed the 2^2, 3^3 sequence and surmised out loud, "This is the letter with the clues."

Fitz interjected, "Yes."

"Help me out here, where did you get the Executive Order out of this?"

"The dots to the left of 'Bye Nary' represent the letters 'E' and 'O' in Morse code."

Annie didn't seem too convinced, "Okay."

345

"'Bye Nary' represents the binary system. You were the one who brought that to my attention."

"But I didn't see it in this context. All I saw was the puzzle you had written down, not the actual source of the puzzle. To me this is clearly 'Bye Mary' – meaning your mother -- and the pen just misfired on ink when the point should have been marking the paper."

"It didn't misfire when he wrote the other letters. And the '30' should be pretty self-explanatory."

"But what you see as '30', I see as a nearly closed heart and a teardrop. His heart is breaking and he is shedding a tear because the end is near. 'Alex, I'll take 1960's Presidential Emoticons for $200'"

"Well, I still interpret that as Executive Order 11110. The other numbers on the paper, you solved before and concluded that it was a date – the date my father gave the speech on secret societies."

"Again, now that I can observe the source document, it is clearly not written by your father. The ink maybe similar, but your father's writing is slanted to the right. The numbers are pretty upright or may lean slightly to the left." Annie the schoolteacher continued, "Plus your father's handwriting was atrocious, this looks much cleaner."

Confused but undeterred, Fitz continued, "But the date is the date of that speech he gave on secret societies. Combine that with an Executive Order that issued *debt-free* money -- a direct threat to the root cause of all our problems: the Federal Reserve. The Federal Reserve and its related organizations (the Bank of International Settlements, the World Bank, the International Monetary Fund, and the Council on Foreign Relations) are the public face of the 'secret societies' that my father was referring to on April, 27, 1961. His father Joe hated central banking and surely instilled this conviction into Jack."

Annie, at this point, viewing Fitz's position as 'often wrong, but never in doubt', retorted, "No silly. Let's assume that you are right about the messages in the letter and that they refer to these specific events relating to your father. Have you examined Executive Order 11110 closely?" Fitz remained silent, curious, but still confident. "It was issued on June 4, 1963, the same day that he signed bill 88-36 into law. In essence, 88-63 repealed the Silver Purchase Act of 1934. The executive order was simply a housekeeping measure. The Silver Purchase Act had authorized and required the Secretary of the Treasury to buy silver and issue silver certificates. With its repeal, your father was now the only one with that authority (from the Agricultural Adjustment Act). He needed to delegate to the Treasury Secretary his own authority, which was accomplished with Executive Order 11110."

"What about the silver certificates that were issued?"

"$768 million worth of certificates were issued in 1963 and 1964, but probably just to match up what they had in reserves at the Treasury. It was the smallest issuance since 1935. Remember, Public Law 88-36 also gave the Federal Reserve the authority to issue $1 and $2 notes, which it started doing in 1964. That was a power they did not have up until the passage of 88-36. You see the combined action of Public Law 88-36 and Executive Order 11110 was to bring the issuance of Silver Certificates to an end and grant the Federal Reserve *more* power, not less. If your father was hell bent on destroying the Fed -- as you are -- he wouldn't have given it more power. Listen -- having done some research in this area, your father was obviously killed by a conspiracy, but not likely this one. You understand a lot more about the true root cause of suffering on this planet – debt-based money – than your father ever did."

Slightly crestfallen, Fitz replied, "So you're saying that EO 11110, in the note to my mother – the reason I desired to attain the office of President of the United States -- is the by-product of a faulty pen?"

"He appears to have been sloppy with a dip pen. That created the dot and dashes and the 'N' instead of the 'M'. Sometimes the genius is in the interpretation, not the message."

"Then what does the date at the top of the page mean?"

"I'm not sure. But the conspiracy referred to by Kennedy in his speech was communism. It was right after the Bay of Pigs incident."

"But communism, at its core, is a creation of the central bankers. Communism is all about a centralized, or monopoly government -- all of our supposed great 'capitalists' were really communists in disguise. They didn't want competition, they wanted monopolies. Central banking is all about the monopolization of the money supply. The Federal Reserve Act was birthed so that the moneyed interests could accelerate their wealth accumulation. It was done behind the smokescreen of stabilizing the nation's credit and currency supply, which is impossible in a debt-based money creation model, the instability of which is further accentuated through fractional reserve banking. Communism was created so that banks and big industry only had to deal with one authority in each country to obtain a monopoly in that country. My father wrote this to my mother two and a half years after he gave the speech."

"That is true, but it isn't what Kennedy was referring to in his speech. He was implicating the Soviet Union and the countries under its influence, not the banking conspiracy behind its creation. Besides, Kennedy didn't write those numbers on the note to your mother."

"Well, why would it refer to that specific date? Is that not a very large coincidence?"

"It doesn't have to be a date. It could be a message that your mother wrote to herself and the date was an additional reminder, perhaps to a passcode or combination."

All of a sudden, Fitz felt like Wile E. Coyote, just as he was about to be hit with an object that he had earlier pushed off a cliff: "*The safe*!!"

"What?"

"The safe – my Grandma Gert had a safe in her house. I sold it when I sold the house. I'll bet any amount of money that is the combination to the safe: 4-27-19-61. I never knew it. And I totally discounted the fact that there would be anything in the safe. It had been decades since Gert was communicating with the world. That safe hasn't been open for at least twenty-five years."

"When did you sell the house?"

"I had it on the market before I identified myself to the world and sold it about two months later. I agreed to a price and gave my lawyer

348

power of attorney to settle everything else. The money was transferred into my account and I never gave it any thought, until now."

"Can you get a hold of the buyer?"

"I probably could, but since I need to open the safe in person anyway, I might as well just show up at their house. Tomorrow is Sunday and you are heading back to the New Jersey area anyway..."

Annie cut him off, "Honey, as the President of the United States, you can't just show up at people's houses randomly and ask to come in."

Surrendering, Fitz said kiddingly, "Why not – I could show up with balloons, just like Ed McMahon and Publisher's Clearing House?"

"Except that you won't be carrying a life altering check."

"Okay. I will call the lawyer – I think I have his cell." After several Saturday evening phone calls, Fitz was patched into the owner of the house; an Indian immigrant named Daaruk, whose voice could have doubled for Apu on *The Simpsons*. After Fitz had supplied enough information about the sale of the house to Daaruk to convince him that the 45th President of the United States was indeed the executor of Gertrude Scott's estate, he divulged that he was still in possession of the safe and agreed to the visit. The whole episode didn't sink in with Daaruk until Fitz informed him that the Secret Service would be arriving at his house before the president – standard operating procedure. The Secret Service was just as startled to find out that Fitz would be traveling with Annie to New Jersey, but taking separate transportation home.

What is in that safe?

****

Daaruk Patel's family of four (wife, son, and daughter) were dressed in their Sunday best upon President Cavendish's arrival. Since Oceanport, New Jersey was only an hour out of the way and since Fitz wanted to say hello to his future mother-in-law with Annie, she joined Fitz on the detour. The Patel family laid out a very nice Indian-themed Sunday brunch that Fitz and Annie were more than happy to sample. Some of the neighbors peeked out their windows at a number of black security vehicles parked on the street, not to mention the Secret Service detail. Fitz apologized to the Patel family for turning their day upside down and said that if there were any valuables in the safe, they were the property of the Patel's – that is if he could open the safe. If the valuables had any sentimental value, like a bracelet, Fitz would compensate them. He was only after personal affects.

Daaruk escorted Fitz and Annie up to the office that contained the safe. The safe hadn't moved -- not surprising considering its extreme weight. Fitz knelt down before the safe and turned the dial four complete rotations to the right before stopping at 4; three complete rotations to the left before stopping on 27; two complete rotations right before stopping at 19; one complete rotation left before stopping on 61. He pulled on the handle and the safe opened, solving two mysterious family deaths.

Chapter 40 (9/11)

BBC Newsman Phil Hayton in his London newsroom, September 11, 2001 5:00pm EST: "The forty-seven story Salomon Brothers Building [World Trade Center Tower 7], situated very close to the World Trade Center, has also just collapsed. Now more on the latest building collapse in New York – you might have heard a few moments ago, us talking about the Salomon Brothers Building collapsing – and indeed it has. Apparently that's only a few hundred yards [wouldn't the BBC script read "meters"?] from where the World Trade Center Towers [1 & 2] were. And it seems that this was not the result of a new attack; it was because the building had been weakened during this morning's attacks. We'll probably find out more about that from our correspondent Jane Standley. Jane, what more can you tell us about the Salomon Brothers Building and its collapse?"

[Cut to Jane Standley with a shot of lower Manhattan in the background. World Trade Center Tower 7 (the Salomon Brothers Building) is clearly still standing in the background. The footer on the screen says, "World Trade Centre destroyed by hijacked planes. Pentagon hit and burning"]

Standley: "Well only what you really already know. Details are very, very sketchy. There's almost a sense downtown in New York behind me [she points over her right shoulder], down by the World Trade Centre, just an area completely closed off as rescue workers try to do their jobs. But this isn't the first building that has suffered as a result. Know that part of the Marriott Hotel, next to the World Trade Centre, also collapsed as a result of huge amounts of falling debris from 110 floors of two twin towers of the World Trade Centre. As you can see behind me, the Trade Centre still seems to be burning. We see these huge clouds of smoke and ash. And we know that behind that an empty piece of what was a very familiar New York skyline, symbol of the financial prosperity of this city, but it has completely disappeared now [footer changes to "Jane Standley New York"] and New York is still not able to take on board what has happened to them today."

[Cut back to the London studio with a screen of Jane Standley in the background with WTC 7 in the background, clear as day.]

> Hayton: "Presumably, there were very few people in the Salomon building when it collapsed. I mean, there were, I suppose, fears that of possible further collapses around the area?"

[Cut back to full screen shot of Standley. The footer now reads, "The 47 storey Salomon Brothers Building close to the World Trade Centre has also collapsed". The building, of course, is still standing in the background.]

> Standley: "That's what you would hope because this whole downtown area behind me has been completely sealed off and evacuated, apart from the emergency workers. That was done by the mayor, Rudy Giuliani, much earlier today, because of course because of the dreadful collapse of the twin towers at the World Trade Centre. But New York, the city still in a chaos: phones are not working properly; the subway lines are not working properly; and we know that down there, near the World Trade Centre, there are three schools that are being turned into triage centres for emergency treatment. And I know this: over in New York Harbor, where the famous Statue of Liberty is, is a field hospital where 1,500 people have been treated. And we have heard, though it is unconfirmed as of yet, that over one hundred New York City police officers have been taken there as well for treatment, but we do need to confirm those figures for the officers."

[The conversation between Standley and Hayton continues for another four minutes.]

> Hayton: "Jane, I think many of us, when we heard the news, perhaps on the radio earlier today, were ah completely flabbergasted by it and just couldn't comprehend it. It's almost sounded too farfetched. I was wondering what it felt like for you, being in Manhattan... [Screen showing Standley completely cuts out. Someone finally figured out that WTC 7 is still standing.] Well, unfortunately, I think we have lost the line with Jane Standley in Manhattan. We will follow that up later."

Someone missed the rehearsal…

To be sure, WTC 7, the Salomon Brothers building, collapsed about ten minutes after the live feed cut out. Based on where Jane Standley was reporting from, it seems odd that she would be reporting on a building collapse that, unless she was deaf, she would have heard. The excuse given for 'jumping the gun' is that reports indicating WTC 7 was going to collapse were somehow juxtaposed into 'it had collapsed', yet Ms. Standley seemed so intent on emphasizing that reports about the number of police officers being treated at Liberty Island were "unconfirmed", a relatively unimportant tidbit, given the events of the day. On any other day, the collapse of a 47-story building would be the biggest news event of the entire year, so you would think that she would have that "confirmed". How did they know it was going to collapse? Never in the history of the world had a building over fifteen stories collapsed from a fire. Only 43% of Americans are aware of the fact that a third skyscraper collapsed on 9/11.

Also, for the avoidance of doubt, Ms. Standley was correct: WTC 7 was hit with falling debris when WTC 1 collapsed – a lot of very heavy pieces of metal – that did considerable damage to the south and west side of the building. However, the reason given – actually no reason was given for seven years – was that falling debris from the collapse of WTC 1 initiated fires in WTC 7, which spread to ten floors, weakened the structure, causing its collapse. Even National Institute of Standards and Technology's (NIST's) lead investigator, Syham Sunder, admitted that it was the first time in history where fire was the primary cause of a progressive collapse in a building over fifteen stories. There are problems with the NIST narrative, which will be addressed later.

9/11 was as a tipping point on many levels. What changed after 9/11? 1. The United States used it as an excuse to invade Afghanistan and eventually Iraq. 2. A mothballed pipeline project running from the Caspian oil basin to the Indian Ocean through Afghanistan suddenly sprung back to life. 3. The recently dormant poppy trade (necessary for heroin production) in Afghanistan suddenly sprung back with a vengeance. 4. The United States became engaged in a war with a concept (terrorism) not a country, which can last indefinitely. 5. The citizens of the United States lost many of their Constitutional rights with the passage of the

Patriot Act. 6. The Department of Homeland Security was created. 7. Many Americans dislike and fear Muslims. 8. Large groups of Muslim terrorists, who hate the United States and Western Europe as much as Israel, now actually exist.

Who benefitted from 9/11? 1. The military-industrial complex received most of the money that goes to pay for the conduct of war -- it always does. 2. The debt-based money cabal was able to increase the debt of the United States by $2 trillion while putting into place the ability to call you an "enemy combatant" if you don't obey its orders in a time of a real or make-believe crisis. 3. The Homeland Security apparatus (i.e. police state), which did not exist before 9/11, took $1 trillion of taxpayer money in order to more efficiently round up those same taxpayers in a time of crisis. 4. The CIA could be a member of any of the three organizations previously listed, but deserves special mention since it is responsible for most of the world's poppy trade, with Afghanistan being its largest producer. It needs the poppy money to run its shadow government operations around the globe. It's tough to get funding from Congress when the debt is $18 trillion. 5. Israel benefits because the United States is exhausting its capital and manpower to fight a common enemy: Jew hating Muslim "terrorists".

Who didn't benefit from 9/11? 1. The alleged terrorist organizations that perpetuated 9/11 as they have been carpet bombed into an alternate universe. 2. Osama bin Laden, who died of kidney and lung failure a few months after 9/11. You see, it is very difficult running around in forbidding terrain conducting a war when you need kidney dialysis a couple of times a week. Did the mainstream media tell you that? Funny how there was no public physical proof of Bin Laden's May 2, 2011 death. You see, Egyptian newspaper *al-Wafd* mentioned his passing and funeral in its December 26, 2001 addition. Additionally, Pakistani newspaper *Abou Zofar* detailed the funeral in Tora Bora that was attended by thirty Al-Qaeda fighters, some Bin Laden family members, and a few Taliban friends. A hail of bullets was fired to see him off to his final resting place. This funeral took place on or about December 15, 2001. This matches up nicely with the fact that on December 13, 2001, his regularly intercepted messages stopped. 3. Saddam Hussein, whose biggest crime was that he wanted to sell oil for currency other than the U.S. dollar. He was also sitting on a massively underexploited Kirkuk oil field. 4. The Unocal-led

354

oil consortium that wanted to put that pipeline through Afghanistan. As it turned out, the initial projections for the Caspian oil basin turned out to be way over-inflated, obviating the importance of the pipeline. Since this small nugget of information was unknown at the time, all of the military bases in Afghanistan were located along the propose route of the pipeline. 5. The American military personnel didn't fare very well – they never do. They die or are permanently disabled in the name of keeping your country safe from "terrorism" and are largely forgotten once they return home. You see, it's hard to spend money on your veterans when you are $18 trillion in debt. 6. The American citizens, who gave up some freedoms in the name of security.

The official version of events states that four airliners were hijacked by Muslim (Al Qaeda) terrorists. Two were flown into the World Trade Center Towers 1 & 2, causing their collapses; one was flown into Pentagon, causing great damage; and one crashed in Shanksville, Pennsylvania as passengers attempted to wrest control of the plane from the terrorists. This seems reasonable enough. You saw it with your own two eyes – at least the planes flying into the World Trade Center. Regarding the 9/11 Commission study that purports this version of events, it is a question of what it left out.

For example, it did not provide any proof that Osama bin Laden was behind the attacks, except for statements extracted in 2003 from waterboarding Khalid Sheikh Mohammed and some poorly produced CIA videos. The "FBI Ten Most Wanted Fugitives" poster does not list 9/11 as one of his crimes. Bin Laden issued a statement to Al Jazeera that was posted on CNN Sept 17, 2001:

> "The U.S. government has consistently blamed me for being behind every occasion its enemies attack it. I would like to assure the world that I did not plan the recent attacks, which seems to have been planned by people for personal reasons. I have been living in the Islamic emirate of Afghanistan and following its leaders' rules. The current leader does not allow me to exercise such operations."

Even though his *modus operandi* until 9/11 had been to take credit for his terrorist attacks, American law enforcement wasn't buying it. In a

September 28, 2001 interview with Pakistani newspaper *Ummat* Bin Laden repeated his innocence:

> "I have already said that I am not involved in the 11 September attacks in the United States. As a Muslim, I try my best to avoid telling a lie. I had no knowledge of these attacks, nor do I consider the killing of innocent women, children and other humans as an appreciable act. Islam strictly forbids causing harm to innocent women, children and other people."

A couple of months after these denials, the United States government produced a video in which someone dressed up as Osama bin Laden admits to the 9/11 attacks. There are many problems with the video including the fact, according to the FBI, bin Laden is left-handed. He is writing right-handed in the video. He is also wearing a gold ring in the video which is forbidden by Islamic Law. The video was released on December 13, 2011 – the same date that Bin Laden's transmissions, and possibly Osama himself, ceased. You would think that would be ample time for the CIA to produce a better quality video.

As another example of omission, what does the 9/11 Commission Report state about the bombs in the basements of the World Trade Center *before* the first plane hit the North Tower (WTC 1)? William Rodriguez, who worked in the North Tower, said,

> "I was a janitor in the building [Rodriguez was in sub-basement 1]…There was an explosion in the basement and this is *prior* to the building got [sic] hit by the plane. And then the plane hit and there was a series of explosions afterwards…"

He testified as much in front of a closed-door 9/11 Commission and provided a list of others who would corroborate his testimony. Not only were the people on Rodriguez's list not called to testify, his testimony was omitted from the 9/11 Commission Report. Finally, in January 2009, after buckling to public pressure, the Commission's investigation records were released. William's testimony was among those marked "restricted," and thus still inaccessible to the public. Why?

One of the people on Rodriguez's list was John Mongello. He was in the lobby of the South Tower when the North Tower was struck.

Mongello claims that within a minute of the first plane hitting the North Tower, an elevator in the *South Tower* exploded right in front of him. Mongello (and according to him, others) were blown back by the blast, which took place fifteen minutes *before* the second plane hit the South Tower.

Evalle Sweezer said, "There was no [North Tower] lobby. So I believe that the bomb hit the lobby first and a couple of seconds then the first plane hit." Others, including an unidentified, but clearly soot covered witness from the impact area, stated, "I think a bomb went off in the lobby first, then a plane hit the building." Another identified man caught on tape said, "The building shook and I thought there was an earthquake...and then there was a huge explosion."

You are told by the report that a jet fuel induced fireball traveled a fifth of a mile down elevator shafts causing the explosions that blew out the lobby windows of the WTC 1. How did the fireballs know to get off at the lobby? Out of the one-hundred elevators servicing the WTC 1, only three went from the point of impact down to the lobby. Certainly, elevators caught fire from jet fuel traveling down the elevator shafts, and certainly elevators with their cables cut plummeted to their landings. However, it seems more plausible that the bomb claimed by Rodriguez was the culprit in the lobby destruction.

For the avoidance of doubt, these explosions did not bring down WTC 1 & 2, nor did they affect how the towers came crashing down. If it was an attempt to bring the towers down just as the planes hit the buildings, it was a failure. The point of Rodriguez's testimony (and Mongello's and other eyewitness claims) is that there has to be more to the story than the nineteen hijackers on four airplanes.

As far as the destruction of WTC 1 & 2 is concerned, 2,398 Architects & Engineers for 9/11 Truth don't believe that the buildings could have fallen in the manner claimed by the NIST, which was tasked by the 9/11 Commission with ascertaining the cause of the collapses. NIST's conclusions were not substantiated by its physical experiments. In fact, the physical tests performed by NIST showed that the fire temperatures were generally too low and that the WTC floor trusses should have easily withstood the fires they experienced on 9/11. Additionally, the physical

357

tests were improperly modeled (e.g. the fire tests were not ventilation limited). Unable to prove anything through physical testing, NIST had to rely on computer modeling. When NIST did its modeling, it plugged in its best guess based on observables and what it knew about the planes and the building. When that failed to induce a collapse, NIST modified the model. For example, for the North Tower, NIST admitted that it increased the speed of the plane by 29mph; increased its weight by 5%; decreased its approach angle by $3°$; increased the aircraft strength by 25%; and decreased the building's strength by 20%. In other words, NIST manipulated the input data until it achieved the desired results. What appears to be a conclusion is actually a premise. Even more curious is that NIST didn't bother simulating the collapse. It is assumed that collapse initiation automatically leads to global collapse. The content of NIST's models is anyone's guess. You see, its models are not available for public consumption, nor does NIST publish any of the data sets generated by its models. It must be a national security issue....

The Architects and Engineers for 9/11 Truth point out the presence of squibs shooting out below the collapsing floors. They point out the presence of thermite in the WTC dust. These are signatures of explosive devices in a controlled demolition. Also, they specify the presence of molten metal in the rubble weeks after 9/11. Captain Philip Ruvolo, a firefighter involved in the recovery stated, "You'd get down below and you'd see molten steel, molten steel running down the channel rails, like you're in a foundry -- like lava." Leslie Robertson, a member of the WTC engineering team, stated "As of 21 days after the attack, the fires were still burning and molten steel was still running." Greg Fuchek, vice president of a company that provided computer equipment to identify human remains, stated: "sometimes when a worker would pull a steel beam from the wreckage, the end of the beam would be dripping molten metal." William Langewiesche, the only journalist who had unrestricted access to Ground Zero, mentioned "areas where underground fires still burned and steel flowed in molten streams." What did NIST have to say about the molten metal?

"The condition of the steel in the wreckage of the WTC towers (i.e., whether it was in a molten state or not) was irrelevant to the investigation of the collapse since it does not provide any conclusive information on the condition of the steel when the WTC towers were standing."

That is not a very "scientific" rationalization.

Susan Lindauer claimed that the U.S. intelligence community had advance knowledge of the 9/11 attacks on the World Trade Center. She was the back-channel liaison between the United States and Iraq at the United Nations prior to 9/11. (Incidentally, the Iraqis *were cooperating* with the United States in order to get crippling economic sanctions lifted over the weapons of mass destruction issue.) In the months preceding 9/11, her bosses at the CIA were demanding information from the Iraqis about that specific plot. (They had none.) In fact, on August 2nd, her CIA handler, Dr. Richard Fuisz, warned her not to travel to New York because the attack on the World Trade Center involving airplane hijackings was "considered imminent," with the potential for "mass human casualties" and a "possible miniature thermo-nuclear device". She called Attorney General John Ashcroft's office on either August 7th or 8th to warn of the impending attack. After the attacks, Susan learned through a contact at the State Department that unmarked white vans entered the World Trade Center each morning at 3:00am (after the custodial vans had left) and exited at 5:00am (before the Wall Street employees would arrive) from August 23th until September 4th. When she attempted to go public with her revelations, she was arrested under the Patriot Act on March 11, 2004. In 2005, she was incarcerated at Carswell Air Force Base in Fort Worth, Texas, for psychological evaluation. She was released in 2006 after judge (and future Attorney General) Michael Mukasey declared her mentally unfit to stand trial. In 2008, the Federal District Court in New York City reaffirmed her inability to stand trial. Discredited.... Want to know more? Read *Extreme Prejudice: The Terrifying Story of the Patriot Act and the Cover-Ups of 9/11 and Iraq.*

Sibel Edmonds also has a story to tell. She was hired by the FBI as a translator just after 9/11. From her work she discovered that the Sept. 11 hijackers were in the country and plotting to use airplanes as missiles. She said documents also included information relating to their financial activities. More importantly, she discovered that the FBI was aware of the plot. Once she attempted to go public with this information, she was fired. She filed a whistle blower lawsuit. Her allegations of FBI misconduct led to the Senate Judiciary Committee asking for an independent audit of the FBI's translation unit. Attorney General Ashcroft retaliated by invoking the States secrets privilege over Ms. Edmonds on October 28, 2002, stating that her deposition "would cause serious damage to the national security and foreign policy interests of the United States". In February 2004, she did appear in front of the 9/11 Commission, but her three hour testimony was behind closed doors and was never mentioned in the report. She was scheduled to testify for a 9/11 victims' class action lawsuit on April 27, 2004, but Ashcroft stepped in again, quashing her testimony. She couldn't even be deposed in her own whistle blower lawsuit. What was Ashcroft hiding? History is a lie – a lie of omission. Silenced.... Want to know more? Read *Classified Woman – The Sibel Edmonds Story*.

Another example of omission in the 9/11 report is the failure to mention chief of Inter-Services Intelligence (ISI -- Pakistan's CIA), Lt. Gen. Mahmoud Ahmed's $100,000 wire transfer to Mohammed Atta in their final report, even though it was reported by the *Washington Post*, *Agence France Presse*, and *The Times of India* in late September and early October 2001. Perhaps this omission was due to the fact that Ahmed met with the Chairmen of the Senate and House Intelligence Committees, Senator Bob Graham and Representative Porter Goss, CIA Director George Tenet, and U.S. Under Secretary of State for Political Affairs Marc Grossman during his weeklong visit to Washington D.C. the week *before* the 9/11 attacks. Would not the money trail of 9/11 be of some importance? Why is this not questioned?

Why did President George W. Bush and Dick Cheney testify *together*, *not* under oath, with *no* press or victims' family members in attendance, and with *no* notes taken? Senate Majority Leader and anthrax recipient Tom Daschle appeared on NBC's "Meet the Press" in May 2002, and said Cheney had, on January 24th of that year, urged him not to investigate the events of 9/11. Daschle added that four days later Bush made the same request. When program moderator Tim Russert asked: "No investigation by anyone, period'?" Daschle replied: "That's correct." He added that the request had been repeated on "other dates following." Even though they were unable to squash an investigation, Cheney and Bush successfully avoided publically disclosing their actions on this rather important date in American history. It would have been interesting for

America to see Cheney explain his part in Secretary of Transportation Norman Mineta's testimony:

> Vice-Chairman of the 9/11 Commission Lee Hamilton: "...were you there when that order [to shoot down planes] was given?"
>
> Mineta: "No I was not. I was made aware of it during the time that the airplane [was] coming into the Pentagon. There was a young man who had come in and said to the Vice President, 'The plane is 50 miles out. The plane is 30 miles out.' And when it got down to, 'The plane is 10 miles out,' the young man also said to the Vice-President, 'Do the orders still stand?' And the Vice-President turned and whipped his neck around and said, 'Of course the orders still stand. Have you heard anything to the contrary?' Well, at the time I didn't know what all that meant. And..."
>
> Lee Hamilton: "The flight you're referring to is the..."
>
> Mineta: "The flight that came into the Pentagon."

Looks like Dick Cheney, like Ashcroft and NIST, played the "national security" card – again.

It seems as if the 9/11 Commission was no different than FDR's Roberts Commission or the Warren Commission; it was a complete farce. Not buying that William Rodriquez's and Sibel Edmonds' suppressed depositions and the strange circumstances surrounding the Bush and Cheney testimonies don't add up to a farce? Two 9/11 commissioners and a senior counsel seem to think so.

> 9/11 Commission Vice-Chairman Lee Hamilton: "...there are all kinds of reasons we thought we were set up to fail. We got started late. We had a very short time frame -- indeed, we had to get it extended. We did not have enough money. They were afraid we were going to hang somebody; that we would point the finger."
>
> 9/11 Commission Chairman Tom Kean: "Lee [Hamilton] and I write in our book that we think the Commission, in many ways, was set up to fail, because we had not enough money. We didn't

have enough time. We were appointed by the most partisan people in Washington: the leaders of the House and Senate."

Senior Counsel to the 9/11 Commission, John Farmer: "[The Commission] discovered that what had occurred that morning — that is, what government and military officials had told Congress, the Commission, the media, and the public about who knew what when — was almost entirely, and inexplicably, untrue.... At some level of the government, at some point in time ... there was a decision not to tell the truth about what happened."

You would think that for the crime of the 21st Century, our government would be interested in getting to the truth, expenses and time be damned – especially considering America spent $1 trillion setting up its national security apparatus and $2 trillion on the subsequent "War on Terrorism", which seems to have been as successful as the "War on Drugs". That is, of course, unless they had something to hide. The wool is being pulled over your eyes.

As for WTC 7, it seemed to be almost completely evacuated by the time the second tower was struck – rather odd. Unfortunately, city staffers Barry Jennings and Michael Hess didn't get the message when they entered the building around 9:00 am. When they arrived at the Office of Emergency Management on the 23rd floor, they found no one. Jennings phoned other staffers and a supervisor, who told him to "get out of there now." Deciding to heed orders, Jennings and Hess left for the elevator bank, but the power was now out in the building [why?], forcing them to take the stairs. On their way down, one of the landings on the stairway they were descending gave way after being rocked by an explosion below. Trapped on the 8th floor, Jennings and Hess broke a window and yelled to firefighters below to initiate a rescue. This was allegedly one hour *before* the North Tower – which caused significant damage to WTC 7 – collapsed. Jennings reported multiple explosions and Hess said that there was thick smoke around them. After an hour and a half, the rescue was accomplished. If their claims are correct then something else started the fires in WTC 7. Hess would later change his version of events. Jennings did not. Jennings died two days before NIST released the draft of its final report on WTC 7 on August 19, 2008. When filmmaker Dylan Avery hired a private investigator to look into the cause of Jennings' death, he received a message back from him: "Due to some of the information I have uncovered, I have determined that this is a job for the police. I have refunded your credit card. Please do not contact me again about this individual."

When NIST released the draft of its final report – over seven years, 200,000 man-hours, and 10,000 plus pages in the making – it gave the public *three weeks* to make a scientific review of the document. What were they hiding?

According to NIST, the heat from the uncontrolled fires caused steel floor beams and girders to thermally expand, leading to a chain of events that caused a key structural column to fail. Specifically, a girder on Floor 13 lost its connection to a critical column, Column 79, that provided support for the long floor spans on the east side of the building. That triggered a cascade of floor failures down to the fifth floor, reducing support for Column 79, causing it to buckle and fail, which set off a chain reaction resulting in the progressive and global collapse of the building. This certainly sounds reasonable until you realize that for the girder on Floor 13 to lose its connection to Column 79, NIST had to assume that only the steel heated and expanded while the concrete floor did not. Given that steel and concrete have nearly the same coefficient of thermal expansion, this explanation holds no water. It also had to remove girder shear studs from its model to create the disconnection of Floor 13 from Column 79 by removing lateral restraint from its models. In other words, NIST doctored its model to achieve maximum differential thermal expansion and maximum lateral motion in order to produce a progressive collapse. Again, no explanation was offered as to the molten steel under WTC 7. Maybe that's what they were hiding.

Nicholas Rockefeller (CFR) wasn't hiding anything from his (then) friend, filmmaker and former politician, Aaron Russo when he was discussing a future event with him eleven months before 9/11. Rockefeller, it can be argued, is informed. In addition to being a Rockefeller, Nicholas is a member of the following round tables and think tanks: the International Institute of Strategic Studies; the Advisory Board of RAND; the Corporate Advisory Board of the Pacific Council on International Relations; the Board of the Western Justice Center Foundation; and the Central China Development Council. He has served as a participant in the World Economic Forum and the Aspen Institute. According to Russo:

> "[Rockefeller said] 'There's gonna be an event, Aaron. And out of that event you're gonna see we are going to go into Afghanistan so we can run the pipelines from the Caspian Sea, we are going to go into Iraq to take the oil and establish a base in the Middle-East, and we are going to go into Venezuela and try to get rid of Chavez.' And the first two they've accomplished, Chavez they didn't accomplish. And he said, 'you're gonna see guys going into caves, looking for people that they're never gonna find.' You know, he's laughing about the fact that you have this war on terror and there's no real enemy. He's talking about how by 'having this war on terror you can never win it 'cause it's an eternal war, so you can always keep taking people's liberties away'. I said, 'How are you gonna convince people that this war is real?' He said, 'By the media. The media can convince everybody it's real. You know, it's just that you keep talking about things, you keep saying it over and over and over again and eventually people believe it.' ... And I would say to him, 'What are you doing this for? What's the point of this thing? You have all the money in the world you'd ever want, you have all the power.' I said, 'You know, you're hurting people, it's not a good thing.' And he would say, 'What do you care about the people for? Take care of yourself, and take care of your family.' And then I said to him, 'What are the ultimate goals here?' He said, 'The ultimate goal is to get everybody in this world chipped with an RFID chip and to have all the money to be on those chips, and everything on those chips. And if anybody wants to protest what we do or violate what we want, we just turn off their chip.'"

Enough said.

Chapter 41 (January 22, 2017)

The first letter appeared to be a copy generated by inserting a sheet of carbon paper between two pieces of paper and then inserting all three into a typewriter's cylindrical platen. The note was addressed to the District Attorney's Office of Orleans Parish, Louisiana. It was dated August 1, 1968. It read,

"Dear District Attorney Garrison,

"My name is David A. Scott. I am an accountant for PepsiCo in Manhattan, New York. I was in Dallas attending a national soda bottling convention in late November 1963. My schedule was light on Friday, November 22nd, so I headed out towards Dealey Plaza in hopes of seeing the president. I had a special connection to him (the nature of which is not germane to my story) and wanted to catch a glimpse of him in person. Because I wasn't familiar with Dallas, I made a wrong turn. I ended up parking my car in a lot on Pacific Avenue and what I now believe to be N. Record Street. I got out of my car and walked to where Pacific dead ends on Houston Street.

"I heard the roar of the crowd on Main Street indicating the approach of the president. Realizing that I wasn't going to make it to Main Street in time to see him, I made my way onto the railroad tracks that ended right where Pacific dead ends with Houston. (In essence, I continued walking on Pacific, which was now railroad tracks.) My actions were a last-ditch attempt to view the president. I never saw him. But when shots rang out – I thought they were firecrackers – I had a good view of the activity behind the Texas School Book Depository and the "grassy knoll". It is this activity which I think maybe pertinent to your investigation.

"Without getting into too many details, I saw two people exit through a loading dock. One was male and looked to be of dark skin. The other was a dark haired, young Latin woman that was holding a device that looked like a radio. I saw another young man run close by carrying a head set. Further towards the triple overpass, by the grassy knoll I saw two well-dressed men and I saw two men who looked to be railway employees. I witnessed one of the well-dressed men throw what looked to be a gun to one of the railway employees. He appeared to break it down into an attaché case, and pass it down to someone who appeared to be below ground. The other railway worker was also walking with a briefcase in the direction of Houston Street. The other three men appeared to linger when people started to converge on the area.

"Unaware as to what had just transpired, and disappointed that I missed the president, I returned to my car and drove to a 2:00pm meeting in Fort Worth, which was canceled when it was announced that the president had been killed. Not knowing that the murder took place in Dealey Plaza and not comprehending that the "firecrackers" I heard were the shots that killed Kennedy, I never filed an affidavit and left town the following day. Because of my special connection to Kennedy, I had other matters to attend to and never gave the Warren Commission findings much thought. Upon further reflection, I believe that my account, because of my unique vantage point, may be of some value.

"If you would like to discuss this matter further, please contact me at the address and phone number provided above.

"Yours Truly,

David A. Scott"

The other sheet of paper was a copy of a handwritten note addressed from Fitz's mother to director Oliver Stone. It was dated July 17, 1990.

"Dear Mr. Stone,

"Through a friend of mine at Yale University, I was informed that you were directing a movie on the JFK assassination. I have information on – actually from -- JFK of which no one is aware and I also possess a copy of a letter that my father (David Scott) sent to New Orleans District Attorney Jim Garrison concerning the assassination. My father died suddenly a few weeks after he sent the note to Garrison, but to the best of my knowledge, no attempt was ever made by Garrison's office to reach my father. His eyewitness account of the assassination, detailed in the letter, provide a whole new perspective on the events at Dealey Plaza. If you are interested in discussing this matter further feel free to contact me at 555-500-8245.

"Yours Truly,

Mary Scott"

Fitz handed the letters to Annie, contemplated their implications given the events of the past year plus, posed for a photo with the Patel's, thanked them for their indulgences, and returned to the limo for the drive to Jersey City. Once in transit, Fitz clarified his thoughts about the notes to Annie. "My grandfather's death was also not an accident. I had read where the CIA had infiltrated Garrison's investigative staff with the hopes of thwarting any revelations that would contradict the accepted dogma. This certainly qualifies as a revelation. I was told by my mother that he died of a stroke – more likely a severe stroke to the head with a blunt object. I had just turned five when he passed and would not have understood the truth anyway. When it became apparent that I was going to win the election and I was pulled in by the globalists who offered me that bribe to get out of the election…"

Annie cut in, "So that was true?"

"Yes, but the disturbing part about it, is that when I left, I said something to the effect of, 'I would never take money from people who were responsible for my father's death.' The next morning there was a note under my door, that said, 'and your mother too.'"

"So these people killed your father, mother, and grandfather?"

"Not directly. The one man in the room was too young to have any prior knowledge of the events surrounding my father's (or likely my uncle's) death. Of the other two, both were probably aware, and one may have been involved in ordering the assassination. I'm sure the FBI or CIA or Mafia killed my grandfather before he could talk to Garrison. As far as my mother is concerned, I remember now that she was heading to the airport to fly to Dallas to be part of a movie. I doubt she meant in the letter to Oliver Stone that she was going to reveal the affair that led to me, but maybe she was going to show Grandpa Scott's letter to Garrison and the last letter from my father to her, the one you decoded twice.'"

"What are you going to do?"

"I don't know if there is anything that I can do. I could reopen the investigation to my father's death with this new revelation, but it's not like we can bring my grandfather back to life. All we have is his letter, which is a lot, but maybe with the release of the other assassination related documents this year – and I will make sure that they are released – I will add this to the bounty. I'm quite sure these men are behind the disappearance of Polly, but I can't do anything until there is a break in the case."

Annie, without a modicum of irony or humor said, "It's been quite an eventful forty-eight hours."

It was about to get more so.

****

Fitz was as very excited to see Annie's mother and Oliver. The visit appeared like an abeyance in the space time continuum, where Fitz was allowed to return to the past and experience life one last time, as it was before his public revelation about the identity of his father – that is of course, except for all the security. Mafia Mike seemed excited to see Annie's mother. Fitz kidded Annie about the budding relationship. Mrs. Van claimed she was only coming down to help Annie get settled, but once under the spell of the Hotel White House, Fitz had the feeling that his future mother-in-law would take up permanent residency. He offered to take Oliver back to the White House, but Annie was having none of it. Oliver's reign as the First Dog would have to wait a couple more days.

Fitz kissed Annie, Oliver, and Mrs. Van good-bye, gave Mafia Mike the keys to his place in SoHo, hopped in the limo, and reemerged in the present. He apologized to the Secret Service for all of the last minute logistical acrobatics required to move a president and said that he would likely not be leaving the White House anytime soon. His phone buzzed. It was Chuck Schilling, who, in addition to his Press Secretary role, was rapidly assuming Chief of Staff responsibilities since Polly went missing. Evan Spring was still getting settled on the grounds of the U.S. Naval Observatory. Fitz felt guilty that Chuck was getting overloaded with the extra burden. That emotion vanished the second he answered the device.

"Chuck. Any news?"

"They just found Polly's body."

"Oh, dear God – are there any details."

"They found her just beyond the boundaries of Fort Bragg. Someone called; claiming to be a representative of an organization called Muslims of the Holy Eternal Rite, and said where we could find her." Chuck's voice started to crack, "She was beheaded. There was a disk and a cell phone that accompanied the body. The Department of Homeland Security took the disc and phone into its possession and is reviewing it as we speak."

"Has anyone contacted Polly's parents? Is the media aware?"

"No and No, but they will hold off the media pending notification of next of kin."

"I have Polly's parents' number. Are you absolutely sure it's her?"

"I didn't see the body, the head, or the video, but the DHS said it was her."

"Okay. I will make that call. I will call you back."

Fitz hung up before Chuck said goodbye. He immediately dialed Polly's parents. Having zero experience in these matters, he acted on instinct and didn't hesitate.

"Hello."

"Mr. Preston, this is Fitz, Fitzgerald Cavendish."

The staidness of Fitz's voice made Paul Preston blurt out, "Oh no. She's dead."

"I'm so sorry Mr. Preston." Fitz heard the uncontrollable sobbing of Paul, joined seconds later by Polly's mother higher pitched wailing. Fitz, so consumed by the utter poignancy of their despair, broke down. Thirty seconds elapsed before anyone could say anything. Fitz, still choked up, was able to force out, "I know who did this. Don't believe anything you hear or see on TV. Justice will not be swift, but it will be severe. There are deeds, crimes that can be forgiven, but this is not among them."

"She loved working for you."

"And I loved working with her. She's the one who put me in the White House. The success of my campaign put her in danger. I should have been more protective of her. I am so sorry." Fitz started breaking up again.

"Do you know how she died?"

Holy Lord. How do I tell these people that their daughter was decapitated by some people dressed up as Muslim extremists? "I don't have all of the details yet. My guess is that we will all know very shortly." Fitz could hear Polly's mother choking up in the background. "This may seem so hollow right now, but is there anything I can do for you two?"

"Justice…justice."

"You have my word."

"Let us go for now. I really appreciate you breaking the news…" Paul Preston's broke down again and hung up the phone.

For thirty seconds after the conversation terminated, overwhelmed with guilt, Fitz desired to crawl out of his skin, out of the car, back into that brief tear in the space time continuum, never to reemerge. His run for the White House was a crusade. He not only wanted to expose the conspiracy, but also terminate it. The conspiracy just fought back – brilliantly. And for a half minute, Fitz wanted to run and hide. Polly's murder was not only his burden; it was now his *casus belli*. He discussed the potential dangers of the assignment to Polly and was serious when he did, but she never shared his concern. Only until he experienced the destruction of Polly and her parent's lives, did it dawn on him that he would have to compartmentalize to deal with the emotional weight of his mission. If he didn't, he might lose the war.

Recomposed, he called Chuck back.

"How did it go?"

"Except finding out my mother died, it was maybe the single worst experience of my life."

"How do you want to respond?"

"As utterly heartless and vicious as it was, it was a message from the cabal that they were still in charge."

"I don't know if I follow."

"Chuck, I'm sorry. I will explain everything when I get back. Can you get Caroline and Evan to meet later this evening? We'll have a dinner meeting at the White House."

"I'm on it. Eight?"

"Fine."

"One last thing: can you arrange a meeting early this week with Chaz Wyckoff -- I think I gave you his contact information -- and with Robert Atkinson, my attorney?"

"Done."

"Thanks."

After Fitz hung up with Chuck, he informed the Secret Service escorts in his car that a trip to San Diego was likely in the cards at the end of the week.

At the White House dinner meeting, Fitz explained to Chuck, Caroline, and Evan that the terrorist organization that allegedly killed Polly was made-up. The name of the organization was simply a message to Fitz. He then went on to explain his meeting at the Council on Foreign Relations and the "and your mother too" note. "Muslims of the Holy Eternal Rite is an anagram for 'Mother.' If the perception is that we have Muslim terrorists on American soil committing heinous acts ala Polly Preston, there will be no appetite to negotiate with terrorists since anti-Muslim sentiment will be off the charts."

Evan quickly grasped everything, "They sent you a message while at the same time crippling your ability to end the war on terrorism."

Fitz replied, "Indeed. If I go out and tell America my tale, and convey that this is all an illusion, I am likely to look like Ben Carson and his Pyramid grain silos, or worse yet, look like I am not in control."

Caroline added, "Fort Bragg houses the U.S. Army John F. Kennedy Special Warfare Center and School – adding to your 'they're sending you a message' theory."

Chuck wasn't completely on board, "Who would they get to commit such an atrocity?"

Fitz replied, "Possibly someone from Mossad or some other foreign intelligence asset that trains at Fort Bragg. You are aware of the fact that the CIA has assassins? They don't ask questions, they just follow orders. As far as I know, they still train them at Fort Bragg. This cabal that we're fighting has assets like this all over the world."

Chuck replied, "It's just hard for me to digest that someone in America could do this to a beautiful young woman."

Fitz returned, "It's hard for you to digest because you have been taught that only Muslim terrorists would do such a thing. Get out of the Matrix."

Caroline asked the question that was point of the gathering, "How do we handle this publically?"

"I'll tell America what I told Polly's parents. I will also add that we will do a thorough investigation. I'll denounce terrorism. Given that the State Department is presently infested with CFR members, we don't try to use any back channels to communicate with any of these terrorist organizations – that will be leaked to the press and only weaken our hand.

I will proclaim that this act, if it was actually committed by terrorists, only strengthens my belief that they should have their own caliphate, so that they can leave this country."

Vice-President Spring critiqued, "You may want to lay off any rhetoric that hints of sympathy for terrorists for a little while."

Fitz complied, "I understand. They have painted me...us into a corner early on. I will hold a news conference on this matter tomorrow noontime. I will have prepared remarks and then take questions only on the Preston matter. Chuck, I need to meet with senior officials at the IRS, the Department of Treasury – tell them to bring the head of the Bureau of Engraving and Printing, CEO's of the top payment processing companies, and the Social Security Administration."

Chuck queried, "What time?"

"All separate meetings. At some point, we may all get together." It was time to implement his plan.

Chapter 42 (Terrorism by Drone)

"We didn't really know who we were firing at." Since 2001, the United States has been meting out justice this way. You would expect that quote to come from an ISIS terrorist (if one had survived) after he walked into the Bataclan concert hall in Paris and randomly snuffed out young, innocent lives. However, that quote is from former US drone sensor operator Brandon Bryant, who claims to be responsible for the deaths of 1,626 people. In a country that occasionally and unfortunately sends innocent people to prison after a court trial and decision rendered by a jury of his or her peers, its central intelligence service decides the fate of people in Afghanistan, Iraq, Pakistan, Yemen, Somalia, and other God forsaken places from an airbase in Nevada (amongst other locations), based on unconfirmed intelligence that a paid local informant looking to feed his family has passed along. To that part of the world, drones represent American terrorism. Yes, you are the ones sponsoring terrorism with your tax dollars, according to the Islamic world.

There are two types of drone strikes: personality strikes that target known terrorist leaders and signature strikes that target groups of men "believed" to be militants. The threshold for evidence purporting that a group of men are "militant" is absolutely zero. Their identities are not even known. They could be walking together to play soccer or in a wedding procession. Regarding the decision making process, Bryant said, "There was no oversight...or accountability." Six out of every seven drone strikes are signature strikes. In Pakistan alone, contingent upon the source of the estimate, between four hundred and eight hundred civilians have been killed in American drone strikes. But you are so indoctrinated by the elite-owned media that you believe that that these strikes are making you, America, and the world safer. If such acts were conducted in the United States, they would be illegal. If they were conducted by a foreign power, would you not want retribution against that foreign power for killing your mother, daughter, grandmother, brother, father, aunt, uncle, etc.? Would an undying hatred not be incubated in you for the perpetrators of this act? Would you, at the very least, want the daily menace to end? But what if you live in abject squalor and don't have the means to fire a missile from your aircraft carrier? You are going to form groups to get your revenge, eventually manifesting your anger and frustration in acts like Bataclan.

The more drone strikes, the more likely you will be drawn to these groups like a moth to a flame. This is NOT a defense of terrorism. This is an argument that drones make the situation worse, not better; putting you in more danger, not less. This is NOT an anti-American rant. This is the other perspective: anti-American. Paris is all by design, and your designers are laughing all the way to the bank.

The way you solve terrorism is by making the terrorists not want to kill you, not by indiscriminately killing people in their homeland; not by installing puppet governments in place of freely elected ones; not by raping its citizens of their natural resources; not by invading their countries under false pretenses like weapons of mass destruction. It's been so long since America invaded Iraq that you probably forgot that Iraq didn't have any terrorists. Now they do.

Here is the quick 411 on Syria. It has a government-owned central bank, not a privately held one. It has no IMF debt and it does not allow GMOs. It is blocking a natural gas pipeline from Qatar to Western Europe that would allow the Saudis and the Qataris to access the very lucrative European natural gas market. Instead, Syria has agreed to a pipeline that would instead give Iran and Iraq access to the European natural gas market, which would likely sell that gas for currency other than the dollar. The United States business interests are aligned with the Saudis and the Qataris. Russia's interests are aligned with its ally, Bashar al-Assad, current President of Syria. The conflict is not a civil war in which both sides are committing atrocities, but a geopolitical money grab between opposing sides of the pipeline power play. It is a proxy war in which the United States funnels money and weapons to the Free Syrian Army (FSA) and Turkey. For what it is worth, Russia claims that the FSA doesn't even exist. They, in turn, take the military and financial bounty received from America and truck it to ISIS to fight al-Assad. In other words, the United States supports ISIS in Syria. That's not all. The United States, France, Great Britain, and the UAE trained fighters who would become ISIS in Jordan. However, when a journalist uncovers this inconvenient truth, she is accused of being a spy and is murdered (or "accidented" by a cement truck going the wrong way down a three lane highway in Turkey). Such is the case of American born Serena Shim, who worked for Iranian based Press TV.

Do you remember when Muammar al-Gaddafi, former leader of Libya, then head of the African Union, proposed that the continent adopt a new currency, the Gold Dinar, and accept exclusively that medium of exchange for the payment of oil, instead of dollars? You probably don't. It occurred in 2009. The CIA and banking elite acted decisively in removing him and others from power in the so called Arab Spring uprisings that swept away leaders from Libya, Egypt, Tunisia, and Yemen. Funny how one of the first items of business for the rebels (a.k.a. National Transitional Council of Libya) was scrapping the state-owned monetary authority in favor of a central bank tied into the BIS while they were still trying to establish control amidst the chaos. This dynamic is likely to play out in Syria as well if Assad is removed from power.

Do you remember the 100 Orders enacted by L. Paul Bremer, III, former head of the now defunct Coalition Provisional Authority in Iraq? You probably don't because they weren't given much attention by the media. And even if you had heard about them, you probably thought that the Orders ended with the transfer of power to the new Prime Minister, Ayad Allawi on June 1, 2004. That would be an incorrect assumption. The orders just transferred under Allawi's control. Allawi, for his part, had strong ties to British and American intelligence organizations and was a thirty-year exile of Iraq. Each Ministry in the new government was staffed with U.S. appointed officials staked to five-year terms, ensuring the implementation of the Orders. Order 39 allows U.S. corporations operating in Iraq to own every business, perform all of the work, and send the profits home tax-free. Nothing needs to be reinvested locally to service the Iraqi economy and no Iraqi need be hired. Order 40 turns the state run central bank into a privately held entity tied into the Bank of International Settlements. Order 81 forbids Iraqi farmers from storing their own seeds, developed over hundreds of years. Instead, they must buy GMO seeds which have to be bought annually from Frankenseed corporations like Monsanto. These seeds have terminator genes which ensure that the seeds can only be used for one season. If a crop fails, they can't reach into their store for next year's planting, but instead go into debt to buy more Monsanto seed. And of course, oil transactions would be conducted in U.S. dollars. Orders like these would likely go into effect if Assad is removed from power. Are you beginning to understand why the Islamic world hates America? It's not about some holy religious war garbledy gook cooked up by the mainstream media or some interpretation of a line in the Quran. It is about money and control.

The atrocities in Paris are by design, or at least the inevitable by-product of the never ending war on terrorism: more terrorism. The elite running the planet know this. The debt-based banking cabal wants terrorism to provoke a visceral response from the American public which will call for greater involvement in Syria. The irony is that the United States is arming ISIS in Syria, but the media in the United States will make you believe anything. The actual desired outcomes of the conflict in Syria are as follows:

1- To implement a Syrian central bank tied into the BIS.

2- To turn Syria into a corporate socialistic playground for energy and food interests.

3- To line the pockets of the military industrial complex through proxy wars.

4- To instigate more terrorism through the United States' involvement in places where it is not wanted.

5- To foment fear in the United States through the threat of terrorism. This allows the elite to remove your Constitutional rights in the name of security with your cowardly blessing.

6- To incite Donald Trump-led hatred of Islam, 1.8 billion strong, allowing any xenophobic action in the name of security, even though less than one one-hundredth of one percent of them possesses any militant hatred of the United States. That number was orders of magnitude lower before the Gulf War.

7- To tear the United States apart on the gun control issue.

Bryant, reflecting on his time killing militants and innocents nearly 9,000 miles away from his office in Nevada described the controlling apparatus as a "black hole putrid system that is either going to crush you or you're going to conform to it". So when you send out your love and support to those who needlessly died in Paris, remember your government's (or the CIA shadow government's) actions provoked it, and your tax dollars financed it.

Chapter 43 (January – February 2017)

The Monday press conference was even more brutal than Fitz had imagined. It was as if they had turned completely against all of his policies that had carried him into the White House. It was somehow as if Polly's kidnapping was a failure on his part – it was, but not in the way that the media portrayed it. He tried to remind the assembled throng that he was not yet the President of the United States when Polly was abducted, but they were having none of it. "How could you defend a policy of negotiating with terrorists?" "Why would you give these sub-humans a country of their own?" "Are you reconsidering your stance on terrorists?" "Is your present policy not foolhardy?" Fitz was left with no alternative except to endure it; answer every question and outlast the press corps, no matter how stupid or ignorant the question posed. Appear strong and saddened – which wasn't too difficult since that is how he felt – and move on. Don't tell them who the real killers are, because if he did, no one would believe him anyway. No need to have his credibility chipped away any more than necessary.

****

Fitz's Tuesday meeting with Lt. Gen. Chaz Wyckoff proved very informative and productive. Wyckoff was the mole inside the secret societies such as the Bilderberg Group, and slightly less secret organizations such as the Club of Rome, the Trilateral Commission – which was responsible for Jimmy Carter's rapid accent to the presidency -- the Council on Foreign Relations, and Bohemian Grove. He was a frequent attendee at these meetings, and with his overt role as CIA liaison, Chaz was likely the most informed decent man on the planet regarding the actions of the globalists. The good news (as far as Fitz was concerned) was that the internationalists still thought Wyckoff was one of them. When he heard Cavendish speak at the first presidential debate, he finally found someone who wasn't bought and sold by the elite and who shared his 'America First' view. After listening to Fitz converse with Alex Jones, Wyckoff reached out to the radio host, whom he periodically slipped information to (as an unnamed source) regarding the one-world agenda. As a result, his brief introduction to Fitz at the Inaugural Parade stand was not completely unexpected.

Fitz shared with Chaz the actual circumstances behind Polly Preston's death. Chaz shared the globalists' goal to sterilize the African continent through vaccines and GMOs. Fitz shared his plan to control population growth and Chaz agreed that it was a lot less Machiavellian.

He also discussed the aerosolizing of the atmosphere over the Pacific with chemtrails, resulting in above average moisture in the eastern part of the United States, yet drought conditions west of the Mississippi River. Wyckoff said that geo-engineering was responsible for ice nucleation which caused 100,000 cattle to die during a freak early October 2013 storm in South Dakota during which massive snow fell when temperatures were in the mid-forties. When Fitz inquired as to how cattle could die in mid-forty degree temperatures, Wyckoff explained that ice nucleation is an endothermic (heat absorbing) reaction caused by a mixture of sprayed chemicals (such as barium hydroxide and ammonium), which can cause temperatures to plummet when introduced into the atmosphere. Even though the temperature is forty-five degrees, the temperature of the snow covered cattle's hide might be twenty below zero, resulting in massive deaths. This NASA-patented ice nucleation was the cause of the seventy-five pound ice balls washing up on the shores of Lake Michigan. Wyckoff emphasized that all of the United States weather was now geo-engineered and was largely responsible for birds falling out of the sky. He went on to explain that 5.2 million years ago, carbon levels were 25% higher than today, yet the planet thrived because it could adjust – it just rained more. Now it can't respond because of all the geo-engineering. He also stated that the Fukushima reactors were still dumping nuclear water into the Pacific, yet it continued to be the most underreported story on the planet.

Wyckoff then demonstrated the latest in predator drone technology through his tablet. The planes were getting exponentially bigger and faster, with greater range and carrying capacity – one could now be outfitted with the equivalent of a daisy cutter. They could also be pre-programmed to a destination and controlled by devices as simple as a tablet. They were almost idiot proof. When the demonstration ended, Fitz discussed a couple of ideas requiring Chaz's engineering expertise. Chaz agreed to assist.

After that meeting concluded, Fitz sat with Robert Atkinson Esq., who had made the journey from New Jersey, to discuss his impending nuptials, the revisions to his will, and the acquisition of additional insurance.

The rest of his week was filled with meetings that Chuck Schilling had arranged with various departments of the government and companies such as GS1. These would be the first round of many before the State of the Union.

At the end of his first week in office, Fitz and Annie flew off to the memorial service for Polly Preston in San Diego. They met with Mr. and Mrs. Paul Preston privately and did not attend the actual service, not wishing to be an enormous distraction to an already circus-like atmosphere. If Fitzgerald Cavendish was the Kim Kardashian of 2016, Polly Preston was a solid contender for runner-up. As a result, her service was not only attended by friends and families, but also by the mainstream media, the Hollywood press, the paparazzi, Muslim haters, and perfect strangers that grew attached to her through the media and had nothing better to do. 6th Avenue outside St. Paul's Episcopal Cathedral was a mob scene, only adding to Mr. and Mrs. Preston's suffering. After Fitz saw news reports about the chaos, he surmised that it would have been better if he had stayed and attended -- at least the Secret Service could have cordoned off the area and kept the voyeurs away.

****

And there it was, when he awoke, the date on the calendar – February 16, 2017 -- staring Fitz in the face. The State of the Union address was going to be the potential *coup de grâce*. With the media conditioned to having the speech leaked in advance – it wasn't this time -- Fitz knew the reaction would be visceral, not only from the floor of Congress, but from every 'pundit' who would analyze his message. Fitz was more concerned with the reaction from the populace. He was worried that the men who controlled the planet had eroded his popularity down to the level of a Democrat or a Republican, but in the end, there was nothing else to do but go for it. After all, this was the agenda on which they had voted him into office. But, as Polly had told him the evening he was elected, over one-quarter of the people who elected Fitz did so because he was either good looking or 'presidential' looking, not because he had exposed the two hundred fifty year old fraud to the masses. In other words, his popularity was potentially fleeting. The most confrontational State of the Union address in the history of the United States was about to begin. Fitz girded himself -- he was usurping the Constitution while at the same time restoring it. With Annie watching from the White House with Oliver and Mrs. Van, Fitzgerald Cavendish assumed the podium.

"Members of the U.S. Congress, esteemed guests in attendance, and fellow Americans watching from your homes, I thank you for your indulgence. I have postponed the State of the Union because it was my hope to actually have something accomplished before I stood in front of America. I find it silly to stand in front of America, as your newly elected president, and present a critique littered with hope. In my inauguration speech I outlined seven items that needed to be addressed. What follows is an attempt to address all of these issues directly or indirectly. I have come here with a message of change, a message of real change; not the garbage that has been presented has hope to the populace since my father was assassinated. What I have started in motion is truly transformative.

"First off, as your president, by definition, my job is to enforce laws, treaties, and court rulings; develop federal policies; prepare the national budget; and appoint federal officials. I also approve or veto acts of Congress and grant pardons. But also, as an extension, I cannot enforce laws that are technically or obviously unconstitutional. To that end, I have issued a series of executive orders to keep the government functioning while I don't enforce those laws that are unconstitutional. With regards to the sixteenth amendment to the Constitution, not enough states properly ratified it in a way congruent with the tenants of the Constitution, and as a result, I cannot, in good faith, enforce this law. As a result, anyone who has paid income tax in 2017 will be refunded his money. Since I was not your chief law enforcer in 2016, you will be bound to make amends for that tax year. 2017 is a completely different story. Anyone with a previous outstanding tax issue will be bound by the law prior to January 1, 2017. If you have already paid taxes in 2017, which most working Americans have, you will receive a refund not only for your income taxes, but also for any Medicare and Social Security taxes paid in 2017. In other words, if you earn $75,000 this year, you will take home $75,000 this year, except for state income taxes and other state or city level programs. For the avoidance of doubt, the capital gains tax is no longer. [A stunned clamor enveloped the floor of Congress.]

"In place of the income tax, to keep the government functioning, I have issued Executive Order 13750, which creates a federal sales tax. I have worked with many companies over the past three weeks to make sure that a federal sales tax of 30% will be instated by April 1st of this year. If the product that you purchase is destructive in some way shape or form, be it to your health or to the environment, it will be taxed at 150%. If it is something that enhances life on this planet, it will be taxed at 5% or 0%. For example, in the area of food, if it is organic, or is proven to be beneficial to life, it will be taxed at 5%. If it is all-natural, or yet determined to be a detriment or benefit to mankind, it will be taxed at 30%. If it contains non-approved, artificial, or poisonous ingredients that cause degenerative disease, it will be taxed at 150%. To better define it, and I don't mean to single them out, Dairy Queen will be taxed at 150%. Because the 150% tax is quite harsh and some industries will not have sufficient time to get compliant with a 30% tax rate, all goods, except for example, organic goods, will be taxed at 30% starting April 1st. If your goods are destructive to the planet or human condition, they will be taxed at 40% starting May 1st; starting June 1st, they will be taxed at 50%, and so on until they reach 150% at this time next year. With regards to gasoline, the federal tax rate will increase from 18.4 cents per gallon to 25.0 cents per gallon and from 24.4 cents per gallon to 30.0 cents per gallon for diesel. If you are a retailer, you will be forced to file a federal application and pay monthly federal taxes, much in the same way a refiner or producer of alcohol does already. As far as the service industry is concerned, you will also have to charge and pay the 30% federal tax for your services. For those on a fixed income with programs like Social Security, or receiving government subsidies, you will receive a 10% jump in your benefits to offset all of the bogus cost of living adjustments you've received in the last decade. This will keep the sales tax from becoming too regressive, unless of course you are purchasing items that bear a 150% tax. As you will see shortly, there is another phase to this program that will make the tax non-regressive. Social Security will eventually be phased out as no one will be paying into it anymore. This phase out is very long term in nature and anyone who has paid into these programs will be entitled to their fair share of the proceeds. A list will be available later this evening detailing what goods and services are subject to the national sales tax and at what rate.

"This is a lot for my fellow citizens to digest. And don't get me wrong, it is a massive change. As part of this change and in return for your indulgence, I have signed Executive Order 13751 authorizing the U.S. Treasury to send out checks in the amount of $10,000 to every man and woman eighteen years and older immediately. The cutoff date for those checks is December 31, 2015. In other words, if you turned eighteen in 2016, you will have to wait another year for your check. Those checks, over 200 million in total, are being processed in large batches, with the first batch being mailed as we speak. You will need to have a Social Security number to receive a check. There is one catch: if you attempt to cash your check (as opposed to depositing it) you will receive money that looks exactly like your current money, [Fitz pulls out a freshly minted $100 US Government Money bill and shows it to a stunned Congress.] except where it says "Federal Reserve Note", it will now say "US Government Money". These bills will be accepted as legal tender for all debts public and private. This money has been in print at the U.S. Treasury for the last two weeks and will be sent out to all banks and credit unions to make sure that there are no disruptions in the system. This was accomplished through Executive Order 13749. This is not a one-time event. A check will go out each year on or around January 1st to defeat the regressive nature of the sales tax. When the good citizens of this nation receive these checks, the banking system will be flooded with money, which is technically inflationary. As a result, I have issued Executive Order 13752 authorizing that the fractional reserve requirement be increased at all banks from 10.3% to 15%. This will have the effect of taking money out of the economy, thus counterbalancing the increased money in circulation as a result of all of the $10,000 checks being issued. This is not a perfect science, and as a result, banks will have a ninety day window to borrow U.S. Government Money from the Treasury at initially low rates to stay compliant with the 15% fractional reserve requirement. As more debt is retired, the fractional reserve rate will continually be ratcheted up, and different ninety day windows for compliance will apply.

"For those of you that say the Federal Reserve is the arbiter of the fractional reserve requirement, and not your newly-elected President, I submit to you that the Federal Reserve Act of 1913 and the National Banking Act of 1863 so amended in 1864 are unconstitutional, in violation of Article I, Section 8, Clause 5 of the Constitution. Without boring the TV audience to tears, "the Congress shall have Power to...coin Money, regulate the Value thereof..." not the Federal Reserve. Hamilton argued that the necessary and proper clause gave Congress implied powers -- the power to enact any law that is necessary to execute its specific powers. However, that would imply the creation of an entity which is beholden to Congress. The Federal Reserve is a private bank, with shareholders. It is not answerable to Congress. The only way that Congress carries any clout over the Fed is with the threat of the act's repeal. Any bank that defies Executive Order 13572 will be shut down. Depositors will have one week to withdraw their deposits from those banks after non-compliance is revealed. The U.S. Treasury will then assume any outstanding loans.

"As the federal debt comes due -- for example, $50 billion three year notes – it will be paid off with U.S. Government Money plus interest due. It will not be rolled over. For those that say that the checks going out to the citizens, not the illegal aliens of the United States, will violate the debt ceiling, I submit that the money being issued is *debt-free*, and is not going to affect the debt. In fact it will be the vehicle by which all debt will be retired. To repeat, U.S. Government Money is *debt-free*, not debt-based, like Federal Reserve Notes, and as a result, is not in violation of the debt ceiling and therefore is lawful, just like Lincoln's Greenbacks

385

during the Civil War. It is not loaned into existence and therefore does not have to be paid back. I know this is confounding to many of you watching and listening, but it should not be to the banking system. If the major banks wish to challenge me on this issue, it will be at their peril. The retirement of the debt with U.S. Government Money will make the issuance of new debt unnecessary; therefore the Treasury calendar of new offerings is hereby suspended.

"For the avoidance of doubt, we are decoupling from the Bank of International Settlements. Former President Bush – W – made a famous Axis of Evil speech regarding North Korea, Iran, and Iraq. Do you know why he gave them that title? Not because they were housing terrorists or 'hated our freedoms' – no, it was that these three countries didn't have a central bank tied into the Bank of International Settlements. In 2000, there were seven countries without a central bank – or at least one tied into the BIS. Now there are only three: Iran, Cuba, and North Korea. To be sure, America will have a central bank with the reestablishment of an independent United States Treasury where the Government will keep its own money under lock and key in the building that its citizens provided for that purpose.

"For those that proclaim our currency will collapse, you might be correct for a few weeks, until the rest of the world understands what we are doing, at which point the U.S. dollar will be as strong as it has ever been. As an aside, the strength of the dollar versus other currencies is irrelevant, unless of course, you speculate in currencies or are planning on traveling abroad in the near future. If you own a multinational business and are worried about wild gyrations in the value of the dollar, I suggest you hedge yourself in the currency markets.

"For the time being, corporations will pay no taxes. Once we have a couple of months of tax proceeds to see how the sales tax program is performing, we will use a 10% income tax on business income above $1 million, if necessary. Your government will continue to tweak the yearly 'refund', currently at $10,000, and the sales tax rates to create a fairer redistribution of wealth and a better tool for policy implementation. I will also submit to Congress legislation imposing massive fines on any corporations that pollute the environment or harm the human condition, many multiples greater than any current fine.

"Your checks are in the mail so you should receive them no later than March 1st. Anyone who believes that he or she should have received a check and has not should contact the IRS. Once these checks have been processed, the IRS will be refunding any income tax money paid in 2017. That operation should commence in approximately two weeks. An announcement will be made when those checks are in the mail. When you pull up the website, the contact information will be displayed. If you do not own a computer, just contact the IRS by phone and you will be directed to the proper department for processing. The sales tax will not be enforced until April 1, 2017. That will give not only citizens, but also businesses time to get adjusted and compliant to the new revenue laws of the land.

"The reason that I have been forced to take such drastic measures is that the congressmen and women sitting before me, whom you have elected, but are bought and sold by the central bankers and one-world government organizations, have told me in meetings that they have no intention of approving any of my Cabinet appointments or any of the policies on which you elected me into office. Your Congress is bought by special interests and as a result is inimical to you. I strongly suggest you vote these people, [Fitz gestures with his arm] whom I stand in front of this evening, out of office. [Congress begins to boo.]

"Based on what I have just laid out to you here, I will be introducing legislation to repeal the National Banking Acts of 1863 and 1864 along with the Federal Reserve Act of 1913. The back office functions, like clearing checks, will continue to exist, and the whole process should be seamless to the depositor or creditor of any bank. I will also be introducing legislation that submits the 16th Amendment to the Constitution is not legal since it was never properly enacted, and therefore, should be repealed.

"In addition to these important measures, I ran on a platform of choice. To that end, I will be introducing legislation that will make the following legal, and depending on the vice, taxable: prostitution, all drugs, gambling, and all non-approved treatments for degenerative diseases. For example, laetrile will be available to anyone who wishes to use it. If it is demonstrated to be a poison -- which it isn't -- it will either be taxed at 150% or pulled from the marketplace. For those of you that are worried you're your children will be subjected to formally illegal drugs, I submit that you teach your children well. Just because heroin is legal, I am not going out tomorrow to purchase it. I will introduce legislation making vaccines a state-mandated issue. I am strongly against forced vaccination. If you are extremely pro-vaccination, get vaccinated and you will have nothing to worry about.

"I have issued Executive Order 13753 that repeals the unconstitutional provisions of the Patriot Act and greatly restrict the powers of the Department of Homeland Security. As I have said in the past, those who are willing to give up freedom for security, are worthy of neither. Please don't view this as a weak stance on my part. We must have very strong defenses: against potential nuclear threats, against cyber-attacks, against biological and terroristic threats. But we can be much stronger by keeping our nose out of other countries' business and bringing our resources home to defend the homeland, not force our will on people abroad. To that end, our soldiers will be returning home from conflict abroad, be it in Iraq, Syria, Afghanistan, or any other place that we have no right to be. Along these same lines, Andrew Snowden will be welcomed home with open arms and will be pardoned if indicted on any matter relating to the NSA.

"I don't have a problem with our National Security apparatus trying to keep us safe by monitoring calls in bulk in order to find tendencies that could indicate a threat within our borders. If there is a potential threat based on the call monitoring, then the national security apparatus can apply for a search warrant – which has been the standard operating procedure. I do have a massive problem with that monitoring being conducted by companies that are not based in the United States. That procedure,

388

under the bill that I will be introducing to Congress, will end. If I find that reliance on foreign companies has compromised our security, those responsible will be brought to justice.

"On the international front, I will be introducing a bill to Congress providing scholarships ROTC-style for people who wish to spend the first three years out of college abroad, helping others, like the Peace Corps. Almost fifty-six years ago, my father signed Executive Order 10924 that officially started the Peace Corps. The bill will look to link these scholarships with the Peace Corps. [Finally, the first smattering of applause]

"I will stop right there. Once we have our domestic house in order, I will focus more heavily on our foreign relations. However, by ending our days as the bully on the block, I think we will be viewed in a much more favorable light abroad. Also, there will be some legislation that I will be proposing that will encroach on your pursuit of happiness at some point in the near future, but that is for another time. Because of the radical changes being implemented, disruptions will occur; checks will get lost; and certain items will not be scanned at the proper sales tax rate. I have redeployed government resources in an attempt to make the transition as smooth as possible and certain agencies such as the IRS will be hiring more people immediately. You can apply on line with the IRS. I will apologize in advance for any inconvenience suffered as a result of this unprecedented exercise. But please remember, these changes are why you elected me into office.

"Goodnight and be well."

A collective "holy shit, that didn't just happen" enveloped the country. The political pundits asked if Cavendish was mad. They claimed his executive orders were in violation of the Constitution – for all his bloviating about the sacred document. They yawped that he was president, not king. Some declared that the 16th Amendment was not unconstitutional and that Fitz's claims to the contrary were technical and purely rubbish – they were correct. Some argued about the constitutionality of the Federal Reserve Act, while others made idiotic observations that this was no way to endear himself to Congress. Some said that the debt would be soaring to over $22 trillion – they were wrong. Some said that he might be impeached before any of his Cabinet appointees were approved. "Don't get too comfortable in the Oval Office," one angry commentator vociferated. "We are pulling out of Syria?" asked one. "Prostitution legal?" queried another. "How is he getting rid of Social Security?" asked still another. Mostly however, a state of utter shock had seized the media and the country. It was as if the election was a guilty pleasure, a protest. It was a dare to take a jump off a very high bridge that most guessed Fitz would never do – or if he did, an uncooperative Congress would act as a bungee cord. And here he was, diving head first into the unknown, taking the American population with him. You could hear a giant, "no he didn't" echo throughout the land.

Most Americans were just excited about the prospect of not paying income tax and receiving a check in the amount of $10,000. Diane Van's reaction summed it up best, "Ooooh, I'm getting a check for ten thousand dollars?" Annie tried to put a lid on her excitement, "Yes, but everything you buy is going to be 30% more expensive."

CNBC gurus were busy speculating Friday morning. Some forecasted that a portion of the $2.3 trillion in checks being sent out would find its way into the marketplace, which would obviously benefit the market; others, said that the inflation of the currency, and the creation of a new one would greatly tarnish the credibility of the U.S. markets in the eyes of the world. Some predicted a monumental buying spree in March that would benefit retailers, since this would be the time of no sales tax; others wondered how the government would function and tabulated what the abolition of income tax would mean for the deficit and debt. Not one was singing the overhaul's praises. The financial markets initially reacted with cautious pessimism. An orderly early morning sell off in the fixed income and stock markets degenerated into a mad panic by day's end, with the Dow Jones Industrial Average registering its single biggest daily point loss ever: 1,764 points, making it the second biggest percentage drop in the history of the Dow Jones. Fixed income markets, normally a recipient of safe haven buying during stock market panics, fared no better. Investors wanted out of everything American. The dollar sold off by nearly ten percent against the Euro and Yen. The post mortem on CNBC featured catch-all phrases such as "protest sell-off" and "a vote of no confidence" for Cavendish.

****

Reverend Trace Vonada wasn't sure it was a hoax, but with the arrival of a limousine carrying the Presidential Seal, his incredulousness gave way to genuine excitement and nervousness. Mafia Mike, outfitted in a tuxedo, got out of the car to approach the residence – a rather opulent house in Alexandria, Virginia – but Justice of the Peace Vonada was already moving his large frame rather eagerly in the direction of the limousine. His long, flowing cassock appeared as a muumuu to Mike, forcing an uncomfortably large smile on his face when he introduced himself to the reverend with a handshake. Vonada still wasn't convinced that he wouldn't end up on the receiving end of a practical joke. It was an odd time to conduct a ceremony – 10:00pm, Saturday evening – but Vonada figured his going rate would triple if this turned out not to be a sophomoric prank courtesy of his college buddies who couldn't believe that this was his new "hobby". His wife made a very good living and with his kids off at college, Vonada figured he could earn some spending money 'officiating' some future divorces. The item of note his friends found most humorous on his webpage was that he had been "trained to respect all backgrounds and beliefs". Now here he was, off to marry the President of the United States.

The next morning, Fitz and Annie sent out an Instagram picture of their extremely private ceremony, witnessed only by Mrs. Van, Mafia Mike, Oliver, and two Secret Service agents in the White House Blue Room. The picture was a headshot of the smiling bride and groom with Oliver in between, brandishing a black bow tie. Vonada managed a couple of shots with the bride and groom, whose offer to play golf at Camp David was quickly accepted.

When Fitz awoke at 5:30am with Annie and Oliver, he fed Oliver and took him for his morning constitutional on the North Lawn of the White House. On his way out he noticed that the missing Inauguration invitation was framed, waiting to be hung on their bedroom wall – it was simply put in the wrong mailbox. Annie would be asleep for many more hours. He loved his morning walk with the First Dog as it gave him the opportunity to clear his head, which was still tired from the nuptials and consummation of the night before. Observing his Jack Russell smelling and peeing on everything in sight gave Fitz an idea. He got back into bed. It was Sunday and his 'honeymoon' after all.

****

The Blonde Jew, Wheelchair Man, and the Old German met at the Council on Foreign Relations headquarters Saturday afternoon. Their post-State of the Union address cynicism was replaced with hope when the markets retreated in spectacular fashion. Even though Fitz had set in motion a mechanism that would eliminate their instrument of financial domination, the markets' inability to digest or comprehend the ultimate result of Fitz's executive orders buoyed the men with the possibility that Fitz would be run out of office, or at the very least, be forced to reverse course if the markets didn't rally. However, Wheelchair Man was the least sanguine about the prospects of a policy U-turn, "The markets are eventually going to figure out what he is doing. Even if they don't, the laws of supply and demand dictate that a rally in the fixed income market is in the offing."

Old German: "Even with all of the buying done by the central banks to keep rates artificially low?'

The Old German was referring to the massive purchasing by the Federal Reserve (and other central banks) of U.S. Treasury securities. This had the effect of propping up the market, allowing the U.S. Government to conduct its financing at artificially low rates. The average rate has been in the low to mid two percent range despite the fact that total debt of the United States government was over 100 percent of GDP. Compare this with a mid-six percent interest rate average on the debt over the 1990s when debt to GDP ran slightly less than 60%. For the avoidance of doubt, there are many factors affecting supply and demand for Treasury securities, but without the Fed's buying spree, it can be reasoned that financing the debt would be much more expensive. If the Fed walked away, rates could soar, which means that interest on the debt could grow from $400 billion to $1 trillion, if rates reached 5% on the intermediate and long ends of the yield curve for a protracted period of time. That could eat up a great deal of the $3 trillion plus in receipts that the government brings in. It also gives the Fed the power to control the government, using the tacit threat of non-participation in the auctions or selling to raise rates as a silent trapdoor at the gallows. Where did the Fed get all of its money? It created it out of thin air. Fitz's executive orders essentially neutered the Fed's control over the government.

Blonde Jew: "I have reached out to Caruana, Noyer, Draghi, and Merkel. They will be making statements calling his actions irresponsible. I have others who are going to call the White House to apply pressure. I have also spoken to the board, and every major publication in the country will be denouncing his moves."

Old German: "The media is practically calling for this guy's head now, between his financial policies," he hesitated and looked knowingly at the Blonde Jew, "and his stance on terrorism. He is beginning to appear as a loon on the worldwide stage. I'm curious as to his next job approval rating."

Wheelchair Man: "When the 200 million plus receive their checks, it is likely to go higher. I'm afraid that we have a real problem: the media and the world leaders can call him whatever they like, but he has convinced many in the United States that they are the problem, so their criticism is likely to fall on deaf ears, unless of course, the markets continue to crater."

Blond Jew: "Can we get him impeached?"

Wheelchair Man: "I have made a few calls, but it will take at least a month before Congress is organized enough to act, and as far as the courts are concerned, it will be many months before the executive orders are reviewed."

Old German: "Can the central banks intervene?"

Wheelchair Man: "I'm not sure what a coordinated intervention on the part of the central banks will accomplish – we will crater the U.S. markets by short selling the hell out of it if it tries to rebound on Monday, but we also run the risk of losing trillions. I thought about the international community not accepting the new currency as payment, but since everything is just a stroke of the keyboard anyway, I don't see international

393

commerce grinding to a halt just to make a statement. We control a lot, but we don't control everything."

Old German: "Is he planning on traveling any time soon?"

Blond Jew: "Nothing on his itinerary."

Wheelchair Man: "Nothing to do, but wait and see."

****

The salesmen on the Credit Suisse fixed income desk got to work early Monday morning. Managing Director John Brett was having a discussion with one of his clients who said that he had already received the funds for his 4-week Treasury bills that were coming due that day in his short term bond account – an account that he ran as part of a larger portfolio for Homefield Capital. It just felt strange that he couldn't roll it over (i.e. he couldn't use those proceeds from the 4-week bill that had just matured to purchase an equal amount of 4-week bills in the next auction), since the auction for that day was cancelled, as was the entire U.S. Treasury security calendar. John's client joked that his statement still showed a '$' next to the amount. It all felt the same, except that the money could not be used to purchase any Treasury securities in auction. Intrigued, Brett started calling traders on his desk, calculating roughly how much of the debt was being retired in the next three months. He calculated that all of the $160 billion in 4-week securities would be retired by month's end; all $325 billion of the 3-month bills would be retired; $300 billion of approximately $600 billion of 6-months bills would be retired; $75 billion of 1-year bills; $78 billion of 2-year notes; $89 billion of 3-year notes; $105 billion of 5-year notes; $95 billion of 7-year notes; $21 billion of 10-year notes. His long bond (30-year) trader was in a meeting, so he didn't have that information. He arrived at $1.248 trillion. Cavendish was essentially paying out one and a quarter trillion dollars plus interest in new U.S. government money to retire the debt coming due over the next three months. For the first time in a long time, the U.S. debt clock would move in reverse. Brett quickly surmised that it would be one and a quarter trillion dollars with no place to go, except into other securities, investments, or a bank account – likely increasing the value of all three. Add to it the $2 trillion plus that Americans were receiving in the form of

$10,000 checks and M3 (i.e. a broad definition of the money supply) was going to grow by 15% in three months. No wonder why he had to change the fractional reserve requirements – that was the only way to keep the level of M3 (and by extension, inflation) relatively constant. Brett, starting to completely grasp what the new president was implementing, begrudgingly told his client that it was a masterful stroke. With that, Brett walked into the Fixed Income Division Manager's office, and informed him that he was taking the early retirement package.

At long last, nearly five months after Fitz announced his strategy at the debate to eliminate the debt, someone at CNBC commented that his plan amounted to the end of the U.S. Treasury securities market. Fitz had said as much previously, but it was finally starting to take hold: with one and a quarter trillion dollars less of U.S. Treasury securities in the marketplace over the next three months, the remaining seventeen plus trillion in debt instruments would become even dearer to investors, especially since the amount outstanding would continue to decrease. With 58% of the $19 plus trillion in debt coming due in the next four years, the debt would shrink to $8 trillion by the end of Fitz's first term. With 88% of the debt coming due over the next ten years, the US government debt outstanding would shrink to $2 trillion, making securities such as the 7-year note, 10-year note, and the 30-year bond much more appealing to investors as they would be the only Treasury instruments available in a couple of years. This paradigm shift resulted in a massive buying spree in the government securities market, erasing nearly all of the losses from Friday's selloff in the front end of the curve (i.e. the shorter maturity securities like the 3-month bill) and creating a net gain from Thursday's closing prices in the back end of the curve (i.e. the longer maturity securities like the 10-year note). The stock market continued to gyrate. It rallied 700 points on the back of the paradigm shift in the bond market, but every time it got its sea legs, massive selling would return, keeping the market flat and deeply in bear market territory.

Chapter 44 (The Bilderberg Group)

Show of hands – before the advent of the internet, how many of you heard of the Bilderberg Group? The answer is probably zero. The amount now is probably less than one in fifty. For the uninitiated, the Bilderberg Group is a gathering of 120 to 150 of the elite from the United States and Western Europe. "Elite" means the political elite – generally those who control the puppets, like your president, from behind the curtain of Oz – and the top drawer from industry, finance, academia, and the media. This group has been financed by the CIA, the Ford Foundation, and the Rockefeller Foundation since its inception in 1954. David Rockefeller is the only known attendee of nearly all the meetings. The name Bilderberg comes from the Bilderberg Hotel in the Netherlands, where the first conference was held. Because the top of the food chain in media is in attendance there has been a media blackout from day one. This amounts to a gathering of the ultra-rich and the ultra-powerful deciding the future of the planet, with none of its inhabitants in mind, without your consent, knowledge, or input; likely in violation of the Logan Act, which forbids unauthorized citizens from negotiating with foreign governments having a dispute with the United States. The security at these events is such that if you get within a certain distance of the resort that is hosting the event, you will be shot on site.

These are people who have been born with a silver spoon up their ass, like banking titan and internationalist David Rockefeller and Queen Beatrix of the Netherlands; or suck-up political recruits like Barack Obama; or titans of business like Bill Gates, Chairman of Royal Dutch Shell, plc Jorma Ollila, and president of pharmaceutical company Lundbeck Jorgen Huno Rasmussen; or titans in politics like Angela Merkel, Bill Clinton, and Henry Kissinger; or titans in the media like Rupert Murdoch and Editor-in-Chief of The Economist John Micklethwait; or titans in the military like NATO Secretary General Anders Fogh Rasmussen [the NATO Secretary General attends every meeting], Supreme Allied Commander Europe Philip M. Breedlove, and Former Commander of United States Central Command and CIA Director General David Petraeus; or titans in international law like EU Commissioner for Justice Viviane Reding; or former president and CIA Director George H.W. Bush; or of course, banking titans such as director of the International Monetary

Fund, Christine Lagarde and president of the European Central Bank, Mario Draghi. These are the people who are responsible for and benefit from your suffering, yet their clandestine gatherings are censored by the media. These people are the puppet masters of your supposed elected officials. These are the people, who through their slightly more public faces like the Council on Foreign Relations, are responsible for your illusion of choice in America between a religious right, pro-gun, anti-abortion, pro-business, anti-welfare, anti-immigration Republican and an anti-religion, gun control, pro-life, help the poor, help the illegal aliens Democrat. These are the people who are responsible for the Euro. The Bilderberg Group engineered the Yom Kippur War, the subsequent OPEC Oil Embargo, and the rise of the petrodollar – all for the attendees benefit. These are the people that decide that Germans have to work a few more years so the Greeks can slack off all in the name of keeping the Euro alive and well. These are the people who mandate the boundaries of debate in the United States through your television set. These are your one-world government communist loving criminals who hate humanity. And you are the people who are ignorant of it all. Watch another reality show, consume some more high-fructose corn syrup; take another prescription drug; and die a slow painful death, while these pompous, self-serving, plotting gangsters dance on your grave.

Thanks to some true investigative journalism by Daniel Estulin and Alex Jones (amongst others), this self-important cabal has been outed to a very small degree over the past decade. They generally meet in late May or early June for approximately one week to decide on such matters as assassinating Ron Paul or how to keep the European community together or how to reduce the population, all in the name of one-world government.

From an American perspective, the Rockefeller interests are always represented. As mentioned previously, David Rockefeller's attendance at Bilderberg is near perfect. When he doesn't get his way, such as when he wished to bring the Japanese into the fold at Bilderberg, he simply starts another organization, the Trilateral Commission. His foundations have also financed hugely influential think tanks such as G30 or its predecessor, the Bellagio Group, which debate issues of international trade and finance – you assuredly haven't heard of them. It is absolutely amazing that a group such as G30 (a.k.a. Consultative Group on International Economic and Monetary Affairs, Inc.), whose membership (of thirty) includes chairmen and members of the Bank of International Settlements, governors of the Bank of England, the Federal Reserve, and central banks throughout the world, former directors and chairmen of major Wall Street banks, can conduct discussions on the foreign exchange market, international capital markets, international financial institutions, central banks and their supervision of financial services and markets, and macroeconomic issues such as product and labor markets without EVER putting *debt-free* money on the fault line. Debt-based money, when laid on the fault line, will eventually split the earth in two. *Debt-free* money will secure the fault line, making it impervious to monetary earthquakes, but it is not ever a topic of discussion. Are they that stupid? No – they are just that ruthless. Political leaders worldwide take their cue from this group, but yet again, you've never heard of them and their policies are inimical to you!

Chapter 45 (March – June 2017)

The weeks moved along at a frantic pace. The Department of Homeland Security concluded nothing in the case of Polly Preston. Fitz couldn't find anyone he could trust in the agency that he was trying to restructure, or possibly dismantle. Fitz surmised that it was better not to broadcast his knowledge of the perpetrators as that information could be potentially used against him and not the killers. To be sure, the DHS was broadcasting messages about MotHER, claiming that the leader had some tie to some new form of Islam – or some nonsense. To Fitz's dismay, the populace was still slurping this balderdash out the media's hand – thus the reason for his reticence on the matter. In spite of all the media attention paid to terrorism, Fitz made good on his promise to bring home troops from the Muslim-dominated section of the world. The radical Muslims claimed victory over the infidels and Fitz let Chuck Schilling deal with the quizzical press corps.

His stance on terrorism was about the only platform item that the citizens were still in a state of uncertainty over. Fitz's monetary reforms were beginning to gain traction in the markets. The fixed income market continued rallying from its Friday, February 17th lows. The stock market, as measured by the Dow Jones Industrial Average, gyrated for two weeks between 12 and 13 thousand, before rallying to 14,800 as a combination of *debt-free* money flooding the market and debt statistics confirming the effectiveness of Fitz's radical departure from the central banking model gave the equity markets a much needed shot in the arm. The following ten weeks featured a steady climb to 17,000. People around the globe, witnessing the American vanishing debt miracle, were looking to dismantle the debt-based money creation model, which did not sit well with Old German, Blonde Jew, Wheelchair Man, and other globalists.

The populace was in a good mood during March as most were $10,000 to the better. Reality set in when sticker shock appeared in April. Unlike Obamacare, the sales tax launch went relatively smoothly. Medical insurance premiums were not taxed – a rare exception. This was done in deference to the hike that many Americans experienced when Obamacare was initiated. It was too early to tell whether tax receipts were going to match expenditures. Fitz knew that he was going to run a deficit because of the interest on the debt. Even though he was retiring the debt, the

American taxpayers still owed interest payments on the debt that remained. Since a good portion of debt being retired in the first year of his presidency was going to be shorter term securities that carried much lower interest payments – in fact, U.S. Treasury bills don't pay interest, but are sold at a discount to face value -- the amount of interest due on the debt would not come down as fast as the debt.

Small business owners had mixed feelings about Fitz's plan. They were happy that they would not be subjected (at least for the time being) to corporate income tax, but their ability to write all of their expenses off against their business had vanished, raising their effective tax rate.

Homeowners were also ambivalent as their mortgage interest deduction would no longer exist, but the $10,000 checks helped sooth over that loss.

Despite the positive response from the financial markets and opinion polls, the Senate refused to confirm any of Fitz's Cabinet nominees, except Caroline Kennedy as the Secretary of State. Fitz's other nominees, by and large, were playing golf with Trace Vonada daily at Camp David, while the lawmakers dragged their feet. Caroline Kennedy traveled to visit dignitaries while Fitz managed the domestic front from the White House. He rarely stepped outside the office, except to walk Oliver in the morning.

With an approval rating consistently hovering near 80% -- thanks in large part to the $10,000 disbursements -- Congress dared not attempt impeachment proceedings. The judiciary review of his executive orders had not yet been placed on the docket.

The first high ranking foreign official Fitz hosted was the Mexican president. The two leaders had a problem to resolve: the new American tax code – or lack thereof – was going to force illegal immigrants back to the countries from which they originated, leaving four million U.S. children, who were the offspring of illegal immigrants, parentless. Illegals tended to purchase products that would be eventually taxed at 150%, hastening their exodus dilemma. Mexico was the source of 62% of the approximately 11.4 million illegals. In the meeting, the leaders agreed that in return for a pledge from the Mexican president allowing U.S. citizen children of illegal Mexican immigrants to obtain Mexican citizenship, Fitz offered to increase Mexican aid fourfold to $3.0 billion for four years. Fitz knew he would have to repeat similar, yet smaller offers to the Central American countries as well. Fitz admitted that he was 'buying' his way out of the crisis, but it wasn't a crisis that he had created.

Business leaders of companies that didn't produce garbage that harmed the world or its citizens welcomed the tax code change with open arms. The Monsantos of the corporate world were completely up in arms, airing commercials claiming that the administration had no right to 'arbitrarily' declare an exorbitant sales tax on products without proof of their environmental or health impacts, comminating retribution if 'fairer' tax policies weren't implemented. Monsanto warned that crop yields would be severely impacted without the use of such insecticides such as Round-Up. In a nationally televised speech from the Oval Office, Fitz responded that healthy human being yields were being severely impacted by Round-Up, citing the latest study from the Center for Disease Control stating that autism was now inflicting one in forty children, up from one in five thousand in 1975.

The makers of junk food saw a huge uptick in purchases at bulk retailers such as Costco in the month of March. It seemed that it was going to take a while for the country to ween its way off of Ring Dings, pop tarts, and Cheetos. Fast food companies were furious, but scrambling to get their recipes compliant with the 30% code. The sugar lobby was beside itself as Fitz declared any food that contained refined sugar or high-fructose corn syrup would be taxed at 150%. When they aired their commercials claiming that people were being stripped of their freedom of choice because of Fitz's policies, the Chief Executive responded in that same nationally televised address that choice was still offered, but if citizens were going to consume garbage that would lead to degenerative diseases and burden the medical system, they would have to pay more into the system.

Fitz hired nutritional and holistic practitioners to dismantle the Food and Drug Administration. All available remedies would be available to the populace, be it hemp oil, BHT, Gerson therapy, laetrile, etc. Vaccines could not be administered if they contained preservatives such as mercury, aluminum, and formaldehyde. In the future, FDA panelists in charge of approving drugs could not have been a compensation recipient from a pharmaceutical company for the previous three years.

He proposed legislation for a magnetic-levitation transportation feasibility study that would eventually convert all modes of ground conveyance into magnetic-levitation devises utilizing the current rail and roadway infrastructure. This didn't sit well with the oil industry or the automobile manufacturers.

Fitz also announced plans to cut the defense budget, saying that this could be accomplished easily by not conducting illegal wars abroad. He also promised to shift money within the defense budget towards protecting the homeland and taking care of the neglected veterans.

The debt dropped (predictably) from over $19 trillion to slightly under $18 trillion with only a small spike in inflation due to the $2.3 trillion of checks mailed out at the end of February. The fractional reserve requirement now stood at 18%, eventually (in forty years) on its way to 100%. Fitz instructed the populace, that without fractional reserve banking, the U.S. financial system would be deleveraged, meaning that the wild swings in the economy such as the Great Depression or the Great Recession would be far less likely. For those critics that claimed debt-based fractional reserve banking was necessary to grow commerce, Fitz answered that fractional reserve banking was essentially a one-time event and a deception, arguing that real GDP had grown essentially with population growth plus increases in productivity for the past two-hundred years. If fractional reserve banking disappeared immediately, the amount of money in circulation would drop by ninety percent, but if you replaced that money (which had been loaned into existence) with *debt-free* money, the amount of money in circulation would be equal to the monetary base. Instead of banks having $1 million in deposits making $10 million in loans, they would eventually have $10 million in deposits making $10 million in loans; thus deleveraging the system without impacting the economy. That is what he was doing by retiring the debt with U.S. Government Money. Without debt-based money in the system, inflation would be a dynamic of the past.

Fitz said that he hoped to keep the per capita net worth constant by running an annual budget deficit equal to population growth. It was on this subject of population growth that Fitz introduced an unpopular concept, potentially unconstitutional. He said that as much as he hated the globalists, he agreed with them on their attempts to control the population. Fitz explained that if the world's population was 1,000 and the lake that supported the population could sustain life for 1,200, then the its inhabitants would live in harmony. But if the population swelled to 1,500, life in the lake would rapidly deplete from overfishing, causing starvation, breeding desperation and eventually violence as everyone scrambles to survive. The United States was blessed with many great natural resources such as the Ogallala aquifer, which yields about 30% of the ground water used for irrigation in the United States. Since 1950, the saturated volume of the aquifer has been reduced by 9% and that rate was accelerating. As a result, Fitz argued, it was important to keep the population under control. The tax code that would remove many of the eleven million illegals was a start.

But Fitz didn't stop there. He issued an executive order declaring that every child born after January 1, 2018 would be assigned to either the father or mother. Each parent could be assigned up to one child. If you were married and had two children, each parent would be assigned one of the children. If the couple decided to have another child, one of them would lose his or her annual check (presently at $10,000) from the government. If they decided to have two additional children for a total of four, both parents would lose their government compensation. Once an adult had a second child assigned to him or her, he or she could not collect the annual government check, ever again. It could be contended that this was a penalty on the poor, but what it really was, Fitz argued, was another redistribution of the wealth. If a wealthy couple decided to have four children, they would be foregoing $20,000 per year ad mortem. If a couple were to divorce, the child assignment would follow them into the next relationship. In other words, if you already had one child assigned to you from a previous relationship, you will lose your government benefit if you have another child with another partner and that child is assigned to you. Fitz figured that this order would be unpopular – and the one most likely challenged in the courts. That is why he waited until everything else related to his sweeping changes began to settle down before being the bearer of bad news. Given his popularity, it was a good time to spend some of his political capital.

Although popular with his citizens, in the space of three months, Fitz, like his old man, had managed to make enemies in big business, the military, most of Congress, the homeland security apparatus, central banking, and finance. The mob wasn't too keen on his idea of legalizing prostitution and all drugs either, but that proposal was a long way from becoming law. And he was already in a war with the globalists. It seemed that the only difference between Fitz's and his father's enemies lied with the Vice-President. Evan Spring did not have any interest stepping into Fitz's shoes.

The public couldn't get enough of Annie and Oliver. Although she rarely left the White House, anytime she made a social appearance it was front page news. If it was during the day, Oliver accompanied her in an oversized beach tote. She frequently visited local animal rescues when Fitz was bogged down running the country. She embraced the idea that incubated in Fitz's mind while walking Oliver. If Nancy Reagan was going to say no to drugs, Annie was going to say yes to animals in need of a permanent home. Fitz proposed the idea of opening a giant animal rescue on a recently decommissioned military base. He had spoken to several governors about the idea and was hopeful that he could find a spot relatively close to New York City, possibly Fort Monmouth in New Jersey, so Annie could pursue her passion. Annie had never thought about being a First Lady until she received the text from Mafia Mike and when push came to shove, she would rather just play the part of Fitz's wife. She found herself in the kitchen helping out the staff because that made her comfortable. Her mother was taken equally by both the White House and Mafia Mike. Even though she claimed she wasn't becoming a permanent resident, Ms. Van had spent four of the last six weeks in Washington D.C. with Mike providing the transportation back and forth.

****

The imperial view of Lake Como from the front terrace of the Villa d'Este's Cardinal Suite was enough to make any ordinary man's problems wash away. But the four titans sitting around the terrace's glass table did not consider themselves -- or their problems -- ordinary. The apricot awnings were fully unfurled so the late May sunlight could not be a witness to their discussion. Even though their cups were filled with hot water, none of the men had immersed their teabags. They were staring out over the lake; plotting. Unlike Mussolini staring out over Lake Garda in January 1945, these badly beaten men didn't consider themselves, or their plans, corpses. They discussed the attitudes towards central banking in Western Europe. It seemed as if Fitz had awoken the world to the source of its suffering by pulling that suffering weed out by the root. If their plans of the last sixty years, and their ancestor's schemes of the past two hundred fifty years, were to be salvaged, swift and drastic measures were necessary. The Old German, the Blonde Jew, and Wheelchair Man seemed to be taking their cue from a man they referred to as Spartacus. Spartacus was the wealthiest man on the planet, and by his definition of power, the most potent. Fitzgerald Cavendish was dismantling his power source one *debt-free* U.S. Government Money dollar bill at a time. After another thirty seconds of contemplation, Spartacus indignantly queried, "Who does this guy think he is – God?" Not seeking a reply, Spartacus dropped his teabag in the teacup. The other gentlemen followed suit. It had been decided. The bald security guard with the massive hands from the Council of Foreign Relations building was standing twenty feet away, attired in an unhappy black suit and earpiece. Wheelchair Man summoned him over to the table. A few words were spoken in hushed tones and shortly thereafter, Security Man was on his military grade mobile communication device.

Chapter 46 (Bohemian Grove)

If a group of people in your community secreted away into a nearby wooded area for two weeks of meetings, parties, and general debauchery would you stand for it? What if they held an opening evening ceremony dressed in robes, lighting fires around a pond, where they paid homage to a thirty-five foot owl statue, and as part of this ritual, they performed a mock sacrifice of a four year old child? What if the participants were members of the local Board of Education or the Town Council or taught in your school system? Would you just ignore it? No you wouldn't. You'd run them out of town and wouldn't let them near your children.

What if these men have been meeting for over 140 years in Sonoma County, California in a forest that now encompasses 2,700 acres? What if the 1,500 or so men who attend this event are the top leaders in business, defense, politics, banking, media, the arts, etc.? This celebratory assemblage is known as Bohemian Grove. What law are they breaking by getting together in the woods? Don't they have a right to privacy, you ask? Isn't this just a carefree rustic return to their frat house days in college? To be sure, no women or blacks are allowed (only as servants – a couple of token members don't count). The forest is its members' urinal. Within Bohemian Grove, there exist approximately 120 'camps', which could be considered fraternity houses, each with ten to one hundred 'members' and their guests. One former employee of the Grove remarked, "It's as if…all the board rooms, the Supreme Court, major law firms, are all emptied out onto Fraternity Row and was somehow transposed into a redwood forest." You get the idea. It is where the globalists go to unwind.

A big part of the afternoon festivities include the lakeside speeches. They are off the record, approximately thirty minutes in length, and are given by titans in their respective fields. The likes of Supreme Court Justice (and token black) Clarence Thomas – yes, he does speak, but only outside open court -- former Governor of New Mexico and Ambassador to the United Nations Bill Richardson (CFR), MSNBC anchor Chris Matthews, former Secretary of Defense and Vice-President Dick Cheney (CFR), and other 'experts' in their fields including CIA directors, bank CEOs, and major military commanders have orated at the lake. Although no formal discussions are allegedly held and no decisions are allegedly made, it was at this gathering that Ronald Regan agreed to put aside his presidential aspirations in deference to Richard Nixon in July 1967. Nixon also credited his informal lakeside speech at Bohemian Grove as his springboard to the presidency:

> "If I were to choose the speech that gave me the most pleasure and satisfaction in my political career, it would be my Lakeside Speech at the Bohemian Grove in July 1967. Because this speech traditionally was off the record it received no publicity at the time. But in many important ways it marked the first milestone on my road to the presidency."

(Nixon, for his part, didn't like attending: "The Bohemian Grove that I attend from time to time…is the most faggiest God damn thing you could ever imagine with that San Francisco crowd that goes there. It's just terrible!") George H.W. Bush (CFR) and George W. Bush gave a lakeside speech in 1995 where Senior said his son would make a great future president.

Exposed in print by Philip Weiss in the November 1989 *Spy* magazine article entitled, "Inside Bohemian Grove", the private elite gathering has since been infiltrated by Alex Jones and Mike Hanson, who filmed the opening evening Cremation of Care ceremony involving the aforementioned mock child sacrifice (symbolizing "Care", or the burdens and responsibilities that the weary, overstressed Bohemians wish to shed before their sixteen day party). There have also been brief TV News vignettes on Bohemian Grove since 1984. To answer the privacy question, when public officials participate in bizarre (some say, satanic) rituals and at the same time are accountable for running your government -- by the people and for the people -- you have a right to know. As far as the private citizens who are the CEOs of major multi-national corporations, national news anchors, editors, and bankers, that is a matter of debate. What isn't up for debate is that Bohemian Grove is another convention of the wealthy and powerful, which is, for all intents and purposes, blacked out by your mainstream media.

If all that transpired at Bohemian Grove was a reunion of well-to-do comrades in the woods and the making of new ones as Grovesmen frat-hop from campsite to campsite, there is no cause for alarm. What better way to settle philosophical or political differences than around a campfire with a couple of beers? A relaxed, informal environment is almost always preferable to the uptight formality of the boardroom, the courtroom, or the floor of Congress. The problem begins when dark, abhorrent stories begin to leak out about a group that is essentially shrouded in secrecy. Couple the deeply disturbing story of Paul Bonacci with the Grove's rituals and a recipe for a very bad tasting stew is in the offing.

Paul Bonacci was abducted into a pedophilia ring at a very young age. The head of the ring was a man named Lawrence King, who used the kids for sex, drug dealing, compromising politicians, and corrupting government institutions. King rose rapidly through the Republican Party ranks, becoming leader of the National Black Republican Council in the 1980s. He was also the General Manager of a small bank, the Franklin Federal Credit Union. He would eventually go to jail for stealing $40 million from the bank. He is not a good guy. He would invite orphans from Boys Town to lavish parties where he would operate them as sex toys for the depraved older male attendees, while arranging for unseemly pictures of the lubricity as a vehicle for blackmail.

John DeCamp, a highly decorated Vietnam War veteran and 16-year Nebraska state senator, started investigating allegations of child abuse that stemmed from a Senator Loran Schmit-led Nebraska legislative inquiry into the collapse of the Franklin Credit Union. DeCamp's lead private detective, Gary Caradori, developed 271 leads of victims, witnesses, and predators by May 1990. In June 1990, Caradori complained to Loran Schmit's subcommittee that the FBI – to which he was forced to supply his findings -- was deliberately sabotaging his investigation. Senator Schmit had also been warned anonymously to not thoroughly examine the Franklin allegations because, "it will reach to the highest levels of the Republican Party and we're both good Republicans."

On July 7, 1990, Caradori flew his Piper Saratoga to Chicago to rendezvous with Rusty Nelson, who had photographed the politicians and business leaders in compromising positions with the kids as part of Larry King's extortion scheme. Upon receipt of the career ending photos, Caradori called Schmit to brag, "We got them by the shorthairs!" Just like Dorothy Kilgallen after her interviews with Jack Ruby, Gary Caradori never got the opportunity to blow the case wide open. On return from

Chicago, during the early morning of July 11th, with his eight year old son on board, Gary's plane exploded in mid-air, killing both. Remarkably, most of Caradori's possessions, like his briefcase that likely contained the incriminating pictures, were never found. The FBI essentially raided the grieving widow's home two days later by serving her a subpoena demanding all of his files relating to the Franklin scandal. The investigation turned into a power play of the absurd with victims being intimidated by FBI agents and made to feel criminal. The teenagers (and by the time of the investigation, young adults) who did come forward were threatened -- and in the case of Alicia Owens, were charged with perjury and sentenced to nine to fifteen years in jail, when evidence that corroborated her accusations of prominent men sexually abusing her when she was a teenager was suppressed by the FBI. These charges and Caradori's death were a message to the other people on the list of 271 who desired to come forward with further allegations. Owens was released after serving four and a half years and has never wavered from her story.

DeCamp was involved in the production of a documentary called "Conspiracy of Silence" that was to air May 3, 1994 on the Discovery Channel. This documentary reported the story of his investigation and detailed his findings, much of which had been suppressed by the local and national media. It was listed in the TV Guide, but it never aired. You see, certain congressmen threatened the cable industry with restrictive legislation – just like Big Pharma threatening to pull ads from the networks – if the show aired. The show was canceled, the producers were paid a half a million dollars for their production costs, and all copies of the program were supposed to be destroyed. Fortunately, someone with a conscious kept a copy, and it can now be viewed on the internet. DeCamp also authored a book on the investigation, *The Franklin Cover-Up*. Watch it, read it, and ask yourself if justice was done.

Getting back to Paul Bonacci, he kept a diary of his horrific abuse. He was also recorded by Caradori before the investigator's death. Although he did not know what it was called, Bonacci led John DeCamp to a location in the Sonoma County redwoods that was the scene of unspeakable horror. What follows is an excerpt from Paul's diary about his (and another boy, Nicholas') visit to Bohemian Grove:

"In or on July 26th [1984] I went to Sacramento, Ca. King flew me out on a private plane from Eppley Airfield [in Omaha] to Denver where we picked up Nicholas, a boy who was about 12 or 13. Then we flew to Las Vegas to a desert strip and drove in to Las Vegas and to some ranch and got something -- then flew on to Sacramento.

"We were picked up by a white limo and taken to a hotel. I don't remember the name of it. We meaning Nicholas and I were driven to a[n] area that had big trees, it took about an hour to get there. There was a cage with a boy in it who was not wearing anything. Nicholas and I were given these Tarzan things to put around us and stuff.

"They told me to f--- the boy and stuff. At first I said no and they held a gun to my balls and said do it or else lose them or something like that. I began doing it to the boy and stuff. And Nicholas had anal sex and stuff with him. We were told to f--- him and stuff and beat on him. I didn't try to hurt him. We were told to put our d---s in his mouth and stuff and sit on the boys penis and stuff and they filmed it. We did this stuff to the boy for about 30 minutes or an hour when a man came in and kicked us and stuff in the balls and picked us up and threw us. He grabbed the boy and started f---ing him and stuff. The man was about 10 inches long and the boy screamed and stuff and the man was forcing his d--- into the boy all the way. The boy was bleeding from his rectum and the men tossed him and me and stuff and put the boy right next to me and grabbed a gun and blew the boys head off.

"The boys blood was all over me and I started yelling and crying. The men grabbed Nicholas and I and forced us to lie down. They put the boy on top of Nicholas who was crying and they were putting Nicholas hands on the boys ass. They put the boy on top of me and did the same thing. They then forced me to f--- the dead boy up his ass and also Nicholas they put a gun to our heads to make us do it. His blood was all over us. They made us kiss the boys lips and to eat him out. Then they made me do something I don't want to even write so I won't.

410

"After that the men grabbed Nicholas and drug him off screaming they put me up against a tree and put a gun to my head but fired into the air. I heard another shot from somewhere. I then saw the man who killed the boy drag him like a toy. Everything including when the men put the boy in a trunk was filmed. They took me with them and we went up in a plane. I saw the bag the boy was in. We went over a very thick brush area with a clearing in it. Over the clearing they dropped the boy. One said the men with the hoods would take care of the body for them.

"I didn't see Nicholas until that night at the hotel. He and I hugged and held each other for a long while. About two hours later the men or Larry King came in and told us to go take a shower since we had only been hosed off at some guys house. We took a shower together and then were told to put on the Tarzan things. After we were cleaned up and dressed in these things we were told to put on shorts, socks and a shirt and shoes and driven to a house where the men were at with some others. They had the film and they played it. As the men watched they passed Nicholas and I around as if we were toys and sexually abused us.

"They made Nicholas and I screw each other and one of the men put the dead boy's penis in mine and Nicholas' mouth. I didn't want to write this because the man forced me to bite the boys' penis and balls off. It was gross and I saw the film where it happened and started freaking out remembering what they made us do afterwards to the boy. They showed us doing everything to the boy. I was there for about 5 days attending parties but only recall cutting my wrist which is why I stayed two days in a hospital under a name I can't recall. Some guy paid for me."

In the fall of 1992, Paul Bonacci was shown a black and white photo of the moss-covered owl at the Grove and quickly identified it as the site of the July 1984 snuff film described in DeCamp's book.

Apparently, a man identifying himself as Hunter S. Thompson was the cameraman for the snuff film. Although Bonacci couldn't identify Thompson and DeCamp had a hard time believing that someone shooting a snuff film would give his real name, Thompson's moral compass at times wasn't pointing south; because of the monumental intake of drugs and scotch, it was missing. It is wholly possible that his participation in this event is true. In a post mortem, Hunter S. Thompson's assistant Nickole Brown claimed that, "he threw me out of the house for refusing to watch a snuff film." In a weird and wholly uncomfortable interview with David Letterman back on November 25, 1988, Thompson claimed that, "I like to kill." When Letterman jokingly pressed him for further clarity, Thompson replied, "We don't want to talk about this -- shooting people, do we?" When Letterman, who now appeared to be sitting on a thousand thumbtacks, attempted to clean up the awkward mess by insinuating that he was only teasing, Thompson replied, "No, I'm not teasing. I used to like to kill. When I realized that I was hunting... [Letterman interrupts before Thompson resumes.] I quit because I realized I was not hunting for meat. I was hunting because I like to kill."

Former Satanic high priest and Bohemian Grove attendee Zachary King claims the all-male shindig is frequented by Satanists. He also claims that in addition to the Cremation of Care kickoff, other rituals take place both publically at the Owl and privately at the some of the campsites. For the avoidance of doubt, the Satanists are probably a very low percentage of the participants, but exist nonetheless. When you are born without a soul, or through an extremely poor upbringing, you disengage from it, or allow it to darken by ennui induced journeys to necromancy, you end up as Lawrence King and others, committing crimes that can't be forgiven. When leaders in this country, be it governmental, judicial, media, military, business, financial, etc., attend ceremonies worshiping owls while repulsive acts are being committed, it logically follows that you should be deeply concerned.

Chapter 47 (June 6 – 12, 2017)

Magnus Graabak couldn't believe his good fortune. He had just arrived in the United States on a mission – a mission that he would have three weeks to complete; a mission that would pay him $20 million if successfully executed; a mission that could end his life; a mission that would be near impossible to accomplish -- if it wasn't for his good fortune. Standing on the ninth floor (the top floor) of the Hay Adams Hotel with its commanding perspective of the North Lawn of the White House, Magnus witnessed the President of the United States walking his dog just as daylight was making an appearance. All he had to do was walk to the southeast end of the ninth floor banquet room   in fact the entire ninth floor was a series of small banquet rooms, which would be vacant at sunrise -- open the doors to a balcony with a black railing, and *voila*, the President of the United States, approximately 800 feet away, waiting to be assassinated. And best he could tell, there were no security cameras situated anywhere in the hotel. This would be an easy shot, especially for a former silver medalist in the Olympic biathlon.

Magnus was still smarting over the loss in the biathlon. He was the best shot in the world (or so he thought), but not the best cross-country skier. This was his third assassination attempt. The other two were obviously successful, otherwise he'd be dead. The organization he was working for was unknown – he knew he was operating through at least one cut out -- but he knew that it was of the utmost penetralia. He was recruited out of the Norwegian Defence Security Department, his employer when he wasn't preparing for the biathlon. He was offered four million krone (approximately $500,000 US) to take out a business executive after the World Economic Forum meeting in Davos, Switzerland. He wasn't fed a lot of patriotic malarkey such as the person was a threat to Norwegian interests. He was just called into the Captain's office one day and was told to speak with a man who was waiting in the snow, in the dark. Four million krone was his ticket out of Oslo's long and dreary winters. After successfully carrying out his mission, a bank account in Monaco was at Magnus' disposal. He liked the French Riviera so much that he decided to make it his home. It was really expensive to live there, but he was addicted to the Cote d'Azur party scene. He portrayed himself as an international playboy, and even though he didn't own a yacht, the silver medalist was invited to the soirées.

His second assignment involved the killing of an American military advisor in Copenhagen, Denmark in early June of 2014. Magnus never heard of the official, nor did he care. All he cared about were the two million Euros that would be deposited in his account upon the successful completion of his mission. He was passed along information about the target's week long vacation that would commence after his meeting in Copenhagen, making his physical liquidation relatively easy. He rationalized that the person he was killing was a dead man anyway. It didn't matter if he pulled the trigger or someone else. It was the heroin dealer's justification: "I'm just filling a demand that someone else would fill if I wasn't here."

$20 million US was enough to keep Magnus in the French Riviera party scene for the foreseeable future. Hell, he'd kill his mother for that much money. When he accepted the mission he was told that failure was not an option – as before – but was not given any additional information. He really didn't need any. It was the President of the United States of America. The irony was that Magnus had met Fitzgerald Cavendish at a party during the Cannes Film Festival in May 2014, right before he was tapped for his second assassination. He liked Fitz, but that wasn't an issue. The issue occupying Mr. Graabak's mind was not the morality of killing a suddenly world famous figure that he once hung out with for an evening in Cannes; nor was it the Secret Service. It was the fact that Cavendish was a total recluse. He never came out of the White House. It was as if he knew that someone was going to hunt him down if he made a public appearance. Graabak, for all his skills, wasn't going to be able to penetrate the White House, kill Cavendish, and still be alive to enjoy his $20 million. He needed an opportunity and he just got one. He would return the following morning prepared to act.

****

"C'mon Stinky Boy," Fitz lightly urged the First Pooch with bad breath. For some reason Oliver was a little hesitant to get out of bed. Maybe he felt that he was shorted a bit on the ritual morning belly rub; maybe he wanted to cuddle up against his Mommy; maybe he had a sense of foreboding. Whatever his reason, he couldn't resist when Fitz whispered, "Are you starvin' Marvin?" It was time to be fed and that meant organic B.A.R.F. dog food that Oliver absolutely loved. After Oliver ravaged the contents of his dog dish, Fitz strapped on his harness for his morning constitutional out on the North Lawn of the White House.

Special Agent Quint Dravis was assigned the duty of watching the president walk his dog most mornings. He knew his job and performed it well. He and fellow agent John Nidds were supposed to keep close proximity to the president, but when he was walking Oliver, Dravis and whoever else was "walking the president" gave him a little more space. In Dravis' mind the rationale was twofold. First, besides showering or going to the bathroom, he viewed this as Fitz's only alone time all day. Second, Fitz would usually have conversations with his dog, in a voice that assaulted Dravis' sense of what is presidential. This calm morning was no exception.

"You know Oliver; theoretically I'm the leader of the free world. So when the aliens land and they say, 'take me to your leader', they are going to come to the White House." Oliver lifted his left leg and peed on the grape hyacinth that edged the tulips that surrounded the North Lawn pool. Fitz continued in a foolish sounding voice, "When the aliens see me picking up your poop, they are going to assume that you're in charge. So I just want you to know that the fate of the Earth and all of its creatures will be in your paws. Are you up to that awesome responsibility?" [Fade to black.]

The bullet from the Magnus' newly released Remington M40A7 with folding stock and suppressor hit Cavendish square in his left eye killing him instantly. Taking a split second longer to confirm his kill, Graabak quickly pulled himself and his rifle inside the banquet room of the Hay Adams, closing the door to the outside. Once inside, it was only a few steps to the elevator that was waiting on the top floor. On the ride down, Magnus folded up his rifle and stuffed it into his red Wilson Federer Team 6 Pack Tennis Bag that already contained clothes that he wore when he had entered the Hay Adams an hour prior. At 5:35am, he calmly walked out the front door of the hotel, clad in tennis whites, tennis bag slung over his shoulder, walked across the street to where his rented Mercedes was parked, headed out toward the beltway on 16th Street NW and into total anonymity.

The scene on the North Lawn went from shock to chaotic in three seconds. Oliver was the first to react by whimpering as Fitz's lifeless body hit the ground. Agent Dravis hesitated for a split second, processing what had just transpired. A dim light had enveloped the North Lawn as the sun was still ten minutes from rising. After the split second delay, he immediately took three steps and lunged towards the fallen president in an ineffectual attempt to shield him. Agent Nidds immediately followed suit. Oliver was still whimpering. Dravis saw that the president was not responding. *Holy Shit! I just lost the President!* He checked for a pulse, but already knew the verdict when he noticed his left eye was just a bleeding hole. Agent Nidds radioed for assistance, "POTUS has been hit. Repeat, POTUS has been hit – North Lawn. Immediate assistance required." It was too late for Fitz and the brief chaos made it too late for the Secret Service to get a good read on where the kill shot originated. Nidds pulled out his gun, ran haplessly north towards the end of the property near Lafayette Square, but saw nothing suspicious. From his vantage point he could not see Graabak exit the Hay Adams. Fitz's lifeless shell would be hauled into an ambulance within two minutes and an inadequate dragnet would cover Washington D.C. within fifteen minutes.

Annie, who slept through the initial pandemonium, was awakened by Mafia Mike and Oliver fifteen minutes after the fatal shot. She couldn't process the news. Fitz was just next to her and now he was dead? Her mind was still in a post-sleep fog. She kept assuming a fetal position, attempting to jolt herself back to the nightmare, reawaken, and pass the last few minutes off as a bad dream. But it wasn't working. She was in a state of utter disbelief. She couldn't speak. She couldn't cry. When she finally dared to face the day, she walked around in a cloudy dull torpor. Her mother and Mafia Mike tried to comfort her, but she was utterly despondent. Her only comfort was Oliver, but even he could not induce any emotion, any voice, only instinctual physical motions, such as holding him tight to her chest.

The media did not have any problem reporting the truth, because they did not know what had transpired – nor did anyone else. No terrorist groups claimed responsibility, although they were the early focus of suspicion. Unlike prior major catastrophic or shocking events, the media had no cue cards off which to read. They were not being fed any fairy tale by the law enforcement division of the Department of Homeland Security. The only witnesses to Fitz's death were two dumbfounded Secret Service agents and a dog. Unlike his father's death which involved a bunch of high-level players receiving permission from the elite powers, Fitz's assassination was ordered by the top of the pyramid. It was a message to America (and the world) that there were forces greater than the will of the population. Natural resource interests, the NATO-CIA controlled heroin trade, the military-industrial complex, debt-based currency, and one-world government goals were not going to be stopped by the actions of one person, even if he was the President of the United States, the so-called leader of the free world. The message was clear: you are no longer in control of your country's destiny. Your country has been hijacked. Anyone who wishes to get in the way will be eliminated.

****

News of the assassination reached the gathering at the Villa D'Este before lunch. Fitzgerald Cavendish was dead. No suspects and only two witnesses. Unlike the rest of the world, which shut down upon hearing the news, the conference continued on with its schedule of discussions on geopolitical matters – of course, with a slightly modified landscape. Spartacus was never impressed -- except with himself -- but the speed and efficiency of the assassin mildly thrilled the eighty-five year old. He had hoped for Fitz's elimination before July 1st; he never dreamed that it would be accomplished before the conference concluded – impressive indeed. There was a tacit mid-day toast on the Cardinal's Suite balcony, this time with four Bond Street martinis.

****

It was a beautiful day for a funeral – sunny, 80 degrees, with low humidity. Fitz's body had been returned to the White House by 5:00pm the day of his assassination – the autopsy was quick. One bullet through the eye – there wasn't much to examine. After lying in repose in the East Room of the White House for 24 hours, nearly a half million people watched a horse-drawn caisson make its way along Pennsylvania Avenue to the Capitol Rotunda, where Fitz would lie in state for another 39 hours.

The building never closed to accommodate the 350,000 people who waited, in some instances through the night, to pay their respects to their fallen hero. After the mourners had passed, a brief service was held at the Capitol. The funeral procession traveled west along the National Mall past the Washington Monument, eventually past the Lincoln Memorial, and onto Arlington National Bridge. The cortege on the bridge was the opening of an eerie time capsule that most Americans just as well never revisit. Annie walked alone in a long black skirt, a standard black blouse, black heels, and a long black veil, with her mother and Mafia Mike close behind. President Evan Spring – who was awoken and sworn in by 7:00am the morning of the murder – was next with his wife Tracy and Caroline Kennedy flanking him. Behind them were the cabinet appointees – the Camp David Golf Group – who were never approved by the Senate, along with their fast friend Reverend Vonada. Behind them, dignitaries from one hundred nation states walked the route. It was dead silent, except for the sound of horse hooves hitting the pavement, and the occasional whimpering from those who lined the bridge. Almost entirely across the bridge, the flood of sorrow in Annie Van's body finally overwhelmed the dam of shock blocking the receptors in her brain, and she collapsed to her knees, hands covering her face as she sobbed uncontrollably. Fifty million Americans, watching from their homes, and most of the world, followed suit.

****

Robert Atkinson traveled to the White House to read the will of the most famous man on the planet, dead or alive. Assembled in the Oval Office were President of the United States Evan Spring, his newly appointed Vice President Caroline Kennedy, Annie Van, her mother Diane, Mafia Mike, Lieutenant General Chaz Wyckoff, and Oliver. The reading of the will went swiftly. Mafia Mike received $500,000. $2 million would be donated in Oliver's name for an animal rescue, the land for which had been already been purchased by Fitz. Annie Van would be the executor of the rescue's trust. The will explained that this was Fitz's insurance policy that Annie would have an animal rescue to run in the event his untimely death preceded his ability to transform part of a dormant military base into an animal habitat. The balance of the estate, valued at slightly over $15 million, would be Annie's.

Atkinson then pulled out six envelopes – each envelope was numbered. He consulted an algorithmic chart that detailed instructions for the handling of each envelope. He gave the first one to President Spring. Inside was a note simply stating, "Hang tough. Help is coming. Fitz." After Evan read the note, Atkinson handed him envelope #2 which had instructions not be opened until July 16th.

Atkinson referenced the chart, kept envelope #3 and passed envelope #4 to Wyckoff, which had instructions to be opened on July 14th.

Envelope #5 was a FedEx envelope addressed to the parents of Polly Preston with instructions for Atkinson to overnight on July 12th.

Envelope #6 was for Annie. It simply said, "Open when you are up to it." And with that, the affairs of the second shortest tenured President of the United States were complete.

Epilogue 1 (July 15 - 18, 2017)

President Evan Spring was under siege. He had gone from obscure private equity partner to President of the United States in the span of seven months. He was the most unknown president of all-time, and probably desired the office less than even James A. Garfield, who had not even sought the Republican nomination in 1880. The power play that was Cavendish's assassination was not lost on Spring. With a wife and two children he was scared for their well-being. The judicial reviews of the constitutionality of Fitz's executive orders were now scheduled when the Supreme Court term commenced in October. If ruled unconstitutional, Evan would be stuck in the middle of a massive transition back to income tax. He felt that the Federal Reserve Act was unconstitutional, but if the Supreme Court ruled that Fitz's actions regarding the dismantling of it were unconstitutional, Spring would be facing another enormous headache. The Congress was completely uncooperative, still delaying confirmation hearings on Spring's appointments, which were essentially Fitz's appointments.

Almost zero foreign policy was in place, except one of almost complete isolation from the rest of the world. Fitz had brought most of America's military presence from conflicted regions of the world home, be it from Syria, Iraq, Afghanistan, or the thirteen countries in Central Africa. He had kept the navy in its role of protecting oil tanker routes, but was reviewing the military bases around the globe for possible closure, with an eye towards the Mideast. Fitz employed a litmus test for the State Department staff: if an employee was a member of any one-world government organization such as the Council on Foreign Relations or the Trilateral Commission, he or she would not be serving the Cavendish administration. If he or she was a dual-citizen, he or she would not be serving the Cavendish administration. Since the Obama administration State Department contained hundreds of CFR members, his move essentially gutted the international relations arm of the government. Fortunately for Spring, Vice-President Caroline Kennedy, who was mandated by Fitz to preside over its house cleaning, continued on with that duty during this unexpected re-transition period.

The shock and sadness regarding Fitz's death had given way to insecurity and impatience. There were no solid leads in Fitz's death.

There were no patsies. Since only two Secret Service agents witnessed the 2nd Crime of the 21st Century, conspiracy theories developed that Fitz actually hadn't died and the assassination was all a ruse or that the Secret Service was responsible for Fitz's death. Spring let the investigators perform their work, but he was being criticized for not finding the killer. He had been making millions as a partner in private equity and now he was being paid $400,000 to deal with the weight of the world. In six weeks at the helm, he felt that he had aged six years.

****

The mood of the congregation in the Sonoma forest was simply ebullient. The frat party was about to get started. The biggest obstacle to their short-term and long-term objectives (since JFK) had been removed. The fact that it was JFK's love child only made them giddier. Normally, the affair was predominantly American, but many guests had arrived from Europe including Spartacus, who was received by the Old German. The American hosts were going to show their European guests how to drink beer and urinate on trees.

As a result, the attendance for the opening evening ceremony would be huge. The celebration looked like an outdoor version of what took place inside a beer hall during Oktoberfest in Munich: hundreds of banquet tables occupied by approximately 1,800 of the most powerful and famous men in the United States and the world. The difference was that this congregation would also be entertained by outdoor theatre. Dusk had settled in. The double headed gaslights at the ends of each table provided sylvan illumination.

****

The desert opened up like the deck of an aircraft carrier. Emerging from a small underground hanger was the latest in drone technology. General Atomics had really outdone itself with the MQ -12 Reaper, which was a quantum leap improvement over its very effective predecessor MQ – 9. It could carry nearly 20,000 lbs. at takeoff (versus approximately 10,000 for the MQ – 9) and fly at slightly over 400 mph (versus less than 300 mph for the MQ – 9). Because it could carry so much more weight, the reaper could forsake the GBU – 12 Paveway II bombs for much larger ones, including the retired BLU – 82/B that was attached -- in this instance retrofitted. More commonly known as the Daisy Cutter, this bomb had been scrapped in 2008 for more effective killing devices after only 225 were made. The pre-programmed drone headed out on to an empty, unpaved, unmarked, airstrip at the northeast corner of Edwards Air Force base at dusk and took off without anyone initially noticing.

****

The wailing sounds of a funeral dirge drew the attention of the seated. Men in red robes and red pointed hoods slowly and purposefully approached the congregation. Some performed the sad tune; some carried giant torches that allowed the gathering to espy the silhouetted majesty of the redwoods; others carried an open coffin. A few in the crowd whispered wickedly that it contained the remains of Fitzgerald Cavendish. It actually housed the body of Care. As the priests, pallbearers, torchbearers, and musicians passed through, the observers fell into line behind them, forming a parade down a rustic trail towards a small lake. After five minutes, the pseudo-solemn cavalcade arrived at their destination. The performers moved to the right in the direction of a large altar facing the lake, presided over by the imposing thirty-five foot high moss covered totem animal of Bohemia: the Owl. The followers moved to the left in the direction of a large grassy meadow on the other side of the lake. The lake was ringed with torches; the altar alit from the Lamp of Fellowship burning at the base of the Owl. The priests, pallbearers, and others continued past the Owl and towards a boat landing, chanting, "cre-MAY-shun, cre-MAY-shun".

Chaz Wyckoff was inside the redwood forest, but not at the ceremony. He was gathering up as many workers and support staff as he could – most of whom were cleaning up at the dinner circle -- making sure that none would be anywhere near the lakeside ceremony.

****

When the drone entered the California airspace, it confused the air traffic controllers, who actually attempted to make radio contact with it. Once it was properly identified as a drone, the military air command was contacted. They were already aware of its presence. Edwards Air Force Base was contacted. No one seemed to know anything about this craft or why it was menacing the airspace. The craft, with a 75ft wingspan could cause serious damage if it crashed on land. One half hour after its takeoff, a decision was made to scramble fighter planes that would intercept the drone and take it down if a suitable area could be found. Complicating this course of action was nighttime. By the time fighters were airborne, the drone was near San Francisco.

****

At the boat landing on the lake, the catafalque was loaded onto the Ferry of Care. All music seized and all torches were extinguished. The only flame that remained emanated on the altar from the base of the Owl (the Lamp of Fellowship). A spotlight then shined on a redwood near the Owl, from which a hamadryad emerged, accompanied by a chorus of other woodland spirits. The tree spirit cantillated, instructing the audience to, "cast your grief to the fires and be strong with the holy trees and the spirit of the Grove." After the performance, all lights were shuttered as the Blonde Jew, playing the role of high priest, and his entourage approached the stage before the Owl.

"The Owl is in his leafy temple," intoned the high priest. "Let all within the Grove be reverent before him." The high priest continued with more inspiring speech, followed by other priests and a brief song from the choir. The Ferry of Care approached the altar. Everything went quiet, save the cricket music. The high priest shouted, "Our funeral pyre awaits the corpse of Care!" A horn sounded and the Ferry of Care arrived at the altar serenaded by Venetian gondolier music. The high priest then commanded, "Bring Fire!"

Suddenly, loud speakers crackled like uranium orchids. Through them, Dull Care's voice blared, "Fools! Fools! Fools! When will ye learn that me ye cannot slay? Year after year ye burn me in this Grove, lifting your puny shouts of triumph to the stars. But when again ye turn your feet toward the marketplace, am I not waiting for you, as of old? Fools! Fools! To dream ye conquer Care!"

A discussion between the high priest and the voice continued, until the high priest, clearly frustrated, turned to the Owl for guidance, "Oh thou, great symbol of all mortal wisdom," he cried. "Owl of Bohemia, we do beseech thee, grant us thy counsel!"

The Owl, in the voice of Walter Cronkite, explained that the only way Care can be cremated is with the flame from the Lamp of Fellowship, "Hail, Fellowship and thou, Dull Care, begone!" The high priest returned to his feet, grabbed an extinguished torch from one of the torchbearers, relit it in the Lamp of Fellowship, and with it, ignited the funeral pyre. Orchestral music, which started to play quietly when the conversation commenced, reached a feverish crescendo.

The MQ – 12, followed by two F-16s, released its payload over a ceremony in the Sonoma forest.

As the high priest threw the torch back into The Lamp of Fellowship, the Daisy Cutter detonated above the lake. The ear shattering concussion was followed seconds later by the thunderous collapse of the Owl.

****

President Spring addressed a stunned and frightened nation on July 16, 2017.

"I received a message posthumously, from former President Cavendish, the contents of which I read this morning. That correspondence included an address to the nation. With some hesitancy, I will read it to you now."

"'Fellow citizens, you are rightfully concerned about the events of the past few months: the beheading of Polly Preston, my assassination, and the recent incident in Northern California. You probably believe that Muslim terrorists are at work. They are not. I want you to know that all of the events are related. The people assembled in Northern California were behind my murder and the death of Polly Preston, not some group of religious fanatics. I, and I want to emphasize, I alone was behind the death and destruction in the Sonoma forest. It was an act of revenge, pure and simple. When I was offered the bribe from the three men at the Council of Foreign Relations headquarters, I knew that its rejection would

424

probably result in my demise. It was a form of Russian roulette that I was willing to play, but when they included Ms. Preston as collateral damage, the darkness of their souls was exposed, and I sought revenge. Polly's death was not at the hands of a group called MotHER. That entire acronym represented a message to me from them. If I came on TV, a day into my presidency and started blaming these men for Polly's death, my credibility would likely have been questioned. It was a brilliantly disgraceful move on their part.

"'Part of the problem that we as Americans have is that we try to view everything as black and white. The terrorists wear the black hats and our intelligence agencies wear the white ones. It's not that simple – not by a long shot. When we are told that it is not that simple, we shut off the central processing unit in our brains as a defense mechanism. The psychologists refer to this as cognitive dissonance.

"For example, there were two other reasons that I wanted to negotiate with terrorists, which I did not make abundantly clear during my time on Earth. One you will understand and one you will have a hard time processing. First, if we give the religious extremists a caliphate, not only will it attract radicals from other spots on the globe, but also give them a piece of real estate that we can bomb back to the Stone Age if they continue to attack our citizens. That is a concept that I think most can understand. But secondly, if we negotiated with terrorists, if we talked to them, you might find out a lot of things that you don't want to hear, such as they are heroin mules for a NATO/CIA led cartel. In return for their services, the CIA provides them with weapons through a cutout country or some organization that we, through an act of Congress, set up in a place like Tajikistan, under the false guise of increasing tourism or education. These items never make the news. The CIA uses the proceeds from the heroin and cocaine trade to finance its black ops and in some cases, line the orchestrators' pockets, in the process bypassing Congress and the American public. They are running a shadow government that you are not privy to. If you want to know the truth about this other world that you never hear about, how about having one of the major news outlets put a reporter on a plane to Holland, and have him or her interview Huseyin Baybasin, the heroin Pablo Escobar of Europe? He'll tell you how the whole operation works and how he was on the books at NATO. What's wrong *60 Minutes*? Are you scared? You shouldn't be any more since your puppeteers are likely dead. That is the other unspoken logic for legalizing all drugs that you would likely have a hard time comprehending: it would cut off funding for the shadow government. Why doesn't the press report about Operation Gladio or Gladio B?

"'As you noticed in scenario two, *everyone* is wearing a black hat. These are the scenarios that you have a hard time comprehending – the ones in which your government is nothing more than a criminal organization at the behest of the uber-elite. What I attempted to do in my campaign for the presidency is to point out the cancer and then implement policies that would eradicate it at its root. Many of you will respond that there is nothing that you can do about it. You already did -- by voting for me. But you must understand the evil in its entirety in order to stop its next advance – having your brain short circuit is not an option. These are the people that killed not only Polly and me, but also my father, my mother, and my grandfather. Circumstantial evidence backing these claims will be released along with all of the remaining documents relating to my father's assassination shortly. These are the organizations that have controlled the planet since my father was assassinated. These are the organizations that are feeding you crap for news, crap for food, and crap for healthcare. When you are sedated enough or scared enough from that crap, you will accept their next step in their march towards world government. I won't allow you to accept that. I didn't. Northern California is proof of my word. Don't view the blow that I struck at Bohemian Grove as a sockdolager. It is a major step towards the citizens of this country reclaiming what is rightfully theirs, which is a government by the people, for the people, a proper money creation system, a real news media, and a proper healthcare system. But don't lose the momentum generated by the incident in Northern California. To that end, I have two more drones pointed at strategic locations on the planet that are pre-programmed to go off if certain anti-American events occur such as the debt clock increasing. It is my way of holding the hostage takers hostage.

"'You may think I'm insane because people just lost fathers and uncles and sons. Did we think about that when we were fighting the enemy in Japan or Germany or Vietnam? The answer is no, because they were the enemy. The men who died in Northern California are the enemy. They wear the black hats. They killed not only Polly and me, but were attempting to kill the United States Constitution.

"'It was a pleasure and honor serving you. Be well.'"

The 46th President of the United States said nothing more. Instead, he retired to his office to meet with Vice-President Kennedy. There was an assessment being conducted to determine how many congressmen perished in Northern California. Three Supreme Court justices were killed and with two more retiring, President Spring had the power to change the course of the nation by installing justices who would decree Cavendish's executive orders constitutional. Even if that didn't work, the apparatus that controlled Congress was crippled. He would likely get his Cabinet installed and some of Fitz's legislation pushed through. The nation was happy with the new tax law and the new money system. Most still didn't understand it, but were happy when they heard the debt was declining. Now that the horrible events of the past six months had been explained, the country was less likely to be on edge, except for people who worked at places like the United Nations, NATO, or the Bank of International Settlements. The remaining puppeteers were on the run now that Fitz had two more weapons pointed at strategic one-world government locations, whatever or wherever they may be.

As a side note, compellingly positive anecdotes were starting to emerge regarding the effectiveness of certain cancer remedies. People were consuming more food that didn't contain aluminum, high fructose corn syrup, and other garbage.

Somehow, the reading of that bizarre message from the grave had the effect of putting a spine back into Spring's resolve. For the first time since he had the job, Evan felt like everything was going to be alright.

427

****

Situated in an Adirondack chair overlooking the Hudson River, Annie Van was beginning to glue back the pieces of the vase that was her psyche. The animal rescue, located in upstate New York, was a perfect retreat from all of the insanity that had consumed her life from the day Fitzgerald Cavendish initially walked out of it. Her first two rescue dogs were due to arrive the following afternoon. Annie figured that she would have capacity for one hundred dogs with the facility provided by Fitz. She communicated with next to no one since the day of the assassination, but she was almost ready. She agreed to attend two weddings in the late summer/early autumn: her mother's to Mafia Mike and her friend Wendy to Chuck Schilling.

She contemplated the randomness of life. *What if we had went to the Clocktower Bar, like we were supposed to, and not the lobby bar at the Edition Hotel? What if I hadn't solved that riddle for Fitz? What if Fitz hadn't misinterpreted the note or the speech's meaning?* Sometimes there *are* coincidences and fate intervenes. She had read the note from Fitz which ended with, "Even in death, my heart will never leave you. Forever…Fitz." Fitz's recent posthumous address to the country was also a lot to digest. Thinking of her beloved Fitz as a mass murderer (or executioner) and extortionist (or protector) was something that she would rather avoid. That bumpy road was somewhat paved when she heard that Mr. and Mrs. Preston were satisfied with Fitz's modus operandi and explanation and they were ready to move on with their lives as best they could. She sat there questioning a lot, and understanding that there weren't always answers.

Oliver walked over and hopped up in her lap. He may not have been able to save all of humanity from the aliens, but with his unconditional love he was saving Annie Van. He buried his nose in her jugular notch and for the first time in a long time she whispered sweet nothings in his ears.

Epilogue 2 (Be Free)

No more history lessons. You can go home. I'm dead. How do I know? The history lessons were my bequest to you. Maybe someday, they will be part of your high school curriculum.

You may be wondering why this history isn't taught in U.S. schools today. The short answer: as you learned in the first lesson, history is written by the winners.

The long answer is a little more compelling. From November 1, 1953 to April 30, 1954, a special committee of the House of Representatives set out to investigate tax-exempt foundations. It is sometimes referred to the Reece Committee on Foundations in deference to its chairman, Tennessee Republican B. Carroll Reece. What the committee discovered – and more specifically its Director of Research, Norman Dodd – was that the tax-exempt foundations had embarked on a project to gain control over the content of American education. The biggest part of this was a determination to rewrite the history books.

Katherine Casey, a member of Dodd's staff, was selected to review nearly fifty years' worth of minutes from the Carnegie Endowment meetings. After World War I, she found that the members of the endowment concluded that it "must control education in the United States" to manipulate the population. In Norman Dodd's own words,

> "They realize that that's a pretty big task. It is too big for them alone, so they approach the Rockefeller Foundation with the suggestion that that portion of education which could be considered domestic be handled by the Rockefeller Foundation and that portion which is international should be handled by the Endowment. They then decide that the key to success of these two operations lay in the alteration of the teaching of American history.

> "So they approach four of the then-most prominent teachers of American history in the country – people like Charles and Mary Byrd – and their suggestion to them is: will they alter the manner in which they present their subject? And they got turned down flat. So they then decide that it is necessary for them to do as they say, 'build our own stable of historians.'

"Then they approach the Guggenheim Foundation, which specializes in fellowships, and say: 'When we find young men in the process of studying for doctorates in the field of American history and we feel that they are the right caliber, will you grant them fellowships on our say-so?' And the answer is yes. So, under that condition, eventually they assembled…twenty, and they take this twenty potential teachers of American history to London, and there they're briefed on what is expected of them when, as, and if they secure appointments in keeping with the doctorates they will have earned. That group of twenty historians ultimately becomes the nucleus of the American Historical Association.

"Toward the end of the 1920's, the Endowment grants to the American Historical Association $400,000 for a study of our history….That culminates in a seven-volume study, the last volume of which is, of course, in essence a summary of the contents of the other six. The essence of the last volume is: The future of this country belongs to collectivism administered with characteristic American efficiency. That's the story that ultimately grew out of and, of course, was what could have been presented by the members of this Congressional committee to the Congress as a whole for just exactly what it said. They never got to that point."

That's right. The investigation was squelched and the committee disbanded under absurd accusations of anti-Semitism. What the repressors didn't want exposed was that the Rockefeller Foundation, Ford Foundation, Carnegie Endowment, and the Guggenheim Foundation were all secretly endorsing the advancement of Communism in the United States and around the world. Why? Again in Dodd's words,

"because to them, Communism represents a means of developing what we call a monopoly, that is, an organization of, say, a large-scale industry into an administrable unit….[and the foundations]…will be the beneficiaries of it."

From these self-serving tax-free institutions, your history has become a lie.

Oh, you have other unanswered questions? Well, you can't be the judge of my actions in Northern California, only God can now. I didn't kill while I was alive on Earth, so I'm hoping to skate by on a technicality.

You have questions regarding the envelopes? Simple – the instructions to Robert Atkinson Esq. were as follows: if I was assassinated or died under suspicious circumstances, President Spring would receive Envelopes 1 and 2. Envelope 2 contained the address to the nation and a note regarding the ramifications of the bombing in Northern California and instructions to release all of the information regarding the death of my father (including my mother's and grandfather's letters) – not that he needed a roadmap drawn. IF I had died under non-suspicious circumstances, he would have received nothing. Being in good health, I viewed the possibility of dying under non-suspicious circumstances as nil. Envelope 3 was for Chaz Wyckoff IF I died under non-suspicious circumstances. It had the location of my tablet – I had Mafia Mike take it to Diane Van's house in Jersey City -- and the code to shut off the pre-programmed drone strike. Chaz was responsible for obtaining the latest in drone technology – which, with a keystroke, was deemed "decommissioned". Chaz retrofitted the drone with the Daisy Cutter and knew of a spot where it could be hidden away. He helped the Israelis construct an underground air base in the middle of the desert back in the seventies, so the notion of an underground desert hanger was nothing new to Wyckoff. He had NO idea what my intentions were with the drone. I pre-programmed it to drop its payload at a certain date, time, and location. If I wasn't alive to forward the clock to the following year, it would go to its destination. The Cremation of Care ceremony is always the middle Saturday in July. Envelope 4 contained instructions to Wyckoff to remove as many staff people as possible from the ceremony at Bohemian Grove, so as little as possible collateral damage would occur. I sincerely hope he was successful. Envelope 5 was simply a note to Mr. and Mrs. Preston that justice for their daughter's murder was near, as I promised when I last spoke to them. Envelope 6 contained the note which I struggled most to write.

One other item: the story of the other two planes pointed at targets is a lie, but should serve to keep what's left of the elite off of Evan while he forges a new path for America. Do you have any idea how hard it was stealing, hiding, and programming one drone?

I leveled the playing field for you. No more debt-based money and eventually, very little degenerative disease. So class is dismissed. You are free to watch reality TV; free to participate in hot dog eating contests [just remember those hot dogs are a lot more expensive now and cause degenerative disease]; free to pursue your passions; free to explore your spirituality; free to seek the truth; and free to screw it up all over again.

Fitzgerald Cavendish

Appendix A (Debt-Based Money under a Central Banking and Fractional Reserve Model)

[Author's note: The example provided below is very simplistic – although, because of my deficiencies as an instructor, many of you will find it confusing. It is technically incorrect in certain areas and it makes some unrealistic assumptions. However, it is a fairly accurate depiction of how the money creation system works worldwide. It is the sham of the ages.]

Let's assume that no one has any money and barter is the only form of commerce. If I make iPads and you raise goats and I need a goat, but you don't want an iPad, I'm going to have to find someone who not only wants an iPad, but also has something that the goat farmer wants. That is a pretty difficult way to conduct business. What is needed is money to make the process a lot less cumbersome.

The government is also itching to have a system of money in place as it is a pain in the backside storing goats and iPads that are received as tax payments, never mind redistributing those goats and iPads. Under our current insane money system, our government unconstitutionally sets up a central bank, which is owned by private individuals. That central bank takes out a printing press and produces Federal Reserve Notes, which are what most people refer to as money or dollar bills. The government takes out a printing press and produces treasury securities – bills, bonds, and notes – which are essentially IOUs. It then exchanges the IOUs for the Federal Reserve Notes. For example, the government of the United States wishes to borrow $100,000,000. It issues $100,000,000 worth of five-year notes and delivers it to the Federal Reserve, the United States' central bank, which in return produces $100,000,000 of Federal Reserve Notes (debt-based money) and gives it to the United States government. To make the example easy, let's assume that the notes carry a 10% annual coupon, which means that on the anniversary of the issuance, the United States government owes an interest payment of $10,000,000 to the bond holders each year for five years. At the end of the fifth year, the principle of $100,000,000 is due. That is a total of $150,000,000 in payments of principle and interest over five years on a $100,000,000 loan. Keep that thought in the back of your head as we move on with this example.

The U.S. government takes the $100,000,000 and deposits it into a bank. Since this is the first "money" in circulation, a bank is set up to receive the money. We will call it Bank A. It is one of only two banks in existence – besides, of course, the central bank which controls the printing press and currently holds the five year notes that the government issued. With current fractional reserve requirements, Bank A can make $90 million in loans with the deposit it has just received. To make the example easy, let's assume Citizen 1 takes out a $90 million dollar loan to pay for a massive widget manufacturing facility. Citizen 1 borrows the money at 10% from Bank A for five years and the loan is structured in the same manner that the U.S. government loan, except for the fact it may have to pledge collateral (such as real estate, goats, and iPads) in order to obtain the loan. Citizen 1 will owe $9 million interest payments on the anniversary of the loan issuance for five years and the principle of $90 million at the end of the fifth year.

Citizen 2, who is the general contractor in charge of building the manufacturing facility, receives $90 million from Citizen 1 and deposits it in Bank B. Bank B is able to make $81 million in loans with this deposit. Citizen 3 takes out an $81 million loan (at the same 5 year, 10% terms) to purchase a giant plot of farmland from Citizen 4. Citizen 4 deposits the $81 million in Bank A. Bank A can now make $72.9 million in loans with this deposit. Citizen 5 borrows $72.9 million to buy a small grocery store chain from Citizen 6. Citizen 6 deposits this money in Bank B, which can then make $65.61 million in loans. This is the concept known as fractional reserve banking. If this example were to continue in perpetuity, the initial $100 million deposit by the U.S. government into Bank A has generated $900 million of money in circulation. [Let's assume that all of these transactions – the initial government loan and deposit along with all of the bank loans and deposits occur on the same day.] This doesn't sound like a bad idea, since fractional reserve banking was responsible for making the economy grow more quickly. Citizen 3 and Citizen 5 would not have been able to conduct their business without loans that would not have been available if Bank A was only allowed to make a one-time loan for $100 million, matching what it had on its books in deposits.

Here's the problem: there is $900 million in circulation off of a "monetary base" – the original money created by the Federal Reserve's printing press – of $100 million, all of which has been *loaned into existence.* In other words, the $900 million in circulation has annual interest payments of $90 million attached to it – at least for five years. The government borrowed $100 million and owes $10 million in annual interest payments. That makes a total of $100 million in annual interest payments off of the $900 million in circulation. [Again, to make the example easy, let's assume that the banks don't pay any interest on deposits. They barely do nowadays.] At the end of year four, $400 million in interest payments have been made. Once an interest payment is made, that money is no longer in circulation. That leaves $500 million in circulation to pay off $1 billion in principle and $100 million in interest payments at the end of year five. This is a game of musical chairs. Citizen 1 may be able to pay off his loan because his manufacturing concern is a big success. Citizen 3 may not be able to pay off his loan because the crops he planted on his plot of land failed. All we know for sure is that the amount of money in circulation (now $500 million) is not sufficient to pay off the $1.1 billion due at the end of year five. *The level of debt is greater than the level of money in circulation.* One of two events will occur for those who do not have enough money to pay off their loans: 1. the bank will foreclose on their property and assume the assets. 2. The borrower will borrow more money in order to pay off the initial loan.

When scenario 2 occurs with the government, it increases the monetary base by increasing its debt level to pay off the initial five year loan. For example, the government collects $50 million in tax receipts and provides $50 million in goods and services for the population with those tax receipts. The problem is that the government has a $10 million interest payment due at the end of the year, so it can only spend $40 million on goods and services for its population. If it wishes to spend more, the government can withdraw money it has in Bank A; but if it does that, there will be less money in the bank to pay off the loan's principle at the end of year five. This is what is known as deficit spending. In real life, the government is constantly borrowing and constantly retiring debt, but because of the effect of interest payments, the level of debt is always increasing (unless the government spends less on its population -- making their wealth decline – and more on interest payments.)

As a result of this dynamic of loaning money into existence, the level of money in circulation is always increasing. And so is the level of debt. This is known as inflation.

I hope you found this example confusing as hell, because it is completely absurd. Sadly, it is our present system of money creation. This is the money system that we fought against in the Revolutionary War. We won the war, but the money system found its way back into the United States. As a result, U.S. citizens will pony up $400 billion, or $3,300 per tax payer in fiscal 2015, just on the interest for the debt. The average citizen owes $58,054 towards the debt, with the average tax payer owing $156,639. That is absolute madness. The only ones who win are the owners of the central banks, the owners of the Bank A's and Bank B's of the world, and the other owners of the debt. [The Federal Reserve does not keep all of the treasury securities, but rather auctions off a good chunk of it through its broker dealer network. I told you the example above was very simplistic.] You can clearly see that this isn't going to get paid off as we keep kicking the can down the road. The United States careens more quickly down the path to bankruptcy with each passing day.

[Note: If you would like to see Appendix A in a clearer, more understandable animated format, I strongly suggest that you go to youtube.com and watch the *Money as Debt* series.]

The correct way for money to function in an economy is in Appendix B.

Appendix B (How Money Should Actually Work or a Sane System of Money Creation)

Let's assume the same example as above. Our country is using barter as a means of facilitating commerce and we need to change over to a system of money. However, in this example, our Congress isn't bribed or bamboozled into creating an unconstitutional central bank. The government holds the printing press for money. It is decided that the total amount of money that is needed in circulation to adequately facilitate commerce is $900 million. The government would first stop collecting taxes for a period of time and as it needs to pay for goods and services, it would start printing U.S. Government Money (a.k.a. dollar bills) and exchange them for the goods and services. Determining what a good or service is worth will initially be difficult, but price discovery will occur as more money enters the economy. The U.S. Government money will be declared "legal tender" for all debts public and private. Once the government has spent $900 million, essentially introducing it into the economy, it will return to its role as tax collector.

As citizens receive money from the government, they may deposit it into a Bank A or Bank B from the example in Appendix A. However, Bank A and Bank B can only make loans equal to the amount of their deposits. In the example in Appendix A, bank A and Bank B were able to make $900 million in loans off of an initial $100 million deposit into Bank A. In *this* scenario Bank A and Bank B will collectively have $900 million in deposits, but will only be able to make $900 million in loans. As a result, the financial system will not be leveraged, greatly diminishing the possibilities of booms and busts in business cycles.

In this example, none of the money has been "loaned into existence". The U.S. government just printed it and introduced it into the economy. It did not borrow it from some ridiculous central bank. Bank A and Bank B are making loans, but they are not making loans with money that they do not have.

There is no game of musical chairs associated with this money system. There will be successes and failures, but there will always be enough money in circulation to pay off all the money that is loaned out.

Let's assume that the population of the United States is 9,000, so the average net worth of an American citizen is $100,000. If the government wishes to maintain this "standard", all it has to do is deficit spend when the population grows. If the population grows 11% to 10,000, the government can spend more than it takes in by $100 million. The government will not borrow this $100 million, but rather simply take out the printing press, print it, and spend it. The per capita net worth of the American citizen will stay constant at $100,000, as the amount of money in circulation has increased from $900 million to $1 billion in lock step with the population increase. As a result, there will be very little inflation or deflation.

This example has some unresolved issues, such as what happens when this money starts going overseas. The answer is that the government will produce more to keep the per capita amount in the country constant, but obviously, if the United States isn't producing goods and services as efficiently as our trading partners, and as a result we run up a trade deficit, the value of our currency will drop in international currency markets. That is how markets are supposed to work: the most productive countries have the strongest currencies. But given that our country will no longer be saddled with debt, I think we will stand our ground. It will only matter if you travel outside the country, purchase imports, or operate a multi-national corporation.

The response to all this might be, "That is great, but how do we get from the mess in Appendix A to the utopia in Appendix B?" Enter Appendix C.

Appendix C (How to Transform the Mess in Appendix A into the Utopia in Appendix B)

I really want to take credit for the solution laid out below, but it appears that Bill Still beat me to the punch by approximately eight years. Still has written 22 books and two documentary videos, including *The Money Masters* (1996), which is the seminal work on monetary reform and should be core curriculum in every high school.

To move from our present situation where we are $18 trillion in debt to zero debt and from fractional reserve banking to no fractional reserve banking requires the following:

1. Have Congress repeal the Federal Reserve Act of 1913 and the National Banking Act of 1863 and as amended in 1864.

2. Move the printing press from the now defunct Federal Reserve to the U.S. Treasury. The Treasury will produce U.S. Government Money instead of Federal Reserve Notes. The Treasury will also be in charge of the banking system in the United States.

3. As the debt comes due, pay it off with U.S. Government Money, principal and interest.

4. As the debt is monetized (i.e. paid off with cash), money will flood the banking system. To offset this inflationary dynamic, the U.S. Treasury will gradually increase the fractional reserve requirements for banks (Bank A and Bank B from the previous examples). When all of the debt is retired the fractional reserve requirement will be 100%, up from its present 10%.

5. Retire the Federal Reserve Notes in circulation just like you retire old $100 bills: by replacing them when they enter the banking system.

6. To keep the per capita money in circulation constant, run a deficit when the population increases; run a surplus when the population decreases.

THE END

Dedication

To my mother, for always being an inspiration.

To my father, whose work ethic was only surpassed by his enjoyment of life.

Acknowledgements

I would like to thank the people without whose sundry support this undertaking would have been impossible. They include Rick Crosby, David Scott, Robert DiFazio, Jeff Krupnick, Trace Vonada, Bob Atkinson, Emil Woods, John McNear, and James Mather.

I would also like to thank the numerous people who picked up "The Bag Man of Point Pleasant", shuttling me to my car, in the second half of 2015. They include Tim Hughes, John Esckow, Joe Hanney, Danny Ottmer, Janice Christensen, Wendy Dravis, and Suzanne Binette.

Charles Wahlheim's contribution was invaluable. I strongly suggest you read his book, *The Truth, Claiming Your Birthright to Health.* I was also the recipient of some heady advice from Adam Coyle, Bette Hughes, and Kerry Zukus.

I would also like to thank David Quale, Thom Zimny, David Talbot, Frank Forbes, and Casey Gesser who taught me in high school that genius comes in many different forms and to respect it unconditionally.

I would like to acknowledge Matt O'Brien for dealing with all of this nonsense for the past year.

I would like to acknowledge all truth seekers, especially WeAreChange.org, Sharyl Attkisson, Jesse Ventura, James Corbett, and Sibel Edmonds.

I would also like to thank my dog, Oliver, who allowed me to use his likeness for the book. Additionally, I'd like to recognize my long departed dog (and Oliver's littermate), Bruno. He wasn't as cute as his brother – some would say he looked like a platapigapottumus – but he was a wonderful dog.

About the Author

Stephen L Rodenbeck holds a B.A. in Economics from Bucknell University. (He was rejected at Brown.) He worked 14 years on Wall Street as a sales trader on Institutional Equity Trading desks, his last job being Senior Vice President of Equity Trading at Prudential Securities. He has authored a book on blackjack under a nom de plume. He currently co-owns various alcohol related businesses and spends most of his free time playing golf. He is a full member of GenerIQ Society.

He is available for speaking engagements. He can be contacted at srodenbeck2016@yahoo.com.

Proof

Made in the USA
Charleston, SC
11 March 2016